Rodantha's Road

Joyce Hilliard Stotts

Flint Hills Publishing

Flint Hills Publishing

Topeka, Kansas
Tucson, Arizona
www.flinthillspublishing.com

Printed in the U.S.A.

Paperback Book ISBN: 978-1-966323-38-9
Electronic Book ISBN: 978-1-966323-39-6

Library of Congress Control Number: 9781966323389

Dedication

This book is dedicated to all our grandmothers, standing behind us.

Table of Contents

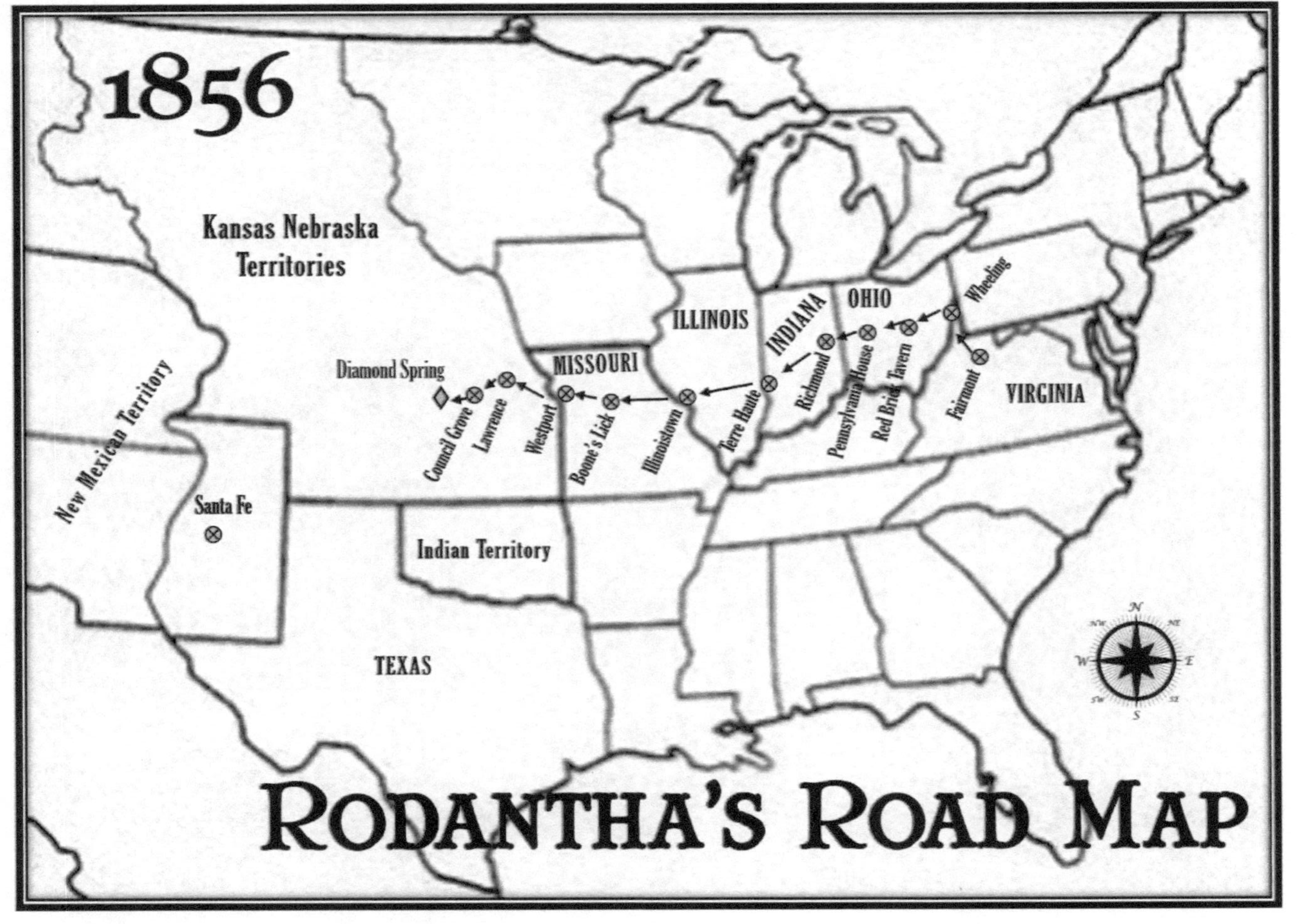
1856
RODANTHA'S ROAD MAP
Kansas Nebraska Territories
New Mexican Territory
Indian Territory
TEXAS
ILLINOIS
INDIANA
OHIO
MISSOURI
VIRGINIA
Diamond Spring
Council Grove
Lawrence
Westport
Boone's Lick
Illinoistown
Terre Haute
Richmond
Pennsylvania House
Red Brick Tavern
Wheeling
Fairmont
Santa Fe

Mountains and Maps

She had been walking since sunup—climbing, stumbling, scrambling through rocks and brush that scratched her cheeks. Out of breath, Rodantha stopped to rest her aching legs. The wind chapped her face and cracked her lips. Her eyes stung and her nose ran. Grit crunched between her teeth. She had promised to go with William when they married, having no idea what that meant. Against Aunt Zelda's objections, she had left the farm just after her eighteenth birthday for this unknown wilderness. She did know why—she had nothing to lose.

The newlyweds gingerly led their packhorse, Molly, along the Indian trails and narrow lanes. Rodantha prayed that Molly wouldn't break a leg or go tumbling down the mountainside. Two dead, half-eaten mules lay in one ravine drawing the circling buzzards. They stopped at the edge of a clear, swift creek and dipped up water almost too cold to drink. Mist turned to sleet and back again and mostly ran off her oiled canvas poncho but soaked her skirt and petticoat. She wrung them out and tied them up with her apron strings under the poncho. Shoes soggy. Feet cold. Blisters raw.

After finding a good campsite, they searched for dry tinder and built a fire, its warmth easing aching muscles a little. As Rodantha pitched the tent, William made coffee in the blue enamel pot. They spread their ponchos down under the gutta percha tent and unloaded the burden from the packhorse, piling it up at one end of the tent. They had repeated this exhausting work every night of the journey to the wagonmaker's farm.

William and Rodantha carefully followed the map, drawn on some sturdy rag paper by Rodantha's Uncle Joe, a lifelong Appalachian mountain man. Up out of Fairmont, Virginia, they followed Buffalo Creek, then Pyle's Fork and Fish Creek, and then struck out across the Appalachian ridgetops to the Waynesburg Pike Road that brought them easily to Moundsville at the Ohio River.

William and his bride got lost twice, but both times soon found their way again with Uncle Joe's map. The weather was cold, and snow still lay in the northern slopes and gullies, but the sun came out, trying mightily to bring the dogwoods to an early spring bloom. The long wilderness trek kept the newlyweds away from crowds and main roads, which she thought curious. On this northbound trip, William pointed out familiar landmarks that he remembered from traveling southward on his way to Fairmont a few months earlier. The map saved them several times from taking dead ends and switchbacks.

In the evening, William entertained her with his bagpipe, circling the campfire in a slow march, tassels blowing in the wind. The newlyweds, now officially Mr. and Mrs. William Hywell, tried to sleep on the cold ground, snuggled together for warmth under the quilts. By firelight, little by little, they gradually revealed their young bodies to each other. She loved his square bulk and the feeling of his strong muscles tightening around her.

When sister Silvie cried the day Rodantha left, Rodantha told her, "I got to get away, Silvie. I got to get free. I want to get some of that gold in California. Staying on this here worthless farm will kill me shor. I just cain't marry no farmer. William is my best chance. He says he loves me, sis."

Marriage, Rodantha thought, did not seem like "submitting," as Reverend Smythe said in his sermons, nor like Aunt Zelda's warnings not to be headstrong and selfish. "Married life won't feel like your normal way of doing things, Rodantha!" Aunt Zelda had said the day before her wedding. "You won't always get what you want."

Right now, all Rodantha wanted was to hear what the big secret was— the one she overheard William telling Reverend Smythe at the wedding. "Yes, I'll tell her all about it, Reverend, as soon as we are out on the road alone and I can find the proper words."

Rodantha found it extremely difficult holding her tongue since the wedding, but she didn't want William to know she had listened in on his private conversation. *Is this what marriage is all about?* she thought.

The last morning in the wilds, they awoke to bright sun and bird song. After William boiled a fresh pot of coffee and warmed the last johnnycake over the fire, they talked excitedly, knowing that today they would reach the Amish wagonmaker's farm. They would soon be on their way to the Kansas-Nebraska Territories. That was nearly all William talked about.

She thought that the territories would be at least halfway to her dream. She hadn't exactly told him about the California gold. But she would—soon.

As they descended out of the last of the mountains, Rodantha saw two bear cubs tumbling around in play near a large stand of timber and a rushing stream. They were some distance off the path that William was on up ahead of her. He was leading Molly and whistling a little tune.

Rodantha paused for a moment to watch the cubs play and take in the beautiful scene. She heard something in the underbrush: rustling, branches snapping, birds flushing and flying up. She looked back up the trail to see Molly rear and heard her scream. The pack horse bucked and jumped sideways. Boxes and bundles went flying off her back as she bolted back up the hill.

Then Rodantha heard a roar. As she turned to look in that direction, a gigantic bear barreled out of the underbrush toward her. In an instant, she knew the bear was headed straight for her and she tried to scream. Before Rodantha could make a sound the bear was on her. Rodantha could feel the bear's hot breath and smell the strong musky odor of the gigantic beast. One huge paw pressed down on her arm.

William turned to see the bear as it slammed into his bride knocking her to the ground. He quickly unholstered his Colt Navy revolver and fired off two shots at the bear, grazing the hind quarters. This seemed to distract the bear from Rodantha. The bear stood up on hind legs and looked in William's direction. Will fired again, emptying his gun. At this, the bear raced toward the two cubs who were crying out in feeble attempts to get their mother's attention. Rodantha lay motionless on the ground, bleeding from a gash on her arm.

The bear and her cubs went crashing through the timber back up the mountainside away from the Hywells. William bent over his precious

Rodantha, tears streaming down his cheeks. "Danna, Danna, wake up. Are you all right? Say something, please!"

He poured a little canteen water onto his kerchief and pressed it onto her forehead. Slowly, she opened her eyes, and as he lifted her head he felt blood on her neck and back. "Can you see me, Danna? Do you hear me?"

In a whisper, Rodantha replied, "Yes, Will, I can hear you, but I, I, cain't catch, my … my … breath."

"That momma bear thought you were after her cubs, she did. She's knocked the wind out of you. It will come back in a few seconds now, don't you worry."

When Rodantha could breathe and sit up, he saw there was blood on the rocks where she had landed. William carefully felt her head, neck, and back to make sure nothing was broken. The wound at the back of her head bled down onto her dress. "You rest whilst I catch Molly and gather the supplies she bucked off. Hold my kerchief against your head and I'll bind up your arm after I get her back down here."

Will built a fire and set up the tent. When the water had warmed he washed the blood out of her hair and dress and tied his clean kerchief tightly around her arm. He gently settled Rodantha inside and covered her with one of Aunt Zelda's quilts. He watched her all night, occasionally dozing off next to her, keeping her warm.

In the morning when he brought her johnnycakes and coffee she was sitting up braiding her hair. "Do you think you can travel on today, Danna? We'll stay right here if you don't. That bear is long gone, and this is a good campsite by this little stream."

"I think I can walk a while. We are getting into level ground now, so it should be some easier."

"We will stop and rest when you need to," he said as he began breaking camp and loading everything onto Molly again.

"My head aches and my arm is sore where that she bear stomped me. I don't fault her none. She was just protecting her young ones. Next time I see cubs, I'll know momma is watching out!"

They followed the narrow track that wound along the east side of the Ohio River, sometimes within sight of the water, sometimes veering out into the trees and meadows, dipping into small washes and ravines where creeks fed the Ohio. William pointed out their destination on the map.

"What a way to spend our honeymoon! I'll never forget this for shor," Rodantha laughed as they stopped for a rest.

"Our honeymoon, you say," William said with a big grin. "I hadn't stopped to think about our journey that way. Not been mindful of a woman's ways. Too focused on the practical work, and our safety, I am. Especially after that mother bear hurt you." He swung around to her, hugged her gently, avoiding her bandaged arm. He kissed her on the lips and shouted. "Our honeymoon, it is!"

The Wagon

February 1856

Rodantha and William trudged into the neat lane curving up to a handsome two-story, white clapboard house. The air was crisp, but the morning sun showed its power to warm the near-spring air to gentle comfort.

"This is the place, Danna," William said. "Fits the map and directions right down to the windmill, it does." A whitewashed wooden windmill stood a short distance to the side of the house, creaking as its wide blades slowly turned. Laundry wash tubs were lined up on wooden benches along a flat rock terrace edged by a freshly-raked flower bed. Little sticks poked up their hand-lettered signals of what was to come—zinnia, sunflower, marigold. The washing flapped in the breeze from a series of rope lines in the crisp morning air.

A brown and white beagle hound came scuttling, wagging, and bellowing, but once it reached William's side, just looked up with soulful eyes. William stooped and offered the back of his hand for a sniff. Then the little dog's tail seemed to wag his whole body, and he smiled his wide beagle smile with tongue slipping in and out. William folded the map and put it back in his vest pocket.

William left his bride holding the sturdy pack horse's reins and bounded up the wide steps onto the front porch accompanied by the ever-friendly beagle.

He peered in at the screen-covered door, then tipped his hat toward the woman standing in its shadow. Shortly, he descended the stairs again. His boots left little clods of dirt behind as he pointed toward a big red barn beyond the tilled and waiting soil of the garden patch. "We'll find Mr. Troyer at the barn, she says."

"Who says?"

"Mrs. Troyer. There, see her waving? She's stepped onto the front porch, she has."

Rodantha waved back to the plump woman wearing a miniature white bonnet and woolen shawl, then followed William as he led Molly back toward the biggest barn she had ever seen. Through the huge open doorway, she could see a bearded and bent old man as he came out of the shadowy, darker interior. His black apron had wood shavings and curls stuck to it. His straw hat shielded light-gray eyes, and his white shirt was crossed by black braces holding up heavy black trousers. A dusty barn coat was loose about his shoulders. He extended his hand to William in greeting.

"Well, what have we here then?" he said in a thick German accent.

William shook the old man's hand and then reached into his vest pocket and drew out the letter and map that he had so carefully handled. "I am William Hywell. Here is a letter of introduction from Pastor Smythe at the Congregational Church of Fairmont, Virginia. The folks there say you are the best wainwright this side of the Ohio."

"Well, second time this very month I have letter from the good Reverend Smythe. Just finish up work on wagon there. The good pastor said this what you need," he said, as he pointed back into the shadowy interior. "Smythe sent funds from the New England Emigrant Aid Society to build the wagon. Said they want to make sure like-minded folks can go to Kansas to vote for Free State government when it joins the Union." He took the letter in his gnarled hands. Looking down, he said haltingly, "Says here you two bride and groom?"

Will interrupted. "But ... but ... how can this be? Reverend Smythe sent money ... for us?"

"That he did sir, and more left beside. He says you take whatever is left and pass along to the church where you are going in town called Lawrence. This to aid in fight against slavery. I built the wagon on his say-so."

Will and Rodantha looked at each other in disbelief as they stepped into the cavernous barn. As Rodantha's eyes adjusted to the darker interior, she could see in a far corner the new wagon he was pointing toward. Light slanted in from windows along the side of the barn, and lanterns burned above a row of sawhorses. Several conveyances were in various stages of construction. A tall, square carriage was half-painted black. Shiny brass lanterns gleamed from each side. Big, curved sleigh runners were laid out on the sawhorses where they were being shaved and sanded. A potbelly stove warmed the workspace.

"I'm sorry … well … sir, ah, this is my … my wife, Rodantha Morgan, er, I mean, Hywell." William gestured toward Rodantha. As she smiled back, she felt the grit between her teeth, remnants of the dusty paths they had traveled on in the last few days and a reminder of her lack of diligence in cleaning her teeth as Silvie had taught her.

"Ma'am," the old Amish man said as he tipped his straw hat in her direction.

"We was married by Pastor Smythe first of January," Rodantha offered as they walked through the springy sawdust toward the new wagon. The barn smelled of newly-sawn wood, pungent pine pitch, and cedar. Where normally there would be stalls and a hay mow, this barn had racks of varying lengths of lumber, buckets of bolts and hardware, kegs of square nails, leather strapping, various sized lanterns, and a huge dark brown log with the bark stripped off. Saws, planes, and tools of every sort were hung or leaning along one wall.

"Now, mind, I call this wagon Conestoga since it is built with curved top, but this, it is about half-size of originals. Yah, you'd need a hitch of a half-dozen to pull one of those old freighters," continued Mr. Troyer. "I think this is stable and dependable wagon for the overlanders. Some folks call them schooners—says look like sails of tall ships going across flat prairies.

"See here? Yah? Extra-wide iron bands on the wheels, riveted so they will not separate from the wood. These might save you the toll over Wheeling Bridge since they pack and level the roadbeds as they roll. Will make your wheels last longer too. The bridge is open again now, so no need to take the ferry.

"All my wagons come with tar bucket and axle grease can. The shovel and axe fasten just here," he said as he pointed down the long side. "Two strong lariats in the jockey box and extra bolts, parts, and tools to keep wagon rolling." He paused, "You like?"

Kind Strangers

While Rodantha was admiring the wagon, Mr. Troyer's son, Jeremiah, rushed into the barn. "I have two very fine oxen to pull this wagon Da built for you. Come outside to see for yourselves," he said excitedly. "Da said you were coming soon, but this is really good timing. I have a Dutch Belted and an Ayrshire ox."

Jeremiah explained that he was in the midst of building a brand-new barn just a half mile down the road. That very day it was being raised with the help of his neighbors. Owing to the construction, the corral where the two oxen were penned had twice the number of animals in it than he liked.

"The Belted and the Shire are two of my best animals." Jeremiah beamed. "They have been handled kindly since they were born. These big brutes pull loads quite willingly around the farm and have had a good education." Jeremiah's speech was nearly devoid of the German influence. But when he spoke to the boy leading the oxen, in the strange sounding German language, Jeremiah seemed to her like a totally different person. Rodantha stood amazed that he could convert himself into a German with his change of language.

Rodantha wasn't sure that all the glowing language was true, though the huge animals did look strong and well cared for. William seemed to her a bit too eager to buy them. She had expected to buy a wagon to travel in but never thought much about the mules or oxen that would pull it. But since she was still shocked about the already-paid-for wagon, she didn't object.

She learned something about William too. She could clearly see that William was not a "save-for-a-rainy-day" man. She could almost hear her Pa's often repeated line: "Just spendin' money with a prodigal hand." Dear old Pa, how she missed him since he passed. At least, Pa would have dickered with Mr. Troyer on the price.

Jeremiah boasted, "I estimate the Shire is eighteen-hundred pounds if he is an ounce. The Belted, well, he will be bigger than that when he comes to his full weight in a year or so. His pap was a huge beast. We finally butchered old pap to be shut of that huge appetite." Jeremiah gushed on and on about the lovely attributes of his animals, how they were trained to follow the short commands—gee, haw, whoa, and back. He went on about how you barely had to poke them with the goad to get them to pay attention. The big bells that Jeremiah buckled around their massive necks were handmade by a Troyer cousin in his blacksmith shop.

"A dream come true, it is," William beamed. "I have been longing for this day since I left home in the Rhondda Valley of Wales. My father risked everything he owned on the long journey to this country. Against many trials, he made it possible for me to be here today."

The wagon and team were the most important equipment for the newlyweds' journey west. William called it their "big investment," though not as big as they had thought due to the generosity of the Fairmont Congregational Church and Emigrant Aid Society. This would be their home for the next many months until they got to the Kansas-Nebraska Territories.

Euphoric from the sale of the oxen, Jeremiah invited the Hywells to the barn-raising dinner at noon. The newlyweds walked the half mile toward the sounds of hammers, shouting, and frantic activity at the new barn, all framed in and at least half finished. A dozen women and girls in plain dark-colored dresses and little white bonnets over tightly-controlled hair worked out of a big, dark green wagon. They carried plates and steaming bowls of food from a muslin-tented "kitchen" sailing out of one end of the wagon. The early spring sun was unseasonably strong and warmed the whole affair, to the point that Rodantha took off her shawl and tied it around her waist.

"I never seen so much food," Rodantha whispered as they walked down the long plank tables filling their plates—fried chicken, mashed potatoes, scalloped potatoes, sweet potatoes, corn, green beans, cheese (a half-dozen different kinds), roast beef, baked beans, huge loaves of fresh bread, and spongy dinner rolls. The cinnamon rolls stood four inches high in giant black pans dripping icing along their sides. The pies at the end of that line were the most incredible part: pumpkin, cherry, peach, pecan, rhubarb, shoofly, and custard. There were a couple of kinds they weren't sure of.

The German-speaking crowd welcomed them. The men tipped their straw hats and pumped William's hand, saying over and over, "Welcome, welcome." Rodantha smiled and nodded. One little girl clung to the stranger's skirt as though to her own mother's.

They ate to bursting. After two weeks of walking through the cold Appalachian Mountains from Fairmont, near the old mill on the Monongahela River, this ordinary Amish dinner was near to heaven. After William went off to hitch up the team, three young women close to her own age came toward Rodantha, smiling, dish towels thrown over their shoulders. The tall one said, "Excuse us, but we heard you speaking English, and we like to practice ours whenever we can. Da says your name is Radinta? We just wondered where you come from?"

The younger girl with a scar on her chin immediately asked, "And where you going to?"

"Well—it's Ro-dan-THA," she said slowly, emphasizing the TH sound on the end. Rodantha's friendly nature and lack of female companionship opened the flood gates, and she began to talk as fast as she could, telling the girls her story of life in the Virginia hills, the Congregational Church, Aunt Zelda, and the long trip west to the territories. They seemed amazed that she had left home and come all this way without any of her blood family. William, they allowed, was a handsome fellow, but did Rodantha really know him that well?

"Exactly where is this 'territories' you been telling us about anyway?" asked the tall one. "Is it farther than Wheeling?"

Rodantha smiled indulgently and explained that she and William had much farther to go than they had already come. "William says it's near eight hundred miles just to the Missouri River, and we will go beyond that quite a ways." At this their eyes widened in amazement. The quiet one at last said, "It'll snow on you for sure before you get there. Aren't you scared, Rodantha?"

"No, I ain't afraid at all. I got my William and now this good wagon and ox team. I only miss home from time to time. And now, well … I'm bound to miss you three shor. Why, you has gave me a right new look-out just sitting and talking women-folk-like. You know one thing is, I shor will try to be as clean and scrubbed as you three. Puts me to shame in my old dress and apron. Your shoes are so fine too!"

This made them laugh. The tall one spoke up again. "Well, our secret is … our Da makes us brush our shoes every night and put new polish on them Sundays before church. We wouldn't care so much if Da didn't." Then they laughed again.

The Troyers sent them off with a new water barrel attached to the side platform, along with a smaller filling bucket, saying this was a wedding gift and an absolute necessity for a long trip. "I make these out of scraps of wagons," Mr. Troyer said proudly, "and they won't leak, long as you keep them wet." Two strapping young fellows relayed buckets of water from the well into the barrel and then adjusted the lid down tight.

William seemed anxious to be underway. So, as Danna reluctantly waved goodbye, her new husband walked beside the oxen, slowly making the Troyer's barn disappear behind them. As she rode along on the high seat, she had time to think about everything that had happened that day. She was sure that they would have done this even if it had taken every last one of their shiny new Flying Eagle cents, though she still didn't like parting with any of her wedding money. Their Congregational Church friends and neighbors had been caring and generous in giving them a letter of introduction and the location of the Troyer farm on the east side of the Ohio River. Then to know that the Emigrant Aid folks had also sent money for their wagon was encouraging far beyond the monetary value. It had some deeper purpose she couldn't quite understand. Now, with just a little distance to Wheeling and the storied bridge, Rodantha felt exhilaration and something new: freedom. They were finally on their way to the Kansas-Nebraska territories.

Rodantha had learned so much, just since breakfast, about wagons and oxen, about traveling the dusty trails and roads, about William, and the surprising generosity of strangers. She wanted to remember it all, to understand and to somehow bear witness. She secretly vowed to write in her new diary about the three Amish girls and how good she felt around them. The afternoon breeze fluttered her yellow bonnet and lifted the corners of her muslin apron. From the high seat of the covered wagon, she could see the Ohio River sliding past. The wagon bumped along, jarring her back and legs and making her breasts sore from the bouncing, so she crawled back into the wagon bed and found a quilt to sit on, which helped a little.

From the age of nine, Danna had been convinced that she could go to California like her Uncle Jim, a forty-niner, seeking his fortune in the gold fields. She had heard Jim tell stories of a place called Rich Bar where he had dug up an old tree stump and gathered $5,000 worth of gold out of the hole. When he came back to Virginia to visit Ma before she died, he gave Rodantha his copy of *The Emigrants Guide to California*, in which the author, a Mr. Ware, wrote something she had memorized: "Make provisions for the forthcoming millions…righteousness exalteth a nation."

That had been her dream, since she had been able to dream and think of the future—to have millions—not $122 and a bunch of Eagle pennies. Everyone in her family rolled their eyes when she started up about the gold. Uncle Jim said that the easy picking gold claims were playing out though, and now you might have to look for the next gold strike to come along. That is what she intended to do. She felt sure that William was going to like the idea.

Rodantha was still somewhat amazed that she had met this Welshman, William Hywell, whose vastly-different dreams seemed to promote her own. Her sister Sylvie called her dreams, "most certainly selfish," but she didn't care what Sylvie said. She kept that wonderful golden dream in her heart. Now more than at any time in her life, she felt as though her dreams could surely come true. A path of her own making—her road—lay ahead, clear and sharp in her mind's eye. She allowed no dispirited thoughts to enter her head. She just kept thinking about all that gold.

Dutch and Shire

February 1856

At dusk Rodantha and William arrived at a little clearing on the east bank of the Ohio River, just a little south of Wheeling, Virginia. The sun glowed its last faint warmth to the west across the water, tipping the ripples a rosy gold. The wagon smelled of new wood and pine pitch and rolled stiffly on wide iron tread wheels, oozing black axle grease from the hubs.

They had tried to follow all of Jeremiah's advice, but being new at this ox venture, the afternoon had been filled with minor mishaps and balking animals. William had some experience handling the farm oxen back in Maryland, but Danna was still not at ease around them, and the oxen seemed to know that.

The oxen continued a slow march down the bank at an angle. William hollered, "Whoa there, Dutch! Whoa, Shire!"

The Dutch Belted was the more pliant and cooperative of the two. Dutch came to a stop as soon as he saw William stop beside him. This forced the Ayrshire to do the same. The two European breed oxen were as different in personality as they were in looks. Dutch with his wide white "belt" on a black body looked respectable, like a nun in habit. The Shire's menacing long horns and mottled reddish-brown and tan coat gave him a haphazard and unpredictable air.

Rodantha nimbly climbed down, bracing herself against the spokes of the wagon wheel and bravely talked quietly and reassuringly to the Shire ox as he snorted and shook his head from side to side. She stayed behind the horns that stood well above her own head by two feet, just as Jeremiah Troyer had instructed her when he sold the giant beasts to them that morning. "They don't like me much," she said under her breath.

"Let's try to get them headed back up the bank a ways, Danna. I do not want to camp down this close to the river. You go on back up and I'll lead Dutch. I think Shire will behave better with a little tap of the goad." This tactic worked well enough, and soon the two giants had pulled the new covered wagon back up the bank to a flat patch where many black campfire rings were burned into the grass. "Looks like lots of other folks have camped here. Stop right here for the night, we will."

He peered around at the forest edge and warily back up the trail the way they had come. "Good," he said. "Seems nah one camping here this evening," as though he expected to see someone. Danna wondered about this as she always looked forward to seeing other overlanders about. A sense of isolation had begun to creep up on her, even after all the excitement at the Troyers had enlivened the day.

Rodantha and William worked for the next hour unhitching Dutch and Shire, hauling water up from the river, and building a blazing fire to keep the chill night air at bay. There was plenty of tall grass at the edges of the flat clearing where the oxen could graze. Rodantha unloaded the rest of their possessions from the pack horse, Molly, and stowed them in the four-by-ten-foot wagon bed: the iron skillet, Dutch oven, and kettle, lantern, tin of lard for the lantern and cooking, sacks of flour and corn meal, salt, dry beans, jar of honey, side of bacon, and William's precious coffee. Rodantha was lithe and strong muscled from an upbringing of work on the farm, but the day's efforts were beginning to weigh heavily on her.

The tin box of garden seeds and William's bagpipe wrapped in the quilts were the most precious. Those she tucked into the corner, and then hung William's shotgun on the inside hooks as he had instructed. As she looked through tins and supplies, she noticed there was only a little of the essential sody sallyratus left for biscuits. Soon they would need more supplies.

"Look here, William. Mrs. Troyer, she gave me a big loaf of bread and some cheese. How's about we just eat that. I'm plumb tired out. I just want to set by the fire a spell." They sat up against the taller back wheel of the wagon, looked up at the starry night sky in wonder, listened to the cold river gliding by and owls hoo-hooing in the trees along the bank. The campfire seemed to gather in light around them rather than radiate it outwards. Sparks flew up like magical sprites of light.

Lights from the houses and factories glowed faintly along the opposite riverbank, both north and south, and gave Danna a comforting feeling, just knowing there were other folks nearby. One of the wedding guests had pressed an advertising flyer about the iron suspension bridge into Rodantha's hand saying, "You will be amazed when you see the bridge, my dear. They claim it was made using materials from the local iron and coke foundries." Rodantha looked forward to seeing such a big industrious place, this Wheeling, Virginia.

She hadn't thought much about the actual journey she was going to take, but had worried mightily about her clothes and shoes, her precious wedding gifts, especially the gilt-edge diary and square cedar pencil.

Her teacher, Miss Quimper, had given her the diary, insisting that Danna's nearly five grades worth of education was not even a might too much. Miss Quimper handed her the diary at the wedding saying, "Pay close attention to the way folks speak to you and try to fashion your speech like unto the Reverend Smythe or even your new husband's clipped Welsh English. The diary will be the very best way to practice your spelling and punctuation. My best advice is this: Just write down what you see and hear and put your feelings on the paper." Rodantha had promised to record the exciting happenings that were bound to occur. She now realized that she would probably just record life as she was living it without much effort. So far, little was exciting. Most was dull boredom and grueling work that was repeated day after day.

Rodantha had been disappointed when William said there wasn't space for everything she wanted to take on the trip. She left the bluebird China tea set with her sister, Sylvie, for safekeeping. She tried to pack only the most useful and practical items but kept a few precious possessions that she didn't think she could ever give up.

"Is that thunder I hear in the distance, Danna?"

"I think so. Off a ways north, but no clouds or lightning anywhere close, that I can see."

"Listen, there it is again."

"It'll be a wonder to sleep in our new wagon tonight," she said with a wide grin. "'Snug as a bug in a rug,' Aunt Zelda always said. No chance we can get even a little wet." Then, with an air of importance, and a display of her new knowledge, she went on. "Mr. Troyer says the wagon has a double layer of canvas, to make it shed the water and keep out the cold."

Unwinding the colorful quilts from around William's bagpipe in the corner, she spread them out on the bed of the wagon, the heavy one on the bottom for a cushion. "Sure am ever so grateful to Aunt Zelda for these quilts. It's a right nice touch of home. I feel her love in every stitch," she said as she snuggled in close to William, who smelled of lye soap. She smiled into the darkness and thought, *He is trying to please me, scrubbing all over and washing out his shirt every night despite the chilly mountain air.*

His youthful zeal for her showed in his every word and deed. So far, her hopes and dreams had not been trod upon. She had no thought of disappointment, or hardship, or pain, only for the adventure with her handsome new husband. He had rescued her from a life of drudgery on Aunt Zelda's farm, or worse, a marriage to some poor coal miner covered in perpetual black. At first, she had been unsure about how to relate to him, reluctant to touch his male parts. But now as his clear blue eyes searched hers, he caressed her tenderly. She gradually responded to these new and strange passions, like a glowing ember within her, though little understood, growing stronger than any mere campfire.

Each night that fire intensified and engulfed her. Each morning, she was less embarrassed to scrub her bare neck and breasts in front of him. These new feelings were the only things that made up for the drudgery and loneliness of the trek through the mountains. In her heart she knew that wonderful adventures awaited.

William now proved every day his promise of freedom and adventure when they married.

He had ten years of age on her, ten years of experience, ten years of dreaming, and of seeing the world and knowing what he wanted from life. She loved that about him, even though she was not sure if she loved him, the person of him. He seemed so overly cautious and wary of strangers.

She wasn't sure what people meant by this word *love* when applied to someone outside of your family. Her pangs of longing for Pappy and Ma were most definitely love, but this … well, she felt an irresistible attraction to William and enjoyed his company and conversation immensely. Just now she could feel his arms tight around her and his hard body next to hers. This was all so new and strange. The thunder rumbled.

"My sweet girl, Danna," he said, "you make my heart flutter like a duck in a puddle."

-5-

Suspension Bridge

February 1856

Rodantha first smelled the coffee and then heard the thunder rumbling again to the northwest. She quickly slipped the blue calico dress over her camisole and bloomers. She had washed it out the night before and it had dried overnight hanging from the stays of the canvas top. It smelled ever so slightly of the sweetly-scented blue flowers she had picked along the road and tied up next to it. During the night, the blue flowers had given up their lives to her dress, infusing it with their sweet scent. The flowers, now limp and dry, tumbled down with her dress.

She wound her long, dark brown braids into a knot at the back of her head, tied the butter-yellow bonnet loosely around her neck, and silently thanked her sister Sylvie again for that most thoughtful gift. She stuffed her feet into her sturdy boots, the shine she'd put on earlier now scuffed away by the rocks, mud, and miles through the mountains. Good serviceable shoes held a high priority on her list of necessities. She hadn't even owned a pair of shoes until her fourth birthday, when Pappy had presented her with a pair of cast-offs from sister Sylvie that he had re-tacked and sewn. She remembered how Pap had shined them and put little caps over the worn heels. Fresh cut rawhide laces gave them an air of newness. Though they were too big for her feet, she put them on and didn't take them off except to sleep, until her sixth birthday when she could no longer get her feet inside. She wore big holes in the soles.

Rodantha was eager for the day ahead and hoped that the rain would stay off to the northwest. Traveling in wet weather was difficult at best and downright impossible if the roads became too soggy. They had been lucky so far with only light dustings of snow during the two-week walk to

Wheeling, but the memory of shivering under their little gutta percha canvas tent threatened to darken her mood. "Rain, rain, go away, come again 'nother day," she chanted quietly and poked her head out of the end flap to see a cloudless blue sky with great relief, the sun just gilding the hilltops.

William had already yoked Dutch and Shire and walked them down the bank for a labor-free drink of the swift Ohio River. He had promised Jeremiah that he would take the animals on a walk-about before hitching them for pulling, to allow their bulky stomachs to work up a proper defecation before the work of the day began. Jeremiah said this would prevent much trouble, make for a more pleasant ride, and probably make the animals last for eternity. Rodantha could hear Will calling, "Gee Dutch, Gee Shire, step up, step up." Their bells clanged gently in a kind of harmony. When the massive horned heads appeared above the bank, William gave her a big grin of accomplishment. She offered the dried flowers to Dutch, hoping to be his friend. He chomped gratefully.

William repeated the recipe again as he prepared the coffee. "Listen now, Danna! Here is how to make the best coffee. Whilst you wait for the water to a boil, grind the coffee. Once the water boils, throw in the coffee and remove immediately from the fire as it foams up. Swirl the whole thing around and drip a bit of cold water on top to settle the grounds. Pour the coffee off carefully so as not to agitate the grounds settled at the bottom."

"You just make it your way, William, and I won't never complain." They ate the last of Mrs. Troyer's bread and cheese, washed down with William's wonderful brew, boiled in the blue enamel pot.

She washed the pot with boiled Ohio water and lye soap and packed everything away in the wagon while William stomped out the last of the fire and turned over all the rocks to make sure no embers hid underneath. They were ready to go. William stood a few minutes with the handmade map spread out on the tailgate. He had made a column of figures and placenames on the back of the heavy paper with the stub of an old cedar pencil he carried in his vest pocket.

"Look here, Danna, I'll show you the way we're going." He pointed toward an extension he had drawn on the back of Uncle Joe's map, starting his map with Wheeling. "If we can make ten miles a day, we should cover the eight hundred miles to Westport where the Kansas and Missouri Rivers meet, I estimate, in three or four months, even allowing for a rest 'on the Lord's Day. We'll take Boone's Lick Road through Missouri. I don't really know what to expect on the rough trail after Westport, but by my generous estimate, that should put us in Lawrence, Kansas, in late summer or early fall."

Rodantha peered at the map as William pointed out the way points. "What's does it mean that you penciled in my name there, Will?" she said, curious why she should see her name on his map.

"Well, I've named our route in your honor, ma'am. It's really the National Road and Boone's Lick and the Santa Fe Trail. But ..." He paused a moment to reflect, "belongs to you, it does. You know, when we met in Fairmont, I was alone, all my courage gone. Providence surely guided us to each other. Count you the best partner a man could have, I do."

"Why, Will, that's about the nicest thing you ever said to me, except of course, 'I do.'" She leaned into him and kissed his cheek.

He squeezed her waist tight and said, "It has a nice sound too, this—Rodantha's Road."

They kept Molly tethered to the back of the wagon. This was the horse's first relief from carrying all their belongings, and Molly seemed happy as she ambled along, a light breeze from the south blowing her tail. Danna walked along beside William as he kept Dutch and Shire plodding in the right direction, encouraged by the goad from time to time. The oxen were most cooperative when they could see him.

The houses became more numerous as they traveled into the town of Wheeling. Brick and stone buildings had been built close to each side of the road. Rodantha wondered aloud, "Some of these buildings are huge, William. Whatever do the folks do in there?"

"Well, some look like homes to me or maybe boarding houses. Some might be factories. See that big place, I think they make thread and cloth from the look of the machines you see there through the high windows. There's a dentist office, and that one has a sign, *Attorney At Law*. Lots of people live close by where there is work for them to do. Reminds me of Swansea in the old country, Wales, it does. An industrious sort of place."

Up ahead they saw a commotion in the road. A horse reared up above the throng, and a man in a top hat held the harness, attempting to calm the animal. A knot of people, horses, wagons, carriages, and dust had formed in the middle of the road.

"What's that, Will? Can we turn the team away from all this?" But it was too late. There were three wagons following them close behind now, and the road was nearly full of rolling stock, animals and humanity—a strong stench rising. All wagons had stopped. The people around them attempted to calm their animals and dipped out water for the children and animals alike.

"Stay with the team, Danna, while I go ahead to see what the trouble might be. You'll be fine now, don't worry," he said, looking earnestly at her for agreement. "I know we're very close to the bridge now. This looks familiar. It has not changed all that much since I made the trip from Maryland. I think the bridge is just out of sight that way, I do," he said pointing to the left.

"Listen! Are you listening, Danna? That is the bridge rumbling, not thunder! I should have known. But when I came here before the bridge was closed and I went south."

"I cain't understand how the bridge can make that sound though, Will. But, yes sir, you go on now to see what the trouble is. Dutch is my friend since just this morning when I gave him the sweet blue flowers." The Ayrshire still tossed his head side to side and snorted his displeasure. With the wagons stopped, the rumbling bridge seemed even louder.

A little boy ran up to her crying and wiping his runny nose on his sleeve. "Ma'am, could I have a drink of your water? Please?" He was the dirtiest child she had ever seen, covered in dust head to toe except for streaks made by his tears and runny nose. His shirt had only one button and one knee of his trousers was torn. The torn piece hung down in a little flap to the top of his boot that looked two sizes too large. A lump bulged just above his right eye, dried blood clogged a gash across this eyebrow, and his right eye watered at the corners.

"Why shor, little fella, you just stand here where Dutch can see you and I'll dip up." She hurried to Mr. Troyer's water barrel—*Now **my** barrel,* she thought—and brought back a big dipper full of the boiled Ohio water to the little boy. He was sitting cross-legged with his head in his hands beside the Dutch Belted ox who was contentedly chewing cud. She let the boy drink all he wanted, then poured the rest over his head, and gently wiped the dirt away from his eyes with her apron, revealing sunburned skin and ginger hair. He smiled wanly and began crying softly, shoulders heaving.

"You still thirsty?"

"No, ma'am, thank you kindly." He sniffed loudly and drew his dirty shirtsleeve across his face. "My mam passed yesterday and we's left her in a hole over by a big tree. I want my mam to come back," he wailed. "But she cain't come no more." He put his head in his hands and heaved great sobs of grief.

"What's your name, little man?"

"I … I'm called Jake," he said weakly, still holding his head.

"Well, my name is Rodantha Hywell. I'm pleased to meet you, Jake,"

"Ro … dan … ta …?" He looked up.

"Just call me Danna. That's easier. Where's your people, Jake?"

"I don't rightly know." he said, looking around blankly. "I think I *would* take another drink ma'am, if you don't mind."

She fetched more water and soaked her blue handkerchief saying, "Now, you just hold this here cool hankie to your sore eye. It'll take the swell down and make you feel better." She washed his hands with the remainder after he had drunk his fill. With surprising strength, she boosted him up onto the high seat in the wagon, and said, "Just look around from up there to find your Pa, Jake. I need to water these other fellas here," she said pointing to the oxen who were both chewing cud by this time, though Shire still stamped his hoof impatiently.

William ran up to her with the news. "Just as I thought. The turn-off to the bridge is about a mile on. A buggy has turned over, and a woman hurt. My guess is we'll start back up shortly, though it will be slow going, Danna, since there are hundreds of people all crowded up together. Tempers are short."

She looked up toward the high wagon seat, but Jake had disappeared. "Well, that boy must've found his kin. Poor little fella lost his ma, and I gave him a drink. But he's gone now."

Whips cracked, wagons creaked, dogs barked, men shouted, babies cried. The wagons began to move out slowly. "Giddup, Dutch. Haw, Shire," William commanded. Dust rose all around them in a great cloud. William trudged straight ahead with his eyes high and searching, ignoring the steaming, pungent manure piles.

Danna tried her best to hop and straddle them, her slim frame looking like a child playing hopscotch. She tied up the bottom hem of her skirt with her apron strings and rolled her bloomers up out of reach of the stinking mess. She doubted her boots would be wearable after this. If only William had let her bring another pair.

Rodantha carefully picked her way along on the side with Dutch, her new friend. William stayed close to Shire, who was once again tossing his head ominously. She could see a wide intersection ahead with buildings close to the road, where most of the wagons had turned to the left and gone out of sight. As soon as the Hywells turned their team, Danna saw the giant limestone pillars about a quarter mile off, rising up to what looked comparable to the three-story buildings she had seen on the way in. Thick iron cables stretched from somewhere beneath the bridge and under the street up toward the tops of the towers. She counted twelve huge cables swaying down on the river side of the towers and back up to two matching towers way over on the other side of the river. Danna looked up in awe as they passed under the near archway between the cable towers. *Who could build such a thing*? Now she understood what the wedding guest had meant—this was truly amazing—and impossible. How did they string those cables across the Ohio? How long did it take to build it? A small sign posted on the right side of the bridge said it would carry the weight of an army of 4,000 men.

They were in the middle of a great seething mass of humanity that was now out over the Ohio River. The wagons rolled over the huge wood planks. She was amazed that all the people acted as though this was a fine way to cross a river, a fine way to get where they were going, a fine way to satisfy their need to get to the land on the other side.

"This is most rightly a dangerous contraption, Will," she shouted. But she could see there was no chance now to get off the thing. She would just have to endure the quarter mile trip out over the water. Those iron links that connected the twelve iron cables to the roadway deck surely contained a weak link somewhere—most definitely not safe out there walking over the water. The rumbling "thunder" of the bridge now engulfed them as their wagon followed those in front and was followed by those behind as close as a few feet between each.

At the middle of the bridge, the suspension cables dipped to near eye level before curving gracefully back upwards toward the towers on the western side of the Ohio River. "Look back now quickly, Danna," William shouted. "Look up the hill opposite to the way we came in. See the road to the north, on that hill? That is the National Pike that goes back east to Cumberland, to Maryland. Do you remember I told you about my trip?"

"I see it, Will," she shouted back. "All the way back to your family."

"That's right ..." but the rest of his words were lost in the chaos.

The Ohio River rushed beneath them, and gave her a strange sensation, like the descriptions her mother had given when she was so ill—the circling, tilting, and disorientation of vertigo. There was a chest-high railing where people leaned out and pointed down. Rodantha stayed in the wagon and prayed for the ride to be over.

The hills rose sharply on both sides of the river. Danna saw a steamboat downstream, belching smoke on its way to some other destination. She thought, *Where are those people going? Where did they come from? Where did they get on the boat?*

They passed under the limestone archway on the west side of the river, which Danna thought might be even taller than the one on the east. At the end of the bridge, to the left, along the opposite side of the road, a throng of wagons, single riders, a drove of sheep, and a fine stagecoach waited impatiently. They were lined up beside and behind a ramshackle building, waiting their turn to cross over the river into Virginia. As soon as the Hywells were off the bridge planks and back on solid ground on the Ohio side, the rumbling faded so that they no longer had to shout.

A small sign at the front of the line of people commanded: Pay Toll Here. Below were rates hand-lettered on plain paper, as though they had been posted just that morning.

FOOT PASSENGERS, 5 C FOR ROUND TRIP
MAN AND HORSE, 10c
SIX-HORSE WAGON, 75c
MONTHLY TICKET FOR FOOT PASSENGER, 50c

William stared at the toll house sign and slowed the oxen. He said slowly. "I guess the people of Ohio have to pay a toll to use the Virginian bridge. I read that a special Wheeling bridge company footed the bill and organized the effort to build it. Trying to get some of that money back, they are."

"Well," Danna said, "you can see right there—not many schooners with oxen are a-coming back from the west. There is not even a toll on that notice for covered wagons. I do hope we can come back if we want to, William."

"Well, yes we can, Danna…" he broke off abruptly, looking back over his shoulder

Quickly he added, "Remember what Mr. Troyer said, these wide iron wheels help to smooth and compact the roads. That's probably the reason right there. Nah need for a charge for most overlander wagons."

Rodantha frowned. Her mouth puckered out defiantly. "Pappy would-'ve said, 'This is a huckleberry over my persimmon,' and then he would have balked and not gone a step further."

Danna lost a little of her confidence. She felt affronted, taken aback, trodden upon for the first time since she'd left Fairmont. Maybe she never would come back to Virginia, visit her parents' graves under the dogwoods that dappled the mountainside. What if she were never to see Sylvie again? *Maybe things don't always turn out the way you plan.*

William goaded Dutch and walked ahead tugging on the nose ring lead. "Haw Dutch, Giddup Shire," he shouted. "Come out of the wagon, Danna, to lighten the load."

"What is wrong, Will? The team is exhausted and needs to stop. Why are you hurrying on?"

"There is danger here and we must keep moving," he said, goading Shire to pick up the pace.

"Danger?" She looked around and saw a rider crossing the verge and angling toward them. He rode a handsome roan horse. He flashed past them and galloped at full speed up a side road. His pistol was drawn, and he fired at some unseen foe in the trees. All the while, Will goaded the oxen onward as fast as they would go away from the danger she had not seen. He was quiet, his hat pulled low.

They continued for half an hour, without stopping, first crossing Zane's Island and the smaller, covered bridge over the Ohio back channel. After that, wagons lined the roadsides as people stopped to rest and eat. They climbed a steep uphill grade until the Ayrshire began to loll his tongue out like a great gray, wet rope. His eyes bulged. His steps slowed even more from the usual ox pace. Just beyond the last few houses of Bridgeport, William nudged the team off to the left into a thinned-out glade of hickory trees. Big stumps dotted the little swale and campfire rings showed the marks of previous overlanders.

William stopped the wagon in the shade of a large hickory and immediately began unhitching the oxen. "The walk will cool them, it will. And then they can drink their fill," he said. He led them down slowly toward the small creek running along the far side of the glade. He still said nothing about the man on the roan firing his pistol.

Rodantha knew something was wrong, but filled the kettle, set her tripod, and easily found kindling for a fire. By the time William returned and bedded the oxen, her biscuits were baking in the big Dutch oven and bacon sizzled in the black skillet. "Smells like heaven itself, Danna," he said with his usual good humor. He thrust a big log he'd dragged up from the creek onto the fire and sat down. She sat next to him and said, "Are you going to tell me what that was all about, Will? I never saw you treat the team that way before. Were you afraid of that man?"

"I saw his pistol was drawn. I thought maybe I had seen him somewhere before, so I wanted to get you away safely. A lot of reckless bounty men ply these roads looking for runaways and thieves, you know. Safe, we are now. Don't fret."

"You shor know a lot about all these dangers. The best man a woman could have!"

The next day they traveled through the wooded valley along Wheeling Creek, which looked much like her native Virginia but with shorter, gentler versions of the beloved Appalachians. Low hills rose on both sides. It was a most pleasant day: bright sun, cool air, the few early flies blown away by a slight breeze, and the steady ox-pace. Even the oxen seemed more content to do their work. The snorting, stamping, and head shaking had dissolved into a resolute amble.

It was twilight when they reached what Will said surely had to be Lansing, and where he'd been told the creek was spittin' distance from the road. As the road followed the bend of the creek, there was a grassy spot with a gentle incline off the National Pike. Several other wagons were already stopped there, friendly campfires burning. Will pulled to the far end of the grass and put the rear end of the wagon as far from the others as possible.

The Hywells repeated the now familiar ritual of unhitching the oxen, watering, and hobbling out on the fringe of the tall grass. Danna built a fire, baked cornbread, and opened a jar of peaches given to them as a wedding present. She parched some corn in the big black skillet and filled the buckskin pouch full for the next day.

Memories flooded back as she worked. Rodantha remembered her early years like they were yesterday. From ten years of age, she had cooked, cleaned, scraped, and scrambled for everything. When Ma died, she quickly learned to do every job that needed doing. Some girls at school didn't even understand what she was talking about when she described her chores. Her schooling was cut short, and she felt cheated.

Rodantha craved nearly anything of beauty or value, especially all that gold in California. She knew that selfishness was a sin, and often sorrowfully repented in silent prayers, but never could manage to change much in the everyday practice of things. She hoped that the Almighty understood her intentions. But what if He couldn't overlook these things? What if she wasn't allowed into Heaven? Then she would surely never see Ma and Pa again. "I repent of my sin, Lord," she said out loud. But her golden California dream was silently alive in her heart.

-6-

William Tells His Story

February 1856

As they walked along the National Pike, the oxen seemed to know just what to do now and kept a steady pace in the middle of the road. "We're sure to make it a tidy ten-mile day, Missus Hywell," William pronounced in his proper Welsh-English.

"Tidy ten-mile day, Missus Hywell," she parroted smiling. "Just trying to copy your accent, Will," she giggled.

William smiled down at his new bride. He wanted her to understand the feeling of peace he hadn't known since he had left his father in Maryland. He wanted to tell her everything. On the trip to Fairmont, before he met Rodantha, he had traveled mostly at night and rested during the day in quiet out-of-the-way corners. He had followed his father's detailed instructions to the Fairmont, Virginia, Congregational Church, not stopping to talk to anyone. He found Reverend Smythe on the very day he arrived in Fairmont and showed the good reverend the letter from his father explaining why he was there and the importance of secrecy.

The wise reverend said right away, "From what you've told me about yourself, young man, I think I'll just put you in the choir and explain to the choir master that you are a visiting Welshman who knows his way around the hymns. And that you will soon be on your way west. We've had a lot of that kind of thing from time to time, natural as anything. No need to say anything about going to jail or running from the law. Safer that way."

William hugged her shoulders as they walked and said, "Meeting you, Rodantha Morgan, was a bit of luck I never expected."

He remembered how Rodantha had come to the Congregational Church choir practice to walk home with her older sister, Sylvie, who also sang in the choir. Right away, William was in awe of Danna's young charms, her lively conversation and easy laugh, her long shiny hair hanging loose and wavy from braiding. When she said yes, she would marry him, it was beyond his dreams. Part of the proposal had been that she would come with him on a trip to the Kansas Territory where his prospects for work were good, where a new Congregational church was forming. When Danna had said yes, Silvie was immediately against the idea and told William she did not approve.

Despite objections, not quite a month after William and Rodantha met, they were married, and two weeks after that they started the trip to the territories. He marked down the day on the back of his father's hand-made map: January 16, 1856. He was anxious to be on his way before his past could catch up to him. They had so many other things to talk about that it was easy for William to avoid talking about his trouble with the law in Maryland.

"Since the Wheeling Bridge, I've been thinking about my father back in Maryland. When I saw that road again … well … made me think how I miss him, and my sisters, it does."

"Just like I think about Sylvie and Aunt Zelda every time I snuggle in her quilts, I reckon."

"Yes, like that, it is."

"Why did you ever leave there, Will?"

"It's quite a story, Danna, if you are interested. I think this might be the right time to tell you more about my life before I met you. That reckless man shooting his pistol out on the road made me realize the danger and my part in it if we are drawn into some trouble."

"Oh, I'm powerful interested, Will. We're both needing to get to know all about the other one."

"Well, I hardly know where to start, but I guess the story would really begin with my dear mother, brought up in the Quaker religion and an abolitionist by—well—by experience, I guess."

"This word 'a-bo-lish-tion-ist'—I heard Reverend Smythe talking about these people in a most favorable way, Will, but I'm still not sure what it means."

"A person who is against slavery, someone who wants to end it—abolish it."

"Are you one of these abolishioners, Will?"

"Why, yes, I guess I am, Danna. That's how I ended up in Fairmont.

The good reverend is a friend of my father's and like-minded to my whole family in the hatred of slavery. We knew Reverend Smythe worked on the Underground Railroad, helping slaves to escape to a better life, to freedom."

"Underground Railroad? That'd be a curious thing."

"Well, this system of secret stops in cellars, tunnels, hiding places, became the stations on the Underground Railroad. This was just a group of good people who wanted to help slaves escape their lives of misery. The underground part just means unknown, unseen, secret. It's not a real railroad with cars on a track. It's just the community, the believers, the helpers; they became known as railroad agents and conductors, each one knowing the next one on down the line."

"But I still don't understand what that's to do with *why* you left Mary Land."

"I told you it was quite a story, Danna."

"Oh, please do go on, Will, please," she said hiking up her skirts out of the way of a tree stump.

William had already said more than he had intended and was quiet for some time. Finally, he said, "Think you deserve to know the truth about me, I do. Reason I did not say anything before … I was afraid you wouldn't accept me since I broke the law." As they plodded along beside Dutch and Shire, he continued his story.

"My mother had been acquainted with Arimintha Ross, a slave, and a child of slaves. The whole Ross family worked on a tobacco plantation in Maryland. People called her Minty before she changed her name. Well, Minty was a force, a strong Christian woman, who got the idea that she could get her people out of slavery. So, she started talking to folks like my mother and father. Some called her Moses, after the Biblical leader of the Israelites fleeing from the Egyptians and crossing the river Jordan. The Ohio River became known as that River Jordan—slaves wanted to cross over into the Promised Land of the North.

"Mother had left the Quakers when she married Father back in Wales, but her *feelings* were always saintly Quaker, though she'd joined Father's Congregational Church."

"Well, I de-clare. I never heard of people changing their religion right smack in the middle of the stream before." She shook her head and twisted her braids. "But do go on, Will."

"There were lots of Congregationalists around and throughout Maryland, folks who believed strongly in education for all people.

Descended from the pilgrims of Plymouth Rock, is the story I was told. But the wonder is people from all the *different* beliefs formed into a secret group who helped Minty get these slaves out, forming the secret Underground Railroad.

"Reverend Smythe has friends in the New England Immigrant Society and knows some of the folks who have gone to start the town of Lawrence, in Kansas Territory, as a place that promotes Kansas becoming a free state, not a slave state when it joins the Union. That's where I want to go. They even made up a guidebook that I have been using since I left home." The wagon bumped over a loose stone protruding up through the macadam of the Pike roadway, rattling the kitchen box. But the patient oxen just kept up their pace.

"But I got ahead of myself a little bit here, Danna. Let's see now. This Minty got married to a freedman, a Mr. Tubman. She changed her name to Harriet and escaped from the plantation. She helped a lot of other slaves escape too. So far as I know, she has not been caught. But that is where my leaving Maryland comes in.

"I was part of the Underground, and I helped many slaves get from our cellar to the other safe houses. I saw first-hand the cruelty of white men toward their slaves, the results of savage beatings, abuse of women and even little girls, tortures, and the breaking apart of families. I thought the scars on those poor people might never heal. My heart was and still is heavy, and in sympathy with the slaves. The best I could do was help them get away." William paused. He swatted at a big horse fly that buzzed around Shire's head, tormenting the animal into a fit of head shaking. Finally, the fly lay in the dust, and Shire plodded on thankfully.

"Do go on, Will."

"Well, one night as I came back from a secret trip on the underground, the sheriff grabbed me, he did. He asked what I was doing out so late at night. He said I must be helping some runaways that had been reported missing from one of the plantations. I did not admit to anything though. Worst was, he said I was going to jail.

"The sheriff held me for a week while my father pleaded for my release. My poor mother…" but he trailed off and was silent for a several long minutes. "A few other fellows spoke up for me and my good character, but nah one could say what was really going on for fear of breaking down the whole Underground system.

"The magistrate finally came in for a court appearance and after, well, a very quick hearing early in the morning—too quick, mind you, since they did not want any objections, I was fined $1,000 and sentenced to six months in prison for helping runaway slaves. Father said I was the 'example,' and that the magistrate thought this would stop the Railroad in its tracks. When Mother heard this, she was stricken down. She couldn't talk, or walk, or eat properly. I feel the fault is mine … for Mother … I'm sorry, Danna." He drew out a tattered handkerchief from his vest pocket and blew his nose.

Rodantha had turned and was now walking backward in the road to see William's face and to hear every word. "Just you take your time, Will." But then, obviously anxious to hear the story, she blurted out, "Did you pay the fine? How did you get away, Will? How did you get out of prison?"

"Well, first off, we did not have that kind of money. But I never went to the prison, either. The sheriff kept me in the county jail until I could be transferred to a prison, I forget where now. One night he got drunk and fell into a stupor. Father came in to visit me and found the jailer passed out on the floor. Father unlocked the cell.

"Now, I do not know how all this could happen. So, I wonder who might have given the jailer such strong drink that night. Anyway, saw him lying on the floor, I did, not moving a muscle. And I was sure that he was going to wake up and catch us.

"Father had a horse waiting for me, our Molly there, with an old Colt Navy holstered on the saddle. He gave me the Immigrant Aid Society guidebook and threw up a carpet bag of food and ammunition behind me. I raced out of there, and, well, here I am. I know that a lot of people worked together to get me out of Maryland, and the silence of those folks has kept me free and untraced, so far."

"That's the gun you shot that big ole' snake with the other day, is it?"

"Very same, it is. I had to learn how to use it right away, so I practiced on unlucky creatures. It kept me from starving, though Mother might protest this as being against the Quaker peaceable ways."

"Well, I seen you cleaning it of an evening, and I reckon it's like the one Pa had back home." Rodantha paused a moment and reflected on all she had heard but only said, "Well, I got a hundred questions in my own mind, but I would-a been so scared, Will."

"At first, I was so grateful to be out of jail, and with the means to get away from Maryland, I just cut out without thinking much. But as I hid myself in daylight, I had a lot of time to think. A few times I heard people on the roads and trails near me, and I didn't move a muscle for hours, in fear of my life. A man on a roan horse with a long turkey feather in his hat followed me many miles one moonlit evening. I got my pistol out thinking that he was a bounty man hunting for me. I was ready to shoot him if I had to. He finally turned off on a side trail. I know my ma would have been ashamed of me.

"Once Molly whinnied, and I thought I was done for. I had never been so all alone in my life. That was maybe the worst feeling I ever had. As I went racing along during the night, I felt a great relief, since I could not brood over everything. I just wanted to put as many miles between me and Maryland as possible."

He paused a moment, and said, "I've thought about this day and night. Truth is, I have a need to go to the territories for my own reasons too. I need this endless road somehow, the openness of things, all the possibles, the newness, the tomorrows. I hate slavery more every day that I have *my* freedom. I miss my mother and family so much that I think I might understand the heartache of the slaves and the prison of their lives. They have none of this." He swept his arm out over the whole scene and let out a ragged breath.

They walked along in silence a while until Rodantha asked, "Does Reverend Smythe know all this?"

"He knows enough and wanted me to tell you all of it, not keep it secret. The letter my father wrote to him explained what had happened, and seeing as how my father and the reverend were friends of long standing, Smythe helped me by using those same Underground connections he used for helping the slaves. He'd sure be thrown in prison himself if people knew how he was involved in the Underground, or that he protected me and helped get me away too.

"Reverend Smythe gave me letters of introduction to the parson at the new Congregational Church just started in that little settlement in Kansas Territory called Lawrence that I told you about—where we are going. Smythe says I'll be safe when I get to the Kansas-Nebraska Territory. There being nah State law there, he said that I'll be free of the trouble back in Maryland, I will."

"I reckon that explains why you was wanting to go soon as we was married?" she said.

"I didn't plan on you, Danna. I wasn't going to stay in Fairmont but a week, but well, here *you* are too. Are you sorry you married me now? Will you stay with me? Are you ashamed of me?"

Danna didn't answer the questions and simply said, "Your ma?"

"Mother died that very day when I left Maryland." Will choked on these words.

"Don't worry none, Will, I cain't say those words to this day without sobbing. Take your time."

When he could go on, he said, "That's why Father had come to the jail that night—to tell me she was gone—or so he said. It seems to me they schemed and planned for my jail escape just like they planned and schemed to help the slaves escape on the Underground Railroad.

"When my father put me on Molly and gave me the letter for Reverend Smythe, he said that my freedom was what Mother most wanted as she lay dying. I was to carry on with the fight against slavery, make her proud of me looking down from her Quaker heaven. I'll do that, I will."

William sucked in a ragged breath and fell silent. Rodantha still hadn't answered his questions.

The "S" Bridge

March 1856

Next morning, William had the team hitched and ready at daybreak. Cold cornbread with honey made a fine breakfast. They were on the National Road before the other campers had even doused their fires. Rodantha didn't have a chance to strike up any conversations with them, but now she understood why William wanted to avoid strangers, and why he relentlessly kept moving.

Danna watched Will closely as he went steadily about his work: high brown boots with the lace ends stuffed inside, blue stripe, collarless shirt with the long sleeves rolled to his elbows. His odd-looking green and tan canvas braces were buttoned to his heavy duck cloth trousers. He'd told Rodantha that his mother had cut and sewn the braces. They had been made from worn out awnings from his uncle's general store where he worked back in Maryland, shredded by age and sun on top but good usable material under the eaves of the building.

Rodantha admired his broad shoulders, tanned face, and dark brown hair hanging out from under his sweat-stained felt hat. "You'll be a-needing a haircut, Will. We'll set you down one of these evening and clip it up out of your eyes." He nodded his agreement and kept on walking.

After they had passed the last house of a little pike town, Danna noticed another of the strange pillars she had seen the day before—about three feet high with a rounded top. Most had the word *Cumberland* arched across the upper part. Other names and numbers could sometimes be made out along two sides. This one was quite unreadable, and the top was cracked right through the word *Cumberland*.

The next stone pillar Danna saw clearly read *Blaine 1* on one side and *Wheeling 9* on the other. She crossed over the road to look at it closely and then caught up with Will again. "Whatever are those pillars for, Will? Like the one we just passed by. Markers of some sort ain't they?"

"Exactly that. They tell how far we are from Cumberland, where this stretch of the road started."

"Oh, I remember. You told me 'bout that when we crossed over the Wheeling bridge. So, what's the meaning of the other words and numbers—Blaine 1 and Wheeling 9?"

"Well, we are one mile out from the town of Blaine on ahead and nine miles away from Wheeling if you go back the way we have come," he said, pointing backward down the road.

"What a wonder!"

"The guidebook says that when the National Road was built, the government required a signpost to be set each mile," William explained, "so, overlanders could tell where they were and the distance they'd come so far. Surely, some are hard to read now, and others already crumbled down. This road has been building westward since Thomas Jefferson's time as president."

She had heard of Thomas Jefferson, but right now could not remember who he was. She did not let on though, so William wouldn't think less of her.

They trudged on. Just beyond Blaine the road went directly over Wheeling Creek as it meandered back around the little town. As soon as she saw the three sandstone arches of a little bridge and the rocky stream flowing under it, she scampered down the bank and dipped her handkerchief in the icy stream, wiping her face, neck, hands, and arms. She wanted to kick off her boots and wade there in the dappled shady ripples. But she could see that Will had continued on across the curious little bridge, and she didn't want to get too far behind him. The bridge formed a giant letter "S" as it met the road that curved away on either end in opposite directions, reminiscent of a big snake. The willows and oaks bent over the banks, and swallows zipped in and out under the stone arches. She wanted to stay right there all day, maybe forever, and just forget all about slavery, abolition, and running from the law. This was an escape from the worries that overwhelmed her.

As Will and the wagon disappeared off the other end of the "S" bridge around a big bend, she reluctantly wet her kerchief one last time and tied it around her neck for a delicious reminder of the lovely spot.

Rodantha ran across the red bricks to catch up and leaned over the sandstone railings one last time to take in the beauty of the sparkling creek and wooded glade. She vowed to put the "S" bridge in her diary to remember the peace she felt there. The oxen were already toiling up the steep winding hill where water seeped from a sheer wall of limestone. Will urged them on. "Step up, step up there, boys," he repeated. She ran to catch up. She wanted to be with William Hywell more than anything, no matter how scary the road ahead might be.

Diary

March 1856

In late afternoon, after the chores were done, Rodantha crawled up into the wagon and got out the diary that her teacher, Miss Quimper, had given her. She had packed it with her other treasures in the tin seed box, a wedding gift from Aunt Zelda, who said, "I made up this box with the freshest seeds I have been saving. It will start your first garden, and then you can save seeds in it too. It's strong and tight from dampness. Some fine white flour came in it, and I have been using it ever since for my seeds. This will also be a good place to keep other things safe and dry since it is not full. I can only give you a few seeds, but they may save you from starvation just as they have saved me."

William had objected to her even bringing the bulky box. "I don't intend to be a farmer, Danna." But when she told him there was extra salt packed in there for safety from dampness, he relented. Strictly speaking it was true about the salt, but it was in a little ceramic shaker made to look like a rooster. The little rooster had a matching pepper shaker with salt in it too. She would have to admit that Will was right about the bulky flour-tin-turned-seed-keeping box.

She had never been on such a long walk in her life and so couldn't really understand until she had trekked through the Appalachians herself—the steep rocky climbs and descents, fording creeks, scratches and scrapes through the timber. The tin seed box had been burdensome for Molly before they had the wagon, and an extra chore to unload it each night and then tie back onto the top of the bundles each morning. She would never part with the contents of the box, though, no matter how long and difficult the journey was. It was easier now to store in the corner of the wagon.

The diary was near the bottom, so she had to lay out her treasures to get to it. She lovingly handled each one. The Congregational Church hymnbook, the lace cape she had worn at her wedding with daguerreotype button portraits of her family. Aunt Zelda said, "Something old, something new, something borrowed, something blue," and explained that the lace cape would bring her good luck in her marriage—old lace, new blue ribbon, and borrowed buttons. The thin delicate material was crushed down though and didn't take up too much room.

In the rush of leaving home, Rodantha had "forgotten" to return the portrait buttons to her Auntie. These were the only images she had of her parents, and of Aunt Zelda and Uncle Clive. The portraits of Sylvie and herself as children were her favorites. The six buttons were edged in silver, now tarnished in places, surrounding the faintly silver-gray tinted portraits that seemed to float outward from the surface of each button. Also in the box were two of her mother's handkerchiefs and the all-important cedar pencil.

The lovely diary was just on top of her *McGuffey Reader* and the book, *A Narrative of the Life of David Crockett, Written by Himself.* The diary had not been used yet, and Danna was reluctant to ruin the beautiful thing with writing, especially with her now unpracticed hand. The parchment paper had gilt edges, and the tan leather cover was bound by darker brown spine laces. The laces wound around the whole and tied in a loose knot. At the very bottom of the box was the aromatic cedar pencil which she held to her nose before she shaved the end to a point with her pen knife. The shavings released even more of the pungent woodsy fragrance.

Resolutely, she opened to the front page and traced the outline of her left hand, which just fit onto the page with enough to spare at the edges for the tracing. Inside the outline of her hand, she wrote:

Rodantha Morgan Hywell - 1856

On the next pages she wrote:

These pages will bear my witness to the things I seen and done. Events and peoples of my life and my thoughts about them. My trip from Virginia to Kansas Teratory. Places I seen, where me and Will traveled since we was married.

–Fairmont – Me and William Hywell was married at the Congregational Church in my hometown where I grew up and went to school, though not quite long enough to show up well on these pages.

—Manningtin – a railroad town with sawmills and tanneries.

—Old Hundrud – where the oldest couple in the states was sitting on their porch watching for the next train.

—Troyer's Farm – we bought our wagon and oxen and ate a grand dinner with the Germans. I met three smart girls with shiny shoes and clean dresses.

—Wheelling – a big city with an iron bridge hanging over the Ohio River, crush of people, much smoke from the foundrys leaving a sooty black in places. Little Jake lost his ma and I helped to comfort him.

—Blaine – an arched stone S bridge over a butifull creek, water sparking over the rocks and shady along the banks. A steep winding road, scary in spots.

She read back over the few lines and wished that she had an old piece of bread to erase "seen." Instead, she crossed it out and wrote "saw" above it to show that she knew the correct English. Speaking in correct English, well, that was another skill entirely, one she thought perhaps she never would master. Finally, she wrote:

I claim here to be a abolessionast just like my husband, and vow before God and this diary to go again slavery whole heart. I seen that William is a straight forward honest man who has paid dearly for his belief. A big batch of what I see and what happens just cn't be put down, but it is still in my heart. I would need a whole stack of diaryies. I will do my best to write the most important things here.

The light was fading. She hadn't thought to bring the lantern with her, so she put all the treasures back into the tin seed box, the diary on top where she could easily retrieve it. When she picked up the hymnbook, she noticed a little piece of paper sticking out at the top and opened to the page that had been marked. The hymn on page 267 was "Guide Me, O Thou Great Jehovah," a favorite of Will's and one she had heard him play on his bagpipe. She thought, *He must have marked the page whilst he was a-practicing.*

When she read the first verse, it transported her back to Fairmont Congregational Church.

Guide me O thou great Jehovah, Pilgrim through this barren land. / I am weak, but thou are mighty, / Hold me with thy powerful hand. / Bread of Heaven, Bread of Heaven, Feed me till I want no more. Feed me till I want no more.

Tears welled up as she remembered the Sunday morning procession into the Fairmont church. Women marched to the right side and men to the left, the whole parade gaining bulk and strength as each family from their individual homes joined the moving singing group. The women had special descants and the men a rousing bass echo until finally they filed into the church right and left, babes in arms with their mothers, girls with the women, and boys with the men.

She quickly dried her eyes and left the hymnbook out while she stowed the seed box back into its place. She found William's bagpipe wrapped in the old worn quilt in the back corner near the kitchen box and took it out to him. He was sitting by the fire smoking a stogie.

"Play us a tune, Will. Please? I want to hear "Guide Me O Thou Great Jehovah." Play it like you did when we was sparking back in Virgini. I mean the old Welsh tune. You said, from your home in the Rhondda Valley."

Will looked up at her, disinterest in his weary eyes. "Danna girl, I'm too tired to play tonight. I was about to wash up for bed." As her shoulders slumped, she turned away so that he could not see her disappointment. But he quickly changed his mind when he saw this was no idle request. "Now, now, play a tune ere we drift off to sleep, I will."

As she handed him the pipe, she dropped the hymnbook. "What's this?" he said looking up. "A secret stowaway in your treasure box?" She blushed but held up her head defiantly.

"I 'spect I am fond of certain things necessary to life, William."

"I see that, I do," he said softly.

He took up the bagpipe, tucked the leather bag under his arm, placed his fingers over the holes in the wooden pipe with a carved horn end and saw-tooth edges. He blew into the carved wood mouthpiece. The single-drone pipe stood up on his shoulder. A long wail rode out into the night air as he squeezed down on the bag, and then the first notes of the hymn. William stood still for the first strains and then began a slow walking pace around the campfire in time to the music. He began to play the tune again from the beginning, and Rodantha sang along this time. She could just read the words in the hymnbook from the firelight—"pilgrim through this barren land." He stopped with a screech of the pipe exhausting its last air.

"Oh, please, just one more time through, Will. I want to sing the second verse." She was gaining in confidence now and let her voice rise to its fullest capacity (though she knew it lacked the beauty of Sylvie's voice). He played again.

She sang along. "Open now the crystal fountain, Whence the healing stream doth flow; / Let the fire and cloudy pillar Lead me all my journey through; / Strong Deliverer, strong Deliverer, Be thou still my strength and shield, Be thou still my strength and shield."

This time when he stopped, he sang out a long drawn out—Ahhh… men—in his fine baritone. But that was not the end of the music. Far off in the woods somewhere, voices floated back. Rodantha and William stared at each other across the campfire in awe. "Songs of praises, songs of praises, I will ever give to thee, I will ever give to thee."

"Someone else knows this Cwm Rhondda tune, William. More Welsh people about I 'spect."

He smiled and reached up into the wagon to wrap the pipe snugly in the quilt wrapping. "Well," he said, "I can say that the part about 'Pilgrims through a barren land' might have applied to those Israelites in Egypt, but this country is a most plentiful land indeed. But surely pilgrims all the same, we are," he said as he stripped off his shirt.

Rodantha said, "The answer is *no*."

"You don't think we are all pilgrims?"

"I do think we are pilgrims, but *no*, I ain't ashamed of you, *no* I ain't a-going to leave you, and *no* I am not sorry I married you, Mr. Hywell. Fact is, I feel right proud."

William said nothing but just looked long and steadily into her eyes.

"Oh, and I just know your ma is proud of you in her Quaker heaven."

William and Rabbits

March 1856

The next morning a thick fog hung over their camp. A hawk screeched and drew William's attention to a group of circling hunters, faintly visible through the foggy gray light, looking for their breakfast. William made his strong coffee with the last of the boiled water. He started another boil in the Dutch oven of the nearby creek water to replenish the water barrel. Will was the first human being stirring in the cool morning stillness. He whistled a tune as he worked, *Sao Gan*, a Welsh lullaby remembered from his childhood. At least a half dozen rabbits hopped about in the morning mist, munching on grass and forbs at the edge of the woods.

A small, dark-haired woman appeared out of the fog, coughing and holding a handkerchief to her mouth. She began to speak with a distinctly Slavic accent. "Sir, please excusing me. I am wondering if have molasses for trading? A fine sack of potatoes and onions, I'm having to trade. I and my darlings have cough, and I need molasses for cure of sickness."

"Morning, ma'am. I am sorry but we have nah molasses."

"So sorry. Thank you just same, sir." She pulled her shawl tightly around her shoulders, and turned to go, coughing into her handkerchief.

"Wait! We do have some honey, though, and if you need only a little I will trade for your potatoes and onions." Her shabby clothes and obvious illness made him wary, but he truly believed she had sick children to care for.

"I need half cup only. See? I brought for to measure. Is here in sack," she said pulling out a small tin cup.

William made the trade with the strange woman, pouring out the honey into the little cup she had brought. He asked her to turn the vegetables out into the corner of the jockey box. "You keep the sack," he said. "You're sure to make good use of it again."

"Thank you, sir," she said. "I mix honey with vinegar and herbs to cure cough." The woman silently disappeared into the fog again.

He reached quietly into the side of the wagon, lifted his shotgun off the side hooks, and set off toward the forest edge. The half-dozen rabbits he had seen earlier had now increased in number, maybe fifteen or twenty, too numerous to count. It had been weeks since he had seen rabbits come up close enough to shoot one without tramping far away from their campsites. This was a good chance to get one of his favorite meals. One he had not tasted for quite a while.

His 12-gauge double barrel was loaded with the light shot that he used for small game and birds. Will took careful aim and brought down the biggest one with a head shot, trying to keep buckshot out of the meat as much as possible. The others scattered off into the woods. He crouched quietly for a few minutes, and the rabbits again hopped out into full view. He aimed carefully again, but this shot missed the target, the fog making it difficult to sight the critters well. The rabbits scattered away. He reloaded to be ready if he got another chance shot.

Will retrieved his prize and pulled out his always-sharpened hunting knife and leather thongs. He tied the rabbit up in the crook of a small sapling, hind legs splayed wide. He quickly cut the fur around the two back paws and peeled the hide downward to the front paws, which he broke and sliced off. He continued to peel until the fur collected around the head. He cut the head off allowing the blood to drain away and flicked out a couple of buckshot that had errantly gone into the chest flesh. He sliced around the tail and opened the belly. He pulled the entrails and tail down and out and left them all in a heap where the blood continued to drip. "The hawks will have easy pickings today with these," he muttered to himself.

This had taken about five minutes, time enough for the rabbits to lose their fear and hop out again. He drew his bloody hands through the wet grass, wiped them on his kerchief, and then slowly lifted his shotgun. This shot brought down a second rabbit, a bigger one. After he had skinned and gutted it, he headed back up to the wagon with his catch.

Rodantha poured out coffee for herself. As she saw him approaching, she frowned. "I heard you shooting out there. Woke me up, right smart."

"Danna girl, see here—got our nooning fair, I did," he said proudly holding up the skinned rabbits. "You can make us a fine rabbit stew."

"We don't have much to go in a stew, Will, but the rabbits will fry up nicely on their own I reckon."

"Just look in the jockey box and tell me what you see."

"Potatoes!" She pulled one out and inspected it. "And two onions!" These she held to her nose and sniffed. "A miracle, or something close."

She poured the water that had been boiling in the Dutch oven out into the water barrel, adding to their supply of safe water for drinking. Then she put the fresh-killed rabbits into the empty Dutch oven. She salted them down and stowed it all away in the kitchen box. "My mouth is watering just thinking about these vittles. But tell me how you come by this fine fair, Will."

"Traded some of your honey to a woman for the potatoes and onions, I did. She had a cough and sick children who needed a remedy. I think she was very poor by the look of her ragged clothes. Reminded me of gypsies I saw in the Welch countryside one time. But count this as our good fortune, I do."

"I reckon I do too, William Hywell. A fine trade, shor."

"Let's get a move on now. This fog is turning to mist. Want to be ahead of the rain, I do. Time to head out. I think the last marker said the next pike town is St. Clairsville."

The morning passed without rain, but a light mist and fog hung over the travelers like a great gray tent. It was heavy enough to encourage Rodantha to climb up into the wagon and ride for a while, trading the cold and wet for the bumpy jostling and rocking. She did think it was smoother than usual somehow, laying that off on the softening of the road by the moisture of the morning. William donned his old wool coat and poncho and wrung out his felt hat several times. Danna pulled out her mother's heavy, dark green wool shawl as some defense against the intermittent cold drizzle. The soft mud sucked at the oxen's hooves and slowed their pace.

Preparing the rabbit stew at midday took several hours. Rodantha built a big fire that smoked heavily in the damp conditions. She boiled the rabbits in water until the meat fell off the bones. She transferred the meat to the cooking pot and strained and added the flavorful broth. She scrubbed potatoes, sliced onions, and collected coals to rest on the flat-top lid. In about an hour the stew was thick with flavor. The results warmed them and brought some cheer into the gray, wet day. They sat under the wagon on a tarp to eat, where they were comforted by the fire built intentionally close to the wagon. William strung up his coat and Rodantha's shawl under the wagon where they might dry by the time the overlanders needed to put them back on.

They could eat only about a quarter of the huge pot of stew, so Danna left the remainder in the Dutch oven and wrapped the whole thing in a gunnysack to keep warm for their evening meal. It was bound to be late due to the long nooning.

Will scraped the packed mud from the oxen's hooves, sharpened his hunting knife, watered the animals from the nearby creek, and tended the fire. He washed the rabbit blood out of his kerchief with lye soap and hung it up under the canvas top to dry. As they packed up to leave, the rain started in earnest. "You might as well stay dry, Danna," Will insisted. "Nah sense both of us catching our death. Get up there and ride this afternoon. Better put on your poncho."

Rodantha did not argue. She was still cold from the morning drizzle and damp clothes. The rain fell—heavy, constant, sheeting down in windy gusts that sometimes made it hard for her to even see Will up ahead. The wagon slowed. The oxen strained and pushed against the yoke, heads down. She could hear the animals' labored breathing and their bells rattling and ringing from their jerky, halting progress. Occasionally, the wagon paused, almost but not quite at a stop, and then with a sudden jolt the wheels slipped sideways or bumped into a rock or high place in the roadbed.

She rode in the wagon for a few miles this way and noticed the swollen creek that occasionally peeked around a bend, out of its banks. It rushed and foamed, like it had been raining here for a week. An uneasy feeling crept up her spine. Big holes in the road were filled with water. The roadside ditches and depressions were full. As the downpour continued, the wagon wheels sank deeper and deeper into the mud.

Will suddenly appeared next to the front wagon wheel, goad in hand, a worried look on his face. He said, "You'll have to come on out of there, Danna, to lighten the load. I do not want to get stuck, and we're already sinking a good deal. The gravel pack here's washed out and the water is running across the road. This much water, well, it must have been raining here or upstream for quite a while."

Rodantha frowned but said nothing.

"See ahead?" William said, pointing. "I think that is the big hill into St. Clairsville. I'm afraid to let the team stop for fear I can't get them going again. Guidebook said this can get greasy and dangerous."

Rodantha reluctantly prepared to fight the elements. She tied her shawl in a knot at her back, hiked up her bloomers, and tied her skirt up with her apron strings, then tied William's red kerchief around her head and slipped the oiled poncho over all. She jumped out the rear flap since the oxen were still moving the wagon along slowly. She went down on her knees. Her hands sunk into the greasy, black mud. Rodantha had tried to jump clear of Molly toward the side of the road, but that plan had gone all wrong. She could not move at first and was stuck fast.

"William! Stop! Wait!" The rain beat down on her back and ran off the poncho hood. Slowly, she got her hands free and straightened up to a kneeling position.

William slogged back to where she had landed, hollering to the team, "Whoa boys, whoa!" since the team had just continued to move forward. "This is a fine mess, Rodantha Hywell. Sunk farther into the mud than the wagon, you have. You're not hurt now, are you?"

"I don't rightly know, but nothing pains, I guess."

He pulled her to her feet, getting the black mud all over both of them. As she attempted the first step toward him, her boot came off, stuck in the thick gluey muck.

"We'll just have to put you up on Molly. I will give you a lift up. Try to keep that other boot on."

She put her knee into his inter-laced hands, and he boosted her up onto Molly's bare, slick back. She started to slide off to the other side and would have if he had not caught her arm. He retrieved her lost boot and helped her lace it back on. The gritty rainwater sloshed between her toes.

"Hang on tight to Molly's mane—grip her sides with your legs. I have to go back up to get the team going." He slogged toward the oxen and pulled hard on the yoke.

"Haah! you brutes." By some miracle, the oxen went forward. The wagon lurched, but Molly stood stiffly, stubbornly still.

"Get up, Molly," Danna yelled at the top of her lungs, and kicked with all her strength into the horse's sides. Rodantha was now crying uncontrollably. She pleaded, "You was willing to tote my box of treasures, now just try real hard to carry me too, please Molly. I so want out of this here mess." Molly must have wanted out of it too and maybe understood that to stand still might mean the end of things. The stout little horse finally obeyed and pitched side to side violently as she got her footing. Only great effort and wit kept Rodantha on the top side of Molly.

She tilted her face skyward and wailed. "I hate rain. I hate this day. I hate this place. Not fair! Please Lord, I just want to go home."

-10-

Rain and Trouble

March 1856

A cold wind kicked up, and Rodantha could see the steep hill now. Black, greasy mud, deep ruts full of dark rivers flowed down toward their wagon. At the top of the hill was a huge, grand-looking house. Lamps burned in several windows. What a sight that house was! *Like Moses must have felt when he saw the promised land,* she thought. But as they approached, she could see that a throng of wagons had pulled off the road and clustered around the house in every available foot of space. Several wagons had stopped right in the road leaving barely enough room to pass on the left side. None of the marooned overlanders had even unhitched their wagons, and a few slogged about as the rain continued to pour down.

A man with a turkey feather in his hat, sitting on a roan horse, stared at her as the wagon drew past him. He was so close to her she could see a fresh, bloody gash across his cheek. An icy chill ran down her spine. She thought, *Could this be the same man that followed Will as he was escaping from jail? The one that followed Will in the night. His face looks like he has been in a fight.* To her great relief he did not follow them. She silently thanked God for the miserable cold rain instead of cursing it.

Her hopes for even a brief stop were destroyed by the rain-soaked crowd, and she now wanted to get far away from the strange man on the roan. Disappointment made her even more miserable. She felt the cold and wet sinking into her flesh, exhaustion overtaking her body. She tried hard to swallow the lump in her throat.

Somehow William kept the team moving forward, further and further away from the welcoming windows of the big house. He urged the oxen to the side of the road while being careful to keep all four wide iron wheels out of the ditch. Mr. Troyer's wheels again proved their great worth to keep the Hywells moving. The roadside ditches were full, water flowing over the road in places. She felt helpless against the weather and the need to keep moving for fear of becoming permanently trapped in the quagmire.

Hours passed. She tried to stay awake, but repeatedly dozed off right there on Molly's back, waking when her thighs lost their grip and she tilted sideways. She leaned forward, gathered up handfuls of mane, and held on to Molly's neck. To stay awake and give her courage, Rodantha chanted the words of the hymn over and over, "Guide me O Thou Great Jehovah, pilgrim through this barren land. I am weak but thou art mighty, hold me with thy powerful hand."

She became conscious of stillness as her drowsing, not quite sleeping brain came out of the fog of fatigue. She opened her eyes to see that Molly had stopped, jammed up close to the rear of the wagon. Faint morning light glowed in the east. The rain had also stopped, and as she lifted her head off Molly's warm damp neck, she heard William calling her. "Danna! Danna girl, come up here and help us!"

As soon as she could force her stiffened hands to release their grip on Molly's mane, she thankfully slid off the horse's now bristly back, dried from her skirts. She relaxed her jellied, weak legs. In the dim, early morning light, she could just see that she now stood on a ledge of rock, like a little island surrounded by a muddy lake.

Wiser now, she laced her boots tighter at the top and tied her skirts up under the poncho with her apron strings, all heavy with rain and mud. She plunged down off the rock ledge into the mud taking big, long steps toward the sound of voices raised alternately in curses and laments. "Ah, here she is now—my wife, Rodantha." Will hollered, as he waved his arm in her direction. "Danna, come meet Oliver Peterson and his Missus ... Eliza, I think it is."

"Ma'am," the tall, bearded man nodded toward Rodantha.

A large, square, red-faced woman just nodded and smiled weakly. Rodantha nodded back as politely as she could, still groggy and stiff from all night on horseback. Danna could see that the woman was in the family way, surely in the last weeks or even days of her nine months. About half of her tangled, reddish-brown hair had escaped the pins and straggled down her sturdy neck.

William pointed toward the big wagon mired in mud up to the axle hubs. "Got a broken wheel under that mud, they have. Broke up when they fell into the ditch from a sudden current across the road, or maybe while they were trying to pull out again. I have proposed we hitch our team in front of their horses. I think Dutch and Shire can pull them out, if we can just get these big grays to work with our team. There's another rock ledge just ahead for a bit of traction for the oxen."

Peterson said. "If we can do that, maybe we can fix the dern thing right on that big old flat rock, before we go plunging back into the muck."

The two men set to work immediately. They hitched, unhitched, aligned, pushed, and hauled. This required every last mite of their combined strength, every cunning trick that they ever heard of in the handling of draft animals, and quite a bit of taking the Lord's name vainly. Mud was the chief hindrance, where men and beasts could not get a good footing let alone move. Eliza pressed on her back and moaned, "I just hope the stork don't decide to leave me a bundle today. I'll lay down a while," she said as she began climbing inside of their big wagon."

Hunger pangs stabbed Rodantha's stomach, and she remembered her rabbit stew from yesterday's nooning. "I have just the thing for you, Eliza. We'll feed that child of yours to make him wait a while longer."

By stretching and leaning in, she could just reach the kitchen box from the back flap of her wagon, keeping her muddy boots and skirts on the outside. She dished out a bowl of cold stew and took it to Eliza, who ate about half of it and lay back down. "Thank you, Rodantha, but I can't hold too much at one time these days. Give the rest of it to my Oliver. He's eaten nary a morsel since yesterday morning. I don't see how he can stay upright."

Rodantha refilled the half-empty bowl and dipped another for William. She whistled sharply to get the men's attention, and William came sloshing back to where she was now perched on the back wheel of the wagon. "You all right, girl?" he said with a worried frown. But right away he saw the stew and grinned. "Didn't know you could whistle like a drover, Danna."

"Here's stew for you and Mr. Peterson. Now you take a short spell to eat it up. I'll stay right here to eat mine. Now get going."

"Yes ma'am, right away. I couldn't refuse such a tidy meal." He disappeared with the bowls.

Rodantha bolted the last of the cold stew straight out of the Dutch oven, sloshed water into the bottom of the pot, and poured out the thinned broth into a cup. She drank half of the broth and took the other half to Eliza who was now sitting up, looking a little less red in the face. Eliza drank it all. Rodantha wasn't exactly full, but she thought that she might be able to go on now, maybe even help the men to get the Peterson wagon out of the muddy ditch.

She collected their bowls and spoons and took a dipper of water up to Eliza, who was once again asleep. She offered the water to Mr. Peterson instead, who drank it in one enormous swallow. One more slog back to the water bucket for a dipperful for William made her sure of what to do next.

What she needed was a pair of trousers instead of yards of skirts to drag through the muck. She knew that this was not "fitting" for a woman, and her ma and Aunt Zelda would have been mortified. But Rodantha knew it was necessary, and thought, *I'll do whatever's needed to survive this. I don't care what other folk might think.* She quickly undressed and left her wet muddy dress and apron dripping over the tall back wagon wheel. She kicked off her muddy boots, climbed into the wagon, and found William's old, patched canvas trousers in her sewing basket. They needed mending again. She pulled the trousers on over her bloomers. Since she couldn't find William's torn shirt, she wound Ma's shawl around her camisole for propriety in the company of others and tucked the ends securely in the top of the trousers. Pulling her boots back on, she approved her attire appropriate to the day and the task at hand.

She woke Eliza and explained to the yawning woman, "Eliza, you're going to need to come out of your wagon. There's about to be a big dangerous effort put on to pull out of the mud. There could be a lot of jolting, the wagon might even break up or wheels come off. Now just to be safe, ma'am, you should rest in our wagon a spell while we get this big rig of yours out of the ditch."

Rodantha watched as Eliza hiked her skirts and waddled back to the Hywell's wagon. Eliza kicked her muddy boots off one at a time as she climbed up the wagon spokes with bare feet. She slowly hoisted her bulging body over the high front seat and safely inside. Rodantha then climbed up onto the high driver seat of the Peterson's wagon and unwound the reins behind the big gray Percheron draft horses.

She called out to whoever might be listening, "I think I can drive these here animals, if that's some help."

William turned and grinned at her wearing his old, patched trousers. Peterson shook his head and burst out laughing. "Didn't know you had an extra hired man with you, Hywell. This here fellow should come in right handy. This ah … Dan fellow, why he's going to have to crack the whip to get my Bess and Bob to move out. He sure has a determined look on his face."

Rodantha snapped the reins, took the whip out of its holster, and cracked it over the big horses—weakly at first, and then with a desperate vengeance. She hollered with all her might at Bess and Bob. With Dutch and Shire out in front of the horses on a makeshift tongue extension, she had to crack the whip out as far as it would go to get their attention. She repeatedly snapped the reins that now connected both teams. The oxen understood what was needed and pushed forward on their yokes. William moved forward to get the team moving and then backed up to heave on the front wheel spokes. The big gray horses lunged forward, flanks quivering under the strain. The men pushed repeatedly on counts of three. Dutch stepped up. Shire stepped up. The whole affair came cracking and creaking out of the ditch up onto the flat rock ledge in the middle of the muddy road.

"Whoa Dutch, Whoa Shire," William called when all four wheels of the wagon had reached a level, relatively-stable spot. The reliable oxen came to a halt. Danna pulled back on the reins and the Percherons stood still, their haunches still quivering. The wagon was now well out of the ditch and rested on the flat rocks that went along the middle of the road.

Three spokes of one back wheel were broken and the felloe to which they were attached was splintered, but the hub held fast to the remaining spokes. The iron rim had stayed in place, though it was flattened out over the splintered felloe. The men sat down on the back of the wagon, exhausted.

After a little rest, they lit their stogies and discussed what to do next. The sun peeked out, and then a bright blue sky favored the overlanders for the first time in three days. Eliza reappeared with her boots back on, still bracing her back with arms akimbo. She climbed back into her own wagon, moaning, and kicking the boots off again.

Finally, after rummaging and rooting in the rag bag, Rodantha found William's torn brown shirt stuffed in with the scraps destined for her next crocheted rag rug. She rolled up the torn sleeves and tied the tails around her middle to hold up the trousers a little better. *Prepared for anything*, she thought. *Never mind what Aunt Zelda would say!*

After the oxen were unhitched and hobbled, and the Percherons tied to a tree, a whirl of activity broke out: chopping of wood, clanging of hammers, scraping of saws. Mr. Peterson chopped down a dead tree and scraped off all the bark to get to underlying dry wood. Part was used for wagon spokes and felloe, the rest for the roaring fire that William built on the far side of the flat rock. Peterson knew just what he was about too. He explained that he hand-built his wagon and had a wide array of wood-working tools. He performed this specialized labor with little difficulty.

The men set to their work to repair the wheel, and Rodantha went to work cooking enough food for four hungry overlanders. Eliza slept through most of the afternoon. By sundown, their combined efforts had produced a workable wagon wheel and a huge meal. While quality was not part of the equation for this fare, no one seemed to care as there were plenty of hot vittles by the fire.

The wet conditions produced a lot of smoke as it burned the wet wood. This burned Danna's eyes and made her cough. But everyone agreed that the simple food around that smoky camp was some of the best any of them could ever remember before or ever would again. The beans were still a little too firm, but the bacon flavor was divine. Ashes had drifted into the cornbread.

The Peterson's contributed sweet potatoes from their supplies, and Rodantha buried them in the coals to bake. They ate the potatoes last with a drizzle from Rodantha's honey jar. William made his trail coffee, and they all sat around the fire long after they had consumed every morsel. Eliza had been quiet and sat rubbing her back. She suddenly cried out sharply.

"What's the matter, my sweet?" Oliver said, moving closer to her. "Is the young one giving you a kick?"

"I fear the baby is coming, Oli. The water's done broke all over my skirts." Eliza put her hand on Oliver's shoulder and started to push herself up but immediately sank back down onto the tarp where she had been sitting. "Help me up, Oli. The pains will be sharpish soon."

-11-

The Stork Cometh

March 1856

Rodantha jumped up from her warm seat by the fire and backed away from Eliza, shocked to see the "broke water" and the soiled skirts. Oliver helped his wife into the back of their wagon, rolled out a thick muslin covered pallet, and eased Eliza down onto it.

"Just do what we talked about, Oli," Eliza said. "I got to bear down now. Don't mind if I scream. Remember what I said."

Silent and wide-eyed, Rodantha hung onto William's hand. She had heard other women talk about their water breaking as a sure sign that the birth was imminent. Unsure of what she should do next, Rodantha took all the tin coffee cups and washed them in the enamel basin and dried them as slowly as possible. She watched silently as William put another log on the fire.

Oliver said, "Now Eliza, why she's done this twice before, so she's right smart about birthing. We got our kit ready to go." But Oliver's hands shook, and he bowed his head for a moment before he started rummaging in the front of the big wagon. He issued orders.

"We need hot water in the big basin here. We need some drinking water to sip on, and she is going to clamp down on this knotted cloth when the pains start coming."

Rodantha was glad for something purposeful to do. She helped tote water, towels, and soap. After William had the fire blazing again, he set the kettle on the tripod over the flames. As Eliza groaned, Oliver scrubbed his dirty, work-worn hands, and unrolled a towel revealing scissors, heavy thread, and a bottle of laudanum. He asked the Hywells to stay out by the fire and keep the water boiling, "To give our mother some breathing room."

The Hywells sat by the fire and waited. Will whistled a tune, and then he sang the song in his rich baritone, but Rodantha couldn't understand the strange words. She whispered, "What's the name a-this lovely song, Will?"

"It's pronounced See-O-Gahn in Cymraeg. It means lullaby in English. My mother sang it to me and my sisters many times."

"What are the words in English?"

"Well, I'll try to come close on the meaning, but maybe it won't exactly fit the tune as well as the Cymraeg words. Let's see, it would be something like this, it would." He began very slowly this time to sing the English words and paused slightly before some of the lines.

> "Sleep, my darling, night is falling
> Rest in slumber sound and deep.
> I would know why you are smiling,
> Smiling sweetly as you sleep!
> Do you see the angels smiling?
> As they see your rosy rest,
> So that you must smile an answer
> As you slumber on my breast."

William paused again and then added, "Mother sang other verses, but this is the one I remember best."

"Why, Will, that's the most beautiful thing I ever heard. It's sure to help the baby come soon, and peacefully, I think. Please sing it again! I'll just hum."

But then Eliza wailed into the night again, showing that there wasn't anything peaceful about her baby coming at all. After what seemed to Rodantha a lifetime, they heard it—the baby's first cry. And then Oliver shouted. "It's a boy, it's a boy. A big strapping boy!"

Later that evening, after Eliza and the baby were sleeping, and the bloody muslin pallet had been burned, Oliver spread a tarp under his wagon right on the big flat rocks, sighed his relief, and fell nearly instantly asleep. Rodantha took advantage of the hot water and soap to wash out her horsy smelling bloomers, muddy dress and apron, and both pairs of William's trousers, the one she'd worn and the one he had labored in all the previous night and day. The last pair didn't really come clean, but at least they were no longer stiff with mud. As the Hywells washed themselves of the last of the mud, Danna said tentatively, "What does the laudanum do, Will? When Oliver said Eliza didn't even need it, well, I just didn't understand."

"It dulls pain and helps some ailments like flux and coughs. I've heard that folks can get to depending on it after their illness passes. It's like what's called opium. It seems to me Eliza is a real strong woman and could manage without that bitter stuff."

Rodantha climbed up into the wagon and snuggled into Aunt Zelda's quilts. She listened as William filled the kettle and built up the fire before he crawled in beside her. "That took you ever so long, Will. Why do you insist so on all that boiling?" Rodantha said, muffled under the quilts.

"I believe strongly in Dr. John Snow's ideas about water carrying cholera and other diseases. I told you about all this before we married. Remember? And with a new baby, well, Eliza already lost two children. Don't want it to be three."

"You'll take good care of me when our young ones come, Will? It's a right frightful thing. I ain't ready for that stork coming to me. I don't want no babe to care for."

"I'll sing the Lull Song to you, and the babe will come easily, he will, and boil all the water, I will."

Rodantha heard the baby cry again. She stuffed the hem of the quilt into her ears and prayed for sleep to come.

-12-

Be There with Bells On

March 1856

The Hywells were slower than usual to rise in the morning after the stork came bringing the baby boy to the Petersons. Rodantha and William lay awake a little while, snuggling in the warm quilts, listening to the Petersons as they talked quietly.

"My milk's coming in now, Oli," Eliza said. "Since our boy suckled during the night. Sort of like priming the pump at the old well."

Oli said, "Do you think you can ride in the wagon today?"

"No, it's too soon. I need to be quiet and rest for a few more days now. Can we stay here a while?"

"Well, if Hywell will help to get us out of the middle of this road we can. I'm surprised a wagon hasn't already come along wanting to get by our big mess. If that was to happen right now, well, they'd like as not get stuck just like we did yesterday. We got to find a place to camp out of the middle of the road. Somthing like this here rock ledge we're resting on right now. Something we can build a fire on."

William made a lot of unnecessary noise getting dressed and out of the wagon. He whispered that it would give Eliza fair warning to cover herself as she nursed the baby. Oliver offered the Hywells coffee and roasted sweet potatoes for breakfast. "I am plumb glad to have a hot meal that I didn't have to rustle myself," Rodantha gushed. "I am near starved."

As they ate, Oliver and William discussed how to get the Peterson's wagon out of the middle of the road and still be on firm enough ground to hold the heavy wagon up from sinking into the mud again. The muddy roadsides had dried very little overnight. The men walked up and down the road and reported that they found that the rock ledge widened out after about a half mile. It formed a cliff on the right side of the road. A shallow gorge plunged down to a little creek, full and swift from all the rain. They planned to pull the wagon to this spot where the Hywells could then get past them. Other wagons traveling the National Road should be able to do the same. The men dragged several flat rocks into the lowest, muddiest ruts along with pieces of unburned wood from the previous night's fire. They would try to keep the wagon wheels rolling over this sturdier path.

While the men hitched the horses and positioned the wagon, Eliza wept. Rodantha tried unsuccessfully to comfort her. The older woman had seen so much sorrow over her two dead children, and she tried to explain her feelings. "The first one, well, I was too young, I guess. I never got any milk to speak of, and, well, the baby just got weaker and weaker. The second one, my little Amanda, she lived two years. The doctor said it was the cholera. She was such a delight, and it tore my heart to shreds, even more than the first little boy. I didn't get so attached to him as I was to her."

"I don't rightly know about birthing or takin care of babies," Rodantha said. "But my William has a strong belief in boiling all drinking water to keep the cholera away. He read about this from some doctor in London who's been studying this very problem. I'm powerful sure that if you do that, why you and the boy will be just fine. You said yourself you got the milk coming in?"

"I do. This little fella feeds right strong." Eliza managed a little smile and dabbed her eyes dry. "I best get on up there now." She said quietly, as she pointed to the big wagon hitched and ready to roll up the road. "The baby is sleeping in the wagon and will soon be wanting my attentions."

Keeping carefully to the rocky middle of the road, Peterson drove, and William led the Percherons. The big wagon finally rested on the rocky ledge by the creek. Everyone agreed there was not room for both wagons on the creek cliff, so the Hywells prepared to travel on.

William said, "Confident our lighter wagon will be able to go through the mud, I am, since the road is beginning to dry up in this hot sun." But as they started up, the mud stuck to everything, was flung at them off the wide iron wheel rims as Dutch and Shire pushed against their collars and sank deep into the mire whenever they stepped a hoof off the rocky ledge. Will walked out front where Dutch could see him to guide the team. Danna rode on the high seat since walking in the mud was nearly impossible. Their clothes and faces were smeared with mud. Rodantha was glad she still wore William's trousers and shirt to save her dress from sure destruction.

It was well after noon when the Hywells pulled alongside the Peterson's wagon at the cliff. A big fire blazed, and nappies flapped on a rope tied to a stake in the welcome sunshine. Oliver waved them to stop.

"We are grateful to you folks for helping us out of the ditch and welcoming the baby. Here's our best bell from off our Bob's harness. It come all the way from Sweden. It's been used in my family for generations. I'd say near every day. We'd be honored if you put this bell on your Dutch, as he's descended from that same part of the old cold countries." Tears filled Oliver's eyes as he proudly put the tarnished silver bell into William's hand.

William looked down at the silver bell and started to shake his head, but Peterson continued. "Now you can't refuse since it's our old-time ways, our custom you see, to give a harness bell to good folks who help in time of trouble."

Eliza had come around from the far side of the wagon carrying an old pie tin full of sweet potatoes. "These is special for you, Danna, all boiled after your London doctor's advice. They're ready for eating with no cooking required. I know how powerful an appetite you got."

Rodantha turned the potatoes out into her own pie tin and hugged Eliza's ample body.

"We're going to name our boy Daniel." Eliza said. "It'll be Dan for short in honor of you, Rodantha."

At this, Danna burst into tears. She sobbed, unashamed, just like she did at Ma's graveside. Finally, she blubbered, "I don't know what in the world to say." She fished out her kerchief from her apron pocket, dabbed her eyes, and blew loudly. Her tears and hanky helped to clean off some of the mud smears.

"Only one thing left to say, I reckon," said Oliver. "You be sure now to be there with this old Swedish silver bell still on your team, you hear? If you come to trouble before you get to the territories, then keep the old custom alive and pass the bell on to whatever folks who help you. But we're hoping, we're praying that you'll be there in Kansas Territory with *bells on*!"

-13-

Boredom and
Remedies

Rodantha wrote in her diary about the birth of Daniel Peterson, her namesake, the silver bell, and the custom of *Be There with Bells On*. She tried to capture the nagging worry that caught in her throat when she heard the bell tinkling, the threat of broken wheels, cholera, and the pain of childbirth.

Try as she might, she couldn't capture the agony of traveling all night through the rain and muck, hanging onto Molly for her salvation, her deep sense of unease when she saw the bounty man in the feathered hat and bloody face. Her words didn't seem to carry the loathing she felt during that long night. Finally, she wrote:

> I vow to think of the silver bell as a signal of good fortune,
> not bad. I found some leather harness strapping and Will gave me
> an old used buckle. I strapped it on Dutch and pray that it will stay
> there for the rest of our journey.

Her fear for her new husband, his abolitionist trouble in Maryland from which he was still running, was maybe the worst worry of all. William was more convinced than ever that he was being watched by the bounty man on the roan. He said it was no coincidence that the fellow with the turkey feather in his hat kept appearing, covertly following them. They had received no word from William's family as no one really knew exactly where the newlyweds were, or that William had taken a wife while staying in Fairmont, Virginia.

Writing these worries down in her diary seemed to make them more bearable but didn't keep the dark thoughts at bay. The days ran together, and the drudgery of endless walking and work never ended. The Pike felt like a repeat of itself, over and over. The days blurred to a dull sameness: mosquitos and flies, dust and manure, walking, cooking, and washing laundry—endless walking. The soles of her new high-top shoes were already wearing thin. Boredom engulfed her. She thought, *I feel like my head is covered by a brown gunny sack and I am looking at the world though the loose dusty cloth.*

There were bright spots though. She recorded little incidents, like her surprise and delight when William brought her a tin cup full of elderberry wine from the Black Horse Inn in Morristown where they stopped one evening. She wrote in her diary:

> The sweetest drink I ever had, dark purple red, it left my head as light as a feather. Ladies don't go into the taverns, but Will wanted me to have this treat. Will stayed away from the circle of men who sang songs around the campfire. He is wary of strangers.

In the evenings, Rodantha re-read the *Fourth McGuffey Reader* by the fire. She read her copy of the *Emigrants Guide to California* and practiced penmanship and pronouncing words properly, trying to copy William's speech. But whenever Rodantha met someone she could talk to, her old habits of speech took over, in the sheer excitement of the occasion.

She met a sweet parson's wife in Cambridge, who traded an old two-volume set of the *American Dictionary of the English Language* by Noah Webster for one of Rodantha's crocheted rag rugs. The old couple was going to New Concord, Ohio, to Muskingham College where the Presbyterian parson was going to lecture. They had stopped along the roadside for a rest. The 1828 dictionary was worn on the edges, missing the cover of the second volume and a few pages of the "Z" section. The parson had other dictionaries, the old lady had said. He wouldn't miss this one.

Rodantha wrote of Mr. Webster that evening in her diary:

> The picture of Mr. Webster in the front of the dictionary comforts me and makes me feel like I know him. This is a man who knows a powerful heap of words. Words I never knew were words. The little square books don't take up much space in the treasure box.

She congratulated herself when she wrote *knew* instead of *knowed*. In that month of March 1856, Rodantha wrote several more entries in her diary.

I am mighty thankful to Mr. Troyer for making our wagon wheels so wide. These has <u>protected</u> (this word found in Webster's) us from paying tolls. There are toll houses every 20 miles or so, but we are waved on and never have to pay.

William was <u>amorous</u> last night, (found this word in Webster's) but I am not willing. Since the birth of Daniel, I am scared of having babies, the pain, the blood is awful. I do not think I can survive such a <u>ordeal</u> (Mr. Webster's word). Sylvie said I was to always receive Will's attentions, even when I didn't feel like it. But I turned Will away. I could not explain to him how I felt. I said it was my "time" and have hid this by washing my under clothes each night. I am ashamed for lying. I feel lonely and distant from every other creature on earth. Will deserves better. He is the most dearest person, always polite. He is ever so gentle and kind. I vow not to lie to him but tell him my true feeling.

Should I strike out on my own to California? My gold dream seems poor and selfish, and I can't bring myself to ask Will about it. But I will soon. Was I foolish to marry him just to get away from the farm? I wish I had known about his past more. His worries are much greater than mine. I do love him dearly, but sometimes I just want to get away from all these troubles, for him and for me.

Making rugs and potholders calms me. I found a pile of old calico dresses near the creek. Someone must of intended to wash them, but just left them there. They almost weren't worth washing I reckon, near worn out. No one was around, so I washed them and hung them up in case someone should come along to claim them. No one ever come, so I stowed them in the rag rug bag. Pretty colors—green, blue, faded yellow and dark brown, should make several fine rugs.

When the fire or lantern was too dim to read or write, she crocheted rugs from torn strips of cloth using her oversized wooden hook. She could usually do this from touch without looking. It kept her hands busy and her mind off babies, blood, and pain. The last few nights she had stayed up crocheting until she could hear William snoring, so she didn't have to lie to him. This solution was better than the choking fear that rose in her throat and made her tremble whenever Will kissed her.

Making something useful from the bits and scraps of cloth grounded her and lulled her thoughts. She became more skilled at combining varied colors and could make them thick and tight in various shapes as she gained skill— round, oval, and rectangle. Odds and ends became hot pads that she thought would be of value to the ladies that had homes, tables, and fireplaces. She could trade them for eggs and buttermilk or even sell them at some of the general stores along the Pike. Though, it was sometimes difficult for her to give up her creation, especially if it was handsomely done. The one in greens and blues had been traded for the dictionary. *An excellent trade,* she thought.

Into Licking County, the pike towns and their near identical Main Streets were uninteresting—Brownsville, Linnville, Kirkersville—the names even sounded alike. But after the Hywells passed the small pike town of Amsterdam, they saw a definite change in the land. The hills and curves nearly disappeared. It was like a different country, spacious and wide. Trees were sparse. Farmhouses and barns sat on the edges of large, plowed fields and pastures. Just into this new country, at Jacksontown (or Jacktown as they heard the locals say when they boasted that their fair city was named after the famed Andrew Jackson), William eased the oxen to the side of the road near the door to a blacksmith and stables. It was next to the Headley's Hotel so said the sign above its wide double doors.

"You're stopping mighty early, Will."

"The harness needs some mending, and I don't have the right parts and extra leathers. I want to see if the smithy has what I need. Why don't you take a little walk while I talk to him, Danna? Just be careful who you talk to, and don't give any details about us to these strangers."

The prospect of something new and interesting was enticing, so Rodantha walked into the lobby of the white clapboard hotel on Main Street, the Headley Hotel. A green glass chandelier hung in the large entry, and the dark wood floors were polished and shiny. Next to the hotel was a barber shop with a pole painted red and white outside. The sign in the window read: *Shave – 10 Cents Haircut – 5 Cents*

The town turned out to be a half-dozen short dusty streets that intersected with Main Street, which was also the National Road. Two or three back streets paralleled Main and then the open countryside spread to the horizons. Rodantha had noticed that the National Road had become a series of Main Streets all through Ohio. Jacktown, she estimated, must be near three-hundred people, enough to have a fine two-story white schoolhouse on the back street, a tall steeple and bell attached. A sign read: *High School Second Floor*. Danna said out loud, "I wish I had a chance to go to such a fine higher school as this one." She quickly looked around to make sure that no one was near to hear her talking to herself. Talking to herself had become usual these days, and it troubled her.

As she walked back around by the blacksmith shop, she saw that Will had pulled the wagon up into the open side-bay where the smithy hammered out a ring to fit the harness. Will was pulling down leather strapping from a rack along the end of the workspace. Molly gnawed on the back rail of the wagon where she was hitched. Rodantha boldly walked up behind William and announced, "I got a treat for you, Will. Something I been promising you but not doing. Can you come away from here just now?"

The red-headed smithy looked up from his work and grinned. "Hey, mister, if a saucy lady asked me to have a treat she'd been promising, I'd fall all over myself to get there pronto." His big black apron heaved up and down as he laughed at his own words.

William looked back at the smithy and whispered to Rodantha. "I think this hard-working fellow is nah threat to us. He was busy shoeing some horses for what he said was his 'freedman friend,' but he says those horses can wait for our small little job."

To the smithy William said, "Can our little pack horse and these two brutes wander in your corral for a while, Mr. Nixon? And have a drink from the trough?"

"Why, those two old boys can even have a little hay on the house since you're a paying customer," joked the big, beefy man. "Your pack horse looks a might worn out and maybe needs a little rest too."

"Nimrod, you should meet my wife properly. This is the extra-special Rodantha Hywell."

Nimrod Nixon nodded his delight in Rodantha's direction and laughed again at absolutely nothing. Then he swung his hammer down with a shocking clang onto the iron anvil with his bulging arm. He stomped on a pedal that pumped the bellows to heat the ring again. Sweat rolled off his forehead and sizzled on the coals.

The clanging of the hammer continued as Will turned Dutch and Shire out into the corral, washed his face and hands in the trough, and slicked back his long hair. He threw his sweat-stained hat up into the back of the wagon as Danna fished something out of the treasure box. He gallantly held his arm for Rodantha, and they walked arm in arm down Main Street. This was as close as Danna had been to Will for some days, and it suddenly felt good again.

She stopped in front of the red and white barber pole. "Now, William, I reckon I'll just treat you to a shave and haircut, since I never do get 'round to doing the job myself."

"How would you pay for such a treat, my dear?"

Rodantha jingled the change in her apron pocket. "Don't you worry none. I have money right here from the rugs I been selling." She smiled and urged him up onto the board walkway.

"Don't mind if I do. I look a little ragged, I guess. Just guard what you say in front of the barber, and don't give our last name to anyone, Danna."

Inside the shop, the barber leapt up out of a curious rotating chair and snapped a large white cloth saying, "What'll it be, sir?"

"My wife says I am to get the shave *and* the haircut. I always do what she says."

"Good code to live by, sir. Sit right down."

As the tall, very clean-shaven barber swathed William's face in a wet towel, Rodantha walked along the side of the room where bottles and jars were lined up neatly on a shelf with a mirror behind it: shaving brushes and soap cakes, and the most impressive of all—tall, long-necked bottles of pale green liquid. These bottles had fancy labels that read *Murray and Lanman Florida Water* and underneath this a lavish fountain and pool with the words *Cologne New York*. Birds, flowers, and much scrollwork completed the ornate label. The long neck had a gold seal that read *Trademark Lanman and Kemp*. The barber saw Danna peering at the labels and said, "Here, little lady, I'll sprinkle out some of that Florida Water so you can smell the lovely fragrance. Hold out your hand."

"No, no really, I couldn't...."

But the barber was already at her side, with the bottle tipped up and poised for a sample. Rodantha held out her hand, and the barber splashed a thimble's worth of the pale green liquid into her palm. She could instantly smell the heady fragrance. Like nothing she had ever smelled in her life.

The barber continued, "Now just rub that on your wrists and arms. See the little pink trade card propped up there on the shelf in front? If you can read, just see what it says on the back."

Danna picked up the card to show that she could read. Silently she read:

We have the choicest fragrance of flowers, fresh and invigorating as from a bouquet newly culled. The hot and feverish head, bathed with it, becomes cool and easy. The temples laved with it, relieves the racking nervous headache. Poured into the water of the bath, the weary body and overtaxed brain emerges fresh and vigorous. Inhaled from the handkerchief, it imparts the most exquisite enjoyment, and sprinkled in the sick room it soothes and relieves the restless invalid.

She wasn't sure about the words "invigorating," and "exquisite," but pretended that she did by nodding and smiling, maybe a little too much.

"This is both an aftershave for the men and cologne for the ladies," the barber went on. "It is said to be made from the far southern waters of the fountain of youth, and contains healing properties of lavender, lemon, and orange."

"It has a hint of Aunt Zelda's spice cake," Rodantha said, giggling like a little girl. "Cloves, I think she always put in it."

The barber was shaving the last of William's beard off with his long razor when he said. "Well, ma'am, I have a special sale on the Florida Water today. Normally it sells for twenty cents, but today it is only ten cents. Would you like to have a bottle to take with you?"

"Why no, I think not. But thank you kindly for offering." Rodantha went outside to avoid any further questions from the barber. She sat on a bench in front of the hotel and waited for Will to be finished with his hair cut. Occasionally she lifted her wrist to her nose for a whiff of the spicy "exquisite" Florida Water.

William came out of the barbershop and walked quickly toward her. "Why, you look so fine, Will," she gushed as he stood before her.

"Most glad you approve, I am. Here's a little treat for you in return for your thoughtfulness today." He drew out a tall bottle of the now familiar pale green Florida Water from the pocket on the inside of his vest.

"I just cain't believe this. Thank you, William. This is the most kindest thing." She twisted the top and inhaled the lovely fragrance of oranges and spice. Danna paused, searching for words to express her wonder and amazement at being the owner of such an extravagant gift. Finally, she grinned at him and said, "But here's what I want to know—how did you pay for such a treat, my dear?"

At this William laughed, jingling the coins in his pocket as they went back toward the blacksmith shop. Danna clung closely to his arm, careful to keep perfect step with his. For the first time in a long while, this felt natural and good. She was aching for him, wanting to kiss that square clean-shaven face.

-14-

Love and the Washing

March 1856

The Hywells filled their water barrel at Jacksontown from the smithy's well, and also filled an extra washtub and two buckets full, the chopping board lids clamped tight to prevent sloshing out along the way. "I need some extra water for a big washing tonight, Will," Rodantha explained.

At the crest of a small hill outside of Jacksontown, trees grew densely on the right side of the National Road. On the left, the hill rose a little steeper away from the roadbed. A rutted path led south from a wide clearing which appeared to have been previously used as a camp. From the rise, Rodantha could see wide open lands beyond to the west. The expansive view opened her heart and mind again to the feeling of freedom and independence.

"Haw Dutch, Haw Shire," William commanded, and the oxen slowly edged into the clearing and up the small hill. "There's nah creek near here, but this is once we don't really need one. Looks like the trees and the hill will make a good place to camp with nah one around."

Rodantha gathered wood and built a fire. She watched as William hobbled Dutch and Shire out under the trees. He gave Molly a brush down and pulled swollen bloody ticks off her neck. He carried the two buckets of water out to the animals for a drink. William retrieved his bagpipe from the wagon and hung the wrapping quilt out the back flap to air out. As he quietly fingered the pipe chanter, she felt a longing to be close to him again. Rodantha stripped off her clothes and put on a clean shift, wrapping Ma's green wool shawl around her shoulders. The late spring evenings were still chilly.

"I'm going to wash my hair while the water is clean, and then my dress and underthings. Just you give me a hand hauling this here tub over to the fire and up onto the tripod grating, Will. I can do the rest myself. This here new lye soap we got in Jacktown will surely clean better than my old homemade."

While the water was heating up, Rodantha took out a basin-full of warm water and washed her hair standing close to the fire. She made a rinse from clean water with a little vinegar, and a sprinkle of the sweet Florida Water. She stripped off her shift and shawl and scrubbed all over two times with the old sugar sack she had brought from Virginia. She rinsed off standing over a clean-looking patch of grass. This made her shivering cold, even with the shawl back around her shoulders, so she was glad to get busy with the washing. The longer she worked, the more she longed to be close to William again, to feel his warm touch.

When the tub of water was hot, she pulled it away from the center of the flames with a mighty tug and repositioned it to the edge of the grating where she could reach everything without burning her shift in the roaring fire. The water sloshed out onto the front of her shift. She poured a generous measure of Florida Water into the tub, enjoying its sensuous heady fragrance, and then put her washing in. Vigorously, up and down over the washboard, she scrubbed all their clothes using the lye soap liberally. She hung the washing up on a line William had strung from the wagon to a tree: two muslin sheets and flour sack pillowcases, her blue dress, and the old brown one that was so dirty she had avoided wearing it of late, her bloomers, camisole and stockings, and Will's shirt and heavy boot socks.

"Before I put your trousers to soak, here's a basin of clean water for a bath, Will," she said handing him the lye soap and sugar sack. She pointed toward the chipped enamelware wash basin she had used for her hair. He stripped off his trousers and union suit from which she had cut the frayed arms and legs at the knee and elbows when the weather warmed. She greatly enjoyed watching him scrub and shiver in the cool night air. Every rag and towel she could find went in last for a long soak with the union suit and trousers in the now dirty water.

Rodantha's fears fell away as William pulled her toward their wagon. His skin was still damp as they climbed in and lay down on Aunt Zelda's quilts. She realized how much she had missed this closeness. This felt so good, so right, so freely given. Rodantha truly enjoyed the lovemaking. It was her own choice somehow. Tonight, it belonged to her.

Much later, as they lay in the twilight, listening to the fire crackle and hiss, she said, "I reckon having babies is the natural way of things. I been afraid of getting too close to you these past days. When the stork come to Eliza, and brought little Daniel, I liked to swooned. But I been lonely, pining for you. I declare I do love you, William Hywell, but I just … well ... I'm ever so sorry for the deceit of my actions. Makes me feel awful bad. I…." she broke off and turned her face into his chest.

He stroked her long, loose hair and said, "I could tell you were frightened. Guess I'm getting to know you better, I am. But don't you worry. You are strong and brave, and I've grown to love you even more, Danna girl." They lay there for a long time just enjoying each other's company.

Rodantha finally raised up on one elbow and kissed William again. She retrieved her shift and shawl. "I got to finish the washing, Will. Now didn't I hear a promise of some bag piping this evening?"

"I only need one last cwtch, Danna girl," Will said as he squeezed her tightly to his chest. "So, what do you want to hear?"

"That Welsh Lullaby to start—with the funny name. You sang it when baby Daniel was born."

"Suo Gan." He said carefully pronouncing the Welsh words, see-o-ghan.

"That's it, Will."

"Means 'lull song' in the Cymraeg."

Will came out of the wagon wearing only his old union suit (still clean since he hadn't worn it due to the holes in the underarms and missing buttons) and boots left untied. As she scrubbed, wrung, and hung the washing, Will played the soothing lullaby. He put down the pipe and sang the verses he could remember in his full lyrical baritone, some in Welsh and some in English, the native Welsh for his own pleasure and then to let her in on the meaning of the secret magical words.

"I cain't see how anyone can understand that Welsh, it is so strange to my ears, Will. But I do love your singing no matter the strange words."

"I learned from an early age and joined in with all the congregational singing. My people are fond of singing together, and the men especially apt to sing at any moment, they are."

Next, William played "Guide Me O Thou Great Jehovah," and Rodantha sang the verses from memory as she scrubbed, wrung, and hung the last of the washing. She tipped out the tub of water, now dirty and cold, and washed off the dust and mud on her high-top shoes with the last of it.

"This is surely a hymn for overlanders putting faith in the almighty, and in their selves I dare say. Not really knowing the future."

"I know another one that you might like," he said, as he got up and adjusted the drone pipe back across his shoulder. "I'm sure this is very old, from the Cymraeg folk of ancient times, but a fellow by the name of William Lloyd wrote it down and polished it up into a proper hymn. It was passed around the towns and churches of Wales in the '40s. It's a good walking tempo for the pipes. I know it by the tune name: *Meirionydd,* so named from the mountainous county in North Wales where Lloyd lived. The English title is 'The Voice of God is Calling.' Let's see how you like it."

William circled the fire, the wagon, and the line of washing in a slow rhythmic march and came back around playing the bold tune. But just as he faced the fire again, he stopped abruptly and let the pipe screech to a stop. He walked toward the tree line and shouted abruptly. "Haw, get away! Haw, you devil!" There was a rustling in the woods, and he turned again toward the fire. "An old dog was growling and hiding in the trees just there, enjoying the music. He's gone wild I think, skinny and mangy. I didn't want him to enjoy anything else. I think he understood my meaning. He's gone now."

As he rewrapped the pipe in the quilt he said, "Finish up, Danna, we have a long way to go tomorrow. I hope to be in Columbus by the end of the week." They heard the dog barking in the distance and rustling through the trees after they lay down, but William's warning and the fire kept the sly creature from coming in close again. There, next to William, Rodantha wasn't afraid at all.

-15-

Ohio State House

March 1856

Early the next morning, the newlyweds crossed the Ohio-Erie Canal at a town called Hebron, over a narrow bridge that even steady old Dutch was wary of. He slowed his pace over the uneven bridge deck. Shire tossed his head in protest, but William urged the oxen onward, and the short distance was covered before they could get really riled. Only the well-worn mule towpath running out of sight left and right, and a sign on the toll house, indicated that this was anything other than a creek or small river. Danna looked for boats or barges that she had heard carried freight but saw nothing but fog and low rock walls farther down the canal. The toll operator waved them on when he saw Mr. Troyer's wide iron wheels.

The next few days were long and tedious. A boring sameness unbroken by anything of note. Even the stone mile-markers held little meaning for Rodantha, who felt lost in the unknown, unable to get her bearings or feel any progress being made. When they ate the last of the honey over some johnnycakes, she thought of little Jake and wondered what had become of him. When the blisters on her feet got too painful to walk, she rode on Molly, using a misshapen brown rug she'd crocheted too tightly. It was a surprisingly good make-shift saddle—so tightly crocheted the rug curled in on itself. When thrown over Molly's back, it hugged around her flanks. In her boredom, she fancied that she could intentionally make some rugs this way and claim that they were naturally curving saddle rugs. At night she darned the holes in her stockings and tried crocheting a "saddle rug." She wrote in her diary:

March 1856

I so look forward to the even-time after a long day of walking. Will and I are often found in long embraces, and the sprinkling-on of the sweet Florida Water to improve our <u>countenance</u> (Mr. Webster's word) with each other. All the quilts smell of lavender and cloves. The days are too long and not worthy of note. Walking, walking, sore feet.

When they reached Reynoldsburg, William began talking about the Ohio State House that was being built in Columbus, details that he'd heard from one of the overlanders who asked him about the handsome ox, Dutch, and the Dutch-belted breed. Will evaded more questions and moved the wagon well away from the man's camp.

Will told her about what he had read in one of the penny papers. The governor of Ohio, Salmon Chase, was a member of a new political party that stood against slavery—the Republican Party. Chase had campaigned against slavery as a Senator from Ohio. Mr. Chase was against the Fugitive Slave Law of 1850 and had worked to establish Ohio laws to protect slaves that came into the state.

Rodantha was confused by some of this political talk, but nevertheless understood that this Governor Chase had sparked Will's interest in the Ohio State House because of his open public anti-slavery sentiment. "A man after my own heart, he is," said Will admiringly.

"In my opinion this fugitive slave law has made a whole new gruesome bounty business out of catching and returning slaves," Will said in a hushed voice. "There is good money to be made by dubious characters who ply the roads hunting down their prey. These blackbird slavers use every violence known to man and get paid to do it!"

"Like the bounty man on the roan who we have seen many times?" Rodantha whispered.

"Exactly, Danna. That fellow with the turkey feathered hat is able to combine his work as a bounty hunter for a judge back East, who wants a lawbreaker caught with catching and returning slaves. Slave owners pay handsomely to get their slaves back, sometimes better than the courts pay. I may be small potatoes compared to what a slave will profit the bounty man."

Will turned to face Rodantha, held her by the shoulders, and looked straight into her eyes. "These fellows are the worst kind of mean, Danna.

They will beat, torture, rape, mutilate, starve—everything shy of murder since their prey must be returned alive. I have seen their cruelty first hand."

"What should we do if the bounty man tries to arrest you?" Rodantha asked.

"Shoot to kill," Will said flatly. "We must not fall into his hands. No Quaker kindness."

"So glad you showed me how to shoot your guns a while back. I understand more about your hatred of slavery now and want to be ready to defend you if need be. But maybe I need a little more practice."

Will was excited to see the Ohio state house for himself on the way through Columbus. At first Rodantha wasn't sure what he meant by the "capitol building," but by the time they arrived in the city, she was beginning to comprehend that the state of Ohio had a special building in which to conduct the affairs of its government, and that it was a grand thing built in the Greek style.

Anticipation built up as she began to look forward to this break in the daily drudgery and monotony. They passed by a big colonial style house along the Pike with many side wings. A few sheep grazed in the surrounding fenced yard. They had clipped the grass closely, giving it a well-cared-for appearance. "If this is any likeness to the state house, why I shor see why folks marvel," she said as they passed by the impressive home.

In Columbus at the corner of the National Road and High Street was a five-story building, with a sign that read *Neil House*. Will said it was a hotel. Off the Pike to the left loomed the huge, though obviously unfinished, Ohio Capitol Building, gleaming in bright limestone. This was nothing like the impressive colonial they had passed with the sheep clipping the yard. It definitely was not a house. In fact, it was nothing like anything Rodantha had ever seen.

The crush of workers, wagons, and machinery made it impossible to stop there though, so they traveled on a little way past the Capitol turn-off where William guided the oxen into an open field. Other overlanders' rigs were haphazardly pulled into this space and many people milled about talking, eating, and trading. William pulled the team as far as possible away from the other wagons.

"We'll not be noticed back here. There is quite a crowd here. Don't need anyone getting too curious about us," he mumbled as he unyoked the oxen where they stood and gave the big beasts a drink. They immediately sank to their knees and rested on their haunches. "We'll need to take turns, Danna. You go ahead back to the State House and have a look around. Stay here until you return, I will. You saw all that construction. But I don't know if you can go inside the building."

"Are you sure, Will? I don't rightly know if I want to go there without you."

"You will be fine, Danna. Just go straight back down this same street and then look left. You can't miss it. We can't leave the team untended."

"Well, I reckon I do remember the way, Will. I won't talk to nobody."

Sounds of chisels and hammers grew stronger the closer she got, and soon she could hear the workmen as they shouted and hoisted a limestone block with a big winch. This required several men to operate it. She worked her way around the imposing limestone structure and was amazed by the eight giant stone columns several stories tall. They were like she had seen under the listing for Greek Architecture in Miss Quimper's encyclopedias from her last year of school. As she stopped and stared, that encyclopedia picture sure made more sense now.

From behind her, she heard shouting and clattering of hooves and iron wheels. "Look out there, missy, coming through. Step aside, step aside, quick, quick." A wagon pulled by a four-up team of mules bore down on her. Apparently, she stood squarely in the middle of a driving path. The driver hauled back on the reins momentarily as she quickly jumped aside, then he waved his hat and continued on, shouting to his animals and cracking a whip over their heads. "Get up there, Sue, Hi-ya, Hi-ya, Bill!"

To catch her breath, she leaned on a little sapling tree, her heart pounding. Suddenly, she felt very hungry. Danna hurried back down the street toward William and the wagon, sweat beading up on her forehead.

When she found him resting against the tall back wagon wheel, she gushed about the near collision, and then finally said, "There's a huge silo right on the top of the building with windows all round. I guarantee it's ten times bigger around than any silo I ever saw. Looks like a big top hat to me just a sitting there on top of the limestone. Now you go on, have a look, William, whilst I find us something to eat."

In the front of a wagon near where the Hywells had stopped, a tiny lady jostled a crying baby and smiled weakly. She stood beside a bucket of big, pale red apples with a hand-lettered sign propped in front. It read: *Apples, 3 for 1 cent*. The lady looked friendly enough, so Rodantha climbed into her own wagon and retrieved two of the new 1856 Eagle wedding pennies and promptly bought six apples, picking the best of the lot. She ate one as she stood there in front of the little lady. It was very sweet, no worms, though a few bruises. "Mighty good ma'am," she said quickly to cover her ravenous behavior. The lady just smiled weakly again and thankfully didn't ask any questions. She sat down to nurse her child, who had refused to quit crying. Rodantha fed the apple core to Dutch and waited for William to return.

Half an hour later, she could see him sprinting toward her. "Marvelous building, don't you think, Danna? See here I found a chip of that white limestone from the building site. Put this in your treasure box to remember it by. Just wish we could have seen the inside of the place, but no visitors allowed. Not finished yet."

She handed him an apple and nodded toward the next wagon. "Bought these from a little lady—uh … well—she was there a minute ago. They are right good. It might hold us until supper?"

"Tidy work, Danna girl." He chomped into the apple and continued with his mouth full. "I took a chance and talked to a fellow working up there on the construction. He says we're fifteen to twenty miles from Big Darby Creek, and that the road from here to there is quite fine and well used, easy to travel. Maybe we can make it there by nightfall if we take off right now. The man said there are fish a-plenty, sweet swift water, good grass, and woods for a fire. Got it in my mind to go there today, I have. We have mixed with quite a few people around here, so maybe best to move on to be safe. Think we can do that?"

"I am most certain we can do that. But maybe a few more of these apples could help us get along without stopping? See, the little lady left the rest of that bucketful. I'll find her and get us some more. You got a couple of pennies in your pocket maybe?"

"Yes," he said fishing out two pennies from his vest pocket. "I'll hitch up the team and we'll cut out for Big Darby. I am feeling uneasy about all the people collected here. The bounty man could be in the crowd and hard to spot. I will feel better when we are in open country where we can camp by ourselves."

"There will certainly be a chance for me to target practice a little out there," she said.

Rodantha found the little lady lying on a quilt in the shade on the far side of the wagon fast asleep. Unsure of what to do, Danna sat down beside the lady and asked with a low, quiet voice. "Ma'am? Can I buy some more of your apples?"

The lady opened her eyes, squinted and put her finger to her mouth. She whispered. "Shhhh, baby has the colic and finally is sleeping."

Rodantha pressed the two big pennies into her hand.

The little lady whispered, "You just take all the rest of them apples, dearie. Only small ones left now and I might-a charged too much anyway." She closed her eyes and seemed immediately to be asleep again.

With eight more apples stowed in the jockey box, the Hywells were soon on their way. The road turned to the north, and they crossed over the Scioto River and away from the crush of the houses and buildings of Columbus. The well-maintained open road beckoned.

Up ahead she saw Will pull his hat low as a rider approached. It was the man with the turkey feather in his hat, riding that same roan horse, coming toward them. She turned her head to the right so he could not see her face. After a mile or so away from him, she ran forward to walk with Will as he guided the oxen.

He said without being asked, "Yes, that was the same man who followed me in the night as I fled Maryland. Fetch my Navy and load the shotgun. Just in case he comes back. He surely is a bounty hunter plying these roads to find lawbreakers or runaway slaves." She prayed and prayed as they continued on, intent on putting miles between themselves and the man riding the roan.

-16-

Big Darby to
Red Brick Tavern

March 1856

They arrived at twilight, beasts and human overlanders exhausted. Several campfires sent up curls of smoke and occasional sparks as the Hywells moved slowly along the steep banks of Big Darby Creek. A dog stood guard and barked a loud warning. They pulled in through the heavy woods near a dense thicket. Rodantha built a fire and set up the kettle to be ready for boiling in the morning. They lay down to sleep as soon as William had tended the animals, too tired to cook or eat.

The next thing Rodantha knew, the birds were trilling their morning songs from the plum thicket. She could smell William's coffee on the fire. She did not want to get up, and lay there awhile, feeling a little queasy. Finally, up and dressed, she saw that William had a batch of hot johnnycakes ready in the chipped blue enamel pan, but he was nowhere in sight. She forked out a cake and burned her mouth trying to eat it too fast. Her queasy stomach eased and settled some.

William returned with a string of fish. "Where's that chopping board, Danna? I want to clean these walleye straight away. Better bring out the big skillet too."

Rodantha returned with the board, iron skillet riding on top with a big spoonful of lard for frying. She ate another johnnycake. "I reckon I about ate all your cakes, Will. I was near starved and queasy from all those apples yesterday. I'll make some more whilst you clean your fish."

Will spent a few minutes sharpening his knife before he hacked off the fish heads, removed the tails and scales and split the walleye into filets. He zipped off the bones and plunged them into a shallow pan of water. He threw the guts and scraps into the fire, and Danna set the fish to sizzling in the big iron skillet. Will and Danna sat down on the tarp for a feast of fried fish and johnnycakes and felt like the King and Queen of England, or at least of Darby Creek. After they had eaten, Will leaned into the back of the wagon and drew out a folded newspaper and passed it to Danna. The masthead read: *Anti-Slavery Bugle*.

"I have been waiting until a safe time to show you. A boy was selling these on the street in Columbus. It is only a few weeks old, and though I haven't read all the articles, the headlines show news from Kansas Territory and the anti-slavery Free Soilers' efforts there to admit Kansas to the Union as a free state. I thought we could read it carefully to get some news of the territories and the situation there now. There's a headline about Ohio Governor Chase too."

"Howdy folks." A wiry man and equally wiry boy appeared, visible through the trees just above the top of the steep bank where they were climbing up away from the creek. "Beautiful day for fishing, I'd say," the man said as he lifted his straw hat. Rodantha had started to open the paper but closed it quickly and put it into her apron pocket.

"Greetings, friend," said Will in his most proper English. "Sorry, we cannot offer you breakfast. We have already eaten every last morsel."

"No matter, we've been feasting ourselves and just now got up to take another try at fishing on upstream a bit. Mighty good fishing here. We came down from our little town, Hilliard's Corner, yesterday on a lark. We think this is the best fishing anywhere around. We come every chance we get. But I forget my manners. I'm Clarence Hilliard. My friends just call me Clary. This here's my boy, James."

"Can't help but notice your town and last name are the same. You own the place?" Will inquired, acting oblivious to the fact that this was a stranger.

"Well, we got a big family up there and a couple of good size farms. Where the crossroad is … well … folks just call that Hilliard's Corner, I reckon. Even got a general store now and building a Congregational Church too." This mention of their beloved Congregational brethren opened the flood gates of friendly conversation for William.

As the two men stood talking, the boy, James, walked on a little way up the creek with his fishing pole dangling a hook behind him. His feet were bare, and overalls rolled up to his knees. "That boy's eager to catch his fish. I best get on up there to keep him from mischief. Good day to you sir, missus." He tipped the straw hat in Rodantha's direction. Then, he turned back saying, "You folks look like overlanders. Where you headed if I might ask?"

"Going to the territories, we are. Some Welsh folks have intentions to start up a new church there too. Seems like the Congregational pilgrims might be putting on a Christian effort all around the country," Will said, chuckling and nodding.

"Dag nabbit, that's where my brother Silas keeps going on about. He wants to go out there to see the land around the Kaw and Missouri, where the rivers come together. Supposed to be right fine tillable land on the flats. But I doubt he'll ever do it. We're both a getting a might old to be striking out again."

"That would be the point of land where that Meriwether Lewis and Mr. Clark camped on their grand exploration journey for President Jefferson, I believe," William said. "I hope to see that very spot before we head on west, I do."

"Good thing Silas didn't come along on this fishing trip. He'd be stowing away with you two, just to get out there. Maybe he will make it one day. Well, good day then."

They watched Clary as he hurried along to catch up to his boy, who by this time was just about out of sight. "What a right friendly man, he was. Little James reminds me of Jake. About the same size and age, I reckon," Rodantha mused.

"It was probably careless of me to mention that we are going to the territories, but as you say, he was such a friendly sort of fellow. You never know who might inquire after us. Just because he mentions a Congregational church doesn't make him abolitionist you know. My father suspected a church parishioner of saying too much to the wrong people, betraying me to the Maryland sheriff the night I was hauled in to jail. The church man was killed that same night under strange circumstances." William took a deep breath and squeezed his eyes shut tightly.

"It is hard to know who you can trust. Lots of the church folks and even ministers are strongly in favor of slavery—they think it is the right and natural way of the world—God putting the white man in charge of the lower races, superior intellect some people say. Total hogwash!"

They spent the rest of the day fishing, salting, and drying their catch over the fire, leaving the fish overnight to cure in the smoke. They ate fish again for supper. She washed her dirty apron with the lye soap on the washboard, but the dark stains didn't come out. At least it smelled a little better. By the time Rodantha had cleaned up the chopping board, skillets, and utensils, her hands were raw and bleeding from the day spent working in creek water and salt.

By firelight the Hywells finished reading every tiny word of the four-page *Bugle* and talked well into the night in low voices. They read that the controversies of slavery were heating up as the pro-slavery ruffians in Missouri were raiding over the border into Kansas Territory against anti-slavery groups, referring to them as Jayhawkers. Two free soil towns—Lawrence and Topeka—had recently been established.

"These articles, if they are true, show there is much sympathy in Kansas Territory toward the free-soil side," Will said as they climbed into the wagon.

"But, Will, we'll be going into the middle of these fights, and I am powerful worried. I have an idea that might be safer. Let's just go on to California and pan for gold. That would be a right better thing than getting' in the middle of this boiler. Plus, we could be rich and never want for another thing in our lives. My uncle's the proof of that. I've always wanted to do this. So now might be a good time. What do you think of that?"

"Pan for gold? What a strange thing for you to say. You want me to abandon everything I believe in and go farther west just to get rich?"

"Like I said, I have dreamed of this for a long time. You know how dirt poor my family is. We never had anything. So I guess the only thing I had was this dream, and I didn't know how to tell you. My uncle struck it rich and I thought maybe we could too. And now, with all this fighting in the territories, well…"

"Now, Danna, we've got to stick to our plan, at least until we get to Westport at the Kansas River. I know the way to go through St. Louis and then to Westport. I'd be unsure of changing to a new route. Let's just see what the situation is when we get there. I don't believe all that is printed in this *Bugle* paper anyway, and neither should you."

"Can we just keep it as a second choice? If things don't work out in Kansas Territory, we will have something to fall back on."

"I have to honor my obligation to my dear mother and fulfill her dying wish. This is no light matter, Danna."

"My dream is no light matter either, Will." Rodantha climbed into the wagon and left William by the fire. When he crawled in beside her, she pretended to be asleep. Her raw hands kept her awake all night.

At first light, Will hitched up the team and Rodantha salted down the last of the smoked fish in the wash pail. This was a painful ordeal now that her hands were so raw, and she had some trouble tying on her now permanently-stained apron. A little lard rubbed over her hands helped to sooth them, though.

William said flatly, "Let's head out for Lafayette, Danna."

They soon passed through West Jefferson where they stopped at one of the half-dozen small stores to buy a 30-pound sack of potatoes. A hand-lettered sign propped on a huge stack of the bulging sacks enticed them: *Potatoes 10 Cents.*

They stopped for a rest to watch a bunch of fellas pitching horseshoes in a big open field where a huge fire pit smoldered. Will struck up a conversation with one of the bystanders, who said his name was Melvin. Melvin was shaking hands with a tall Black man, who laughed and said, "I'll bet you a whole dollar I am the champion of this contest!" The tall man grinned and winked at William. Rodantha whispered in William's ear. "Will, what are you doing? You don't know these people." But William shrugged it off.

"Don't worry, Rodantha," William whispered. "It's okay. Slaves and masters never act this way. Equals they are, these two. This does my heart good to see this kind of friendly relations between the races."

This Melvin said that there would be a big feast toward evening. They were roasting an ox in the smoldering pit. The horseshoe game was the entertainment whilst the meat was roasting in the pits. Choosing the champion horseshoe pitcher would be the culmination of the festivities, but as Melvin said, "It's all in good fun. I'm just waiting my turn at the pitching to see if I can best these other pitchers. I could claim the honors. I feel lucky today."

Melvin clapped William on the back and said, "You want to take a turn, young man?"

"Sure would," William said. He lifted the heavy horseshoe and swung it back and forth before giving it a toss at the iron stake at the other end of the playing ground. It missed the stake completely.

"Harder than it looks," he told Melvin. Melvin just smiled and sent the shoe ringing home on the first toss.

As William and Rodantha pressed on toward Lafayette, they could hear those shoes clanging onto their stakes for a mile or more after Melvin was out of sight. After a while, Rodantha had a chance to think about the friendly group of people, both Black and white, laughing and playing together. Her disappointment over Will's rejection of her golden dream had faded a little. As she walked along beside Dutch she thought about the importance of the scene she had witnessed.

"I reckon this is what your abolitionist dream is all about, Will. I see that now," she confessed. "I shor would like to have a country where folks can live like this." William smiled and then started whistling the Welsh lullaby as they walked.

Rodantha felt sure now that she would keep her promise to go against slavery. She said, "Just forget what I said about panning for gold, Will."

It was early Spring now, with the redbuds sprinkling their pink accents through the new green of the trees, like a giant swath of calico before it's been cut up into a dress pattern. The dogwood at the fringes was just beginning to bloom, looking like petticoat lace poking out from that dreamed-of calico dress.

They didn't talk much until mid-afternoon, when they finally stopped to rest the animals in a big field next to the Red Brick Tavern in the little hamlet of Lafayette, Ohio. "I read that the President of the United States stayed here once," William said.

"Now, don't start up any cooking, Danna," he continued as she started to haul out the tripod and kettle. "I intend to eat dinner at the Inn. See it there next to the bar? I can't face another fish just now, and your hands need a rest to heal. Go on over to see what fare they offer whilst I see if I can put Molly and the team in the corral back there by the barn. Looks like they have every convenience for travelers here."

Rodantha walked across the dusty expanse toward the stately three-story brick building, massive chimneys rising on both ends. White columns flanked a heavy wooden door with a window above. In the wide hallway stood dark wood furniture with a look of ornate permanence. To the right she could see the small trunk room and the entrance to the tavern. A stairway led to the upper floors. Dark, polished woodwork trimmed the whole into a picture of deep comfort and invitation. Directly in front of her was the dining room.

There being no one at the front desk, she wandered on into the quiet dining room, where a tall thin man in a white coat was setting up tables with silverware and glasses on starched white tablecloths. His black face was a stark contrast to the white coat. His slightly stooped shoulders reminded her of Pa. A bank of windows let in the afternoon sun and made the dishes sparkle.

"Yes, um, we is not open for dinner for another half-hour," he said as he bowed his slightly graying head. "The evening menu is posted just there." He pointed a crooked finger to a little stand with iron scrollwork legs.

"Well, thank you then," Rodantha said in her most respectful tone, to show that she did not think this man inferior to her in any way. Though she had seen Black folk working the fields or tending to children, she had never really known a Negro person to speak to one. Slaves were only for lazy, heartless, rich people anyway. She thought this dark man looked a sight more prosperous than the grimy red-haired smithy, Mr. Nimrod. His stooped shoulders and thin frame made her think, *Why, he is just a hard-working honorable man like Pa. I bet they'd get on just fine. Pa would want me to help people, not go rushing after gold that I might not even find. And Ma always rolled her eyes when I talked about panning for gold like her brother. I think they would be proud of me to be part of Will's dream of a better way of life.*

"The smells coming from that kitchen back there is making my mouth water," she continued in her friendly open way. But the tall dark man looked down and said nothing.

After William told her his secret—how he helped the slaves in Maryland and worked in the Underground Railroad—she decided to be just like him. She wanted this slavery to end and was sure it was as simple as following the Golden Rule she had learned in Sunday school. It was the only thing that made sense. She thought surely the man she saw here was a freedman, or maybe he had escaped from slavery on the Underground. He didn't seem quite "free," though, in his manners: wary, downcast eyes, not eager to join a conversation. Maybe he really was a slave and belonged to the owner of the hotel. *What a problem this slavery is*, she thought.

She read the scrolling fancy letters swirling and sashaying across the menu board:

Roast Beef or Roast Pork

Side Dishes on all orders
Mashed Potatoes / Green Beans /
Stewed Apples

For Dessert your Choice of
Apple Pie / Cherry Pie /
Pumpkin Pie

All the Coffee you can Drink

Complete Dinner 50¢
Early Birds - Two for the Price of
One

Her belly was grinding and growling. Time to get back to William. As she pushed out the heavy wooden door, a cloud of dust greeted her. A loud bugle horn announced the arrival of a magnificent red stagecoach with gold lettering arched over the doors. It rollicked into the courtyard pulled by four snorting, lathered horses. Passengers began to fall out of both sides of the National Road Stage, coughing. They shook and shrugged the dust from their clothes, which only caused more dust to billow up around them.

The driver, a dandy fellow, wore a wide-brimmed hat, red kerchief at his neck, fancy brocade vest, high-top tooled-leather boots, and fringed driving gloves. A second man with a big black mustache stepped down and hauled out a dark green U.S. Mail chest with a heavy bolted lock. A sawed-off shotgun stood holstered in a wide loop to the side of his rough leather chaps. He stowed it carefully alongside the luggage, and then, holding a short length of chain, he began dragging the chest toward the front of the tavern, making a little trail in the dust.

The travelers, four men and two women, stumbled toward Rodantha, one lady pulling a whimpering child along behind her. They brushed past without even looking at her and then went on through the big heavy door. The driver cracked his long whip over the heads of the horses and gave a short piercing whistle. They bolted toward the fenced corral, where the driver pulled them up short, jumped down, and unhooked the leathers from the stage. Almost simultaneously, another hitch of four horses was being brought up from the corral by a giant of a man with a full beard. He circled the fresh four-up and backed them into place in front of the coach.

Meanwhile, the dandy driver disappeared at a trot, driving the spent, lathered horses around the side of the barn. This whole affair took only a few minutes, and before Rodantha felt brave enough to cross the courtyard, the coach driver was marching back toward her, wiping his face with his red kerchief. He called out to the giant man with the beard, "Buy you a drink when you're finished, Tiny. I'll be at the bar."

Will hurried up beside her. "Saw you got cut off by all this stage ruckus, I did. A hungry man, I am. What's on the menu?"

-17-
Roast Beef Dinner

March 1856

Well, I already know what I want," Rodantha stated emphatically. "The beef and mashed potatoes with some of that cherry pie for dessert." They paused briefly for Will to look at the menu in the wide entrance to the dining room, dark green draping on both sides. She shook off the dust that clung to the hem of her skirt. She wasn't quite sure if they were supposed to sit down or wait, but Will took her elbow and guided her toward a small table in a corner at one end of the bank of windows. His boot heels clicked on the wood plank floor. From their tall ladder-back chairs, they could see out onto a covered rear porch and a little brick well with a hand-cranked bucket rope. Rodantha recognized the other diners—dusty stage travelers sitting across the room.

A tall, thin woman wearing a ruffled white apron appeared from the kitchen. This pale serving woman stood at the open front side of their table. "What'll it be now, folks? Our early birds is sure to get the choicest cuts."

Will glanced around the room nervously. "Aye … we will have the beef, please. And, ah, my wife wants the cherry pie. I'll have the apple." The server nodded, a tight smile not quite hiding several missing teeth. As she disappeared back into the kitchen, Will abruptly got up and moved his chair so that he was facing toward the windows and closer to Rodantha. He whispered in her ear. "Look only at me and not around the room, Danna. This is important."

She could see that he was serious and had an ominous look about his eyes. She smiled at him and said sweetly, "I truly has eyes for only you already, Will." But this did not make him smile back.

"You saw the man at the back tending the coffee urn?"

"Why yes, I done spoke to him earlier when I first come in without you."

"Well, he wouldn't know you at all. But I know him."

"Who is he?" she whispered, leaning forward, afraid to take her eyes off her husband for an instant.

"His name is Moss Washington, a slave. He wanted to take his daughter to safety after he overheard his master's plan to sell her off to another plantation. Moss's wife had died some months before, and his two sons sold. I thought he was going to Mexico to work as a cow camp cook. Last I saw him, I had just stuffed him and his daughter, Cissy, in through a safe house cellar door about ten miles from my old Maryland home."

"Let's us just leave, Will, before he strikes up with you. I don't want no one to know about your Mary Land troubles. Though I am most starved."

"Nah, he will not let on that he knows me in a public place. Like as not, he is more afraid than I am of revealing himself. He won't let on that he knows a white man enough to say hello. Maybe he belongs to the owner of the hotel now. When I met him, he was a house servant and butler on one of the big plantations."

"Strange thing this. Him here just when we are. What should we do?"

Just then, the serving woman returned to their table balancing heavy grey stoneware plates of food on her arms. She deftly placed the huge slabs of roast beef surrounded by potatoes and green beans before the guests and said, "Here's your gravy boat too, folks. I'll just bring the pie when you are ready."

The heavenly smell of the hot food made Danna forget momentarily about the situation, but when she looked up from her tempting plate, the man, Moss, was standing directly behind the serving woman. He carried steaming cups of coffee in big stoneware mugs. Moss waited until the tall woman went back to the kitchen and slowly placed the mugs down on the white tablecloth, carefully turning the handles in toward each guest. He kept his eyes cast downward and gave no hint that he knew Will. He slowly walked back to the coffee urn. Danna was relieved and longed to eat her early bird dinner.

Will picked up his knife and fork and began cutting off a piece of beef. "Better just dig in, Danna girl." And then in a whisper, "We will not let Moss worry us. I can see he will be careful. He is not going to reveal himself or us. I want to enjoy this delicious hot food." Danna felt awkward, as she looked down at this meal prepared by someone else, someone she didn't even know. The silverware felt heavy in her sore hands, and she was reluctant to begin, afraid she wouldn't act correctly, politely, in these strange, elegant surroundings. But the first bite of the roast beef cured her of all her worries.

Moss brought a plate of sliced bread to their table, and as he set it down whispered, "Pay me no mind, Mr. Will."

When their coffee cups were only half empty, Moss took their mugs and refilled them. As he replaced the mugs and once again slowly, methodically turned the handles, he whispered again, "Boss man don't know who I am, and I want to keep it that way. Listen … here … now… You just ask for some cream, Mr. Will. I'll do the rest."

As Moss started away from their table, Will turned in his chair and calmly said, "Please bring the lady some cream for her coffee."

"Yes sir, right away, sir," came the deep-throated resonant reply.

By this time other diners had come into the room. Two men had seated themselves a few tables down at the other end of the bank of windows. One man wore a knee-length black coat with shiny brass buttons. The other gentleman carried his bowler hat and checked his watch from a pocket in his brocade vest as he sat down. One of the women from the stage arrived, practically dragging a small girl by the hand. She was fresh and neat without a trace of the road dust now. She wore a gray serge traveling dress with a short-waist coat, hair in a neat bun, and a hat with little blue-gray wings on top. The little girl whimpered and sniffled until the woman shook her and plopped her down on the floor just under the table. The little girl immediately quieted and began to bounce a ball and collect her jacks in endless repetition. The serving woman brought out a teapot and glass of milk to their table which was near the open doorway.

Moss crossed the dining room and went through the kitchen door. Rodantha had time to finish her meal before he reappeared. As she chewed each savory bite, she expected him to return. Finally, he slowly crossed the dining room again, carrying a small wide-mouth stoneware pitcher of cream. "Sorry for the wait, sir. We had to go down to the cellar, sir."

"Thank you," Rodantha replied, as matter-of-factly as she could, looking directly into his small, yellowed eyes, which he shifted immediately to the pitcher. She raised the pitcher to pour the cream and saw what he was trying to indicate with his eyes. Under the cream was a little square of yellowed paper. She quickly set the pitcher back down on the paper. William nodded and looked at the pitcher too.

Moss went back to his station near the copper coffee urn. Will looked cautiously around the room and then pulled the paper out and looked at it. He quickly put the paper into his vest pocket and leaned in toward Rodantha. "Don't think Moss can read nor write. Someone else has written this and must know about us being here. Note says *Can you help us get away?*" He took a drink of his coffee and said, "Now listen, Danna, I want to try to help. I hope you agree to risk this. My sainted mother would insist, she would."

Rodantha nodded yes as a jolt of fear ran down her spine. She remembered her vow to be against slavery, and knew it was the right thing to do.

The pale serving woman reappeared from the kitchen and took their empty plates, replacing them with huge slabs of thick-crusted pie, sugar dusting their tops. "More coffee here, boy," she said brusquely as she crossed over to the gray-serge lady and served her a piece of pumpkin pie.

Moss took their mugs once again and filled them. While Moss slowly set them down again and turned the handles, Will quietly said, "We will camp to the West of town along the Pike. I'll hang a quilt out the back of the wagon and keep a fire all night. Come when you can."

Moss leaned in low to brush crumbs and adjust the salt and pepper shakers, his hands trembling slightly. In a low throaty whisper, he said only, "We'll be there before morning, Cissy and me."

-18-

Moss and Cissy

March 1856

Awaking with a start, Rodantha heard hushed voices. She realized that Moss must have finally found them camped along the Pike. Will had waited up, but she had been too exhausted, falling asleep with her clothes on. She climbed out of the wagon wrapped in her shawl. Two dark figures stood at the fire warming their hands, hats pulled low, bed rolls at their feet. She sat down on the end of the tarp that William had spread near the fire.

Will was earnestly talking to Moss, saying, "I don't know much about the stations in Ohio. Do you know of a safe house?"

"If we was to get to a town called Richmond just into Indiana, Cissy here knows what we are to do."

"I've been studying this map I picked up at the railroad station." Will said this as he pointed to the route. "Richmond is a good walk from here, Moss, maybe a hundred miles. This could take us a week, maybe ten days if the weather turns."

"The distance does not matter. We can do it if you will help us." These were the first words from the woman, Cissy—clipped, exact, each word measured, considered, precise. This little Black woman's speech sounded like the good Reverend Smythe and nothing like Moss's apologetic slurring.

Will continued, "Aye, Danna and I agree. We will help. Now, though, it's late. We should all get some sleep. I'll stoke up the fire. Spread your bedrolls down over this tarp. Should keep the dampness off. The water will be hot for coffee come morning. Rodantha here," William reached a hand down and pulled Rodantha up and hugged her close, "she'll make you the best biscuits this side of heaven.

"Remember now—if anyone should come up inquiring, just say you are our man and maid servants. There is a bounty man traveling the National Road. We have seen him several times. He rides a roan horse and has a feather stuck in his hat. He might be looking for me, or just unlucky slaves trying to get away. I keep my Navy close. If he happens by, just make some noise and I will come out of the wagon." He said this as he patted the Navy stuck in his belt.

"Do not fret. We will be gone at first light, before anyone even misses you from the Red Brick Tavern. And they won't expect you have followed the very public National Road."

As Will climbed in beside Rodantha, she was already worrying. As if he read her thoughts, Will said. "Be just fine, we will, Danna. Treat the Washingtons as our slaves. It will be as natural as anything. Might just throw off some folks who might be suspicious of us too. Now get some sleep."

She snuggled close to him under the quilts and silently thought over the situation. *Do we have to hide these two? How long will we have to hide them? If it is discovered that Will has helped slaves again, could that old charge from Mary Land be brought right down on him? How am I going to feed four people? Can we walk in the daylight or only at night? Are there slavers in these parts? Should I fix a double or triple batch of biscuits in the morning? Hope my sore hands heal up quick. I don't know if I even want to do all of this. Maybe being an abolitionist is way too dangerous. Maybe I should have said no.* Sleep overtook her and interrupted the worry for a few hours.

Rodantha slept fitfully and rose before anyone else. The eastern horizon was a pale lavender. As quietly as possible, she dressed and put on her work gloves. Her hands felt a little better, but her stomach was unsettled again. She pulled the half-burned log up onto the smoldering embers to ramp up the fire. While she waited for the water to come to a boil, she ground the coffee she had roasted a few days earlier and then dumped it into the top of the blue enamel coffeepot when it boiled. She set it off the fire to settle the grounds.

From under one of the blankets came Cissy's sharpish voice. "The coffee smells divine."

"Sorry, Cissy, didn't mean to wake you. I don't rightly know just what time it is."

"I did not sleep much anyway. I heard every cricket and rustling leaf, and old father here snores and rumbles."

Cissy stretched up out of her bedroll and then shook and rolled it up tight again. Rodantha continued kneading and cutting out the biscuits on the chopping board that William had conveniently attached to the back of the wagon after they had struggled to cut up the fish they had caught on Big Darby. Two old harness rings let it swing up onto a brace leg he had carved out of a tree limb. "Pour yourself a cup. I got my hands in this here biscuit dough and need to keep going so we'll have some warm breakfast before long."

"Need not ask me twice," Cissy said, as she blew into the empty cup that hung at the ready on the tripod.

Cissy sat close to the fire on her bedroll and wrapped her hands around the warm tin cup, sipping slowly and breathing in the delicious aroma. After a while, Rodantha saw her draw a book out of the inside of her brown homespun jacket, obviously meant for a man, but serviceable with the sleeves folded up. Once the big batch of biscuits was settled into the Dutch oven, the lid piled with coals, Rodantha sat down beside Cissy and poured herself a cup of the strong brew. She could now see the gold guilt title of the book in the firelight.

"I see you brought a book Cissy, uh, *Frederick Douglas,* is it? I was told that no slaves was allowed to read. I can see that just ain't true. What's that word 'narrative' mean?"

"It means a story. It is the account of Douglas' life as a slave. It tells about the brutal treatment of slaves, Frederick's struggle to get an education, and his life as a powerful orator and writer. I hope to hear him speak at the school where I want to go."

"You suppose I could borrow your book when you finish? I done read everything I got a couple of times, except some of the Websters."

Turning a page, Cissy said with exacting diction, "Certainly, I will be finished soon. I'll lend it to you."

The four hungry travelers ate the double batch of biscuits and drank all the coffee. While Will hitched the team and got ready to travel, Rodantha made more biscuits for the road, parched some corn, and fried up all the rest of her bacon. They were going to need supplies very soon. To Rodantha's great relief, Cissy washed all the tin plates and cups, scoured the pans, and handed up everything for packing in the kitchen box. Rodantha was glad she didn't have to put her sore hands into the soapy water. As the sun peaked above the horizon, the little caravan was already moving.

Moss wasn't much help though. Rodantha could see now that he favored his left leg and moved slowly. He hardly spoke, but she heard him say quietly to Cissy, "I reckon sleeping on the ground has got my bones to aching this morning."

The traffic on the National Road was heavy by midday. A stagecoach blared its warning bugle and rushed by. Several on-coming wagons passed them going toward Lafayette, and a group of children ambled along listlessly. One carried a little black dog. No one seemed to pay much attention to the Hywells and their "slaves" aside from tipping their hats to William who always walked up front close to Shire's big horns. But Rodantha was glad when it was time to noon the animals and rest near a little creek. Her queasy stomach had returned, and her hands were still sore. After they had eaten the biscuits and bacon, she fell asleep on Aunt Zelda's quilt.

William woke her and said, "Danna, you awake girl? Got to go! Water's been boiled, it has."

They walked again until early evening and Will turned the oxen off just past the small hamlet of Harmony. A sign she saw on a big white-columned house sitting atop a little hill read Buchwalter House – Harmony – Ohio. Will studied his guidebook and drew in more places on the hand-drawn Rodantha's Road map. He said they would be in Springfield soon and could probably find provisions there as it was a bigger town. They ate all the salted fish and roasted the last of the potatoes. As Cissy again washed up the plates and cups, Rodantha gushed, "Thank you, Cissy. I don't know what I was going to do if you wasn't here to save my poor hands from that lye soap. Shor thing, Will would have been complaining about doing woman's work."

Around the campfire that night, Cissy told them about her life and hopes for the future. After much questioning and encouragement, little by little, she also revealed her plans.

She, her father, and all her family had been broken apart, betrayed, and terrorized by white owners. Cissy explained that she had been assigned as companion for the plantation owner's only daughter, Miss Ellen. At first the two little girls just played with dolls and had tea parties in the nursery, but Cissy had also been present at all the lessons and instructions meant for Miss

Ellen. She absorbed everything. She memorized. She imitated the private tutor's Eastern manners and language. The Master and Missus told everyone on the plantation that Cissy's duties were to assist with the whole enterprise of bringing up their only daughter. They were otherwise occupied with the local social scene and overseeing their plantation.

According to Cissy, she had learned to do fancy needlework, play the piano, and write sums accurately. She could ride in the English tradition, sidesaddle, beat everyone at chess, and correct Miss Ellen's feeble attempts at writing an essay. As all this was told matter-of-factly, without bravado or boasting, Rodantha believed every word Cissy said and thought there was only one thing wrong with Cissy—she was a Negro slave, a circumstance not of her own making.

When Miss Ellen got married and moved to New York, Cissy lost her usefulness. Will said that the good Quakers got wind of this through the Underground. About this time was when William had taken Moss and Cissy to an Underground station cellar in Maryland. "I was part of starting Cissy and her father on this perilous journey," Will said proudly. "And I would do it again."

Rodantha tried to remember all the details of Cissy's plan. That night when William was drifting off to sleep, she burned the oil lamp, sharpened the cedar pencil with her pen knife and wrote it all down so that she wouldn't ever forget:

Almost April 1856, somewhere in Ohio.

I know I take a risk writing down this story, but it is the MOST important thing I ever did. (except marry Will)

Cissy Washington wants us to get her to the Earlham Boarding School, run by Quakers in Richmond. She says, located right on the National Road. She and Moss is to meet up with Gabriel Smith, a free black man who conducts fugitives to Canada. Moss is to go north with Gabriel, but Cissy is going in the other direction. Seems like a fool thing to do, but she says there is a school that has invited her to study with them, if she can get there. A curious place called L-luther-in Collige (Cissy says this is a Greek word meaning free and equal), in the village of Lankastur. The miracle is—it allows every race, and women too. Some's already there studying as I write this. Cissy knows a Mr. Hoyt of the Neels Creek Anty Slave group, who has arranged all this. Cissy is the smartest woman I ever met. NO, smartest person I ever met, brave, and bold. Her speech, though, is quiet and well-thought. She might even be presentable looking if she wasn't so skinny. She looks to be about my own age. She has lent me The Narrative of the Life of Frederick Douglas to read, so I got to read fast, since she wants the book back for her studies.

Moss spoke only once all evening. When he worked at the Red Brick Tavern, he had claimed to be a freedman so as to get the job. He said the hotel boss man weren't much to rest on the law when it suited him. So, he was hired on for the dining room without much questioning.

I been feeling poorly at my belly, which I ain't said nothing to Will about yet. I just cant bring myself round to say out loud what I fear. My blue calico dont reach around my waist no more. I wish Sylvie was here to talk to. She would know what I am to do now that I am in the family way. I have passed no blood since just after we was married. Extra tired and hungry. It's worrisome. As Pa was fond of saying – a huckleberry over my persimmon. What will I do out here where there are no doctors? How can I protect a child when we are already in such danger? What if Will is arrested and taken back to Mary Land? I pray that God will protect us. The Lord knows we are doing the good work of abolishion.

-19-
Cissy's Dream

March 1856

Just west of the little hamlet of Harmony, a stagecoach careened around them, bugle horn blaring, creating a cloud of dust. Rodantha could see the bold lettering over the passenger doors as it passed – *Ohio Stage Company*. As Rodantha and Cissy walked beside the slow-moving wagon, they were caught in a cloud of dust. Cissy coughed, wiped her eyes, cleared her throat, and then started over, to answer Rodantha's question: Why didn't slaves just walk away from the plantations?

"My people are kept ignorant of what is going on in the country. They are not allowed to learn anything about geography and are told that the Ohio River is thousands of miles wide and uncrossable. They are told that native tribes eat Africans. Terrible punishments are given, such as chopping off feet and hands, and branding an "R" for runaway into their foreheads. Women and young girls are routinely raped and mutilated. And beatings are common, everyday events. Slave men, women, and children work sunup to sundown, and are always exhausted. Food is terrible. There is no medicine aside from the home remedies. This life is near impossible to *survive*, let alone escape from.

"I am one of a very few slaves that learned enough to plan an escape before I was raped, sold, or branded. I had the good fortune to be put into a situation where I could learn—the three R's they called them—reading, riting, and rithmetic. That is why I am determined to go to the Eleutherian School. With Mr. Hoyt's help, I intend to learn everything that there is to learn there. Then, I will write letters, articles, books, and pamphlets, and get these things into the hands of my people. I will appeal to the government, to the good Quakers, and other church people in sympathy, and see my old father safe into Canada, where I might join him one day. You and William, helping us like this, makes my dreams a little nearer to reality."

Rodantha listened intently and climbed up into the wagon to ride along for a while. She was exhausted already, and it was still morning. Cissy was quiet then, head hung low, as she walked alongside the wagon, with her eyes on the road. Finally, Rodantha said, "But the cruelty, the un-Christian and wicked deeds. I don't rightly understand how…"

"Remember, Rodantha, that slavery is fueled by the sin of greed. It is a business. Slaves are not considered people, they are property, like a cow or horse, and valuable too. Some say slaves are worth over a thousand dollars each, and owners will pay handsomely to get them back when they escape. And now, by a new Fugitive Slave Law, the free state governments and citizens are compelled to return all slaves to their owners, so it will be even harder to get free. Before you and William came along, well, we were so afraid that some blackbird hunters were going to drag us back to Maryland. For once I was glad for the sin of greed, the hotel owner's greed that is. He told everyone we were free blacks under his contract. Ha! We worked for room and board, though it was a dirty rat-infested shack. He did not pay us. He knew a good thing when he found it. Father knew all about the proper handling of food and drinks from years of serving Miss Ellen's family at the plantation big house. I could clean and do the laundry."

"Will was talking about this law the other day and how that is encouraging more patty rollers and bounty hunters. How did you learn about this here Fugitive Law, Cissy? For that matter, how did you learn all of this you done told me?"

"Now, I won't mention this in hearing of old father, but the tutor, the Eastern gentleman that I told you about earlier?" At this Cissy lifted her head and looked up at Rodantha on the wagon seat with the question in her eyes.

Rodantha nodded. "I remember well."

"Stephen was more than a tutor to me. I had strong feelings for him and I believe he was drawn to me in the same way. He made sure that I got all the newspapers that came into the big house before they were used in the outhouse. He explained many things to me when I worked in the garden, and he pretended to lounge on the garden bench reading. He knew about Eleutherian College from some of his family who lives in Indiana. He put me in touch with Mr. Hoyt. Stephen said that I had a 'promising mind.'"

"You should have run off with him, Cissy. I would have done just that."

"I wish I could have. But he had the consumption. Not really too sick in the early years, when I was younger, but he just got worse and worse until finally he could not get out of his bed in the attic of the big house. He died about the time that Miss Ellen went off and got married." Cissy looked up at Rodantha on the high wagon seat, as tears ran down her cheeks, making shiny tracks on her dusty dark skin. She fished in her pocket, wiped her eyes on a tattered pink hanky, and blew her nose. She sucked in a deep ragged breath.

"I'm ever so sorry, Cissy."

Just then the wagon bumped violently down to one side and lurched up again. Rodantha held on tight to the seat, and Cissy jumped clear of the wagon.

Ahead, William whistled sharply and yelled out, "Haw, Dutch. Step up, Shire, step up!" He guided the oxen into an open area beside a big brick building on the left side of the Pike—a stately three-story with white trim and dark shutters at each window. A wide porch with a second-floor balcony ran along the front. A sign on the end of the building read, *General Store*.

-20-

Pennsylvania House, Springfield

April 1856

Looking back the way they had just come, Rodantha saw Moss, now limping noticeably and leaning on a crooked stick. Cissy went back to meet her father while William drove the team toward a big barn at the rear. Molly trotted along behind. He stopped to talk to a man standing near the water tanks, who pointed toward the corral.

When Rodantha caught up to William, he said, "Go on up to the store and see what you might need whilst I tend to the team. I want to talk to the corral hand about an old saddle he might sell. I'll come up to the store shortly, and Moss can look out for the animals. He and Cissy will be taken for our slaves, they will."

Aromas of fresh-roasted coffee greeted her as she opened the door. The store was run by a Mr. Schaffner, who introduced himself and said, "Welcome to Pennsylvania House. How can I help you today? What would you need, ma'am?"

"Thank you, sir! I am Mrs. Hywell. For starters, I need twenty pounds each of flour and cornmeal, ten pounds each of dry beans and coffee beans, a big sack of salt, and two tins of sody sallyratus."

"I have some *Church and Company* baking soda that comes with a recipe. You might like that, Mrs. Hywell?" queried the helpful proprietor. Rodantha nodded yes.

While he collected the supplies from his shelves, Danna walked around and looked in the glass-front cases admiring the scrubbed wood floor. The General Store stocked just about anything the local farmers and townspeople might need: bolts of white muslin, colorful calico and gray serge, thread, needles, and scissors. He had garden tools, hammers, and nails. A little sign said, *Fresh Eggs and Butter Today*. Up high were shelves of oil lamps, dishes, enamelware, and boots. There was a big barrel of crackers, a smaller barrel of shortbread cookies, and pickles in giant jars.

William came in and struck up a bold conversation with Mr. Schaffner. He started out with the weather, progressed to the status of the corn and wheat crops, and ended up with where the Hywells were headed with their "slaves."

"How is business here since the railroad bypassed you?" William wanted to know.

Rodantha thought Will was entirely too friendly with this man and so tried to distract him with a little nudge, hoping to discourage him from any further conversation that could make anyone within ear shot suspicious. She said very quietly, "If they're not too much, I'd shor like to have a tin of those tomatoes and a big sack of the dried peaches. See just there?" Rodantha was glad that the Washingtons were outside with the wagon and team, so as not to draw attention to them in any way.

Will asked Mr. Schaffner to tally up the bill. "Mrs. Hywell will have a few tins of tomatoes and some dried peaches if our bill doesn't get too tall."

They also bought twenty pounds of potatoes, a basket of onions, bacon, two dozen eggs, a tin of lard, bottle of vinegar, a crock of honey, and a most curious little square of rubber. Mr. Schaffner said this would erase pencil marks. (Rodantha had mistakes in her diary that she wanted to erase.) He loaded everything into a rough-sawn, wooden, two-wheel hand cart. They had spent $4.26 which included three tins of tomatoes and two sacks of dried peaches.

"Thank you, folks. You can take this out for your man to load your wagon. I see the stage is just in, and I believe I have a couple of customers over in the tavern, getting a mite impatient." He smiled and shook Will's hand. "I wish you good luck on your trip to the territories."

In the yard stood the same green stagecoach that earlier that morning had careened around them, bugle horn blaring, or maybe one just like it. Before they were finished unloading the supplies, another stately green Ohio Stage Company coach rollicked into the yard. Four men alighted, carrying rectangular brown suitcases. They headed for the reception desk. Most likely to rent rooms for the night—*Maybe in the very room that Charles Dickens was said to have stayed in*, Rodantha thought. A sign at the front desk read: Rooms 50 Cents/Night – Includes Meals.

"Mr. Schaffner cain't let no grass grow in under his feet," Rodantha said, "what with all the business in this here Pennsylvania House."

"I have been thinking that this kind of work might just suit me, Danna. I took a chance to talk to Schaffner about it, I know. But glad I did. He says that his business is good and still lively even since the railroad was built, which took some of his trade over along its route. I do not really want to get into farming."

"Why, you'd make a fine shop keeper, Will. You shor have the head for it."

Rodantha returned the hand cart and met Mr. Schaffner as he came back in the front door of the store. She showed him the big red and blue rug she had finished making just before the Washingtons had come along. "Would you be a-mind to trade for this here hand-crocheted rug? I make these of an evening."

He turned the rug over and looked at the backside of the stitches. "This is fine work, Mrs. Hywell. Close, evenly stitched, and tight. Folks will like this. I will gladly make a trade. What did you have in mind?"

"I want that old saddle out to the barn that your hired hand says could be bought, on account it's near worn out. Does that make a good trade?"

"Why that is more than fair, Mrs. Hywell, for such a fine piece of work as this." The bargain was made, and as Rodantha turned to leave, the kindly proprietor presented two long peppermint sticks. "A little something for the road, Mrs. Hywell," he said with a broad smile. "Just tell old Joe at the corral that I said okay to load up the saddle too."

After a short rest, the Hywells and Washingtons were again on the National Road headed westward toward Richmond, Indiana. When they were out of sight of prying eyes, Rodantha broke the two peppermints in half to share four ways, feeling strangely in command of things. She knew that giving candy to slaves would be suspicious, unacceptable.

The mile marker showed that it was 128 miles to Indianapolis—44 miles backwards to Columbus—2 miles to Springfield—303 to Cumberland. *That goes all the way back to William's home in Mary Land*, she thought. They put Moss up on Molly's back, balanced awkwardly on the worn saddle, to get him off his lame leg. Moss smiled for the first time since Rodantha had met him, and this made her glad she had traded her precious handiwork to ease his painful leg. She thought, *I reckon the way to best my selfish streak is seeing folks in more need than me.*

As they neared the Mad River, a big Conestoga wagon lumbered across the National Pike going south on a dirt track. A scruffy man with a fat stogie clamped in his teeth cracked a whip over a four-up team of huge draft horses. But as the rig passed, Rodantha was shocked to see six slaves, irons chained at their bloody left wrists, ropes tied around their necks, one to another in a line. A tiny, dusty baby slung crudely to its mother tried to suckle her exposed breast as the wretched barefoot group lurched along behind the wagon.

This shock was followed by another as she saw the trailing horseman. It was the bounty man with the turkey feather in his hat. The hat was tipped back slightly to reveal a tight scar that extended up over the evil man's eye, slicing his eyebrow in half. He rode up quickly behind the chained slaves and whipped the last man in the line with a short whip with three lashes on the end. At this, the slave screamed and tried to move ahead stumbling into the woman in front of him and causing the whole group to pick up their pace slightly. The bounty man spurred his roan horse to race up ahead of the Conestoga and fell in ahead of the whole entourage, taking no notice of the Hywells and Washingtons on the main road.

Cissy stood for a moment, wild eyes looking in terror at this scene. She stifled a scream with both hands clamped tightly across her mouth. The last slave in the line, an emaciated naked man, could only look back before he was pulled along by the neck at the pace of the heavy horses. His back now red with fresh blood running down his leg. The scars on his back as he retreated spoke of the lashes he had received previously.

Moss rode toward Cissy, stopped at her side and leaned down. He placed his hand on her shoulder and murmured a few words. She collapsed against Molly and held on to the saddle horn. Their moments of private grief tore at Rodantha's heart and lumped painfully in her throat.

William halted the team and came back to where Rodantha stood sobbing. He hugged her close and said, "That was the same bounty man, Danna. He took no notice of us, thank the Lord. Tending to the gruesome business of the day, he was. That poor last slave will not live through the night. I will pray for the Lord to take him away from this torture soon."

Will held Rodantha by the shoulders and looked straight into her eyes full of tears. "I promise you, Danna, together we will see this cruel slavery comes to an end—now. Now, let's get a move on away from here. You be thinking of the wonderful supper you will cook with your tomatoes. Don't you have a recipe for peach pie in the kitchen box?"

He paused a moment then said, "My boy, here," he gently patted her bulging tummy, "that you are carrying along, he will need all the happiness and good food he can get. Do not cry now, please." For a beat, she stood looking down at her tattered shoes. She swallowed hard and realized that he knew she was carrying their child. She wished she had been able to tell him herself.

Will continued, "My sisters acted just this way, they did. The sickness in the morning time and expanding apron front."

"I'm not scared no more neither, Will."

She dried her eyes and looked back to see that Cissy and Moss had taken their "places" at the back of the wagon once again. Cissy was just not right though. Her eyes were wide and nervous, and she now held tightly to the stirrup straps as she stood beside her father mounted in the old saddle on Molly. His head was bowed, and hands folded in prayer. They moved on in silence until Cissy and Moss started a mournful chant, "Go down, Moses, Way down in Egypt land, Tell ole Pharaoh, To let my people go. When Israel was in Egypt land, Let my people go, Oppressed so hard they could not stand, Let my people go."

-21-

Can the World Be Changed?

Around the campfires in the evenings, the stories of slavery poured out of Cissy. Moss did not say much unless his daughter asked him a direct question. The woeful tales brought on a kind of morbid gloom that slumped down over the camp. Fear was a palpable presence. Will refused to play his pipes, which normally cheered everyone in its hearing. He did not sleep well, getting up several times each night. He said he was just "checking on the animals" or "tending the fire" when Danna asked what the matter was. During daylight hours, Will insisted that Cissy and Moss walk behind the wagon to indicate that they truly were slaves, relegated to travel in the dusty rear away from the "massa."

Will kept his hat on, pulled low. He never greeted other overlanders as he had before, and his usually big appetite was all but gone. He was getting thin, his face lined with worry. When Rodantha wanted to walk beside Cissy at the back, William repeatedly said, "Please, Danna, just keep up this ruse until we reach the Quakers at Earlham Boarding School. We will be safe then, I promise." So Rodantha tried to act as though she was Cissy's owner, but it was a bitter, distasteful thing.

Slowly, as Rodantha's knowledge grew and she understood the reality of the wretched lives Cissy described, she gradually gained a more complete understanding of slavery and its effect on the whole country, the huge conflicts between Northern and Southern ideals—Southerners bent on protecting their very economy and way of life that depended on the slaves; many Northerners dead set against continuing a commerce built on the subjugation and mistreatment of a whole race of people. In Cissy's telling, slavery became real to Rodantha, as though she had experienced the hardship herself. Worst among the stories was the day that Cissy lost her mother. One warm evening after the dishes and pans were washed, they all sat around the campfire. Cissy started slowly.

"That day, I was at the big house helping Miss Ellen recite a lesson in Latin. We usually took lessons in a room near the entrance hall with a big sliding wood door. When the door was shut, the hall runner carpet muffled the sounds from other parts of the house. We had a big upright piano in there, a wall chalkboard and two desks—one for Mr. Stephen and one for Miss Ellen. I usually sat on the floor to collect papers, stack books, find passages for study, and be ready to fetch lemonade and shortbreads when the lessons became too much for Miss Ellen. I just memorized everything I heard since I was not allowed to write notes. I often read over Miss Ellen's papers as I stacked them, so I got very good at quickly spotting mistakes in subtractions and grammar. Miss Ellen's folks did not even know that I could read.

"I will never forget that day … the day Mama died." Cissy took a deep ragged breath and plunged into the story. "The sliding door suddenly moved back a little and old father here stuck his head into the school room."

Looking over at her father in the firelight, Cissy touched his arm and said, "I think you said something like, 'Pardon, Master Stephen. Cissy, you is wanted in the hall to fetch a parcel of maps.'" Moss nodded his gray head in agreement and stared steadily at the fire as Cissy continued.

"I went out into the front hall. There was a parcel all right, but father just whispered low that Mama had been brought in from the field. She had collapsed and was not breathing. Would I go down and see what had happened? I ran straight away to our cabin where our kin had laid her. She was already gone, lifeless, her bare feet hanging over the rope bed. I will never forget her feet—swollen and bloody as if they were about to burst. This remains the worst day of my life, though many trials have since come my way."

Moss's whole frame shook with silent sobs. Cissy got up and threw the little twig she had been pushing around in the dirt onto the fire. She seemed compelled to finish as though it might somehow help. She swallowed hard and quietly continued.

"I washed her face and feet, and after old father came to kiss her goodbye that evening, he dug her grave through the night, our kinfolk helping. Just as the sun was rising in the morning, we put her in the ground.

The birds sang a hymn to heaven for her. Our people brought little wildflowers and laid them down on the freshly-mounded earth as they went into the fields. We could hear them singing as they went, 'We are crossing that River Jordan. I want my crown. I want my crown.'"

"That is when old father and I began to talk earnestly about an escape the next time Minty came back for some more of her family. Old father learned that Miss Ellen was to be married, and I was to be sold to a Mississippi plantation. He knew this by listening intently during meals and at back hallways. We became desperate to go at any cost. We believed that Harriet Tubman could get us out."

Cissy turned toward William who was intently draining the last drop of coffee from the blue pot. "You knew, William? About Minty? That Aramintha took the name Harriet after she married Mr. Tubman?" Will looked up and nodded and then began scouring his coffee pot in preparation for morning, suddenly, obviously, willing to do women's work.

"Those two did not stay together for long, though. Minty, bless her, was obsessed, and wandered far and wide away from Mr. Tubman, helping people.

"We heard that Harriet had never lost even one passenger that she put onto her railroad." Cissy stooped down to kiss the top of her father's graying head and then patted his shoulder as though he were a child. "Harriet is a great woman. I will try to be just as useful to my people as she has been."

Cissy fingered the edges of her Bible and looked intently into the fire. She was silent for a moment, so Rodantha stood and shook out her skirts, thinking Cissy had exhausted herself. But she continued in her elegant diction.

"I will be forever in the debt of Mr. Stephen, God rest his soul. He risked so much for me … his tutoring job … he could have been sent to prison. He gave me transcripts of speeches, books and pamphlets, maps, all sorts of things. Mostly I burned everything as soon as I read it. I sure wanted to keep the maps but was too afraid. My cousin was flogged when he was found to have a piece of paper in his pocket. If Mr. Stephen had been discovered … well, I do not know what might have happened to him—or me. He was helping to educate a slave right under the noses of the plantation owners.

"Mr. Stephen told me about the slave Frederick Douglas, who was also a Marylander. He is now an outspoken and powerful speaker. He goes around the country lecturing to any audience willing to hear him. I loaned you his book, Rodantha, remember, the narrative of his life? You'll need to finish it soon."

Moss stood. This seemed to signal to everyone that the sad tales and painful memories needed to end, but Cissy looked up and said, "I have just one more thing on my mind, old father. Please bear with me. I must keep these things in mind if I am going to be of use to my people." Moss nodded but stood ever straighter, elbows akimbo.

Cissy looked toward her father but with a faraway look in her eyes. "Remember when the Master almost caught me? I was reading that booklet, *Henry Bibb's Narrative*, how he escaped across the Ohio River to Madison, Indiana, and tried unsuccessfully to get his family out, all about his struggles, of being flogged, starved, and imprisoned. He was repeatedly sold and resold. He had to bury his own child and watch his wife being abused."

Then Cissy looked directly at Rodantha to catch her eye and said, "When the Master came unexpectedly one night, I dropped the booklet in a bucket of water and stood in front of it. He took no notice, and when he left, I collapsed. Old father watched over me all that night.

"But the point of this story is that Mr. Bibb finally went to Canada and is now publishing a newspaper there called *The Voice of the Fugitive*." Cissy flipped her Bible open and took out an old clipping she had kept from *The Fugitive*. She looked at it briefly and said, "Like this one," and then carefully put it back in the same place in her Bible.

"I hope to write something worthy to be printed in his paper one day." Cissy lay down then, rolled up in her blanket, and turned her face away from the fire.

As Rodantha was getting ready for bed, she paused and wrote in her diary.

> Will's great sorrow over slavery has now lodged in my heart too. I will not be rid of it until I die or slavery is ended. And I see the impossible problem of it, and the results it has caused. God forgive our cruelty and greed. Cissy forgive me for not understanding until now. I don't see how there is a way for Will's peaceful Quaker ways to solve the differences. I have been target practicing with Will's pistol. It is familiar now and I am no longer afraid to pick it up.

-22-

Indiana Quakers

April 1856

As the Hywells and Washingtons passed into Indiana, Rodantha noticed a difference along the roadside that at first was confusing. She mistook the first one for a cemetery headstone along the verge, until she got close enough to read the inscription. It read: *SL 9M – R 4 ½ – C 1*. She then realized that this was a mile marker, very different in style from the blocky square Ohio markers upon which she had come to depend. The first lines made sense. As the little group of overlanders had passed into Indiana just that morning: State Line 9 Miles, Richmond 4 ½ miles was clearly the distance from the state line. But the *C 1* marking remained a mystery until they plodded through Centerville, Indiana. "Aha," she said out loud, laughing, "Centerville One Mile."

The headstone mile markers comforted her, and made her feel connected to Indiana somehow, and less alone. Road builders, surveyors, and countless travelers had already prepared for and come this way, all helping her directly, somehow. So that she would know where she was along the road and how long it would be until there was a friendly town or village just in case she ran into trouble. The National Road seemed to knit the whole country together, starting out in William's native Maryland, passing through her beloved Virginia, across the Ohio River on the grand suspension bridge, through Ohio, and now into Indiana.

From studying William's map, she knew the Pike went at least to Vandalia, Illinois, hundreds of miles further west of Centerville. As they traveled it, the road seemed to follow the very rhythms of the earth, starting

110

up each day in the eastern sunrise and going arrow straight into the western sunset, unfailing, eternal. The prospect was simultaneously exhilarating and daunting, but somehow, each day she was eager to see what was ahead and what sights would present themselves before the sun set on the western end of the day's travels. She and William followed the rhythms of the sun as it pointed the way.

The traffic on the Pike was heavy. Buggies, carriages, and wagonettes at a brisk trot came toward them in a steady stream, despite the loose stones and ruts. Nearing the outskirts of Richmond, Rodantha saw the source of the traffic. A small plain sign was nearly obscured by the throng of people, horses, and carriages. It read Earlham Boarding School. Cissy ran forward, boldly abandoning her place of servitude at the back of the wagon, to walk alongside the high wagon seat where Rodantha rode. She beamed up a broad smile. The delight on her dark face transformed her.

A plain two-story brick building sat far back from the pike, and in front of it was a yard jammed with vehicles of all sorts like the ones they had seen on the road earlier. People milled about, talking in small groups as they hitched up their conveyances. Young men in shirt sleeves hustled to assist with the horses and hitches. The milling crowd was mostly dressed in dark formal clothing, accented by white collars and shirts, top hats and bonnets in abundance. She thought these people looked like they knew what they were doing, had a solid purpose to carry out their tasks with determination. They all looked so clean and well-fed.

William passed the throng and circled the team in at the far end of the yard where several black buggies sat, horseless. He said, "Not sure what is going on here, but the sign says we've arrived at Earlham. Let's inquire there through the open front door." Just then an eager young man bounded up.

"Are you folks here to pick up someone?"

Will quickly replied, "To the contrary, we have brought you a student that I am told the school leaders are expecting."

"Oh, well … uh … this is actually the Indiana Half-Yearly Meeting of Quakers, just breaking up, sir. No classes this week. Uh … would … uh … you just come with me, miss, and I'll take you to the headmaster." He held out his hand to assist Rodantha down off the high wagon seat.

"Why no, sir, the student is Miss Cecilia Washington, here." Rodantha motioned for Cissy to step forward. "But I reckon as I am the one who brought her, I'll go right along to see that she is proper cared for. A Mr. Hoyt has sent her here for transport to the Eleutherian school."

High color immediately flushed up into the boy's pale face, and he stammered. "Sorry, sorry, I'm just…"

"No need to apologize now. I'm right glad to be mistaken for a student. But I guarantee her head is in a lot better shape for studying than mine."

"Rest here a while, we will," William said, his face relaxed and calm. He patted Shire's neck and picked a burr from his coat. Rodantha stood back and then followed Cissy and the flustered boy. William winked at her and nodded. He took off his hat and wiped his brow with his kerchief.

The boy stopped and whispered to another young man with a ginger-colored beard, who then escorted them up a wide stair in the foyer and said, "I'll let the headmaster know you are here and the nature of your visit. He'll know just what to do."

The ginger-bearded man bounded up the stairs ahead of the two women and then turned back toward them. "The Western Quaker Special Meeting will be concluded today after the noon meal. They called an extra meeting this year in preparation for the 'yearly,' planned to meet in the fall, as usual. We will have plenty of space for you to stay, but please be patient. Beds are being changed and rooms tended now and surely be ready by evening. You are welcome to go into the dining hall when the noon bell rings and partake if you like. Many of the delegates have already left and so there is bound to be a lot of extra food for guests. Now, if you will, just wait here on the benches? Please excuse me."

The young man rushed down one of the two opposite hallways, the one with a carpet runner. The other hallway was well-worn oak; shafts of light and women's voices escaped from the open doors along its length. From their vantage point on the bench, they could see women and girls as they scurried between the rooms. Brooms, dust cloths, pails of water, and scrub brushes were being toted and hauled back and forth.

"No slaves here to do the work," Cissy said matter-of-factly. "All white faces and carefree chatter."

Shortly, the Headmaster came along the quiet carpet runner and introduced himself as Mr. Magersfontein. Bespeckled and balding, he respectfully shook Rodantha's hand, but bowed deeply toward Cissy, and held her hand in both of his. "Miss Cecilia Washington, we have been expecting you. Our good friend, Lymon Hoyt says you are a woman of special intelligence and recommends that we convey you as soon as possible to his home in Lancaster. He has arranged for you to attend Eleutherian in the coming term. The good Quakers at this meeting just allocated funds for your education. Mr. Hoyt's health at present does not allow him to come up here to deliver you himself."

Cissy looked stunned and might have blushed, though Rodantha couldn't tell. About then, the ginger-bearded man bounded up to stand behind the headmaster, who turned and said, "Rusty here will get you settled then, and I will see you a little later when we will have time to talk."

William and Moss joined Rodantha and Cissy in the dining room. In a whirl of activity, the Quakers provided a plentiful, if plain dinner of stew, brown bread, and fresh vegetables. Wondrous vegetables Rodantha had not seen for many months—radishes, green onions, and sweet crunchy snow peas. The young men stabled the oxen, showed them around the school, and answered their questions.

The Hywells and Washingtons were shown into clean spare dormitory rooms, on opposite sides of the very same hall where they had earlier seen the rooms being scrubbed by the young women. Water was heated for baths and drawn out into the tubs, clean towels and bed linens folded up on the cots.

In one of the ladies' washrooms, Rodantha scrubbed and soaked in the worn tin bathtub until it had gone completely cold. She washed her hair twice with the strong lye soap and rinsed with the vinegar from a jar left on the wash stand. A plain white folding screen provided privacy. Afterward, she washed her faded dress in the cold water and hung it by the window to dry. When she returned to the assigned room in only her shift, Will had changed into a blue striped nightshirt, hair wet and slicked back from scrubbing. As she slipped between clean sheets on the folding cot, she felt safe and content, the baby gently stirring in her belly. She and William pushed their cots together and talked until sleep overtook them.

-23-
Parting

April 1856

After the breakfast bell rang, Cissy appeared at their table in the Earlham dining hall. She wore a green serge dress, sturdy-looking but with a touch of elegance, sleeves loosely gathered at the shoulder. She had rolled the overly-long sleeves up into cuffs and the deep bottom ruffle was a slightly darker shade of green, as if it had been turned and resewn to extend the life of this much washed but handsome dress. A light blue gingham apron buttoned in a V at the back and tied at the waist. A tiny white ruffle circled the neck and stood out in contrast to Cissy's dark skin. The dress gathered gracefully around her frame, revealing a shapely young woman. This fact had been wisely disguised in the dirty trousers and baggy shirt she'd worn since Rodantha met her in Ohio. Her formerly bushy, dusty hair was braided and wound into a neat bun. Her smile said everything. Now the clipped diction and strong voice seemed to fit naturally into the scheme of things.

"Why, Cissy, you is downright beautiful," Rodantha said as she touched the rolled cuff.

Moss came late when the rest of the group had nearly finished their breakfast scrapple. He also wore clean clothes: heavy duck trousers, flannel shirt, and a new straw hat, which he took off and placed carefully on the table beside his plate. After eating several helpings of scrapple and apple butter, he pushed back from the table and spoke—more words than in all the rest of the time he had spent with the Hywells.

"I reckon I had the best night sleep I've had since leaving the plantation. My bones is thankful for a real bed. But more than the bed and warm bath, I am mighty grateful to you, Mr. Will." Tears welled up in his yellowed eyes, and he clapped William strongly on the shoulder. In a thick emotional voice, he said, "I can never repay you for saving me, getting us here, like you done. Why just look at the beauty in my Cissy here, never before seen or known. My pride could just cause me to go to the devil, but I am never minding it." Then he pulled out a clean white handkerchief, like a little miracle, from his pocket. He wiped his eyes and lapsed into contented silence as he carefully refolded the miracle, ready for its next use.

Will couldn't let him rest though and wanted to know what the plan was for getting on to Canada. "A long way to go, you still have, Moss."

"Well, sir, it's been proposed that Mr. Gabriel Smith will be coming through hereabouts in a week's time. I have to be patient, wait till the man says it safe. He don't take no chances with his passengers and expects to get all his cargo safely transported to the promised land. They says the conductor man always does this with care. Headmaster says I am to rest up, eat all that's laid out, to get strength enough for the walk, or maybe a mule ride."

Will replied, "Well, Rodantha and I might not be able to stay that long, Moss. But I know Mr. Magersfontein is a man to be trusted, and one who knows his business well, he does."

Cissy fidgeted in her folding chair and ate the last bite of her scrapple. "The dread day has come, old father."

"What do you mean, girl? This is the most happiest day in memory," Moss said, shaking his gray head.

"Well, I am to leave this very day for Eleutherian. I have seen you every day of my life. How can I survive when I cannot?" Cissy looked down and squeezed her eyes closed against the tears.

Moss cleared his throat and wrapped his huge hand over Cissy's shoulder. "Cissy, this is our best chance to go on living and our *only* chance to live free. Why, your mam would be devilish proud of this day, girl. You have to remember her every hour to point yourself to freedom. You have to be our voice crying in the wilderness, to make straight His almighty paths."

No one said anything, but they all knew this would be the last time they saw each other. Rodantha swallowed hard, blinked back the tears, and held Cissy's hand as long as she could.

"T-rah." William said, shaking old Moss's hand. "Be watchful for a man on a roan horse, wearing a hat with a turkey feather. The one I told you about earlier. He's been patty rolling and bounty hunting all along the National Road. Dangerous, he is. Tell Mr. Smith about him too!"

Rodantha felt strongly that each one of them had hopes deep down that must be honored and followed. Her diary entry on that day read:

April 1856

I <u>underlined</u> the words I looked up in Webster's so I could write this. I also underlined some words Cissy spelled for me. Cissy helped me to find words and meanings through the sounds of the words. I sometimes search and search before I find the right word. So many I have never heard before. She has taught me to listen carefully to what people say and look up what I don't understand. It is hard work.

I cried and cried when Cissy left in the night. I could not sleep. She says I am to write to her – In Care Of Lymon Hoyt, <u>Lancaster</u>, Indiana. She says we are sisters now, entwined for eternity no matter where we are. I would rather be entwined here and now, not looking toward eternity, whatever that is. I asked her to draw her hand on the back page of this very diary and sign her name in it. I will <u>cherish</u> this reminder of her always.

Most importantly, I want to remember all she has told us. I got to set down the names of her heroes and <u>heroines</u>—important in the struggle against slavery.

<u>Sojourner Truth</u>, a <u>formidable</u> woman, had been arrested twice in Indiana and tried for violating the Indiana <u>Constitution</u>. It stops blacks from coming into the state. The court dismissed the charges, and Cissy took this to mean that there were many whites who favor abolition in Indiana, even in the courts and among the leaders of the state. (I had to look up a lot of words to write this today.)

A Quaker man, <u>Levi Coffin</u> and his wife <u>Catherine</u> helped thousands of escaped slaves from their home in Fountain City, Indiana. Cissy said that the Coffins had helped Eliza Harris, whose story was told in *Uncle Tom's Cabin* by Harriet Stowe. The Coffins moved to <u>Cincinnati</u> and operated a warehouse that supplied goods to the "free labor" stores throughout the country. William is <u>keenly</u> interested in this <u>enterprise</u>, because of his interest to work as a storekeeper, and in goods produced by freedmen and women.

Abolitionists I know about:

-Quakers, <u>Baptists,</u> and Congregationals who help slaves on the Underground.

-New England <u>Immigrant</u> Aid Society, who has started a Free State town of Lawrence, Kansas, where William intends to go. They gave funds for our wagon.

-Mr. <u>Stephen</u>, Cissy's tutor, risked his life to help her to be an <u>educated</u> woman. I don't know his beliefs, but he promoted abolition by helping Cissy.

-Lymon Hoyt, Cissy's L'ootherian <u>benefactor</u> (I never heard of this word before and still don't know how to spell it.)

-Cissy <u>Washington</u> for all I wrote here, and now my sister.

-William Hywell, he helped Cissy and Moss to be free and gave many others a chance for freedom. He went to jail for his beliefs.

-Rodantha Morgan Hywell—I want to abolish slavery. I know it is foolish to put my name on the list, but no worse than putting William on it. He might not approve.

Last Day of April 1856

I been feeling the baby today shifting around in my belly like a turnip gone bad. It don't hurt none, just makes me know that I am not alone now but have the company of another. I am glad for the company.

-24-

Highwaymen

May 1856

After William and Rodantha parted from Moss, they were once again out walking on the Pike behind the oxen. Rodantha heard a faint tinkling bell. As she looked intently ahead in the evening twilight, she saw a huge Conestoga freighter as it lumbered toward them drawn by six huge mules, long ears erect. As it drew nearer, she saw the source of the ringing—bells were attached to a thin metal arch connecting the lead mules' hames. As the team moved along, the metal arch quivered and swayed, ringing a half dozen cone-shaped bells about the size of small, table service bells. They rang softly in various tones, like a tiny symphony.

In the soft evening air, this majestic outfit captivated her and made her momentarily forget the nagging pain she had felt in her back all day. She turned back to walk alongside the farmer who rode sitting on the left side lazy board. William kept Dutch and Shire moving toward Terre Haute.

"Ma'am," the freighter said simply, as he shifted the thick stogie around in his mouth and exhaled a cloud of rank tobacco smoke. The man himself was as stout and thick as his stogie. His hair stood up in the front and swept to one side slightly. The eyebrow on the upsweep side swept up to create a kind of double wave effect. His eyes were hooded and jowls loose, but a wry smile turned this whole affair into a pleasant and kind face.

"Why, I was just admiring your bells, sir, and wanted to hear them a minute longer." Rodantha practiced her English pronunciation and diction now every chance she got, calling to memory the many things she had learned from Cissy.

"I do get a fair amount of attention from them, and folks around here know when I am in the neighborhood, bringing along ham and bacon from

118

up to my farm. Whoa there, Gert!" He nimbly hopped off the lazy board as his team halted almost instantly, silencing the bells a moment later. Danna felt dwarfed by the big rig. The back wheels were twice her height, her eyes just level with the wheel hubs.

"I don't mean to keep you sir, but what might you sell one of your hams for?"

"The big ones are a dollar and small ones 60 cents. I'll take whatever you have, ma'am – 'dobe dollars or bits, green backs or U.S. coin."

"I would like to have a small one and let you be on your way then. I think I have enough here in my apron." Rodantha untied the secret pocket hidden inside the larger patch pocket on her apron and fished out the coins. She kept small change from trading and selling her rag rugs, having recently sold a set of four chair pads just outside Indianapolis.

He jumped down and retrieved a pungent ham from the sharply-slanted back of the enormous wagon, the hook still attached. "Just hang this up from the canvas bows and it'll keep well for a good long while. Salt and smoke cured, ma'am, mighty good with an egg of a morning. Don't sell those, but just a mile on, at the Hollister place, there's eggs for sale and live chickens if…"

"Don't move," came a sharp voice from the dense stand of trees on the right side of the Pike. Rodantha was just about to drop the coins into the farmer's hand, but instead some fell clattering on the stones of the Pike. The hair on the back of her neck stood up and goose flesh rose on her arms in an instant. Two figures emerged from the trees, guns cocked at the ready. They had crude hoods over their heads made from old gunny sacks. Their dark clothing and gloves presented a complete disguise in the twilight.

"We'll take that, old man, and your strong box too. Now don't fuss if you know what's good," came the high-pitched voice behind one of the hoods, an Irish lilt in evidence.

"No fuss. Now point that weapon away from the lady and I'll get it."

"No sir, we'll keep the lady in our sights whilst you get your chest, so no tricks, hear?"

The farmer went to the front of the big rig, opened the jockey box, and retrieved a wooden box with a bolt on the clasp. The taller of the two figures grabbed the box from the farmer's hands, shook it, holstered his gun, and backed away. The high-pitched Irish voice screeched, "I've a mind to take this here gal along for some sport." The man grabbed Rodantha's arm and tugged hard, as if to drag her along back to the trees. Instead, he just laughed maniacally, and the two disappeared into the trees the way they had come out.

Rodantha's head ached, and the world spun as she sank onto the rough pike. The farmer caught her as her knees started to buckle and lowered her gently to the ground where she sat until William came sprinting toward her. Looking up, she could see William smiling down at her in the twilight. Will scooped her in his arms and carried her to their wagon. He gathered Aunt Zelda's quilts around her seeing that she was shivering and sweating.

"Thank you, Will!" she said, as she reached out to touch him.

"Shhhh!" William held her head and brought a cup of water to her lips. She gratefully sipped.

Somewhere in the woods, a shot rang out. "Is the farmer all right?" Rodantha asked.

"Aye, he is right here. Waiting to see that you are recovered, he is."

The stogie-smoking pork farmer looked in at her over the tail gate of her wagon, serious eyes searching hers in the lamplight. "I was afraid you was scared to your death, ma'am. Those two Irish lads has been menacing this part of the road of late. I heard tell the sheriff thinks they're part of the big road crew working on the Pike along this stretch, almost all Irish fellas. But he has yet to catch them at it or get proof enough to know *which* two boys they are. That was them, just now, shooting up my strong box back in the woods I reckon. They'll be getting a big surprise about now." He grinned in spite of the situation at hand.

"A surprise?" Will said.

"Nothing in that box of value." The farmer chuckled. "All they got this time is some of your dropped coins, little miss, and in their rush to get away, why they left most of the Eagles where they landed on the pike. I brought that imposter box filled with pebbles and washers along after the Pike men at the wagon stand up the way told me about the theiving." He paused a moment and fished in his vest pocket. "Here, this is to remind you to get off the road at dusk and don't go talking to no strangers about their bells." He held out his right hand and reached in toward Rodantha. He cupped Rodantha's hand with his left hand and dropped a shiny Eagle penny into her palm. "This here is one of your dropped Eagles. I reckon it'll show our luck on this day and help you to recover from your shock. This'll be a good omen for that young'un when he comes."

She smiled weakly and held the penny tightly. She whispered, "I'll put this in my treasure box for safe keeping, sir."

-25-
Ague

May 1856

Rodantha didn't recover. When William looked in on her the next morning, he immediately took charge when she awoke to chills, fever, and a tremendous thirst. Her whole body shivered and shook. The familiar dull pain in her back of the last few weeks was now sharp and penetrating.

"You have the ague, Danna. I've had it and know the signs. Brought you some hot coffee. Drink up, girl, and I'll rustle up something to eat." But Rodantha couldn't drink the terrible tasting coffee.

William soon returned with johnnycakes piled up on a tin plate, honey dripping down the sides of the stack. "Wish I had some butter for you," he said smiling. "I looked at the map, and I have an idea what we might do, if you are up to it."

He bent down to whisper, "I need a little cwtch, Danna girl," while drawing her in tightly. But she had no strength to return the hug.

Rodantha rolled up the top cake and ate a few bites, hoping to calm her queasy stomach. "I don't feel real strong just yet." She managed to say through her chattering teeth.

"Thought as much, I did. So, I propose that we pull on up a ways. I found Big Walnut Creek marked on the map, and I think it's only about an hour away. It will be near to water, and stay until you feel better, we can." Unable to eat the rest of her cakes, she lay back down, exhausted. "Don't worry, Danna, I have a plan," he said as he tenderly covered her with a quilt.

William took charge of everything. He cooked, fetched water up from Walnut Creek, and washed all the clothes and bedding not being used. He even washed the extra muslin pillowcase and sprinkled it with the beloved Florida water. This made her smile when he slid it back under her head. He hoped the heavenly scent roused sweet memories. He brought some fine salty turkey soup, and she gradually regained some strength. To cheer her he said, "That old bird just wandered up close so I could get a good shot. He knew he was just what you needed."

Despite the jogging and jostling of the wagon, Rodantha slept as William resumed the regular travel routines. She was roused only when William stopped the wagon and coaxed her to drink a little.

Rodantha opened her eyes and saw the ham hanging near the back flap of the canvas and shuddered. She could feel the hand of the maniacal Irish robber again tugging at her arm. His high-pitched laugh rang in her ears. She screamed and tried to get away from him, but her head ached so much she could barely raise it up off the muslin pillowcase. She again slid into a fitful, feverish limbo.

"Danna girl, are you all right?" Will said as he lifted her head. "Rodantha! Rodantha Morgan Hywell!"

Danna could hear but couldn't quite understand his words until he said *Morgan*. This is what people had called her Pa, rarely using his Christian name. This roused her from limbo. "Pa … pa, is that you?"

"Nah, nah, Danna, it's me—William. Look at me, girl. Here's a tidy drink for you. Drink up!"

William held the vinegar-and honey-laced water to her lips, and she managed to drink a little. Rodantha had no recognition of the time that passed, whether it was day or night, or even where she was.

But when she could get up long enough to sit on the chamber pot, she saw blood in the bowl as she stood up swaying sideways. She screamed. "Will, Will, come quick. There's blood! Will, where are you? Help me. Blood, Will … blood!" He tried to console her, but she cried and wailed until she was exhausted into fitful sleep.

-26-

Dash to Terre Haute

May 1856

At break of the next day, William had Dutch and Shire headed in a steady pace toward Terre Haute, stopping only long enough to minister to his wife and kiss her pale feverish face. He kept going all day and half of the next night and covered the twenty-five miles without a proper rest stop. William urged his team on and told them, "I only ask you to keep pulling because of Danna." They gratefully sucked in the water he brought and started up again when he whistled.

William inquired haltingly at the toll station. "Sir … ah … might there be lodgings for my sick wife in the next town?

"Don't worry, sir. Just continue a short distance westward to the Prairie House Hotel. You won't miss it. It's a four-story monster, and the lamps is always lit on the entry along the Pike. They generally have plenty of rooms to let this time of year," he added. "You won't be needing a toll fee here as I can see your wide wheels, and also, what with your sick missus and all."

"God Bless you, sir," William said and then whistled for the oxen to pull once again, though he had given them neither food nor water. They seemed to know something wasn't right.

The hotel proprietor put them promptly in a room and sent word to the local doctor who grumbled at the early call out. The doctor, about forty, with hollow cheeks; and long, thin brown hair balding on the top, introduced himself to William, "Dr. Watts, Henry Watts. I'll take care of things now." His bright blue eyes roved and rolled about incessantly while he peered through and over gold-rimmed spectacles. Despite his ill humor, the gruff doctor, still half asleep, took charge. He curtly ordered William, "You just wait outside, young man. You can listen at the door, but wait till I call you to come in. This is for the safety of mother and child."

William kissed Rodantha and dutifully waited as other guests gathered in the hall, curious to know what was happening. He left the door cracked a little and could hear Dr. Watts as he coached weak and pale Rodantha to push only at his bidding. The doctor explained that she was not to push while he turned the breach baby. The baby came at 5:00 a.m., in a second floor Prairie House hotel room in Terre Haute, Indiana.

Nervously listening at the door ajar, William heard the doctor's exclamation, "It's a boy!"

William burst through the hotel room doorway as he heard the child's cry, and just as the doctor held up the baby with a slap of glee. This caused Dr. Watts to scowl in disapproval. Other guests at the Prairie House clapped and cheered in the hallway. "Thought I told you to stay put until I called, young man," the doctor said shaking his head.

William paid no attention and cradled his wife's damp head in his arms. Rodantha smiled her great relief. The baby cried weakly until Dr. Watts laid him across Rodantha's breast, where he continued to whimper until he found the nipple. "Now, little lady, suckle him to both breasts until he draws the milk. He is weak and small. He'll do best that way."

After the doctor washed his hands in the porcelain basin and called in a stout maid to assist with the clean-up, he sat down in the corner chair, opened the window, and lit up a long six. The smoke sucked out the window. The maid bustled back and forth, her ample body rolling about the room efficiently, her freckled face ruddy and flushed. She gently moved Rodantha to the edge of the bed and expertly slipped the extra layers of blood-soaked ticking pad out, revealing clean sheets beneath. She bathed Rodantha with hotel soap and warm water.

Dr. Watts quietly puffed his thin cigar for a few minutes and then stood and motioned for William to come outside with him. Rodantha had drifted off to sleep. As the maid patted Rodantha's hand and cooed over the baby, the two men went into the hall.

"My fee is a dollar and a half for house call and delivery," Dr. Watts said bluntly, as he looked at William over his gold spectacles. "I didn't administer laudanum, since I feared from the start about the baby, his small size, early arrival and all, and besides it costs extra. Will this fee be a problem for you, young man? Uh ... I didn't catch your name."

"My name is William Hywell, sir, and I thank you for coming out so early to help my wife with our baby." He held out his hand and pumped Dr. Watts's in appreciation. "I am able to pay. Thank the Lord! And glad to do so, I am."

"Your wife is strong, and after a while when she fully recovers from the ague, should do fine. But the boy, well, as I said, he has come ahead of his nine months, too soon to know the outcome. I just don't know if he can suckle, or profit from the breast milk as he ought to, seeing as how his organs are not complete yet—a wait and see situation. I warn against giving him a name just yet."

"Surely with our good care, he'll be all right, sir?"

"I can't say, Mr. Hywell. Now do you understand all that I have told you? I must be on my way."

William sat by his wife's bedside for two days. He wept bitterly and buried his face in her pillow. Though he talked to her constantly, she often did not respond, obviously unaware of what was happening much of the time. She sometimes rallied and caressed the baby while he attempted to suckle. She hummed a little tune that sounded something like the Welch Lull Song that William had played for her so many times on his pipe. William tenderly ministered to his wife and son the best he could, but felt helpless, hopeless, alone.

The tiny baby nearly fit into one of William's big hands. As he held him and traced the lines of his thin face, William wanted more than anything in the world to give him some of his own strength, and somehow will him to live. The baby was in an obvious fight for his life, breathing more shallowly with each passing hour.

The stout maid was replaced by a series of other maids who knocked quietly at the door, brought food and water, and wept as they turned their backs to go out. One maid, a very young girl sent in to bring a clean chamber pot and remove the used one, also brought a bright bouquet of flowers that she said came from a lady down the hall. The hotel proprietor's wife brought two soft little wrapping gowns and a stack of nappies made from hotel kitchen towels with tying strips sewn on the corners. There was much whispering and soft footfalls up and down the Prairie House second floor hallway.

Dr. Watts came back to encourage Rodantha to wake the babe and try to feed him more often. He told William that Rodantha's fever was finally down, the effects of the ague about gone out of her body. "Just don't make any plans to leave," Dr. Watts said. "You might be here for quite some time."

But now, it was plain to William that Danna was becoming fully aware of their plight. She asked repeatedly, "Why don't he suckle, William? Why?" And later, "He's mighty pale and ever so small. I tell you, Will, I'm the worst kind of terrible mother ever what lived, for letting him suffer." She sobbed and wailed, so that the stout maid brought some warm milk to calm her nerves. William knew his son's life was slipping away when Rodantha woke him and said, "Let's cover him with extra towels against the chill of this room. He's so cold, his little feet is turning blue."

Around midnight, May 18, 1856, the second day of his life, William and Rodantha's son died.

-27-

Morgan Hywell

May 1856

William and Rodantha held the baby between them on the bed until morning, when the maid came in bringing some coffee and biscuits. With a downcast look of recognition, she set the cups and plates on the bedside table and went out without a word, closing the door softly behind her.

Dr. Watts came and listened for breath and heartbeats and shook his head no. He pronounced the baby deceased, bathed him, and wrapped him in a clean white blanket. William and Rodantha looked on helplessly.

"Here is the death certificate," he said, handing over the small card where he had recorded the Hywells names, ages, and a brief history of what he knew to be the truth about this little family. "I have indicated only Baby Hywell unless you want a name affixed."

Rodantha coughed and cleared her throat. "We want it to say Morgan Hywell, sir. Named for my pa, he is." At this the doctor changed the name on the card.

"I keep a file at my office if there is ever a question, but there will be none, as I attest that Morgan Hywell was born too prematurely to survive, as you see there. Do you have plans for his burial?"

William spoke first. "As you know, we are overlanders, traveling through to the Kansas Territory. We have a little money saved. Could we take our boy to the town cemetery for burial?"

"The pauper's field is a couple of miles out of town where you can have one of the staked spaces to bury your son. That is the least expensive option, at one dollar if you have your own tools."

William reached into his vest pocket and then pressed a silver dollar into the doctor's hand. "Here are the instructions and directions to the cemetery," Dr. Watts said matter-of-factly. "I wish you God speed and am truly sorry for your loss."

Rodantha sobbed but then started coughing again, unable to utter a word.

"I must be on my rounds now, but here is the last of your medicine for the ague, Mrs. Hywell. Take it all as directed, drink lots of water, and eat as much as you can hold every day. I expect you to recover just fine."

"But not from the death of my Morgan, sir."

"Well, I recommend that you rest here tonight and set out to the cemetery tomorrow when your strength is recovered," the doctor said, his bright blue eyes peering and roving about over his gold-rimmed glasses.

The next morning William had the wagon and oxen out of the hotel stables and waiting in front of the hotel, water dripping from the water barrel. He packed their meager belongings and then finally guided Rodantha carefully down the stairs carrying the tiny bundle. After settling her in the back of the wagon, he returned to the hotel lobby to pay the inn keeper. The proprietor refused the payment, saying, "It's the least I can do considering your great loss. A guest, who wishes to remain anonymous, paid for the food that we served. Nothing is owed from you."

William just stared at the inn keeper and choked back his tears, nodding and shaking the man's hand with both of his.

William followed the doctor's directions to the cemetery and pulled into a shady spot along the low fence at the side of the pauper's field. He unyoked Dutch and Shire and hobbled them outside the fence. Rodantha chose a staked plot near the fence for Morgan.

William began digging. He worked until noon time when they ate apples and cheese given to them by the maid as they left their room. Rodantha took her medicine and slept all afternoon. In the evening, William built a fire with a nearby downed log.

They buried Morgan just at sunset. Rodantha collapsed when William laid Morgan at the bottom of the hole. He carried her back to the wagon and settled her on Aunt Zelda's quilts. "Be back to check on you, Danna. Just rest now." William refilled the hole and laid down beside it, exhausted. Rodantha found him there the next morning, dirty and shivering from sleeping on the ground all night.

William built up the fire again, boiled water for coffee, and washed the dirt off as best he could. He made a batch of johnnycakes and ate them all but one for Danna. Rodantha sat crocheting, still not up to doing the usual chores. The symptoms of the ague were subsiding, but she was still weak from the effects of childbirth and the emotional ordeal of losing her first born child. "Do you think you can keep up all this work, Will? Doing my chores too? Maybe we just stop here and find a little place to settle on."

"I have thought about this too, Danna," he replied. "I never dreamed of such trouble and misery. I am sorry for getting you into all this. Perhaps in a few days we will know what we should do."

"Will, I wrote some words for Morgan in my diary that are set to the Lull Song tune. The words are a little like those you sing sometimes. Would you play Suo Gan on your pipe? It would make a fitting farewell, I think."

William went to the wagon, unwrapped his pipe, and tucked it under one arm. He helped Rodantha to her feet. She held her precious diary open to the page where she had written the words. They walked side by side to the fresh little grave, where Will played the Lull Song on his bagpipe. He said, "Now you sing your words, Danna, as I play along. This is our farewell to our son."

She sang the words written in her dairy the best she could through tears:

Sleep my darling, angels calling,
Rest in slumber sound and deep.
I can see the angels smiling,
Smiling sweetly as you sleep.

I will love you ever always,
Leave you here so you can rest.
God will watch you with the angels,
So, my journey will be blest.

The closest water well was too far away for Will to carry water back to the cemetery without hitching up the team. The surrounding trees had been cut to build Terre Haute, so firewood was in short supply. William ranged far and wide, riding Molly further and further away across the fields and dirt roads.

He sometimes reported to Rodantha what he had seen as he stopped to look at some farmer's handiwork, a corn field planted in arrow straight rows with barely a weed in between. Birds circling down near a stock pond. A bold red barn that two boys were half-heartedly adding a layer of red to. These stories told aloud seemed to ease the ache in his heart, but Rodantha made no comments or acknowledgment of these efforts. William longed for the quiet peace he saw along the roadsides. He always came back with a load of wood dragging along behind him on a makeshift sled, hard work for Molly, but something for him to do to keep the campfire going. William didn't play his pipe, and the days and nights wandered into each other.

Rodantha was not herself. She thought, *Will I ever be myself again*?

As she sat beside William's campfire she said, "My soul is gone. I think forever. I am lost in a nightmare, Will."

"Stay warm by the fire, Rodantha, and the light will overpower the nightmares. We can sleep out here, and I'll keep it burning bright all night. Make it big and safe from intruders, I will," he said.

Rodantha's body had begun to recover from the physical effects of Morgan's birth, but her mind and heart had not been able to recover from his death. She walked through the gravestones of the adjacent cemetery, where church folk had planted peony bushes and long rows of purple and yellow iris. She picked one flower each time and brought it back to her baby Morgan's grave. She talked less and less, adrift without the familiar rhythms of rising early to hitch the team for the day's travel, nooning, and evening meals, and chores in preparation for the next day of travel.

William began to talk to himself as he ranged out away from her, unashamed, sometimes loudly, angrily, giving voice to his demons. "I cannot stay here. If she won't go, what will I do? I need the open roads, the newness of the days, for looking forward … not back. I love her so much, but I can't even play my pipe. Like I have forgotten how to."

He tried to talk to her about her fears of leaving Morgan's grave, but she refused to talk and crawled into the wagon to sleep alone. William could not reach her, and he grew more despondent each day. Finally, he formed a plan that he was afraid to say out loud, but as the days dragged by, he knew he had to say what was in his heart, even though he might lose Rodantha too.

One evening at the graveside camp, William made johnnycakes and cut the last few bits of meat off the pork farmer's ham to layer between them. Rodantha ate more than usual. He poured freshly-boiled coffee into the tin mugs, handed one to her, and then sat down on the tarp very close at her side. They both faced toward the crackling fire. He poked at the burning wood several times and watched the sparks fly up into the still night.

"Listen now, Danna girl." He started slowly and quietly, as he stared toward the fire. "Don't say anything till I've finished. You know how I've fallen in this habit of going out during the day for longer and longer? Afraid to see your sad face, I am. Can't even say what is in my mind. Now … wait now." He put his finger to her mouth, silently asking for her to just listen. "I know you dread leaving here, and so do I, but try to remember that Morgan was my child too. I am all alone since you have refused to move on, away from here. I long to sleep by your side out on the Pike. This is not just about you and your feelings."

"But, Will, I…" she stared into the fire.

"Now, please just let me finish. If you won't say yes to my plan, I may have to go on without you. I would hate that, but I just cannot stay any longer. This place holds too much pain."

He took another long drink of coffee to fortify himself against the dread proposal. "When this load of wood is gone and we've burned the sled, we will leave the next morning. Nah amount of staying here can bring back our boy. We have to think of ourselves now and what our life together might be, can still be if you want that … like I do."

"I'm all burnt up like this here campfire, Will, shriveled to nothing but ash."

"I know, Danna, I know. I do."

"I don't feel like we can have a life, like what we thought back in Virginny. It's hopeless…" She trailed off.

"Do you want to try?" he asked.

"Well, I reckon I do." She sobbed and cried, "I cain't lose you too, Will."

"My prayer answered, it is," he whispered. "I have prayed night and day," he said, clearing his throat. "God is good."

He paused, drew his handkerchief out of his vest pocket to wipe his eyes and said more confidently, "Then we better not let the summer get past us. Don't want to get caught by bad weather before we can make it out across the Kansas Territory to Lawrence. Feel safer once we cross into the Territories, I will. I fear there's still blackbird slavers around here. But just you wait. See if I'm not right. Do better out on the Pike, we will."

"How could this happen to me? It is just not fair!" she wailed.

"To US!" William said as the tears rolled down his cheeks again.

The next few days of burning up the little pile of wood and the sled were dread itself. Rodantha started to write in her diary about Morgan and the ordeal of losing him, but as soon as she wrote a word or two, her grief overtook her, and she could not continue. Her tears blurred the page and dripped down her nose. She sharpened the cedar pencil several times with her pen knife. On the third try she was able to write a few lines, but then erased everything with the little rubber she had bought from Mr. Schaffner back at the Pennsylvania House.

She looked at the diary's first page where she had traced her hand on the first day that she wrote in it. It didn't seem like it belonged to her anymore. She lovingly touched Cissy's traced hand and signature on the back page and wondered where her friend was at that moment. She needed a friend to talk to right now. She stated flatly, "I'll not write in my diary again, Will. Least ways not until I have some happy thought to put down."

William simmered the pork farmer's ham bone in the big Dutch oven and then cooked all the beans that they had left in the salty broth to make provisions for the journey. "You won't have to cook a thing for the next few days, Danna," he said.

Rodantha Morgan Hywell threw the last piece of wood on the fire.

She sat awkwardly astride Molly, on the old saddle padded with two of her curving crocheted "saddle" rugs. She wore William's old felt hat, which she had washed, blocked, and dried into shape the day before. It had even shrunk slightly out in the sun and was more her size now. She curled the sides up with a long strip of calico left over from a rug and poked holes through for a tie under her chin. She packed her yellow bonnet away, underneath the quilts.

As the oxen started slowly away from their camp, she craned her neck to look back until the little grave was out of sight. Two miles of dirt road to the north lay the National Road where William turned the team west again, toward Illinois. Dutch and Shire plodded resolutely on the now familiar macadam paving of the Pike. After some time, Rodantha said, "See how slow old Dutch is this morning, Will? He don't want to leave neither." Her tears flowed freely and mixed with early morning drizzle.

She did not look back again, but kept her face pointed west, the rising sun behind her, shining through the misty drizzle.

-28-

Bad Road Better Days

June 1856

The last of the macadam pavement gradually played out as they crossed into Illinois, and then totally disappeared, replaced by a rutted dirt trail: loose boulders, potholes, and even tree stumps and grass. Rodantha walked most of the time as the jolting of the wagon was painful for her still-tender body. Every hour or so she had to stop for a rest. William usually kept the team moving ahead. When she was alone, she sobbed and sometimes screamed out in frustration. "I cain't walk very far, I cain't ride in the wagon, I cain't rest, and I can barely get my breath. I cain't get no peace or relief of the pain in my heart. Help me, Lord!" The Lord didn't seem to hear.

Riding Molly for long stretches was almost as bad since she had to sit astride, not having a side saddle. Even her rugs or Aunt Zelda's quilts didn't soften the bumping and swaying as Molly picked her way among the rocks and obstacles in the road.

In many places the road split into a dry weather "low" road, and a "high" road. The high road followed the ridges and hill tops for easier travel in wet weather. These were not marked well, and often were cause for much confusion as to which fork should be taken—this was probably known only by the locals. In some places the low flat areas had been corduroyed with logs laid perpendicular to the route of travel, which provided a bumpy, but dry passage over the bogs.

The normally slow pace of the oxen was even slower, and the Hywells had to stop many times to clear away a log or back up to cross a ditch at a different angle. William often walked ahead of the team a few yards and raised his hands for Rodantha to stop the team when there was an obstacle or problem. This was exhausting work, but she knew that he was also hiding his tears from her. She saw the streaks on his cheeks when he had to turn suddenly to call out to her to stop the team. Seeing this always raised a lump in her throat.

There wasn't much traffic, and what wagons that were on the road crawled along just as the Hywells did, often stopping along a rise or verge to rest, their endurance stretched to the limit. Seeing the struggles of the other overlanders on that road somehow challenged her to go on.

They found a level patch of tall grass where they could noon close to a small pond. A whole choir of bullfrogs sang continuously behind the canebrake at the edge of the pond. As soon as he had unyoked the oxen, William disappeared into the rustling reeds at the edge of the pond carrying his Colt Navy pistol.

Might be snakes out there, she thought.

"If you can get a good fire going, Danna," he yelled back, "I'll get us a treat." As she built the fire, she heard him chopping with his ax, and then the rustling and clacking of the harricane. Before long he came out of the cane, two fat frogs skewered on the sharp-forked bottom of a long pole. Several huge frogs hung from a string on his belt—the size of dinner plates. His trousers were wet up to his knees and boots muddy.

"You got that skillet hot, Danna? Hungry, I am." He slipped the frogs off the end of the gig pole and cut their legs off with his hunting knife. Danna rinsed off the pond mud and slid the legs into the big black skillet. They sizzled and jumped up like popping corn in the hot lard. Will untied the other six and severed their legs. They went jumping after the first two as soon as they touched the hot skillet. Will piled the bloody frog bodies up by a tree. Two huge black buzzards stopped circling and swooped down to rip them apart. They squabbled over the easy lunch Will had provided, and finally picked up the remainders and flew off across the pond out of sight.

When the Hywells had finished eating every morsel of rich meat off those frog legs, Danna said, "That was a mighty good treat, Will. I'm feeling better. Now, mind you, pull off those wet boots and stick your feet up to the fire, so's your trousers will dry out some." She dragged the boots through the tall grass to get the mud off and then hung them up over the tripod to dry. Will had already dozed off. She lay down on the tarp next to him, enjoying the warm sun and the nearly mosquito-free zone near the smoke from their fire. She tilted the old felt hat over her eyes and drifted off to the bull frog chorus, insects buzzing in the grass.

"Get your hands off me!" Will shouted, waking Rodantha with a start.

"What's wrong, Will?" she said, still half asleep but looking around for the danger.

"I had a dream, Danna. The sheriff was after me and I was trying to get away."

"Those old Mary Land troubles, is it?"

"I guess so. I can sometimes forget about all that for a while, but when I was gigging those frogs today, it reminded me of my father. The best frog catcher, he was."

"We're a mighty long ways away from Mary Land now, Will. How could that sheriff find you here? How would he even know where to look?"

"Let's see, it's been over seven months now since father put me on Molly outside that jail. That was the end of '55. Maybe I was never really worth the sheriff's trouble, or the bounty man is going after the higher paying runaway slaves. Except for the time we spent in the Prairie House, we have kept to ourselves since we started out from Fairmont. But you know, I still find myself looking over my shoulder and avoiding strangers. The bounty man on the roan has menaced my thoughts. I am hoping that he stays in Indiana."

He stood up and shook out his still-damp trouser legs. "I've been told that the bounty hunters have a network of informants that they often pay to help them catch lawbreakers. And I hate to admit this, but I was so worried the whole time we had Moss and Cissy with us. I felt sure someone would put two and two together and I'd be discovered for who I really was."

"Well, I will never forget that rainy night just before we rescued the Petersons. Remember? I saw him in the lights from the big house." Rodantha shuddered. "He had a horrible bloody gash across his face. I was so scared he was going to follow us."

"That cold rain probably saved our lives," William said. "Since he couldn't see us very well in the dark and rain. Had a lot of close calls, we have. But, Providence is on our side, Danna."

He threw the spent coffee grounds on the last of the dying fire. "You ready to get going, Missus Hywell? Got to fight that poor road again, we do. It will be slow going to keep from ruining a wheel or breaking an axel. The team will tire quickly trying to pull over all those loose rocks and mud holes. I'll go ahead to scout, but we may not get very far today."

"Let's just quit early Will. I need … we all need a long rest so we can carry on."

-29-

Mr. Lincoln

July 1856

Rodantha's Diary Entry

July 2, 1856 Marshall, Illinois

It has been hard to see Illinois because of the rain. The road has turned to a mud hole, and we have made very slow work of it. It is wet misery. I can't get warm, even though it is July. After a few hours, our Dutch and Shire just stop in their tracks unable (unwilling?) to go on. I know what hard working old boys they are, so I don't fault them none.

The land appears to me nothing much to speak of. Illinois is just a lot of flat grass land, interrupted by groves of trees along the low places and creeks. Mostly it is just mud along the Pike. I been eating mud, scratching mud in my eyes and ears. It seeps in between my toes. Skirts are quickly ruined, so I wear Will's old trousers. The felt hat stays damp even though I dry it near the fire or hang it from a canvas bow. I'll not pull out the yellow bonnet though. It don't suit me no more. There are few travelers. Today we didn't see a soul one on the road.

Tonight, we are staying in a real room, at Archer House Inn in the town of Marshall to get out of the wet. I do enjoy the comfort of these whitewashed solid walls and ceiling. I am laying up here on clean sheets writing this and letting my clothes dry over the bedstead. I washed them in my cold bath water and there was a half inch of mud at the bottom when I was finished. I'll put on my clean blue calico to go down to supper.

Maid says clean hot water will be brought up for Will, and she is having my boots cleaned out to the barn. God help me, this Inn reminds me so of Prairie House where my Morgan came and went from me so soon. But I'll not speak of it to Will.

He has promised me a proper meal in the dining room once he has tended to the animals and had a bath. He says we will have venison cutlets. I <u>determine</u> (Mr. Webster's very good word) to have a cheery face for him no matter how my heart aches for my Baby Morgan. Will is near exhausted too. What with all the hauling on the team and being sucked down to the mire.

The finery of Archer House captivated Danna—cherry wood side tables, walnut rocking chairs, and pewter castors on each dining table with a handle on top for carrying. The castor twirled in a carousel fashion and held the salt and pepper shakers, vinegar, sugar, mustard, spice containers, and a little bell on top to ring for service. The venison cutlets were tasty and tender.

Their sleeping room had white curtains at the windows, and a pink flowered china basin and pitcher for washing up stood on the washstand. They snuggled under the clean sheets, and William made her laugh like a child when he again said, "You make my heart flutter like a duck in a puddle." It was like their first nights together at the beginning.

The rain stopped, and after two nights' sojourn at Archer House, the roads were drying out again. The morning of the Fourth of July was sunny, and the inn bustled with people traveling into the town for the Independence Day parade. William and Rodantha ducked under the red and white bunting that had been draped from the front portico. Mr. Archer, the owner of the inn, stood on the edge of the portico, and spoke in a loud voice above the bustling crowd.

"My friends and neighbors, I have been informed that Mr. Abraham Lincoln will be coming out in a few minutes to speak to us about the newly-formed Republican Party. He has been campaigning in our fair state since the Republican National Convention last month. He will share his views with us regarding his stance against slavery and his support for John Fremont for

President. We all know what a treat it is to hear Mr. Lincoln. We have lemonade right over here for all those who wish to stay for the speech." He swept his arm dramatically toward a long table where pitchers and stacks of hotel glasses were laid out with more bunting. Immediately several children ran up to the table eagerly jostling for their turn at the lemonade. "Just listen for the Congregational Church bell. It will ring when Mr. Lincoln is to begin."

"You suppose Mr. Lincoln stayed overnight here too, Will? Maybe right next door to ours?"

"I guess he might have. I want to hear what he has to say. I read in the lobby papers that Illinois has passed a law against slavery, though all the former slaves have not yet been freed. This was to ease the law into place and avoid problems with what they called 'established commerce.' Mr. Lincoln and the Republicans are loudly proclaiming against slavery, they are."

They drank lemonade and milled about listening to the talk among the Illinoisans gathered there. Rodantha noticed that the ladies in the crowd wore their corsets and layers of clothing despite the heat of the day. On Sundays back home, she had seen Ma and Aunt Zelda putting on a half-dozen layers—chemise, pantaloons, corset and corset cover, crinoline, petticoat, and dress over it all. This memory and the sight of the proper ladies of Marshall, Illinois, made her feel rough in her felt hat and natural waistline. But since she didn't even own a corset and had no liking for them, she soon began to feel sorry for the trussed and laced ladies and their tendency to swoon and sit in the shade fanning. She felt decidedly grateful to be walking to the territories in her serviceable clothes.

Will interrupted her thoughts. "All this makes me feel safe in this crowd, it does." At one table, a smiling man passed out special posters that showed the free and slave states on a colorful map of the nation. Will got one and immediately began to pour over it with a grin on his face. This was the happiest she had seen Will for many days. Boldly across the top was a headliner that read: *Reynolds Political Map of the United States*. At the top were pictures of Republican candidates for President, John Fremont and William Dayton. Right in the middle of it all was a white area labeled Kansas Territory.

"Aye! This is just what I need," Will said, "though the detail is not great, it will be a tidy helper on our way west." The white area showed that the territories were still not aligned with either side of the slavery question. The point of this extravagant free giveaway seemed to be the Republican cause for Kansas to come into the Union as a Free State.

From a block or two away, the church bell rang out, and soon Mr. Lincoln ducked his long lanky frame under the bunting and solemnly looked over the crowd. He stood holding his tall hat in the strong July sun. His thin angular face and steady eyes calmed and quieted even the little ones. He began his speech, boldly declaring: "As I first testified to the people of Illinois in Peoria two years ago, I want to say again here—little by little, but steadily as man's march to the grave, we have been giving up the old for the new faith. Nearly eighty years ago we began by declaring that all men are created equal. But now from that beginning we have run down to the other declaration, that for some men to enslave others is a 'sacred right of self-government.' These principles cannot stand together. They are as opposite as God and Mammon. And whoever holds to the one must despise the other."

He went on to declare that the Republican Party was the party for Illinois and the party for the nation. He and the party stood against slavery. They would work tirelessly to accomplish that, the sure election of John Fremont this year and looking toward the election of 1860 to be a Republican victory as well. And now that the Kansas-Nebraska Law has been passed (against his advice) he would see to it that when the territories are made into states that they should be free. As he progressed through his speech, his words quickened, and his face lit up. His whole body gestured his enthusiasm. His eloquence showed his deep conviction and sincere belief in this cause and gave the crowd a kind of light buoyancy and excitement. This was no ordinary fellow.

As the crowd applauded and moved toward their representative, Will went straight up to him and shook his hand.

Standing just behind her husband, Rodantha smiled up at Mr. Lincoln, who had a surprising twinkle in his eyes as he looked directly at her. He lifted his huge stove pipe hat and nodded to her before the crowd swallowed him in a throng of welcoming greetings.

-30-
Marshall to Greenup

July 1856

As the Hywells passed over the stone arch bridge on the west side of Marshall, the rain began again. The eighty-five miles of prairie between Marshall and Vandalia, Illinois, was a bitter trial of two opposing yet related endeavors—trying to get drinkable water and trying to stay dry. The rain continued off and on, swelling the creeks and ponds. Clean, clear water was impossible to find.

No matter how many times Rodantha strained the water through a muslin cloth, or how long she let the water settle before boiling, it was still muddy and foul tasting. The National Road, now just a dirt trail in the best weather, was this day a quagmire and often had to be avoided all together by angling out into ravines and meadows. The Hywells stopped often to rest the oxen or pull some hapless family out of the mud. Rodantha was thankful for Mr. Troyer's wide iron wheels and Will's considerable skill in navigating unfamiliar terrain that saved them from also being mired in the mud.

At a Greenup general store on Main Street, William left Rodantha standing directly in front of Shire in the middle of the muddy Pike. He said, "Just you wait a minute, Danna. Be right back, I will. Keep the goad handy."

He ducked in under the fancy two-story porch that formed a portico over the front door below a sign that read Mercantile. Hurrying back out, his eyes twinkled as he produced a peppermint stick from under his poncho, where it had miraculously stayed dry while his head took the full brunt of the pelting rain. Her eyes were wide with pleasure and anticipation as she quickly transferred the thick, four-inch stick under her poncho and shot him a wide smile.

"Here is what I was really after, Danna," he said, as he held up a brown paper sack. "Some alum. I'll show you what it's for and how to use it when we can stop for a while. You are going to love this stuff."

The fancy porches, sometimes two stories high and topped with ornate balconies, continued along the Main Street (also the National Road) for a few blocks and made the whole town seem to be coordinated and beautiful, although drenched. People congregated all along the street under the porches where men smoked and children played.

A roan horse was tied up on the railing of the last main street building. This sent a shiver down Rodantha's spine. She thought, *Surely this is not the bounty man. At least it is bad weather for hunting fugitives. But it sure looks like the same horse.*

When they came to the edge of the Embarras River, a herd of sheep was being driven over the wooden floor of a sturdy covered bridge. The shepherd at the back end of the small flock turned to wave his hand and motion for William and Rodantha to come onward. But William waved to the shepherd to go on and cross over to the west side of the river. Through the heavy rain, she could see William walking slowly back and forth along the east side, looking at the two ends of the bridge.

He yelled out to her over the sound of the rain, "Want to see that it is holding fast to both shores, I do." The water flowed just under the floorboards of the bridge and splashed alternately by spits and crashes, then dashed waves up onto the floor. This washed off the sheep dung but was not much of a consolation. After the sheep were out of sight, William finally hollered to his oxen, "Get up there, Shire, Haw Dutch." Rodantha held her breath.

For a magical spell of a few minutes, Rodantha was out of the rain and under the strong protection of the mighty wooden roof cover and trusses. The dashing of the river over and under the floorboards made a kind of thumping roar, which she tried to ignore as she bit off an inch of the peppermint under the dry cover. The reliable oxen plodded across the bridge.

As they approached the far shore, Rodantha heard a loud crack and saw the bridge shudder. She involuntarily jumped sideways on the seat where she was riding. A wave of fear rolled through her body. A huge log had slammed into the side of the bridge near the bank, which the rushing river was trying to suck under the torrent. She choked a little on the peppermint and gulped down the fear in her throat. She peered over the railing at the log as it continued to slam the side of the bridge. She said a quick prayer that God would allow the quaking bridge to hold fast.

She hoped the peppermint would stay dry under the wagon's double canvas cover as she wrapped the sweet candy in several handkerchiefs and stowed it inside the wagon.

That peppermint seemed the sweetest thing she had ever tasted or ever would again. It calmed her lurching stomach and took away her hunger pangs for a short while. Those pangs soon returned, though, reminding her she would have to find a way to cook in the rain yet again.

Will pulled the team just off the Pike onto a slightly-sloping verge in sight of a pond overflowing its downside bank. The team was near exhaustion, and the Hywells were cold and hungry. No other travelers were about.

They could find no dry tinder to get the fire started, so they used a few sticks and some hay slung under the wagon. Rodantha was careful to keep this under cover of the wagon bed in the dry bottom of the black skillet. She uncorked the match bottle, firmly held one match as she recorked the bottle to keep the remaining matches dry. She struck it near the driest of the hay. When a weak fire got started, little by little she transferred the embers to the pile of wet wood William scrounged up under the oilcloth tarp, tented upward toward the wagon on fishing poles they had made at the Big Darby.

The fire smoked more than it flamed, but soon the feeble heat and few sparks got a small fire burning. Will stripped off the wet bark of a big log and laid the dry underside up under the tarp. Rodantha laughed and cried, her raw nerves a jumble in the downpour. When she saw that the fire would burn and the smoke would vent out at the top, she dragged out her tripod and cooking utensils.

"I'll show you how to use the alum rock salt," William said as he began to crush the alum and sprinkle it into the water buckets he had sloshed up from the creek. "Settle the mud to the bottom, it will. It would be best to let the alum work overnight but should help considerable in an hour or so."

Rodantha waited as long as she could stand for the alum to mostly-clear the water for cooking. She poured this clarified water off into the now-heated kettle. It then took a half hour just to get the water boiling. The rain, mist, and drizzle were her constant companions as she sucked on small pieces of the peppermint to stave off her hunger. She barely noticed Will as he tended to the animals and was vaguely aware of the dull thuds of his axe as he chopped more wood for the fire and several drying stakes.

After some hours of heavy labor, she produced a pan of johnnycakes, four boiled potatoes, and a pot of coffee. Strictly speaking, the coffee was Will's doing, but just getting the water to boil made it seem like she had done it all by herself. Having used the tarp for a rain shield for the fire, they stooped and crouched under the wagon to eat, pressing down the weeds and grass into a damp mat. This disturbed a black snake and a hill of ants. The black snake slithered quickly away which settled her nerves a bit. Rodantha stomped on the ants all the while eating her potatoes speared on a fork. The heat radiated toward them and most of the smoke went up the slope of the tarp tent.

They hung their dripping, muddy clothes over the rain-washed wagon wheels and let the rain clean them too. Will worked in his union suit and Rodantha in her camisole and bloomers until they could wring most of the mud out and hang the clothes under the wagon bed to dry. Rodantha wrung out their felt hats and propped them on short stakes out of the rain and nearest the fire. And last, they stripped off their underwear and boots and followed the same routine—underwear strung up on twine and boots on stakes.

Shivering, teeth chattering, Rodantha climbed up into the wagon to snuggle her bare skin under the warmth of Aunt Zelda's quilts, calling out to her husband over the sound of the rain as it pelted down on the canvas top.

"William Hywell! Come on up here now, you hear? I reckon the rest of this work can wait till morning." He soon snuggled in beside her, lending his warmth to hers. They were both asleep almost instantly, staying dry under the double canvas wagon cover. Rodantha roused when Will got up to stoke the fire and move the big log further up into the embers to keep the fire burning all night. His hands were cold and rough on her waist when he slid back in next to her, and she was vaguely aware of a burning itch on her legs.

Dull gray morning light illuminated the canvas roof just enough for Rodantha to find clean dry clothes in the carpet bag. They dressed quickly and found their boots still damp and cold, but thankfully free of grit and mud. Her legs were on fire with hundreds of insect bites. It was all she could do to keep from digging her nails into her flesh. She applied vinegar several times and screamed at the sharp pain but was rewarded by the relief it brought to the burning itch. Will had bites on his arms, but he didn't complain much as she dabbed them with the vinegar-soaked cloth.

The air was still and heavy as the birds half-heartedly started up their morning songs in the trees. She sat by the fire to ward off the mosquitos and focused her attention on the twittering birds while she sipped Will's hot coffee and smelled the bacon he was frying. He went about his chores, yoking up the team and securing the water barrel.

She dreaded the cheerless day ahead. Her mind drifted first to baby Morgan and his lonely little grave in Terre Haute. Then she thought of her dear friend Cissy at Eleutherian School and Moss somewhere in Canada, imagining both as free from slavery. She resolutely refused to let that image go. The morning gloom clamped down over her heart. She couldn't keep her eyes open and nodded off leaning against the trunk of a big tree.

Suddenly she heard Will call her. "Rodantha Hywell! Didn't you hear? What's the matter, gal? Sun is coming up, it is. No clouds!"

She jumped up and gathered the still-damp clothes from under the wagon bed and hung them up on the staves of the wagon canvas to finish drying. Will handed her a slice of bacon wrapped up in a johnnycake, normally one of her favorites. She ate a few bites at a time as she started to pack up the wagon for the next part of the journey, which Will said should take them through a town called Effingham, if he could follow the road. He had taken a couple of wrong turns already, ending up at an abandoned farmhouse at one and a big pond at the other one. Turning the oxen around was always a chore, but in mud and muck it was perilous.

"Thank you, Lord, for giving me a clear sky this morning," Rodantha said out loud. That thanksgiving must have held some weight with the Almighty, as the skies were clear for the next week.

-31-

National Road End

July 1856

The skies were clear blue, the days not yet excessively hot. Strong breezes blew flies and mosquitos away. "Making good time, we are, Danna girl," William said. "Maybe we can stop in Vandalia for a spell.

"The penny paper I picked up in Effingham had a short story about Vandalia, and said it was the former capital of Illinois. Said it is a good place for a rest. Visitors can stroll around the old Capitol grounds and view the Senate chambers. The enterprising folk of Vandalia want visitors to stay in their hotel and board the working animals at their stables. Besides, I would like to see some of Mr. Lincoln's territory."

It was clear that both the original idea and the money for a National Road had played out before the Pike reached its goal of the Mississippi River. There were no more stone bridges crossing the many creeks and ravines along the rolling countryside of Illinois. William had to carefully survey each creek crossing before leading the oxen across, and occasionally he went up or downstream a half mile before he could find a safe place to cross. But the dry weather was a true blessing as the creeks were mostly shallow, and the team could find solid ground beneath the water. They traveled the sixty miles from Effingham to Vandalia in four days with relative ease.

William said, "My knowledge of the road beyond Vandalia is sketchy. I think we will need time to study the route from the end of the National Road onward from here."

They planned to visit the former capitol building where Will said that Mr. Lincoln had served as a state representative until the Capitol of Illinois was moved to Springfield. The more Will read about Mr. Lincoln, the more he talked about his hero as though he knew him, declaring he had a gentle nature, was a shrewd politician, a champion of the law, and careful with words about his anti-slavery views to preserve the rights of all the states regardless of their leanings on the slavery issue.

As soon as the oxen were settled into a corral on the outskirts of Vandalia, William and Rodantha walked to the stately white building where huge pillars at the front portico led to the front hall. High ceilings and tall windows were accented by rich dark floors. Rodantha observed, "This feels so settled and civilized."

Back outside, she continued, "I'm getting hungry, Will. What say let's stop by that general store we saw on the main street and get some potatoes. I'll make us some potato soup for supper." They left the store with ten pounds of potatoes, a sack of dried peas, and a big jar of milk which was marked low because it was already a day old. But the real finds were freshly-ground coffee and a small brown book entitled *The Prairie Traveler*, by a captain in the U.S. Army, Randolph B. Marcy. Thumbing through it, Will commented on a chapter with information concerning the *Habits of Indians*, directions on how to pitch tents military style, and how to ford streams safely.

"Come in handy for the rest of our journey, it will," William said as he paid the extravagant twenty-five cents for the little handbook.

That evening after they had eaten Rodantha's delicious dinner of creamed peas and potatoes, Will read to her from the new book while she washed up the pans and plates. The part about building a bull boat to ford large rivers seemed practical, as long as a buffalo hide was available, which didn't seem likely. When she heard the chapter on "Routes to California and Oregon," she thought, *I just don't need that golden dream like I once did.*

Of late, Will had been worrying aloud about crossing the Mississippi and Missouri Rivers. Each time they crossed a stream it seemed that his trepidation increased. He said, "Those big rivers will not be so easy."

After some thought, Will said, "Thinking about the journey ahead, and I'm convinced that the road will not be well cared for or marked like the National Road. Pretty much a trail from here onward, it is. I am most sure we will need more pulling power than Dutch and Shire can give. I spoke to the livery stable man, and he has a couple of oxen that he says are trail-trained, mature, and docile. He says ten dollars each for them, which is a right fair price, even low. The usual price I have seen is between twenty and thirty a head. We'll need a yoke too. I saw an old dusty one hanging in his barn. That will be extra…" Seeing Rodantha was about to protest he held up a forefinger. "Now, wait, just hear me out.

"Consider this, Danna. Would you agree to trade that big rug you have been working on, the one you say is a proper dining room size? I have said nothing to the livery man about this but think with the right words he might just be persuaded to take that big rug home to his missus, real proudly, he would."

"Well, I am not against trading the rug, but it ain't quite finished yet. If I could spend this evening working it, I reckon I could finish up by morning. I'll use up all my left-over rag strips on a fancy edge." Will washed the dishes, and Rodantha went straight to work on the rug.

The next day, when William returned from trading with the livery man, he had a surprise. "Come out, Danna, and see what I have here." Rodantha poked her head out of the end of the wagon top to see that William had four animals instead of two.

She laughed. "Why, Will, you have a whole herd!"

"Well, that livery man, George was his name. He asked me if I could use a fresh cow and asked only a dollar for her. His helper just up and quit, so George couldn't look after all his animals. Said he would consider it a favor if we took all four to relieve him of the chores and the expense of hay and grain. It's his wife's birthday soon, and your rug is to be her present."

"He must have liked your looks, William Hywell. You got a bargain for shor."

"I suspect he felt guilty. He knew that your rug was worth more than those two oxen."

"Well, I declare! If that is right, I'll need a lot more old clothes and worn bed linens to make up another one." Rodantha giggled and smiled.

"Well, now worried about getting all these animals across the Mississippi River, I am. George said St. Louis is about seventy miles. I figure we will be there in less than a week. George was sure that we'd be able to catch the big ferry at the main crossing for a few dollars and get our whole rig across together. He's been across on that ferry and says it's reliable. If Providence should favor your road, Rodantha, we should be in Lawrence in a month's time. Well ahead of cold weather." He looked up from the *Reynolds Political Map* he had been studying.

"Meantime, the Jersey cow is fresh and will give milk," he said, "and you can have some for breakfast."

"And make some butter! And…"

"Now, Danna, don't let your thoughts go wild. Let's see if she has enough milk for her calf and us too. Kind of small, she is. What will you name her and her little one?"

Without hesitation, Rodantha said, "Well, I think her name should be Dollar, and the calf could be named for this Van-Dalia town. How about Dalia? Hum? Now then, you know, you got to give the two new oxen names too, Will. What'll you call them? You'll be calling out their names to get their attention."

"Let's see. The brown one can be George after the stable man, and the one with the curly white face will be Curly. I think I'll yoke up George and Curly first as the wheelers, with Dutch and Shire out front since they are seasoned. I hope that the new boys can follow along peacefully. They're supposed to be well used and trained. Let's give Dollar some of our oats and find out if she can be driven along behind. Maybe the calf can keep up without ropes. You might have to watch them close for a while to make sure they don't get lost, Danna."

Rodantha wrote in her diary:

July 1856 – 70 miles to St. Louis

We are on an unmarked trail now. I am scared of the <u>Mississippi</u> River. Crossing the Ohio River on a strong bridge was one of the worst things I have ever seen, but now to know that a much wider crossing is coming and there is NO bridge. Will says a flat boat ferry will take us across. All the animals got to go no matter if water is high, or weather is bad. We now have Molly, four oxen, a sweet Jersey cow, Dollar, and her calf. When I milk Dollar, I only take about a quart, so that Dalia will have plenty to grow on. It is nice to have a little fresh milk. We drink it warm. Dollar is calm and easy to milk. She has beautiful long eyelashes.

I pray continually. I sing "Guide me Oh Thou Great Jehovah" as we walk each day. Lord willing, I will not complain or cry. I will have a pleasant face so that William will see my faith is unshaken. Will don't play his pipe much lately, so I know he is worrying even though he says all will be fine. I hope his <u>confidence</u> is real (found that word in Webster's). Curly and George has settled in with Dutch and Shire now and all pull mostly in the same direction—a good team.

Will says we will see Kansas Territory in less than a month!

-32-

The Mighty Mississip

July 1856

When Rodantha saw the wide Mississippi River churning, rushing its way southward, she immediately thought of the old Scottish tune that Will sometimes played, "O Waly, Waly," about the wide water and not knowing if you will sink or swim. It was wider even than she had imagined and more violent. The snags and logs that caught along the edges broke loose to careen with the muddy-brown churn alternately bobbing and sucking them down. She tried to hum a little of the tune, but her throat closed up tight. She mused, "I shor pity any woman who comes to this mess if there aren't any ferry boats."

Illinoistown clustered and hovelled at the river's edge with a great crush of people, livestock, wagons, boats, and machinery-boxes, barrels, lumber, cattle, hogs, sheep, dogs, and cats. The large ferry boat looked strong and ready, but the mighty river acted as though it would swallow anything or anyone who ventured across. A steamboat was departing the wharf, its front pointed to the north. Bystanders said it was going to Minneapolis in a place called Minnesota, not yet a state in the Union.

They and their "herd," as Rodantha called their animals, arrived in late afternoon and then had to turn back a mile or so from the Father-Of-Waters to camp because of the throng; scores of white tops clustered together tightly at the water's edge. Will said, "It might be a couple of days before it is our turn to cross. There are hundreds of wagons here. I must find the captain right away."

On the morning of their departure on the Mississippi River ferry called the *Norma Jean*, Rodantha was up well before dawn. They arrived at the landing at daybreak. Only two other wagons were ahead of them, and they were close enough to the river edge to see that it was a rushing, roiling brown tide. As the sun rose, the crush of people and animals increased, and the ferrymen were in a frenzy of activity unloading kegs and barrels over a side planking. The large flat wooden barge before them was half-covered by a flat roof, on top of which boys were engaged in a spirited card game and a fiddler was tuning up. A plank fence or corral encircled the open deck, and a huge tailgate blocked entry to the boat as it swayed and heaved in the rushing water.

The toll taker came along to collect their one dollar and ninety-five cents for four oxen, one vehicle and driver, one extra person, one horse, a cow, and calf. He called out loudly, "I'll take your greenbacks or your dobe dollar bits but no picayunes. Got no time for that kind of counting."

The gruff old sinner barked orders. "Set your brake, tie your loose stock close to the wagon, keep all water vessels closed tightly, children inside the wagon at all times, firearms holstered or stowed, and all fowl in cages. In a half-hour you be in Misery." He laughed at his own joke, revealing his tobacco stained near-black teeth.

When the toll man got to the back of the line, he gave a sharp whistle. Two men began to lower the tailgate of the *Norma Jean* so that wagons could be loaded across it without wading into the mighty Mississippi river. The mules pulling the first wagon refused to budge and dug in their hooves to the soft, muddy bank, trying to back away. The driver whipped them mercilessly, finally resorting to covering their heads with gunny sacks so they couldn't see their frightening fate. He led them on to the ferry and never lifted those gunny sack hoods. The next wagon had wise, calm oxen driven by an ancient man smoking a corn cob pipe. His open wagon was piled high with cantaloupe and watermelon. When it was the Hywells turn to board, fear rose in Rodantha's throat, sweat dripped from her temples and between her breasts. William had positioned Dutch out front with the new ox Curly and set Shire as the wheeler with George.

"I don't really trust those two new boys to do this without some reliable help from old Dutch. Now you stay on the right close to Curly where he can see you, and I'll guide Dutch, and we will be just fine, Danna." William simply said, "Step up, Dutch," and gave a short whistle. Dutch stepped up, Curly stepped up, and the wagon moved slowly onto the heaving deck.

Rodantha looked back to see Molly sidestep nervously as her hooves hit the decking, but Dollar and her calf moved along without so much as a glance in either direction.

The toll taker motioned for them to keep moving to the middle of the boat, so all the others waiting in line could board. Three more white tops rolled in close to the Hywells, and a small bunch of sheep tethered together took up the last space on the ferry at the rear. A beautiful black and white border collie circled and nipped at the sheep. The dog then sat at attention as though he was the king of the domain, master of all. No growling or barking needed.

Loud whistles shrilled the air, then, "Plank up!"

Two men, either side of the gate, hauled on chains and ropes, and all the other workers scurried into their places. In the center of the ferry were four huge mules standing on a circular treadmill deck, each pair facing in opposite directions on opposite sides of the recessed treadmill. The mule driver whistled, then shouted, "Git up, girls!"

The huge animals started walking. This turned the rotating treadmill wheel which then turned the paddle wheels alongside by cogs and gears, dipping rhythmically into the water with their bucket paddles. Rodantha could hear the turntable creaking and grinding below the deck she stood on. The ferry moved out slowly from the bank and into the rushing water of the Mississippi River. She braced herself, held on tightly to Curly's rope lead, and prayed. But to her surprise, the big boat only swayed and rocked gently, in cooperation with the rushing water. The team boat ferry, *Norma Jean*, was underway.

The young fiddler started a lively tune as the treadmill creaked into motion and the ferry lurched out into the muddy frothing water of the mighty Mississippi River. He started with "Old Dan Tucker," then swept into the sweet "Aura Lee," followed by "Blue Tail Fly." Rodantha concentrated on the music coming from the roof and barely looked out on the water. Her stomach felt unsettled. She hummed along on "Aura Lee" and stroked Curly's white face, then sang all the lyrics that she remembered from "Buffalo Gals." Voices rang out from the other wagons on "Oh Suzanna!" The mules set to braying toward the end of the trip when one of the gunny sacks flew off in the breeze. The fiddler gave up and quit playing.

At last, as the water rushed past and foamed up on the western shore, Rodantha was jolted by the *Norma Jean* as it slammed into the bank. This knocked her to the deck, hammering and lacerating her elbow. William was at her side to help her up and wrap her elbow in his handkerchief. "I was not braced for that, Will! I think I am okay though, just bleeding a little."

The ferry triangle clanged out a loud signal that the ferry had landed. This alerted all on shore that a new batch of immigrants was about to be deposited at the shore. A gate on the opposite end of the ferry was lowered for the wagons to proceed out from under the roof without turning around.

"All ashore!" rang out.

A little girl waved at her from a wagon waiting at water's edge, and Rodantha felt a sense of welcome to this foreign place, though the girl was probably a newcomer too. The Hywells' four oxen plodded away from the bank and up a steep incline with deep ruts and gashes where hundreds of wagons had recently plowed through. Her elbow throbbed and ached. "I'll ride in the high seat for a while to rest my arm a bit," she hollered out over the hubbub of wagons, animals, and people disembarking. She looked back to see that Dollar and Dalia were following calmly along behind, tethered to the back of the wagon.

A few dreary shacks and fishing shanties lined the banks. In the doorway of one shack was a skinny Black boy holding a baby wearing a soiled dress and makeshift diaper. Around the shack sat a dozen or so adults in wrist chains, heads bowed. William looked back at her sharply and shook his head. They passed by without a word, but Rodantha caught the eye of the boy and then "accidentally" dropped the leather corn pouch over the side nearest the boy, just out of the wagon wheel path. She had parched the corn the day before while they were waiting their turn to cross the mighty river.

She looked back and saw that the boy calmly walked to the pouch and stood on it while he put the baby down and removed the soiled diaper. He straightened up and pitched the diaper into a dung heap nearby. He quickly tied a rough square of gunnysack around the baby's bottom. When he turned to go back toward the shack, the pouch was gone. She knew he had it with him.

A great sense of joy and hope engulfed her. Perhaps tonight they would each get a kernel or two of her parched corn (though she couldn't be sure the boy would be generous with his meager little bag of corn). Tears ran down her cheeks and a lump stuck in her throat. *How can I fight this cruelty?* she thought. But she didn't know. The toll taker's joke was right! This certainly was Misery.

Boone's Lick Road

July 1856

On the Missouri side of the Mississippi River, William and Rodantha were immediately in the midst of a great crush of people and frantic activity. Rodantha saw riverboat men, roosters, Indians, Irishmen, painted ladies, and many overlanders in schooners. Freighters in huge rigs were pulled by six-span mules. Farmers drove wagons full of potatoes, watermelon, turnips, and beets. Dirty children scampered and livestock of all kinds were driven or herded: cattle, sheep, hogs, chickens, ducks, and geese. The wharves were piled with boxes, barrels, cordwood, and rusty iron, and a caged bear paced and rattled his cage.

As they traveled on, she saw scattered fishing shanties, and a few proper homes on real streets. Narrow paths led away in all directions. Alternately, the buildings and dwellings clustered together or spread apart separated by a few acres of garden or horse pens and stalls. A neat white clapboard church with a steeple was surrounded by a large cemetery where a few sheep steadily clipped the grass around the headstones.

The twenty miles between St. Louis and St. Charles, Missouri was the dusty, stinking Boone's Lick Road. It was easy to find and follow though, as nearly all roads led to or away from it. The road had been macadamized and marked with a sign that read: St. Charles - 19 Miles.

As William led the team onto the smoother, packed macadam surface, the incessant bumping and jolting of the wagon ceased. Rodantha said, "Will, I am going to ride a spell and rest my feet. The blisters is still paining me some, and my elbow is real sore too." She laid down on Aunt Zelda's quilt and immediately fell asleep. She had no notion of how long she slept. She was jolted awake by gunfire and shouting. Her heart thumped in her chest and the hair on her arms stood up.

She peeked out to see a dozen men on horseback as they galloped past the wagon at breakneck speed, mounts lathered, their mouths foaming at the bits. Their hooves thumped on the macadam. Their pistols were drawn. One man passing on the left fired at something ahead just as he came even with her in the wagon. He rode a roan horse. He had a feather in his hat.

It's him!! she thought, and then instinctively covered her ears against the deafening noise and crouched low behind the high seat. Then, rising on her good elbow she saw a horse go down far ahead and pitch the rider head over heels to the ground. The bounty man and two other riders circled wildly, shooting their pistols into the air. Then they all stopped where the horse and rider had gone down.

"Whoa, Dutch. Whoa, Curly. Easy there, Shire, easy George," William said calmly to the oxen as he crouched on his heels. More riders flashed past, firing their pistols toward some unseen foe. "Danna, Danna, you all right?"

"All right here! Are you hurt, Will?"

"No, by the grace of God," Will said. "But that spooked Molly, it did. She broke away from the wagon. Have to catch her, but she did not go far. Come on down now and hold the team from wandering. That mob is past us now, and I have no wish to continue until they move on a ways farther. Keep a sharp eye on them up ahead. I think the bounty man has joined forces with this bad bunch. If they come back, say we have some folks in our party with the typhoid. They will leave us alone." He sprinted across an open field and grabbed Molly by the halter. As he tied her back to the wagon he said, "We are almost to the Missouri River."

"Oh Will, I don't rightly know if I can go across another river. I ain't over the fright of the Old Mississip yet. And this here mob shooting—well, my heart don't want to quiet down," she said as her wild eyes darted back and forth.

"Looks like those ruffians have started off to the south dragging their catch," William said. "Bad bunch, they are. These senseless bloody attacks— I am against it with whole-heart Quaker beliefs of peacefulness. But, I know I must use my gun in defense or a severe threat to us. Out here, that is the only way to survive, it is.

"Now look here, Danna, just look ahead over that way," he said deflecting her attention to the task at hand. "See the smokestacks just above the horizon? That's a whole line of steam paddle-wheelers waiting for passengers along this south shore of the river. Try to get one of those, we will, but let's pull aside and rest the team for a few minutes, so as to keep good distance from those ruffians."

Another wagon followed them as they rolled onto the siding near a field of corn. Will kept a good distance away from the wagon and then moved ahead a few yards when he saw a boy from the wagon behind go into the field and come out, arms full. "They are stealing the poor farmer's crop, Danna," Will said shaking his head. He immediately whistled to the oxen to start up away from the thief.

The *L. Francis Ferry* was an impressive though worn and much-used wooden paddlewheel boat. It stood three stories at the middle, had two slender smokestacks toward the front, and a round side wheelhouse toward the back. It was tied up alongside the wooden dock at the Missouri River shoreline. Three heavy wooden gang planks tilted out from the main deck side facing the shore. The roosters hurried back and forth carrying sacks, bundles, barrels, and boxes on their backs to be stowed on board. Cord wood was piled up to the second deck all around the smokestacks where a boiler hissed and churned. A crowd of people, mostly ladies it seemed, leaned out of the second story railings waving their handkerchiefs. A boy sat nonchalantly on the railing. He jeered and taunted the roosters as they heaved and sweated at their work. A small pilot's box sat atop the whole, where the pilot stood just under the flapping flag. Cables stretched over poles on the long sides, and a line of overlander and farmer wagons waited on the bank ready to board.

William lined up their wagon and livestock toward the middle of this waiting throng. As soon as each group paid their toll, they were allowed to roll up over the planking and feed in under the second-floor railing, noses pointed toward the opposite long side of the ferry. The calm oxen took all this in stride, but horses and mules reared and balked at the entrance, not wanting to go into the dark, low ceiling interior. Molly screamed her protest, but Rodantha held on tightly to her halter and sang a familiar tune, "Buffalo Gals won't you come out to night, and dance by the light of the moon." Soon their rig was parked deep inside where the deck was slick with dung, stench rising. As she pulled her felt hat low, she thought, *So glad I wore Will's old trousers and shirt today! My blue calico don't quite fit no more anyway.*

Teams of roosters and Irishmen heaved the gang planks onboard like they were broomsticks, and the boilers popped and spat and shuddered. The *L. Francis* moved away from the dock as the wheelhouse sloshed and sang its watery tune, churning up that Big Muddy water. Black smoke choked the sky and trailed downstream. In a short while, maybe fifteen minutes, the *L. Francis* had lined up its nearest long side to the north bank of the Missouri River, where St. Charles sat awaiting its newest visitors. As Dollar and her calf, Dalia, trotted along the planking, Dalia lost footing and splashed down into the water near the dock. This caused Dollar to bellow her displeasure until Dalia scrambled back up the bank and safely rejoined her mother.

"Thar win aus a loocky budtti," William blurted, his Welsh suddenly come to life.

That night, William stopped the team on South Main Street in St. Charles, Missouri, and they camped in a large wagon yard. It was located in the rear of a small store and stage stop that accommodated overlanders as they traveled Boone's Lick Road on their way to Franklin where a ferry operated to cross the Missouri River again.

William wandered into the stage stop office, and when he came back out to the campfire where Rodantha was cooking biscuits and gravy made with Dollar's milk, he said, "There is a large map in the stage lobby that clearly shows the road between here and a couple of old forts that are now grown into the town of Franklin. Map shows the salt enterprises of a company called Bryan and Morrison. Shows all their many salt factories and stores, it does. Helpful information offered by the company in a clever way to show off their business interests."

He continued, "There are a couple of small creeks to cross but the road stays well to the north of the Missouri. We will only need to cross the river at the Arrow Rock ferry near the town of Franklin. I estimate it will take a week to get to Arrow Rock if we can make good time. And the overlanders in the lobby said that a new hotel is planned to be built on this very spot."

"I only wish that it was standing here today, with a feather bed and a warm bath," Rodantha mused. "I'd soak my sore feet and elbow and wash the stench out of my hair."

William talked with the gray-haired smithy in the blacksmith shop, Mr. Benchy, who was working late. The kindly fellow was willing to make a new iron coupling to replace the rusty rigging on Curly's yoke before he left for the day.

Rodantha took Mr. Benchy some of her fresh coffee and struck up a conversation. "Sir, I am just a might curious how this come to be called Boone's Lick Road."

"Well, missy," the smithy said in his country drawl, "the famed trail blazer Daniel Boone and his sons came here and found a natural deer and buffalo salt lick over around Franklin that had been drawing the wild herds. They say the Indians was the first using that. The Boones started boiling down that saline and shipping it out of here on the river. So, people just naturally called it after the Boones, seeing as that was who was doing all the work. Or rather their slaves was doing all the work. Other salines and plantations sprung up that all brought their slaves to work. So, the traffic along here just kind of built up the businesses to where the state fixed the road real good due to all the overlanders going west. They say that old Daniel Boone died somewhere in Missoura, you know. And I heard that Morgan, one of his sons, went to Kansas Territory of late."

"I do love that name, *Morgan*, sir, because that was my son's name too." She looked down and twisted her apron string. "I lost my boy a while back … born too soon."

Mr. Benchy quit pumping his bellows and handed the coupling ring to Rodantha. "Show this to your good husband, ma'am, to make sure it's a fit. He already paid me." He tossed the water in his dunk bucket on the glowing embers and snuffed out the lamp.

"I am so sorry for your loss, little gal. You don't seem old enough for such a tragedy. Though, I lost a son similar. Now, excuse me, ma'am. I'm off home for my supper. Thank you kindly for the excellent coffee." He handed her the tin cup and hobbled off.

Into the dark she said, "Sorrows are everywhere, with all the people."

In her diary she wrote that night in her most proper English and careful penmanship:

There are plenty of tears for the tearful type. I will not be crushed by my sorrows. I am grateful that no blood has passed this month. I hope that in a while I may have a child to call my own.

-34-

Between Civilization and Sundown

July 1856

True to the smithy's words, Boone's Lick Road between St. Charles and Franklin, Missouri, was busy with all manner of vehicles and humanity. Rodantha was relieved that the macadam made traveling the 120 miles a smoother ride. Out front, she could see that William kept his hat low and pulled his kerchief over his nose if suspicious looking characters appeared.

A lean fellow on a huge Percheron led three slave women on neck ropes behind his big black horse. One woman wore only an old rag on her head and a towel around her hips. Her feet were bleeding.

Rodantha understood immediately that this man was a blackbird hunter. He kept one hand on his pistol. Rodantha tried not to look at the slave woman and gave no indication that she cared. She quickly dabbed her eyes and kept her head down. Her heart was still beating wildly when she heard singing faintly in the distance.

"Will! Will! You hear that singing? It's coming from somewhere ahead," Rodantha yelled out, and then was sorry she had acted so brashly, as William only turned and scowled at her, and shook his head. She knew what this meant—she had to be quiet, unsympathetic, uncaring, uninterested, so as not to attract undue attention to their little party.

The singing turned out to be a gang of slave men stripped to their waists and chained to an enormous Conestoga wagon minus its canvas top. The salt merchant's wagon was filled with the rocky gray-white saline stuff. The slaves were singing loudly as they shuffled along, "Jimmy Crack Corn and I don't care, Jimmy Crack Corn and I don't care, my massa gone a-way." They looked only at each other and not at the scenery or the other travelers. As the group drew near, they broke into the most beautiful anthem that repeated the words, "Michael Row Your Boat Ashore, Hallelujah." That night Rodantha wrote in her diary the words that she could remember.

Monday-

I heard a song on the Boones Lick Road today sung by salt slaves. They sang with force and harmony despite the cruelty that kept them there. I pray that they will all soon escape to freedom or go to heaven away from this hopeless life. The miracle is they sing Halleluiah to end each verse like the Lord was listening. Maybe Michael is their guarding angel. I will never forget this.

1. Michael Row the Boat Ashore. Halleluiah.
2. Gabriel blow the trumpet horn…
3. Trumpet sound the jubilee…
4. Brother, lend a helping hand…
5. I wonder if my mother there…
6. Trumpet sound for you and me. Halleluiah.

I know there are more verses. I could still hear the tune but not the words as they went away from us. My heart is aching as though these was Cissy's kin. Tomorrow I'll write her a letter.

Thursday-

We crossed the Missouri River again at Arrow Rock on a new steam ferry that dwarfed all others we been on so far. It was scrubbed and pleasant too. It was called the *Rella Dean.* I was not afraid this time on account of its shiny new look and sturdy sides. I now know that ferry boats are a reliable way to cross rivers. We crossed late in the day after the crowds were already gone over— an easy smooth crossing. Fine boat, this *Rella Dean.*

Friday-

Whilst William was playing his pipes after supper last night, a scruffy black and white dog came to our campfire. He sat politely at the edges until I ~~cokest~~ coaxed him with the left-over johnnycake. He ate it in two bites and laid down at my feet. I didn't have nothing else to give the poor skinny thing, so I boiled up some of Molly's oats and flavored it with some bacon grease. He ate that in short order and slept by the fire. If he is still here in the morning,

I'll take him with us if he will go.

Saturday-

That skinny dog stayed the night and next morning followed me everywhere I went, which is a might bothersome. He has fleas and ticks. I gave him a name, Piper, since he was drawn in by William's pipe playing. William pulled the ticks and dunked him in the creek, which he did <u>not</u> like one bit! Lye soap and vinegar poured over and scrubbed in finished off those fleas. But he will be sleeping outside by the fire in case he gathers more vermin. He's used to it!

Sunday-

Will's map shows that the Santa Fe Trail starts here! We are finally on the way to Westport Landing at the Kansas-Missouri border. This is Will's dream of Kansas Territory where he will be safe from the Maryland bounty hunters. That is, when we finally get west of the Missouri state line. As some say around here, between civilization and sundown.

Jumping Off at Westport

August 15, 1856

"Could I have another drink from your canteen, Will? I just want to sit on this rock for a spell to cool off," Rodantha said as she blew out her cheeks and dabbed at the back of her neck with her hanky.

Hot! An oven. A steamy thermal slithered upward toward their vantage point on the high limestone bluff above the confluence of the Kansas and Missouri Rivers. A group of buzzards circled and glided effortlessly on that rising heat. The Kansas, or Kaw as the locals called the river, flowed in from the west across Kansas Territory. As William had explained earlier, the Missouri River flowed from the northwest and met the Kaw at this very point. The Missouri River then flowed on eastward, across Missouri and finally into the Mississippi River—all downstream from here.

The August heat at the Missouri state line sat on Rodantha's chest. The dread of slavers weighed on her almost as much as the heat. The Kansas Territory lay just beyond. From this high point they could glimpse the promised land they had been traveling for months to see.

A magnificent steaming paddlewheel riverboat churned along the curve of the Missouri River proclaiming in huge letters across the whitewashed wheelhouse Missouri River Packet ARABIA. Two tall smokestacks trailed thick plumes for miles. The decks of the packet were filled with people, boxes, barrels, and cordwood. "That steamer sits so low in the current, must be carrying tons of merchandise and supplies," William mused. "And to go west, it will fight that current upstream all the way."

A smaller flat-bottom boat floated mid-stream in the Kansas River far below. Several men with long poles pushed it slowly across. It carried a wagon and a couple of horses. Three calves were tied to the wagon, wobbly and braced against heaving floorboards.

"The consolation today is that we don't have to cross the river," William said as he tugged Rodantha's hand. "Have a good look, Danna girl. We might not get back this way for quite a while. More magnificent from up here than I imagined. And, as I have said so many times, this has been my dream, so long coming, to see the exact spot where those two explorer chaps, Lewis and Clark, stopped on their journey of discovery across the West. President Jefferson's greatest achievement, it is. Beyond this point are the wild buffalo out on the prairie, the Indian villages and native people. Where the west begins, it is."

After the Hywells had purchased the extra yoke of oxen at Vandalia, navigating the rough terrain was a bit easier on Shire and Rodantha's beloved ox, Dutch. Rodantha had to learn how to keep all four animals moving in the same direction. Her favorite, though, remained old Dutch, and she often talked to him like a dear friend and asked for help in guiding the team of four animals.

They had followed the Santa Fe Trail from Arrow Rock, Missouri, where they had crossed the Missouri River on the *Rella Dean* ferry. When they had safely arrived on the opposite shore, Rodantha let out the breath she had been holding and said to Will, "I declare, William Hywell, this was easier than I thought. I so dreaded crossing the Missouri. But these rivermen know exactly what they're about, don't they? No tipping or surging that I was so afraid of."

They then traveled on the south side of the river through Fort Osage, then to Independence where outfitters bustled and hawked their wares. There they were able to stock up on much needed items: flour, cornmeal, sugar, coffee, and dried peaches. No one took much notice of them, and this calmed their fears of traveling through a slave state now tense with Missouri ruffians who plied the back roads and raided over into Kansas Territory. This whole time William had kept his Colt Navy revolver holstered on his belt as they traveled across Missouri on Boone's Lick Road and the Santa Fe Trail to Westport perched on the western edge of civilization.

"Let's head south now, Danna. I want to stop at Boone's Store before we cross into Kansas Territory. The penny papers in Independence carried their notice. Says they stock all sorts of supplies and ammunition, which I need for my Navy, I do."

"I'm hoping for some fresh eggs. Maybe some really cold milk too," Rodantha huffed as she stood to go, wiping her brow. "Maybe that old Boone has a icehouse? This is powerful hot weather."

As they started south along the Kansas river bluffs above the river, they saw a few signs posted here and there along the State Line Road that declared first that this was the Missouri State line and then further on declared that the travelers should follow an arrow pointing west into Kansas Territory. These hand-lettered signs seemed to have no connection to on-the-ground reality.

"We'll sleep in Kansas Territory tonight for shor, Will!"

About mid-day, William angled the oxen back eastward near the five-story American House Hotel with its wide porches along the river-facing side. Today there were three steamers tied up at the levee. A half-dozen smaller craft came and went below the hotel and other buildings built into the bluff.

Shortly they pulled in front of Boone's Store, a few miles east in the town of Westport, Missouri. "Last stop before we jump off into Kansas Territory, Danna."

"You go on in there, William, for your ammunition. I don't reckon I can move a muscle in this heat, no ways," Rodantha sighed. "I'll just stay with the team after you dip a bucket for them to drink. Please, just find some cold milk and eggs and beg a block of ice if they got one. Here's two dollars I been keeping from selling those rugs at Franklin."

William was gone quite a while when suddenly a dozen or so men road up stirring a cloud of dry August dust into her eyes and nose. They had side arms on their belts and rifles holstered on their saddles. Their sweat-stained clothes and lathered horses smelled sharply acrid. *Those boys need a bath,* she thought. They dismounted and headed in through the open door on the front corner of the building.

She instantly recognized the last one to jump down from his horse. It was the bounty hunter that she feared. He still wore the turkey feather in his hat; his handsome roan was lathered from hard riding. He looked back toward her wagon and then shuffled toward her, spurs clinking with every step. Up close she could see the gash across his face.

He shouted, "Don't I know you, lady?" Rodantha pretended not to notice and turned away. "You just look like someone I seen on the trail."

"Come on Deke, leave that lady alone. She ain't hurting nobody." The men laughed and shouted more curse words than she had ever heard strung together as they trooped inside.

They yelled out, "Death to all the damn Yankees," to no one in particular and everyone in general on the street. Piper growled his displeasure, his hair bristling.

In an instant, she knew what she had to do!

Quickly she grabbed the empty watering bucket and hung it on the hook. She put on her felt hat and rousted the resting oxen, who had already lain down. She secured Molly, Dollar, and Dalia to the back of the wagon with the trailing rope, so they could not wander away.

"Get up now, Dutch! Get up, Shire! Up George, up Curly!" Rodantha released the brake as fear rose in her throat and sweat trickled between her breasts and down her back. She grabbed the ox goad from the wagon and showed it to old Dutch, who she knew and trusted to do her bidding.

The bounty man has joined up with these bushwhackers, the evil Missouri ruffians, she thought as she goaded Curly to get up off his haunches. Piper nipped at their heels to help. *Will is still inside!* She was ready.

What seemed like an eternity passed before William appeared in the doorway carrying a big bundle of supplies and a covered pail. As soon as she saw him, she whistled and urged the team of four oxen to move forward. William fell in behind, hoisted the bundle up into the back of the wagon, and wedged the pail securely between it and the tail gate. He seemed to know exactly what she was doing and ran forward where Shire pawed the dust to get some traction.

"Throw me the goad, Danna," William shouted. "Step up, Shire. Step up, Dutch." He goaded the two new oxen and yelled out, "George! Curly! Haw! Haw!" And all four of those old boys did just that, in spite of the heat, in spite of the shortness of the rest. Did they hear the danger in Will's voice? Her heart pounded in her chest and thumped in her ears. She whistled sharply and then fell behind a little and cracked the whip over their heads. For a moment, she thought she would pass out from the heat but kept her head. Her stomach lurched as the wagon rolled out.

As the road angled toward the southwest, Rodantha climbed up onto the high seat. She cracked the whip and whistled whenever she thought the team was lagging. William repeatedly looked back toward Boone's Store and goaded the team more than he had ever done before. The bushwhackers were not following them!

They kept this pace for a couple of miles before they slowed. To one side they could see a vast flat campground where hundreds of wagons were gathered in groups. Livestock milled and horses whinnied from stout picket lines. Several fires burned, wafting cooking smells out to the road. It reminded her how hungry she was. She could just make out the huge letters scrawled on one white top: California or Bust. William came back and walked alongside the high seat, and Piper circled at a trot.

"We have crossed into Kansas Territory now, Danna. This campground is on the edge of it, according to the poster I saw back at Boone's. Used to be someone's farm. There are three trails out of here. One to Oregon, one to California, and one to Santa Fe. We need to stay on this southwesterly route until we get to the Mahaffie Stage Station." He looked around several times and then told Rodantha what had happened inside Boone's Store.

"That feathered-hat bounty man has joined up with these Missouri ruffians. They called him Deke. This Deke was bragging and said that they were looking for a man by the name of Phillips. The best I could get from their raucous talk was that this William Phillips recently published a paper they called *Conquest of Kansas*. Made that bunch angry, it did. They wanted to string Phillips up to the nearest tree because of his strong anti-slavery views. I was surprised to hear Boone himself congratulate them on their recent burning, looting, and murder at Lawrence. They destroyed the anti-slavery printing shops there and threw the presses into the river. They really laughed about that and acted proud that they had shut down *The Herald of Freedom* paper and stalled efforts of the New England Emigrant Society to bring in anti-slavery voters like us."

"Oh no, William! That is where we was going to go wasn't it? To the Plymouth Congregational Church?"

"Yes, yes, the very same, it is. But now don't you worry, Danna, the Free State Hotel is already being rebuilt. The bushwhackers were downcast about their efforts and said that most folks in Lawrence were not scared off yet. They told Boone they might have to try again."

"Cain't we find some other town?" Rodantha swallowed hard and tried unsuccessfully to keep her voice even. "I am against going there all together now that I've heard this. I'd much rather dig for gold in California."

"Please, let's just strike a bargain, Danna. Visit with the Lawrence church folk and ask them about going further west, we will. Besides, Reverend Smythe has entrusted me with the funds left over from Mr. Troyer's wagon expense. I am to pass that along to the Emigrant Aid Society to help other abolitionists coming to Kansas territory."

"Well, I suppose we do need to know where there might be a good safe place. It's no good just wandering around in this dangerous territory," Rodantha reluctantly agreed.

About an hour later, William pulled the oxen over near a grove of elms. "I want to show you what I got for you at Boone's." He retrieved the covered pail and pried the lid loose to reveal a chunk of ice surrounded by a jar of milk and a box of eggs.

"Why, Will, you brought me a treat, even though…" Tears welled in her eyes, and she buried her head in his chest. "I do love you dearly for thinking of me whilst there was such trouble and…"

"Now, now, Danna girl. Dry your eyes. We'll drink this cold milk right now, before the ice melts, and have these fresh eggs for our supper. We can move on a bit further into Kansas Territory to make camp. Feel safer the further we get away from the Missouri border, I will."

Rodantha had never tasted anything better in her life than that ice cold milk.

-36-

Mahaffie Station
to Lawrence

August 1856

The roads teamed with wagons, stagecoaches, freighters, single horsemen, and women walking behind every kind of conveyance imaginable, pulled by mules, oxen, horses and, occasionally, people. Children skipped along, and babies wailed out protests against hunger, heat, cold, illness, and often, death. Great herds of cattle and horses were constantly circled by cowboys in chaps, spurs, and broad-brimmed hats against the sun, though all of them had leathery tanned or black faces.

At a distance it seemed to Rodantha as though the whole world had come here in search of its dreams. She imagined each covered wagon held immigrant dreams just like hers—a yearning for a better life, one that was perhaps attainable, but much in doubt.

Up close, though, Rodantha saw the hunger in the children's eyes and smelled the stench of too many animals and people crowded together. She couldn't hold back the tears as they passed a family bent over a woman in a green calico dress, lying on the grassy verge, face covered with a gunny sack. Little girls held hands, heads bowed, while a gaunt man read from a little testament.

Many roads converged here. Dust kicked up in all directions: California Road, Oregon Trail, Santa Fe Trail, and many local splits at odd angles. Rodantha's own road on the Santa Fe route led directly past a blacksmith's shop. The Hywells stopped to rest there and inquire about shoeing the oxen. Piles of rocks signaled the beginnings of a rock house. It was staked out around a hole dug out for a cellar. A Mr. Mahaffie said he would soon have a proper stage stop with lodging rooms, eating house, and supply store.

"Well, sir, do you happen to have an ox shoeing stock?" William inquired. "Two of our oxen have tender feet, and no one has been able to do the job. Curly and George here, are new additions to our team. Their hooves haven't hardened yet."

Mr. Mahaffie nodded yes and pointed the way to the stock. "I do this all the time these days. I have a fella here to help too. Should make a quick job of it."

They stopped near the big barn and asked permission to camp overnight while the oxen were shod. While the farriers worked, William bought bacon and smoked beef out of the Mahaffie's smoke house.

Rodantha made a triple batch of biscuits and stirred up peppered cream gravy in the big Dutch oven, flavored with that smoky beef. She had milked Dollar and saved her milk for a few days to make butter, but as it hadn't soured yet, she decided she wanted something to share with all the hungry-looking overlanders nearby. When the gravy bubbled up in the huge Dutch oven, she realized she had enough to feed at least a regiment. As word of mouth spread, she filled cups and bowls for many strangers and new friends, the best being the hungry children who came back for seconds. She gave all the scraps to Piper and a couple of other tame dogs who wandered in close to the cooking smells.

To William she quietly said, "I never knew how good giving away could feel."

"The best gravy you ever made, Danna, maybe the best gravy I ever had, it is."

"Here, have this last bowl, so's I can wash up all these dishes. I used ever last bowl and cup I had. Good thing most people brought their own."

"Mr. Mahaffie says we can get to Lawrence by following this Santa Fe Road until the Oregon Trail turnoff at a place called Gardner, a settlement of the Emigrant Aid Society. Named after the Governor of Massachusetts, it is. The Oregon goes northwest near the town of Lawrence, and Mahaffie says there's a sign at the turnoff to the town that you can't miss. I feel so much better now that we are among many like-minded folks. We will camp at the Gardner settlement tomorrow. Maybe two or three more days we will be in Lawrence, just in time for Sunday services at Plymouth Church."

"If you can, Will, I need all the water you can bring up from that Cedar Creek. I want to do a washing when we get to that Gardner place, so we will have clean clothes for Sunday services. Not sure what the water will be like there. I done used all my boiled water for this huge batch of gravy I made and the washing up. And all my towels and wash rags is dirty too. I'll set to boiling as soon as I can. With all these folks crushed in here, I reckon the water is not the best we seen."

In late evening, near to sunset, Will brought the wagon back with all the water he could get in their barrel, tubs, and buckets. He also borrowed a reach pole and ten-gallon keg from Mr. Mahaffie that he attached at the back of the wagon. Rodantha boiled water nearly all night and finally quit near daybreak when the fire had died down below boiling strength. Piper sat by the fire, alternately sleeping and barking if someone chanced too close while Rodantha slept.

A few hours later, Will handed her a cup of coffee and said, "I think I made a good trade, Danna. I thought we needed the water barrel more than the rug. Hope you are not upset that I traded your four-foot runner rug for it and the reach pole," Will said as he tilted his head with a question in his eyes. "Your rugs are like gold, they are."

"Right proud," she said, "to be compared to gold!"

The southwesterly Santa Fe Trail was a wide, well-worn, and relatively flat swath of many tracks snaking out over the landscape. Rodantha thought it looked like a giant bear had raked his claw across it. The cheery sunflowers that grew in the unused tracks and along all the edges made her smile. It also made the track plain to see and easy to follow—a golden pathway toward the setting sun.

At Gardner, just where the Oregon Trail branched northward from the Santa Fe Trail, they made camp. William built a huge fire to heat the laundry tub and played a little pipe tune for her while she washed all the clothes, towels, and bedding. His piping lifted her spirits and transported her away from the drudgery of the task. Reluctantly, she added the last few drops of her precious Florida Water to the rinse, and once again inhaled a beautiful memory that eased her weary mind. She carefully packed the empty bottle away in the kitchen box for safe keeping. It still smelled so nice.

Next morning, Rodantha awoke refreshed, and after all the clean clothes were folded away, they continued north on the Oregon Road. As they started out, they noticed that almost all the folks traveling this way were settlers with families in schooners. The traders in their heavy wagons had all headed southwest, staying on the Santa Fe Trail to the Mexican lands.

At the ford of the Wakarusa River—a strange sounding, Indian name— a band of Indians offered to ferry them across. William declined right off. "I think we can ford this little stream on our own, thank you." The Wakarusa appeared to be a gentle, picturesque little stream.

But as they waited for the wagon in front of them to cross, the skinny mule pulling the buckboard wagon ahead of them slipped midstream and almost drowned as he tried to swim the wagon to the opposite shore. The Indians pulled the rig out with their horses, and after much arguing and threatening on both sides, the wagon handler paid the Indians half fare. "Damn Shawnees has no right to this stream!" he bellowed.

William shook his head and said, "Think we'll need some help with this ford after all."

These so-called Shawnee Indians took the Hywells over the Wakarusa in two loads. William went first with the wagon and oxen. Then the rest of the livestock went in the second trip with Rodantha and Piper. The Shawnees secured rope lines to both banks and had great skill in getting their paying customers across. William gladly paid them two fifty-cent fares. On the north shore, the Indians helped with their own mules to get the wagon up the steep banks on the far side. "This toll is a bargain, it is, Danna," he stated flatly.

"These people are most curious, ain't they?" she mused.

The men were tall and straight, dressed in trousers like Will's, with moccasins on their feet instead of boots, long hair down their backs and wide headbands tied around their heads. The one woman she saw bent over a fire had a long colorful skirt. White beads hung around her neck, her face leathery. The Indian woman worked next to a little hut of animal skins tending the fire and steaming kettle. Several dogs barked around her fire, and Piper returned this ruckus until they traveled out of sight.

After some time, Will hollered out, "Haw, Dutch. Haw, Shire," and the oxen sauntered left into a narrow lane that led toward a big hill in the distance. The sign said *Lawrence*. "Tomorrow after services at Plymouth Church, I think we will have to go straight over that high bare ridge," Will said pointing to the hill that stood out above all the flatter land around.

"That'll be a hard climb for the herd," she mumbled, feeling glad that was not a task for today. Her legs were tired and sore. She felt a little faint and hunger gnawed at her belly.

-37-

Plymouth
Congregational Church

August 1856, Plymouth Congregation Church meeting, Lawrence, Kansas Territory

On Sunday, the good Reverend Jones, of the Plymouth Congregational Church, stood after the last hymn and said, "I would like to introduce a young man, William Hywell, who has come from Virginia with his wife, Rodantha." Reverend Jones motioned for them to stand and continued. "They are congregants from our sister Church in Fairmont, Virginia, where Reverend Smythe, our beloved friend, and their pastor, is continuing in the fine work of the Massachusetts Emigrant Aid Society, protecting and saving lives of many of our enslaved brethren. Some funds remained after their wagon was paid for by the Fairmont church and the Emigrant Aid Society." A baby in the back of the room started to cry, and Reverend Jones waited a moment for quiet and then continued.

"Fortunately, the Hywells have brought these remaining funds to us to be invested in yet more endeavors to promote a slave-free state of Kansas. We appreciate this gesture of support for the cause and this church from our frugal Welsh friend and his lovely bride. Thank you, Mr. and Mrs. Hywell. These funds will be well used." He folded his paper and nodded toward the Hywells.

"As you can see, William brought his Welsh bagpipe, and at my request, has promised to play a special piece as we end our worship today. William, whenever you are ready."

Rodantha seated herself on the bench, still buoyed by the pastor's lovely words. She watched as William shouldered his pipe, and said, "I will play

'Amazing Grace' by John Newton, a slave holder, who later became an Anglican priest. He preached against slavery and penned several songs that declared his strong belief and repentance."

He blew into the chanter to fill the bag, squeezed inward to start up the drone, and then filled the church with the bagpiping of his native Wales. Rodantha's heart nearly burst with pride. Tears leaked unbidden from the corners of her eyes and a lump swelled in her throat.

William then stopped briefly and asked the congregation to join in singing the words that now held more meaning. "I once was lost but now I'm found, was blind but now I see." Rodantha swallowed hard, but just could not sing.

As William sat down, a loud AMEN arose from the congregation as one. Pastor Jones closed the service with the benediction, *"You take the high road, and I'll take the low road / May God's love abide and sustain you. / Though it is true we may never meet again / We'll soon walk those golden lanes together."*

The parishioners came around to shake William's hand and thank him for playing. As William folded his pipes into Aunt Zelda's quilt, a gentleman introduced himself. "I'm Franklin Haskell, a deacon here at Plymouth. Where are you headed, William? Are you looking for a job?"

William glanced at Rodantha with a little nod and answered, "We thought we might go on west and pre-empt some of the near-free land on offer, but we have no set destination firmly in mind. We hoped that someone here might know of a good place to settle. We want to add our vote for a free Kansas."

"Well, then you won't be interested in the only job I know about," said the handsome old fellow. "It is hard labor and would not include a chance to buy land. But I wish you the best of luck on your journey. Thank you for coming to us and helping our cause." He slowly turned to go.

"Please, sir, wait a moment, Mr. Haskell. I would like to hear about this job and its location, since it could be a start-up anyway. I am not afraid of hard work, and my Rodantha here is just the same, maybe more."

"Well, sir, the stage station west of Council Grove is building out to serve the Santa Fe trade. It is located at Diamond Spring, a watering stop on the Santa Fe road. They need someone to build a limestone-fenced corral to hold cattle and horses while folks stop for the night and temporary pens for the herds of sheep being driven south to Santa Fe. As it is now, there are many losses from marauding Indians, Mexican banditos, and other scoundrels stealing livestock. As I heard tell, the fierce winters alone can kill cattle not able to be kept where folks can watch after them. The other man we sent them already quit and came back here after his little daughter was bit by a rattler and died. He reported that he was asked to stock shelves and keep an account of incoming supplies as well. So, they want someone who reads and cyphers."

"What is the pay for this job, Mr. Haskell?"

"A dollar a week, plus room and board, if your wife can help the cook. Otherwise, its seventy-five cents." Mr. Haskell looked directly at Rodantha, but she looked down at her shoes.

"As a boy, I helped out in my uncle's mercantile back in Wales. I can read and write and know my cyphers too. I would be able to help the station clerk in many ways."

After a moment, William continued, "In whose employ would this be?"

"Waldo-Hall Company is the stage outfit, with a contract for carrying the mails. I don't rightly know the fellow you would answer to, but the company has been begging us to send them someone for some time now. Far as I know, no one has taken them up on the offer yet. Some say it's a dangerous proposition."

William said, "I might be inclined toward this, but not sure about my wife."

William looked askance into Rodantha's eyes and tilted his head down in question. She had just looked up from her fixation on her shoes. She said, "Could we talk this over, Mr. Haskell, and let you know tomorrow? We been in considerable danger on our journey, so I am a might skittish of this proposal."

Mr. Haskell nodded and said, "Tomorrow will be fine. Tell you what, I will prepare a letter of introduction for you and bring it back in the morning, here to the church. That will give you overnight to think about all this. No hard feelings if you decide not to take the job. Is that agreeable to you, William?"

"Agreeable, sir."

"Agreeable to you, Mrs. Hywell?"

"All right, agreeable." She said looking again at her shoes.

Around the campfire that evening, the Hywells talked about their situation, more frankly than at any time since they were married. So much had happened to them and they both agreed that they were now different people than when they married and started this journey to the territories. When they finally lay down to sleep, they had come to an understanding.

Rodantha understood clearly the depth of William's commitment to fulfill what he saw as his duty and destiny to follow the abolitionist way, saying, "That horseshoe game where we met Melvin made me understand the world that you want to live in, Will. The races sharing friendly games and meals."

"I never took your dream of gold seriously, Danna. I see now that having gold and all the things you never had growing up has kept you hungry for a better life. That dream maybe even made you willing to marry me and come on this journey. Grateful for that, I am."

The Hywells decided to take the Waldo-Hall job at Diamond Spring. They would have an income and a settled place to live. They agreed to support the abolitionist cause and earn money at the same time.

William and Rodantha began to yoke up and prepare for the journey to Diamond Spring. They got over to the church very early and were glad to see Mr. Haskell walking out to meet them with the letter in hand.

The letter said:

> To be conveyed to: Waldo Hall Station Overseer at Diamond Spring, Kansas Territory.

> The young man bearing this letter, William Howell, is a musician of note and has played at the Plymouth Congregational Church this past Sunday morning. I believe him to be honest and trustworthy owing to his testimony before the congregation. I send him to you with the highest recommendation to build your stone corral or perform other duties as you see fit. He appears strong and says he is willing for this kind of work. He has experience working in a mercantile, and professes knowledge of reading, writing, and cyphering. His good wife agrees to help the cook in the kitchen.

Regards, Franklin Haskell, Church Deacon,
Plymouth Congregational Church
Lawrence, Kansas – member in good standing.

"I have been thinking about you folks and hoping you would take the job," Mr. Haskell said, "but I just want to give you a bit of advice from what I know of the situation out there. I don't want you to go in blind to something you might not understand or be prepared for. I feel like I should have said this to you yesterday, but I did not know if you would even take the job. It's not too late to change your minds. I will understand completely."

"Well, Mr. Haskell," William said, "we will take the job, and certainly want to hear anything that will help us with this work."

"Most folks from the East think that the troubles we have here in the Territory are over the issue of slavery. And, granted, the fight between abolitionists and slave owners is real and violent. You know, the good Reverend Jones sometimes makes it seem as though this is the only problem, but you have to understand that his passion for that subject is great.

"With so many settlers rushing to stake claims to the Indian lands, it is no surprise that much violence has erupted between the Indians and the settlers, causing predations on both sides. Emigrants and Indians alike are capable of extreme cruelty. But the quest for land by speculators, bank agents, and outright swindlers can far outweigh the issue of slavery, in my opinion. Banditry and personal vendettas are common, and usually in the disguise of the conflict over slavery. Also, throw in the struggles over the promotion of new towns, over the removal of Indians, and over the selection of railroad routes … well … you have opportunities for bloodshed in many corners. It can be a dangerous place. Kansas Territory is bleeding."

Will nodded his understanding and then drew Rodantha in by his side. "Thank you, sir, for your frankness and warnings. We appreciate your thoughtfulness toward our welfare. We have read the penny papers and broadsheets as we traveled through the towns along the way and have been stunned by many of the reports about these things." Here William took Rodantha's hand in his big grasp and continued.

"But our agreement is to stand against slavery and try to be fair and honest in our dealings. We both come from low and narrow beginnings and want to be a part of this new thing, this new country."

Mr. Haskell looked down at Rodantha and posed a question straight to her, in a shocking and unusual way. He simply said, "Little lady, are you willing to risk your very life to continue on?"

Rodantha looked Mr. Haskell straight in the eye and said slowly, "I done risked everything when I married William Hywell, sir. He has not disappointed me neither. I ain't scared of anything, except maybe crossing rivers." She looked up at William and said, "I reckon, we are the best kind of folks for this work."

-38-

Mexican Traders

September 1856

On advice from Mr. Haskell, William decided to go up the Hogback Ridge before turning south again to retrace their path along the Oregon Trail, to the Gardner settlement, where they would turn off onto the Santa Fe Trail toward Diamond Spring. Mr. Haskell said the view from the Ridge was the finest of the surrounding area, and the Kaw River, was not to be missed. To ascend the ridge, William angled the four oxen up along the side on a well-worn diagonal path. The ox team had little trouble pulling up the gentle grade.

At the summit were several burned structures. "I imagine this is the work of Missouri ruffians, Danna, when they also burned the hotel down in the town and destroyed the newspaper press. It's still fresh and has that charred smell and blowing ash."

They stood there and gazed out over the river. A trio of crows cawed and flitted in the treetops. William pulled her close and said, "I thank God for delivering me here and giving you to me to share it with."

"I do love you, William Hywell!"

He smiled and kissed the top of her head. "Now, Danna girl, let's light out for Diamond Spring."

As they slowly went back down the ridge, he applied the brake intermittently to ease the burden on the oxen and prevent the wagon from pushing them too fast. As they entered the town of Lawrence, they passed what was left of the Free State Hotel, where workmen were busy cleaning out charred timbers and bringing in new wood on their wagons.

"This will soon be a hotel again, Danna. These people are a determined lot, they are, and many overlanders are coming in to bolster the ranks in favor of a free state of Kansas."

A long line of settlers going northwest on the Oregon Trail passed the Hywells as they headed back south. William took the outermost track to avoid the stench and congestion. Theirs was the only wagon going south. At Gardner, they camped near where Rodantha had done her laundry a week earlier, and again they boiled water, this time dipped out of the Wakarusa River on the way back. Their wagon was the only one camped that night at the Gardner settlement campground.

In the middle of the night, Rodantha was startled awake by the rattling, creaking, and thundering of a caravan of huge Conestogas as it passed. Bullwhackers yelled out in Spanish, probably curses, into the darkness. They whistled sharply and cracked their whips. When Rodantha looked out the end of the wagon, she could see a moving mass, like a giant snake going up the trail toward Westport or Independence or wherever the traders were taking these wagons piled high with wool, cordwood, and supplies. By the light of the near-full moon, she saw the enormous wagons churning up a choking dust cloud, each pulled by five span of oxen. Lantern lights bobbed as the caravan moved slowly past and formed into a giant circle of many concentric rings.

Rodantha could see William out by the fire heaving a log onto the flames, sparks flying. She wrapped the woolen shawl around her shoulders, jammed her feet into her boots, and climbed down onto the packed ground. A figure in white moved in close to the fire, and Piper barked a warning, but soon quieted. She took this to mean Piper sensed that the man meant no harm. As she approached, she heard the man's mixed English and Mexican words.

"Boss man, Senior Perea says, 'uno stop dia, so we travel mucho en noche.' Our stop aqui … here … is the last before Los Estados. Always safe here. No prairie dog casas y malo indios."

As she approached, the small, brown-skinned man bowed toward her. William said, "Danna, this is Esquipulo, the foreman of this outfit. He says we are about to be surrounded by his wool trading caravan. This is the last stop before they go on to Westport to deliver their wool for storage and transport down the Missouri River. I can hardly believe they will cover the whole distance in one day!

"Esquipulo, this is my wife Rodantha."

"Perdoneme seniorita, do not worry, you will be safe. The men will sleep for a few hours, and rest animales," said Esquipulo, as he bowed again and moved away from the fire and off into the shadows.

Within an hour the whole four-hundred-wagon caravan had stopped, thousands of oxen unyoked, watered, and fed amid Spanish chatter and laughter. A picket of mules, extra oxen, and cows was set up on the perimeter, where young boys constantly rode around them. The bullwhackers spread their bedrolls in every available space near the quickly-built fires made from the piles of wood on the wagons. A great snoring and sighing mingled with spicy cooking smells that drifted from somewhere in the giant circle of wagons to the north where the dogs were still barking furiously. Piper just growled and stood stiff and attentive.

"This is like a whole Mexican village come to Kansas Territory!" Rodantha quipped. "I'll put this in my diary for shor!"

Rodantha and William tried to sleep but were up as soon as the great horde again awakened and prepared to leave, yoked up to the wagon tongues, to head north again. The men carried tin cups of hot food to their individual fires and drank whisky straight from bottles that they passed around. All were dressed in tattered white shirts and pantaloons. Enormous roll-brim hats shielded leathery faces or smooth boyish grins. Around their necks were slung small cords attached to long-necked gourds, from which they often took small sips of water or merely moistened their lips and faces.

One young fellow who said his name was Jose brought two cups of the spicy gruel and offered these politely to the Hywells with a big grin. A rolled flat bread stuck out of the top of the cup. At first Rodantha just smelled its overpowering aroma but could see that William had no qualms about eating the strange stuff. It turned out to be beans and onions, so spicy that it made Rodantha choke and cough, eyes watering.

When she recovered enough to speak, she said, "I shor can see why eating these vittles needs all that whiskey to wash it down." She offered it to Piper, but he wouldn't eat it. Though he happily accepted the bread that Jose' called tor-tee-ya.

After a couple of hours of frenzied activity, the Mexican wool trader wagons rolled north again. As the last wagon went by, four women smiled out of a rolled-up side flap. Their faces were painted a white-ish gray. They chatted and laughed as they tied each other's hair up into buns and braids.

Soon the caravan creaked out of sight to the north. The whole camp area was trampled and stomped, so that no green thing remained save some trees around the perimeter. This made it easy for Rodantha to see two makeshift grave markers that stood against the flattened landscape with stones piled up around the base of each.

As they walked nearer, carefully avoiding the manure, they saw that one was made from a wagon tongue, stuck into the ground on end with carved words that said: *Pedro fell asleep on this tongue. He was trampled. Son of Las Placitas 1856.* The other, carved on a piece of wagon tailgate, said: *Mourned by friends, Our Best Cook, Son of Tejon. 1856.* All around the large carvings were initials and tiny crude drawings. The tiny drawings stood out in beautiful relief and were covered with oil that smelled faintly of the spicy chili gruel Jose had offered them. William said. "Surely these have been left as a remembrance by each man's friends."

William thought out loud. "Curious, that someone did the carvings in English since this whole caravan is made up of Spanish speakers. Even Esquipulo doesn't do too well with English. You know what? I'll bet this train will be going back by the Waldo Station at Diamond Spring after they have traded for the return goods. Perhaps we will see them again."

-39-

Into the Hills

September 1856

Out on the Santa Fe road, the earth was packed and dry, like the campground, and littered with piles of dung from the thousands of oxen, mules, and horses in the wool trader's caravan. William took the outermost track again to stay clear. "If my calculations are right, we have a little over one hundred miles to go, Danna. We should be at Council Grove in a week, and then on to Diamond Spring the next day. We need to buy supplies, but if the job turns out to be as Mr. Haskell has said, we should not need too much, as supplies will be flowing past the Waldo-Hall station on the Santa Fe Trail regularly. No doubt part of the room and board. But I want to be prepared if things do not work out as we hope."

The weather was the finest they had seen on the whole trip, warm sun, cool breeze, cloudless sky, and crisp evenings accompanied by the most spectacular sunsets either one of them had ever seen. At night, a carpet of stars hung above as the whippoorwills called to each other from their hiding places. Rodantha could not get comfortable though and tossed and turned over the quilt padding that night. Her expanding waistline prevented her from sleeping on her stomach. Her back ached. She was afraid to say anything about a baby coming though, afraid she couldn't carry it to term, remembering her little Morgan born too soon.

William drew in all the stops he planned to make on Rodantha's Road Map and labeled each one. Danna looked over the map to see that after Gardner, they would be at Willow Springs, then in two days to Switzler Creek then Havana Stage Station, then Agnes on Bluff Creek, and then across Big John Creek by Big John Spring before stopping in Council Grove, and last Diamond Spring. Will drew in a diamond shape to mark the spot.

The Hywells nooned at the Havana Stage Station to rest the team and cook a midday meal. They drew water from the well and met the station master, Roch Gagnon, a friendly Frenchman, and his Osage Indian wife. A bunch of noisy kids played in the tall grass nearby. "Be wary of Missouri ruffians coming through here. Don't mix with them, ma'am." Roch said in his lovely French accent. "Oui, there was a bunch through just yesterday, riding hard, stopping only for water, and asking me if I kept slaves for field work.

"One guy with a feather in his hat grabbed Blue Cloud here and started dragging her off. I had my rifle handy like I always do. I fired off a round over his head, and he let go of my wife. She's still got the bruise."

Rodantha knew it was safe to talk to him. "Was he riding a roan horse?" she asked.

"Oui, we was! You've seen this bad one before, I guess?"

"We have seen him along the trails and know that he is a bounty man and a blackbird hunter. But we hoped he had stayed over in Missouri with the other slavers."

"This is the first I have seen him around here," Roch said, turning to go into the tall grass toward one of the children who was balling and hollering for help. "These kids are always stepping on burrs and sharp rocks."

Rodantha looked hard at Will and shook her head.

Will built a fire and Rodantha drew and boiled water. Danna baked potatoes in the big Dutch oven with embers piled on top. Roch came back out after they had eaten and struck up a conversation as Will studied his hand-drawn road map. "Where are you folks headed?"

"We hope to be in Council Grove soon," Will said. "How long do you think that will take us?"

"Well, these oxen generally take about three days, with the normal stops in good weather."

"We are going on out to Diamond Spring where I've been recommended for a job building rock fence. Do you know that place?"

"Oui, I heard that the Diamond Spring station is closed since no one could be hired to take care of things. It's not good to leave these stations untended since the western tribes have been more hostile lately with the squatter settlers pouring into their reservation land nearby. No telling what you will find when you get there."

"I was told that there is a Waldo-Hall mail stop in Council Grove also, where I should inquire about this job in Diamond."

"Oui, but the station manager there, name's Ebenezer I think, is often not around. He goes fishing after he sorts the mail, I suspect. So, if Ebenezer is not there, my advice is to see a Mr. Seth Hays at his trading post close to the Neosho River. It is almost always open. Seth knows everyone in Wise County."

Mr. Gagnon headed off toward an outbuilding in back of the station. "God speed to you. Say hello to Seth for me. I have to finish butchering a deer I shot this morning, before it gets rank."

After a few moments to think about all that Mr. Gagnon had said, Rodantha concluded, "Looks like this is a shaky kind of thing, Will. I don't rightly know what is best to do, since we are out here in the middle of nowhere, with that Deke fellow plying the trailways. That dollar-a-day wage does sound inviting. And I might be needing a restful place for this young one here real soon."

Rodantha patted her expanding apron front and gave Will a wry grin. This was the first time she had mentioned that a baby was one the way, though she had known for a number of weeks.

"Well, I think Diamond Spring is still our best bet," Will said, "and we will find out more in Council Grove. It is certainly safer than out here on the open trail, with no one around.

"I knew you were in the family way. Your dress is hiked up in the front and I see you've been walking all the time, and not in that bumpy wagon."

He bent down, kissed her full on the lips, and held her a long time in a bearhug embrace, tears in his eyes. With a catch in his throat, he said, "This child coming is another reason I wanted to take this job. I want to have a home for him."

A steady wind blew, sometimes strong enough to blow her old felt hat off, sometimes softer, along the ground. Rodantha untied the calico strips that usually kept the brim up out of her way and tied them under her chin, so she wouldn't lose the hat all together in a big gust. Her cheeks were dry and red.

The landscape beyond Havana Stage Station gradually changed from uneven flatness with considerable timber to clean rounded expanse of open country and wide vistas. The grass grew thick and much taller. In some places it was waist high. The blue-green of the summer grass was changing here and there to red, giving a kind of glow and a polished look to the hills. These hills were rocky on the tops with heavy ledges in the valleys. Fewer and fewer trees grew as they made their way southwest, most huddled into the low places or by little springs.

At Agnes, they camped by a small cemetery, evidence of deaths among travelers along the Santa Fe Trail. A gentle rain fell, refreshing the grasses along the packed ground of the trail. Down in a ravine, a flock of turkeys, numbering in the thousands, talked together and made a racket like Rodantha had never heard.

William grabbed his gun and walked a little way toward the noise. He took aim at one nearest. His aim was true, and the turkey flopped down. The rest of the flock only skittered slightly at the sound and paid no attention to the dead bird. William aimed again, fired, and brought down a second turkey. "I think I could kill as many birds as I have bullets, Danna. I am surprised that they are not frightened at all. Maybe we are the first people they ever saw, least ways people with guns."

Rodantha spent the next hour plucking and preparing those two big birds. She boiled them into a rich stew using up most of her salt and pepper, retrieving extra salt from her precious ceramic chicken shakers stowed away in her treasure box. It was very late when they ate the most glorious meal they had tasted in weeks. William ate the last biscuit to a coyote serenade under a carpet of stars as they sang, *Hoo-yip, Hoo-yip, Hoo-yip, Hoody hoo-yip, Hoo-yip, Hoo-hooooo.*

"These noisy little critters has got me curious, Will. They've been loping across our path all day and trying to hide in what few trees there are. Their howls is haunting and comforting at once. I wish I could understand their talk since I know they are telling all the tales of their home, this here wild land. I reckon they were after these turkeys we chanced on, for their own supper."

-40-

Council Grove

September 1856

Standing out here on the prairie I feel tiny, like a bug, near to nothing," Rodantha said. "And at the same time, I feel like I am at the dead center of everything on the earth. I cain't explain this feeling of large and small together, Will."

As they dropped down out of the high prairie toward a dense grove of hardwood trees, they passed a village of Indian wigwams and smoke from campfires. In the distance a river sliced across the road.

"What's the river called, Will?

"Mr. Gagnon called it Neosho. Council Grove is just on the other side of it."

"So we got to cross it? Hope there's a ferry."

As they got closer, Rodantha saw that there was no ferry. Her heart sank. Will halted the team at the steep banks of the Neosho and secured the water barrel with extra rope. He asked Rodantha to wedge all the wagon contents as tightly as possible, and then stowed the reach pole and empty extra water barrel inside the wagon.

"The water is nah too deep right now, so I don't think we'll float or drift. Looks like a rocky bottom from here. This should be easy once we get down the bank."

He set the brake to slow the wheels on the incline and said, "Ready, Danna?" Then, without waiting for her answer, he whistled and called out sharply, "Step up there, boys, step up. Haw, Dutch!"

Rodantha wasn't ready but had learned that there was no alternative to crossing creeks and rivers. "It's not too swift, Will." She said confidently though her heart was pounding. "I can likely wade across."

The wagon slowly descended the bank and angled, creaking, into the stream as William led them across. Today Rodantha wore William's old trousers and shirt. She held on to the tailgate as they entered the moving water, staying close to Molly, Dollar, and Dalia at the rear of the little caravan. William released the brake. The water of the Neosho covered the wheels by half and only splashed into the jockey box at the front. The footing was solid rock. Soon the oxen were pulling up the opposite steep bank, working efficiently as a team.

Up on the other side, they stopped to dump the water out of their boots and found themselves among several hundred Indians collected up and down this wide spot along the trail. More congregated around a building that turned out to be a Methodist Mission School, now closed. The Indians took no notice of them whatever.

These Indians were very different in appearance from the Shawnee that she had seen on the Wakarusa. Almost all wore or carried robes. Some had spiked headdresses and rings in their ears. Most of the men had some kind of hat, feather, or fur headdress while the women wore their hair in long braids.

They stopped at what seemed like a place of business, barrels stacked in front and a variety of tools leaning against the front wall. A large Black woman was sweeping the front steps.

"Whoa, Dutch, whoa, boys," William shouted to the oxen. "Ma'am, is this the trading post? I am looking for a man by the name of Hays, Seth Hays."

"Why you shor come to the right place," she said, a wide grin lighting up her round face. "But Mr. Hays is out just now. Should be back before nightfall, though. You and your missus, come on in. We got hot coffee and some fresh pies. Mr. Carson is here helping out and can maybe help you too."

Inside the little cabin, merchandise of all descriptions was piled to the rafters. Behind a low counter stood a small wiry man with a big mustache, blue eyes, and reddish hair above a high forehead.

"Welcome friends, the name's Christopher Carson. Most folks call me Kit. I'm standing in for cousin Seth while he is out tending to his cattle. I see you met Aunt Sally already. You'll have some pie and Ariosa?"

"That sounds mighty fine, Mr. Carson, uhh, Kit. I am plumb starved," Rodantha said boldly. "Might I ask what all these Indians are doing around here?"

"Today is supposed to be allotment day, but there is a hold up, since Seth is their agent and gone for a while. These Kanzas won't molest you none, friendly most of the time."

"What's this allotment day?"

"Well, ma'am, the government pays the Indians regular in bank notes or goods for their land that they give up. Now that the tribes don't have room to spread out to hunt and live in their old ways, they have come to depend on these hand-outs to survive. As I said, Seth is the Indian agent around here and handles all the government payouts."

Aunt Sally bustled out from the back room with a big tray of warm apple pie and steaming mugs of coffee. She set the dishes out on one of the three small tables in the corner and slapped her hip with the tray.

"Come and get it while it's hot, folks," she said.

As they seated themselves, Rodantha continued, "Well, sir, you seem to know all about this allotment business." Rodantha dug into the huge slab of apple pie and William went straight to the coffee.

"Well, I am also Indian Agent to the Apache and Ute tribes down the trail in New Mexican territory. And we have some of the same ways of doing things down there. I'm only up here for a short visit with Seth, trying to close out my sheep business. I'm selling up." Mr. Carson headed back toward the counter as the front door flew open with a bang against the wall.

"Speak of the devil himself! Here's Seth now."

Seth Hays had a full beard and a floppy hat, rough buckskin clothing worn with heavy boots. He nodded toward the Hywells but spoke directly to Aunt Sally who had once again appeared in the back doorway. "Sally, I brought a big beeve to butcher. Let's boil him up to feed all these Kanzas."

Sally nodded and said, "You left it out back for me?"

"One of the youngsters will string him up and carve. You just take care of the cooking, Sally." She disappeared again through the back doorway. Seth followed her out.

Rodantha went over to the counter and whispered to Mr. Carson. "Is Aunt Sally a slave?"

"Not any more, Mr. Seth give her freedom when he brought her out here to Kansas Territory. She can leave anytime she wants, but I reckon she wants to stay. Seth says she's family." Seth returned in a few minutes sipping a cup of steaming coffee out of a dented tin cup.

"Seth, this here is some folks looking for you, stopped in just now," Kit said.

"Yeah, I seen their rig outside. How can I help, folks?"

Once again William introduced himself and Rodantha, and said, "The station agent at Havana, a Mr. Gagnon, said you would know the Waldo-Hall mail station clerk here and perhaps also at Diamond Spring. Is that true?"

"Sure do. Fact is I just saw the clerk on my way in, talking to a lady on the stoop.It's your lucky day! Name is Ebenezer Storrs. You can either post your letters here at the counter, or take them on down to him direct, as he will be putting some mail on the stage tomorrow."

"Oh, no sir, I don't have letters to post. I need to discuss the offer of a job at the Waldo-Hall station at Diamond Spring."

"It's about time! Lucky for Hall that the station is still standing, since being left abandoned and boarded up like they done. Eb will be ever so glad to meet you and get rid of his burden. Waldo-Hall mail is a sort of side light for him. He comes here when he can and has been hoping for some relief. He holds mortgages on several farms here about, and on down on Stribby Creek to the south. He tells me banking is where the real money is, so he wants to do more of that and less station-minding. My advice is to hightail it on down there before he up and leaves again."

The Hywells found Ebenezer Storrs in the tiny mail and stage station made of rough logs. He sat behind a desk stacked high with letters, papers, and packages. Without looking up, Mr. Storrs said, "Be right with you, folks. Rates are posted on the wall there." The hand-lettered sign said:

LETTER RATES

LESS THAN 300 MILES –5 CENTS / HALF-OUNCE
OVER 300 MILES –10 CENTS / HALF-OUNCE
IF SENDING TO CALIFORNIA OR OREGON –SPEAK
TO AGENT

Unsure of exactly what they should do, they waited until he finally did look up. William said, "Mr. Storrs, I believe? Mr. Hays sent us here. We are inquiring about the Waldo-Hall Stage Station at Diamond Spring and a job there."

The thin young man stood up and grinned. That grin changed his whole demeanor, lit up his eyes, and dimpled his cheeks. He strode forward and shook William's hand.

"My wife, Rodantha." William said putting his arm around her shoulders. "My name is William Hywell."

"Rodantha, William, so glad to make your acquaintance."

William once again explained how he learned about the job to build the rock corral from Mr. Haskell at Plymouth Church in Lawrence and handed Ebenezer the letter of introduction. He said, "Rodantha is willing to help the cook. But now, we were told there is no station agent, no cook, and the premises boarded and abandoned. Is there even a job?"

Ebenezer glanced up as he read the letter from Mr. Haskell. "So, I see you are also a muscian, William. You come well recommended from the deacon, an honorable and shrewd man."

He hired the Hywells on the spot as keepers of the Diamond Spring stage stop for Waldo-Hall and Co. provided that William would build the rock corral fence, make repairs as needed, and start receiving stages again and provided that Rodantha would fulfil duties of cook and housekeeper. Rodantha would be paid the full cook/housekeeper wage of fifty cents per week. William would be paid one dollar a week as the station manager. A three-dollar bonus would be paid upon completion of the rock corral fence.

"If you will just go on over there and start on the rock fence for the corral? Yes? Here's the keys to the back door. You have my permission to take off the boards nailed across the doorways. Front is bolted from the inside. I will come next week to show you how to run the business end of things and you can then begin receiving and feeding travelers and selling goods. I will dispatch a letter to Leavenworth for supplies today, and send you a wagon of food from Seth Hays' storehouse tomorrow, if these Kanzas don't clean him out."

Eb Storrs stuck out his hand to shake William's and bowed to Rodantha. "You have no idea how much this means to me!"

-41-

Diamond Spring

October 1856

Golden sun rays shot skyward across a silhouette of the tall grass on the crest of a hill ahead of them. It filled Rodantha with new hope and exhilaration on this very important morning. A little way on west of Council Grove, they saw a woman and a young girl coming toward them along the trail. The girl stumbled along and leaned against the woman. As soon as Rodantha saw the little girl's distress, she filled a tin cup of her boiled water and grabbed her pouch of parched corn. Rodantha hurried as fast as she could without spilling the water and stooped to offer the cup to the little girl. Rodantha looked up at the woman who nodded, yes. The girl drank all of it, careful not to waste a drop.

"You are forgetting your manners, Marion!" the woman said. The girl hung her head and sank to the ground. She sobbed into her hands and then dabbed at her eyes with the corner of the woman's apron.

The woman introduced herself. "I am Marion's mother, Eliza Sloan."

"You just sit down on this rock, and I'll run to get you a drink too, ma'am. It is sweet, boiled water from Council Grove. Munch on this parched corn to give you strength."

Mrs. Sloan said they were trying to get to Council Grove to get help and provisions. They had been stranded at Diamond Spring for two weeks waiting for a stage or caravan so that their group could travel safely to Ft. Leavenworth. They did not feel safe from Indians and banditos without an escort. Mrs. Sloan said that all the windows and doors at the Waldo-Hall station were bolted and boarded up when they got there. Her party was forced to break in while they waited for a larger caravan headed for Ft.

Leavenworth.

"Those men," sighed Mrs. Sloan, "the leaders of our little party, were willing to starve rather than go for help. Well, I could wait no longer. So, I left the others to guard their precious wagons."

Mrs. Sloan explained that ten-year-old Marion wanted to go along. She had bargained and pleaded to go with her mother, not comprehending the trouble, since the distance to Council Grove had mistakenly been calculated at five miles. In reality it was three times that. Mrs. Sloan smiled weakly and said, "Marion usually gets her way."

"Now this girl takes after me, ma'am," Rodantha said. "My own mother always said the same about me!"

When William and the team came even with the ladies standing on the Santa Fe Trail, Rodantha pulled out her leftovers—biscuits from morning baking, and apples and slabs of ham from Aunt Sally. Right there in the middle of the Santa Fe Trail, Marion and her mother sat on the tailgate and ate all the leftovers.

"God bless Aunt Sally for her generosity." Rodantha went on, "She was the most welcoming woman in Council Grove and kept the whole Hays enterprise there running smoothly whilst Mr. Hays went out tending his cattle or managing his other work as Kanza Indian agent. You would really like her, I know."

William excitedly explained that they had just loaded provisions and supplies up to the staves of the white top to resupply the Diamond Spring station. His pride in being hired to build fence and act as station keeper was evident. The stand-in agent, Mr. Storrs from the Council Grove station, would come out soon and get everything running again—both stations being a part of the Waldo-Hall company. "We would be happy to have you and your daughter accompany us on to Diamond Spring, Mrs. Sloan. No need to go over to Council Grove. We can supply your party from our provisions until Mr. Storrs sends along more to stock the storehouse."

"Bless you, William. What a relief this is!" Mrs. Sloan sighed.

William cleared out a little space in the front of the overloaded wagon by putting several bundles on the little pack horse, Molly. He tied everything across Moss's old saddle that they had gotten back in Ohio. Here, just behind the high seat, Marion and her mother slept on Aunt Zelda's quilts until they reached Diamond Spring again that evening.

At the partly-boarded-up station, the folks in the Sloan's party were eager to hear the whole story, which William told and retold by the fire they built in the dining room fireplace of the imposing limestone hotel. Everyone there agreed that Eliza Sloan's chance meeting with the Hywells was a small bit of good fortune among all the hardships along that trail.

Rodantha kept the good feeling in her heart. She had helped Eliza and little Marion to survive. She fed them, bathed Marion's face and hands, lent Eliza some of her clean underwear, and watched them both like a mother hen until safely back with their traveling companions. This generosity felt so good. Caring for other people and helping make a little girl feel safe was a wonderful thing. Mrs. Sloan and her party left two days later with a merchant carrying bayeta cloth and Navajo blankets. Rodantha hugged little Marion Sloan long and hard, reluctant to let go.

As they had rolled down out of the hills that first time, William and Rodantha saw the little hamlet of Diamond Spring situated picturesquely on the slope of a valley where an icy-cold crystal-clear spring bubbled out of the limestone and flint rock. A strong fountain of water gushed like the namesake diamonds out of the earth and rippled brook-like through the nearby valley, down Diamond Creek, also called Otter Creek. Tall grass surrounded the buildings, rustling and whispering in the prairie winds.

The largest building was the two-story hotel and eating house built of limestone where travelers could rest and get a meal. At the side door saloon, the menfolk traditionally gathered to swap stories of their journey and hear the latest news of the Santa Fe trade.

Ebenezer had said that this would again be a regular stage stop, bringing guests and news from the states. At peak travel time, the limestone rock warehouse and store front would be kept busy from shipments of goods up and down the trail, for trading with the local Kanza Indians, and for storage of supplies, timber, wagon parts, and stage leathers.

Two haystacks slumped from disuse just outside the finished part of the rock fence. Out in the back, the partly-finished corral had a temporary split-rail zigzag fence across the open end, along with a blacksmith shop and several small outbuildings: a chicken coop, corn crib, and outhouse. William's first job, the one that had brought him here, was to finish the small rock corral into a four-acre enclosure for securing livestock. An enormous pile of limestone stood waiting in the distance to be used for this purpose.

The first thing Rodantha did was to take the Peterson's silver bell from Sweden off of Dutch's collar. The bell was tarnished, and the collar was blackened from much use, having been around Dutch's neck for many months. She rubbed the bell with a little saleratus she found in the pantries and wrapped it carefully in a square of muslin. She put it in the treasure box with her other treasures—the limestone chip from the Ohio Statehouse, the penny from the pork farmer—that all held memories of important events along the roads.

As she closed the lid, she said, "Be there with bells on." She smiled and knew that was exactly what had happened. The bell *was* good luck just as she had hoped, and she thought, *Bound to bring a lot more*. The bell stood for all the trials she had safely come through, surviving to see this day.

She unbuckled the oxen's big bells made by the Amish blacksmith and stowed them in the back of the wagon. The barnyard was strangely quiet without the constant rattle-y ringing of those big heavy bells as the oxen had formerly moved along the roads and trails and now around the barnyard. The sound of those bells had become a comforting, consistent reminder of their dependable transportation and quiet companionship of the oxen. *Old Dutch deserves a vacation*, she thought.

After Rodantha unpacked all the supplies and put everything away in the pantries and storehouse, she set up the kitchen using her own pots and pans, plus what had been left at the hotel. Cupboards held sets of dishes, serving and mixing bowls. Water kettles hung on swivel hooks near the huge open fireplace. An enormous wood stove with eight burners stood importantly on one wall. A big pile of cord wood stood just outside the back door.

"What a marvel this Diamond Spring is!" she said on first seeing the bubbling, gushing, constant flow out of the hillside up close. "Sweetest water I ever tasted. Wonder if it ever runs dry? Must be a mighty big lake under the ground. And we don't even need an icehouse, Will. Look here at the cold water flowing right on through the stone spring box. Milk and eggs can always be kept cool right here in the little side pool."

Rodantha started cleaning the rooms and washing bed linens. She discovered an infestation of bed bugs in one of the rooms, so she took extra precautions with the mattresses, asking William to take several outside to air in the hot afternoon sun. She scrubbed everything with vinegar and dusted all the rooms with the "sody." She washed every window curtain in the hotel and boiled towels and washcloths. She kept water hot on the huge black wood stove in a copper canning boiler. A tin of soft soap had been left in the pantry with the lid clamped tight. Rodantha dipped this up to wash all the laundry in big tubs in the alcove. She added vinegar to the rinse water.

She collected the lanterns from all the rooms and hallways, filled each with lamp oil left in the supply closet, trimmed the wicks and washed all the glass globes. These would have to do, since there were no candles anywhere. Most housekeeping tools had been left as though the former proprietress was coming right back. Rodantha tried to string new rope to hang the washing, but could not reach the poles and fasteners, so reluctantly asked William for help.

For the first time in her life, she had more luxuries than she could ever dream of. She treasured even the ordinary furnishings and household goods, of no value to most Eastern women. Even a porcelain chamber pot for each room was an extravagance.

After two days' labor, all the rooms were in order, beds made, curtains hung, and lanterns replaced on the stands. Chamber pots were washed, dried in the sun, and returned underneath each bed. Rodantha swept all the dust down the stairs and out the door. The dining room was the last to get a cleaning—walls and floors, chairs and tables scrubbed and polished. Despite being in the family way, Rodantha felt good, energized from the excitement of suddenly being in charge of such a grand establishment. Her trail backache vanished, and she worked long hours to be prepared for the first guests to arrive.

"I reckon I am the chief cook and bottle washer now," she said to William with a big grin. "There will be no bedbugs while I am in charge!"

-42-

William's Work

October 1856

William hauled water from the spring to fill every available container. He filled buckets at the source, emptied them into Mr. Troyer's barrel, and then hauled them in the mostly-empty wagon to the hotel with Dutch's help. Then he transferred the water in the barrel into the smaller buckets, barrels, tubs, and boilers for laundry, bathing, cooking, and drinking. He quickly realized this would have to be repeated every few days, especially when guests stayed at the hotel. He found several clean water barrels in the storehouse that he pressed into service. This cut down the number of trips he had to make from the spring to the hotel.

Will made a pot of his trail coffee on the big stove and rested for a while at the long dining room table. He watched Danna bustling about before he went back out to begin serious work on the neglected station.

Rodantha strained the left-over coffee through a little piece of muslin dish towel and set the thick brew aside in jars to make William a fresh cup quickly throughout the day. She explained, "I need your coffee pot to heat up some of the water really fast. And it's easy to pour out with that bail on."

He put on his hat and bounded out the door. The outhouse had been tipped over and refuse littered over the area, so William pulled it upright with Molly's help. Over the next two days, he cleaned and whitewashed it with supplies in the barn. He dug a second latrine and used boards from the chicken coop siding to build a second outhouse, though he only had enough whitewash for the interior. William found a crib full of corncobs and placed a bucketful just outside of each privy. He placed a ladle and bucket of spring water inside each. He gathered flat rocks scattered about the perimeter of the corral for a fine walkway from the hotel to the privies. "Call this ready for the necessaries of the hotel guests and stage passengers, we will!"

The rock fence was another matter. After the first day of trial and error, his back was sore, two fingers of his left hand bruised and swollen, and the top of his boot sliced open, leaving a gash across the top of his foot. He had many scrapes and bruises. Rodantha brought hot water from the clean laundry rinse water so he could soak in the big washroom tub.

"Wish I had some of that sweet spice Florida Water," she said to him, "to sooth your sore muscles, Will."

He fell asleep as he soaked. Rodantha roused him and helped him hobble to a nice clean bed in their little caretaker's apartment. "I tell you, Danna, if it were not for the fence being the very reason I got this job, I would quit right now. This is the hardest work I have ever tried. No wonder that other fella didn't last long. I have a new respect for those Welsh fence builders whose work I saw as a boy. These are strangely similar. Though the Welsh might have had centuries to complete theirs."

Next day though, William went back to work, boot patched with harness strapping, and fingers wrapped. William used the existing, already-completed part of the rock fence as the model for his fence. He copied the building technique of carefully fitting the limestone rocks together horizontally without mortar, built wider at the base and about four feet high. The top was finished with slightly-tilting upright stones. Will hitched old Dutch to the stone boat and loaded the rocks which the faithful ox then pulled from the big pile to the fence line, staked out with string on pegs.

After a week, he began to make real progress using levers and chisels more wisely. He nearly doubled the corral space and once again blocked the end with the zigzag timbers. He worked out of the back of their covered wagon, which he kept parked inside the barn. This provided a movable workspace where he could keep his most-used tools handy and out of the weather. To ease his aching back he often soaked in the washroom tub.

As he worked on the corral, Rodantha brought him biscuits or johnnycakes with some peach jam from the storehouse cellar, and always a fresh pail of Diamond water, cold from the spring. From the first day at the hotel, Rodantha had strained the left-over coffee through muslin and kept it for later to be diluted with boiling water for an instant drink. She took him "fresh" cups of coffee made this way while he worked.

William kept the four oxen, cow, calf, and pack horse up close to the barn in their own small corral for safety. There was plenty of hay and corn for feed. Dollar started giving lots of milk since Dalia was weaned and now able to live on hay. All of Dollar's energy went into that milk, now that she no longer had to walk all day. Like all Jerseys, her milk was rich with cream. "Dollar gets all the best water in the world that she wants," Will said.

"It makes for the sweetest milk I ever tasted," Rodantha replied. "I do believe it's even better than that Boone's store-bought in Westport, especially when it's cooled in the spring house."

As promised, Ebenezer Storrs arrived on the first scheduled stage out from Council Grove carrying only mail and a strong box of cash supplied by Waldo-Hall. This would allow William to buy goods from traders and make change. William saw the dust from the stage along the Santa Fe Trail to the east and met Mr. Storrs at the back door. William shook Ebenezer's hand as he came out onto the porch.

William took Eb out to look over the rock fence work. "You have made real good progress here, William. I am surprised to see how much you have completed. Another month and you'll have it done?"

"Well, sir, if this weather holds up it will. As you know, it is starting to get cold and has rained me out a couple times. By the look of the clouds to the north might even be an early snow coming. I will keep the temporary fence in place and move it out as I finish more rock work, so we can accommodate the drovers or herds that might come along."

"Mighty fine plan, William."

They nodded, shook hands, and started back toward the hotel. "I notice that the little lady is in the family way. Might she be needing some help in the kitchen and with the laundry?"

"Yes, been fretting about that, she has, sir."

"If you are agreeable, I'll send my sister, Mary Jane, out to help. Waldo-Hall will pay for a helper because they know what a big job this is from the reports of previous station masters," Ebenezer explained. "Sis is strong and a hard worker. Though she might be a bit head-strong too. She has been down on Stribby Creek, helping us out since my wife is ailing with a broken wrist. It would do Mary a world of good to be out from under the thumb of her big brother."

Ebenezer and the stage driver stayed two days. Eb explained how to keep the ledgers, account for incoming supplies, and understand the correct charges for all goods and services, the handling of mail, rates for stage passengers and overnight guests, and a thousand other details. Rodantha practiced her new duties as hotel hostess, cook, and maid to keep the three men comfortable and fed. A few travelers stopped in for meals.

The night before Eb left, Rodantha served everyone in the hotel a special meal of prairie chicken and noodles with dumplings, roasted carrots, and baked sweet potatoes. When it was time for the dessert, she inspected each plate and patiently waited for each person to finish. "Who wants coffee?" she said. She counted the raised hands and promptly added boiling water to half cups of the strong muslin-strained brew she now kept on the sideboard all the time.

"Do you want some dessert, Mr. Storrs?"

"Sure do," he replied.

"Turn that plate right over then. Here you are, some sweet potato pie."

She repeated this for each guest in turn until a curious traveler wanted to know why she used the backs of the plates.

"Don't have a lot of dishes, sir, and sure saves on the washing up," she said with a grin.

As Ebenezer left on a return stage and was out of earshot, William said to Danna, "I think with all these notes I took down on the back of the ledger, I am ready to be the station master. Born to do this kind of work, I was! I love everything about this except building that blasted fence—the very thing that brought us here."

"Well, that fence will soon be finished, Will, and you can forget it," Rodantha said. "It will be there for eternity, shor. I do love the way it looks, sturdy, straight, and strong. Handsome, just like you!"

-43-

Mr. Majors

About mid-day, a respectful soft-spoken gentleman arrived at Diamond introducing himself to William as Alexander Majors. He was one of the Hywells' first customers as proprietors of the Waldo-Hall Station at Diamond Spring. Mr. Majors told William that his wagon train would arrive later in the day and would camp out beyond the spring. He wanted to rent a room for himself for the night.

"Tomorrow being the Sabbath," he explained to William, "my men will observe a day of rest, only doing the necessary labors to replenish our stores of water, before we go out over the Jornada."

"Will your men require hot meals and baths, sir? How many might there be?" William asked.

"No, my thirty-five men are well trained, each man belongs to his own mess and cook, so we just need the space to spread out, since I have a sizable train of twenty-six wagons with six yoke of oxen each. It will just be me needing your services. And yes, I look forward to a hot bath and a meal in your dining room this evening. I will tell you, sir, that I am well pleased that Jacob Hall and his partner, Dave Waldo, have opened this station again, as it is a very important stop for Russell, Majors & Waddell company. I usually come along here several times a year out to Santa Fe or the Rockies. It's the best water we ever get, some years almost the only water."

"Glad to have you staying with us, sir. My wife, Rodantha, is in the kitchen preparing the evening fair. I believe it is a big turkey and all the fixins. I'll show you up to your room. Here's your key. Let me know when you would like to have your bath drawn."

While Mr. Majors soaked in the washroom, his freighters lumbered in and fanned out over the tall grass, organizing into a near-perfect circle, each wagon tongue with oxen attached angled just outside the circle. William watched as the men unyoked, built campfires, and sang songs. Horses and draft animals were put on picket lines with riders circling contantly. The piles of dung were shoveled into a heap on the perimeter. Robust cooking smells from the several campfires wafted through the open back door of the hotel.

During dinner, William and Alexander kept up an effortless conversation, sharing stories from their lives. Rodantha bustled back and forth during the meal, but mostly sat and listened to the men as they spun yarns and laughed at each others quips. That night William and Rodantha learned that they were having dinner with a seasoned freighter who had been plying his trade for the last twenty years all over the West. He now made his permanent home to the north in Nebraska. He told stories about blizzards, grasshopper invasions, cyclones that leveled buildings, the demise of the natural springs that were formerly all over the state of Missouri, and the whole-hearted cutting of timber and ruination of the creeks where trees formerly grew abundantly.

Mr. Majors said, "In the early days, Missouri was considered the last Western frontier and it was thought no settlements would ever be west of that state, save for a little strip on the West Coast of California. Dealings with the Indians were friendly and cordial. Most whites treated the Indians as equals or better and respected their right to their lands. As more Europeans poured into the territories and the newcomers became more covetous of the Indian lands, the Indians were more and more seen as savages, less than human, and better off separated from whites on reservations." Mr. Majors said that he had traded freely with and had friends among the various tribal groups: Wyandotte, Shawnee, Delaware, Kickapoo, Miami, Sac and Fox, Osage, and Iowa, and that peace reigned from 1825 until the last few years, when treaties were broken, land illegally seized, and Indian families broken apart. Mr. Majors believed a full-on war with the western Indians would happen soon since they were more resistant to the white man's ways than the eastern tribes.

"I strongly believe that there will also be a war with the southern states,"

Alexander said as he poked his pipe full of tobacco. "Those are states in favor of slavery for themselves and new territories such as Kansas. Missouri ruffians, in particular, are the most dangerous group.

"I admire your courage, Rodantha, in all of this. William told me about his narrow escape from the Maryland authorities and the bounty hunter who has been nipping at your heels."

Mr. Majors paused a moment and looked directly at Rodantha who was clearing the dishes. "I will not get into the particulars in front of your sweet wife, William, but I have first-hand knowledge of their evil deeds. These ruffians will all go to the devil for what they have done! They continually stir up trouble, and Rodantha should be wary."

Rodantha said, "We had a close call with those rascals at Westport. The station master at Havana stage stop also had a run in with some of the ruffians. We are sure that he saw the same bounty hunter that has been trailing Will. I understand now how all this random violence can become a full on war." As the men smoked by the fire, Rodantha listened as Mr. Majors explained his method of carrying on his freighting business saying, "I make a gift of a Bible as soon as I hire a new hand. Each one must sign an agreement to refrain from using profanity. They must agree to not get drunk, not gamble, not mistreat any animal, and, in general, to act as gentlemen at all times. I have found that this policy, aside from being morally right, prevents fighting and unhappiness and much abuse. So far, I think my success has been built on these ideas. If anyone is found to violate the rules, I do not punish, I simply terminate the offender without pay and will never rehire him."

About midnight, Rodantha excused herself, washed the dishes, and cleaned the kitchen for morning breakfast preparations. The men were still talking when she went up to the caretaker rooms. Her feet hurt and her back ached. The baby was growing. She was vaguely aware of William slipping into bed, but had no idea of the time.

The whole Russell, Majors and Waddell outfit was gone shortly after daybreak. Mr. Majors left Rodantha a big bag of Arbuckle Ariosa coffee on the dining table with a little note attached that said:

> Thank you, Rodantha, for a most pleasant evening. I apologize for the lateness of the hour last night, but William and I had so much to discuss. I enjoyed your company and the delicious food. Here is a sack of the coffee favored by the bullwhackers in

my outfit. I trust you will also like it. They all fight over the peppermint sticks that come in the package, so to prevent squabbles, I want you to have them.

Enjoy, Alexander.

p.s. Just wanted you to know that you remind me so much of my own daughters. You made this the best stay at Diamond Spring in memory.

When William came in from the storehouse about noon, he continued talking about Mr. Majors. "Alexander said that his friend, a Mr. Creighton, is building telegraph cables all through Ohio and will soon start a line from Omaha, Nebraska, out west along the proposed railroad right of way. His work is funded by the U.S. Congress for enormous sums of money. Alex said we will soon be able to send messages over these telegraph wires."

"William, I do declare this is just about the most excited I have seen you since we started west on our honeymoon. You and Mr. Majors got on well, huh?"

"A loocky budtti I am, Danna! I have learned so much from him. Meant for this work, I am!"

-44-

Rodantha's Road House

March – April 1857

Mary Jane Storrs came to help out at Diamond Spring in November, just as Ebenezer had promised. By March she had proved what she said on her first day at the hotel. "I am here to make life easier for you, Rodantha. Just show me what you need me to do."

Ebenezer's sister was hard-working, capable, and knowledgeable about every aspect of keeping a household running. Mary was the blessing Rodantha needed as her time drew near, though at times Mary Jane's take charge attitude felt bossy and annoying. The last week before the birth, Rodantha stayed in bed with swollen feet and legs and could only waddle around a bit trying to balance her huge mid-section. Mary ran everything, did all the cooking, cleaning, and cared for the guests. Rodantha learned quickly to nod and smile and do as she was "told." It was a relief to know that Mary Jane was looking out for her.

On April 13, Rodantha's water broke. As soon as Mary Jane arrived that morning, she came upstairs to help, so William could attend to station business. Mary Jane sat with Rodantha all day reading Walt Whitman's *Leaves of Grass*, and *Walden*, by Henry Thoreau. She said, "I closed the dining room, and posted a notice that says NO VACANCY on the front door, so there will be no interruptions or noise today.

Rodantha delivered two healthy beautiful twin daughters, attended by Mary Jane and William. He sang or hummed the "Welsh Lull Song" during the labor and true to his prediction, the babies were born trouble free.

Mary Jane eased the babies into the world, calmed Rodantha during the labor, and tied the babies' cords. When it was over she said triumphantly,

205

"You know, I helped with my brother's birth and learned from the midwife how to do this and keep things clean."

Mary Jane brought the twin girls in for breast feeding one at a time, changed their nappies, and tenderly cared for Danna. "You are the sister I never had Danna," Mary said. Rodantha felt a bond with Mary like no other in her life, more than Aunt Zelda or her own sister, Sylvie.

The doctor from Council Grove came by the next day and pronounced all in good condition and gave instructions on the finer points of mother and baby care. Rodantha rested for two weeks and nursed Jennie and Ellie with surprising advice from young Mary. "I'll show you how my ma did the nursing for our baby James to prevent soreness. I helped her sometimes."

Every night William played the "Welsh Lull Song" for his infant daughters on his bagpipe or sung it in his fine baritone. "Sleep my darling, night is falling, rest in slumber sound and deep." The little girls grew and thrived even though the atmosphere of the surrounding lands was often hostile and dangerous. Mary Jane was "Auntie Jane" to the twins from their birth.

In addition to the traders and merchants using the Santa Fe trail, some families coming into the territories from the north and east also used the trail, since there were reliable stage stops, and provided the three requirements of the settlers: water, timber, and grass. Overlanders traveling westward as a result of the Kansas-Nebraska Act that opened up land for pre-emption or outright sale routinely stopped at Diamond Spring.

Two brothers coming from Wisconsin used part of the military road from Ft. Leavenworth to Ft. Riley and crossed the Kaw River near Topeka. These German brothers were on foot and had only a pack mule to carry provisions. They told William that they walked south from Topeka and then followed the Santa Fe Trail to Council Grove and then Waldo-Hall station at Diamond Spring.

Henry and Frederick Pracht were on their way to join other families from Wisconsin who had settled further to the south along Diamond and

Middle Creeks. They planned to follow Diamond Creek as it meandered its way southward to where their friends, the Hegwers and Freys, had already settled. They hoped to pre-empt some choice land in those valleys and said they wanted to farm or raise cattle.

On the day the Pracht brothers arrived, Rodantha felt strong enough to do some cooking. Down in the kitchen, hanging above the big black stove, was a surprise waiting for her—a neatly printed sign that read: *RODANTHA'S ROAD HOUSE*. It was hand-lettered on a big piece of packing crate and in the bottom corner was William's signature, which Rodantha had never seen before. She laughed and cried and rocked in the rocking chair, her emotions swelling and ebbing in the way of new mothers. Her heart pumped with pride at this unexpected honor.

Rodantha was anxious to serve her customers again and help the folks who stopped at Diamond Spring station. So, while Mary Jane watched over the baby girls, Danna made prairie chicken and noodles, grilled potatoes and squash on the side. She made a fresh pot of coffee and held a triple batch of biscuits in the warming oven. Those two German fellows sat down and commenced to eat three helpings of everything. Finally, Rodantha asked them if they had any room for dessert. She was fond of playing her little trick on unsuspecting customers in the eatery.

"Just turn your plates over and I'll bring you some apple pie," she said.

"What do you mean, turn our plates over?" Henry said.

"Well, you said you wanted pie, didn't you?"

"Yes," they said in unison.

"Just turn 'em over and you'll see how we do things at Rodantha's Road House," she said as she pointed to the new sign she had propped up on the fireplace mantel in the dining room.

They burst into laughter and made little jokes about "Kansas dessert plates" at "Rodantha's Road House." They each ate two pieces of her apple pie on the clean plate backs and drank several more cups of her strained and reheated coffee. She had seen some good appetites, but these skinny young Pracht brothers were the hungriest in a long time.

As they were about to leave, Mary Jane came down from the nursery, and said, "The little ones are fussing and hungry, Rodantha. You go on up to nurse them and I'll finish up here."

Rodantha finished clearing up the table and later told William, "Mary saw Henry Pracht, Henry saw Mary Jane, and cupid's arrows flew. Those two talked and laughed quite a while. Then Mary Jane followed him outside while he and Frederick loaded supplies onto the pack mule. Henry came back and asked my permission to call on her. He said something like, Mrs. Hywell, may I come to call on Mary Jane next week? And of course, I said yes."

Henry Pracht appeared at the hotel one evening with a single prairie rose for Mary Jane. The two young people sat in the corner by the fire and talked quietly. He held both her hands in his and gazed uncomfortably long into her eyes, which she cast downward from time to time. After that, Henry rode up from Stribby Creek every few days. Love bloomed.

Rodantha boldly declared repeatedly. "Henry would make a fine husband for you, Mary Jane." This always made Mary Jane smile and lose a little of her usual bravado.

"I am just waiting for him to ask me, Danna. He seems a might slow to me, but men have to take their sweet time to know if it is right, I guess."

-45-

Neglected Diary

1859

As Rodantha and Mary Jane worked together to clean and cook and do laundry for hotel guests at the Diamond Spring station on the Santa Fe Trail, they talked of their dreams. They shared their womanly concerns over husbands and suitors, recipes, gold, babies, and a thousand things that they could only discuss with each other. They laughed and sometimes cried.

"Henry has proposed to me, Danna!" Mary Jane said. "The school building will be finished soon, and he and his family want a big wedding there. I said yes, of course."

Rodantha hugged her best friend with tears of joy in her eyes. "The church people will get the first use of the new building since there is no teacher yet, and no books either."

"Would you make a cake, Danna?" Mary Jane asked.

Rodantha nodded yes and hugged Mary Jane again. "I'll try to get some vanilla from one of the merchants this week. Now, what about a dress? You can wear my lace cape if you want. You know—the one I showed you— stowed in the treasure box from my own wedding?"

"Oh, yes, Danna! That would be perfect. I have the loan of my cousin's dress with a lace hem. Your cape would dress up the plain bodice into a splendid finish." They discussed wedding plans on and on all day, with agreement that Rodantha would be maid of honor and William would be best man.

The large Pracht family, along with their neighbors on Stribby Creek, had been building a school for their children. The Methodists gave a donation and provided extra labor and materials to build the school large enough to accommodate their meetings, with the agreement that the congregation would also meet at the school. Benches and desks were movable, and the teacher's desk became the parson's podium on Sunday mornings.

The Pracht wedding was the first in the community and turned out all the neighbors for miles around. The day-long celebration included a potluck dinner, games, and a three-piece string band for dancing. The benches were shoved to the walls where the old folks sat, and the new wood floor was filled with joyous reels, schottisches, and waltzes.

After the wedding, Rodantha dug out her diary to record her thoughts at this most important time. She realized it had been almost two years since she had written anything in it. She devoted several pages to the wedding and then tried to remember and write down the most important happenings in her life that had not been recorded.

1859

I was eighteen when I started writing in this diary that Miss Quimper gave me as a wedding gift. When I put my hand in the tracing I made on the first page, it still fits, though I am now almost twenty-one. I cherish Cissy's hand trace in the back and think of her every time I see it. I have a few empty pages left and I have taken time to write down the important people and events I can remember. I have gotten out of the habit of daily entries since we have settled here at Diamond Spring station. I have gone back through everything I wrote and assigned the dates the best I can remember. Some entries were written earlier, and some just now. I stay so busy with the children, running the hotel, and cooking for the guests. It is hard work, but I enjoy it most of the time. I have finer things here than I ever had in my life, or ever expected to have: big kitchen, well-furnished dining room, proper bed linens, supplies of fresh food, and never-ending pure water. I meet the most interesting people from all over.

1857

I will go back and fill in the last few years, since I have neglected my diary. I just could not keep up with all I had to do, and the writing got left out.

1857 is the year my beautiful daughters were born, Ellie and Jennie. I love them more than my own life, and I reckon the best cure for selfishness I know. They depend completely on me to look after them and make a safe place to grow. I will not follow my foolish dreams of finding gold in California, since what would they do without me?

Will built a four-acre stone-fenced corral and two privy houses. He met all the stages and changed, fed, watered the horses, cared for sick and lame animals. He cleaned out the spring box, so the cold water can run right through it to keep milk, butter, and eggs cool. He has made friends of all comers, Kanza and Osage Indians, Mexican traders, sheep drovers, stage drivers, even a couple of banditos that tried to steal supplies from the storehouse. (He had to catch them first as they was trying to get away in their wagon, then he GAVE them the supplies if they promised to quit thieving.) He kept all the ledgers straight and paid merchants for supplies.

Will has a shotgun, but only uses it to shoot prairie chickens, turkeys, and the occasional deer when they come close. He keeps the Navy pistol handy out in the storehouse in case of banditos or quarrelsome travelers. He says it is more of a peacekeeper than a weapon.

As for me, I always put in a big garden with all kinds of good things—beets, carrots, potatoes, peas, pole beans, chard, okra, and sweet potatoes. I planted all the seeds that Aunt Zelda put in the seed box (now my treasure box) and give me for a wedding gift. I had kept them for over a year, so some were not good and never even sprouted. Aunt Zelda's chard is doing well! I tried to get some tomatoes to grow, but the wind beat the leaves and made the blooms fall.

I always do laundry the day after any guest leaves, empty and clean the chamber pots and make up all the rooms, cook all the meals and keep everything clean and neat—except for what Mary Jane (now Pracht) does, which is considerable. She can do the work of three and does a good measure of cooking, cleaning, and minding the children. We make up big batches of corn bread, cinnamon rolls (when we can get cinnamon from traders), and several loaves of sourdough bread every morning for a good supply for our customers.

Mary Jane is like a sister to me, and I would be lost without her. Since she is married now, I hope she will keep coming to work for such a small wage as W-H Co. pays her. Her Henry farms down on Stribby Creek, so she can still stay with me a few days, and then go home a few days. My little ones miss her when she is not here and are so excited to see her again.

Ebenezer Storrs recently has bought up a lot of farms around here that he held mortgages on, since quite a number of folks left the territory to go back east to their old homes. Severe winters put a lot of folks out of the farming and ranching business. Their stock couldn't survive the harsh winter and crops were destroyed. I am glad Will is not a farmer. It is too <u>unpredictable</u>.

1858

If I remember correctly, Will built a new chicken house in '58 and we got some chicks from a farm at Council Grove, so I have plenty of fresh eggs to eat and extras to sell. We have had some trouble with the coyotes stealing them, but Piper mostly chases them away. I lock all the chickens up in the hen house at night.

Ebenezer's wife was ailing, and she died in '58. I never met her, and I think she was young—a sad thing. Eb was distraught and lonesome. He started coming out to have supper with us. He and Will always had a lot of Waldo-Hall business to discuss. He sometimes stayed overnight after Mrs. Storrs passed.

Eb started bringing his son Riley out to help William with animals. He cleans stalls, milks Dollar, and helps to care for stage horses so they are always ready. His help relieves us of so many daily chores, like toting water up from the spring. Riley is a strapping young man of about fourteen and has continued on as William's helper for several months now. W-H pays him a small wage. He is a mischievous fellow, but good at heart, so I don't mind his little tricks and laziness. He makes me laugh.

Mr. James Mead from over on the Saline River came through the station a few times in 1858 on his hunting trips and his trading trips. He does considerable trading with the various Indian tribes for goods, buffalo hides, and wolf pelts. He goes up to Leavenworth and back. He is a most interesting fellow, very ambitious, and talks of building a town.

In late September a flaming wonder appeared in our night sky for two nights in a row—a comet stretched across the Western sky. I did not know what it was at first, but one of our guests was familiar with this sort of thing and told us all about comets. It was a brilliant star with a long curving tail. On the second night of the comet show, Henry came to pick up Mary Jane and stayed for supper. As we walked out to their wagon that evening, Henry said something like, "God probably sent this flaming star to celebrate our engagement, Mary Jane." He is a romantic fellow and a good match for sweet Mary.

Written in 1859

Gold was found in the Rocky Mountains to the west. I love hearing the gold men talk about their adventures, but my heart stays right here at Diamond Spring, so I do too. The news came late in one of the papers we get from the states. I was shocked to see a bold title "THE NEW ELDORADO!! GOLD IN KANSAS!!" "Pike's Peak or Bust" is a popular phrase among many travelers through Diamond. If I was to go out there, I'd go to Golden City. It just sounds right!

In one of the newspaper articles we read, the report said that the value of goods that went over the SF Trail was $10 million. I am not sure how the newspaper men arrived at this huge number, but I can truthfully say that by William's count we averaged eight wagons a day stopping here for water, supplies, meals, or just coffee and a rest. Everyone gets as much of the Diamond water as they can haul. Usually, the wagons travel together—at least a dozen—and often meet up here to gather into trains for safety. William says Waldo-Hall Company is getting rich. W-H pays us regular, so in a way we are too.

One very large train of more than seventy-five wagons made a <u>rendezvous</u> here in May (they were waiting for others from Council Grove). They usually camp out of their wagons and rarely ask for a room for the night. I met several of their party as they gathered and prepared to go across the Jornada. I was most interested in newlyweds Lydia Ann Kahl and her husband Adam. She has also been keeping a diary of her journey, and we had much in common. Big trains are good protection from Indian attacks and bandito thefts. I do hope she will get safely out to California. There is still a very long way to go, with many dangers and difficult travel through mountains. I gave her a set of my crocheted potholders when she left.

-46-

Canaan Land

1858

Aletter from Cissy came in the spring responding to Rodantha's letter sent to Mr. Hoyt and forwarded on to Cissy at the Eleutherian School. Cissy wrote:

> I have finished my studies at Eleutherian and will soon go to a new underground town in Quindaro, Kansas, near Westport. The Emigrant Aid societies have started a Freedman's School to educate the children of former slaves. Escaped former slaves are pouring into this town and I have been hired to teach their children.
>
> Tell William old father made it to Canada and works in a hotel. You and Will saved our lives. THANK YOU are poor words to express our gratitude.
>
> Enclosed is an article I wrote that was published in the *Quindaro Chindowan*, an abolitionist newspaper. My dream has come true. I hope to write many more to support our cause.
>
> I once again need your help and will explain everything when I see you. I will be coming out to Diamond Spring on a stage from the Mahaffie Stage Station accompanied by another teacher (a fearless Irish lady). It is not safe for a Black woman alone. If all goes as planned, we will be there in late May. I can only stay a few days, as I am supposed to start work at the school this summer to prepare for the fall term.
>
> I was so glad to get your letter about your baby twins. This does not seem possible! I have much news to share also.
>
> I am ever your sister,
> Cecilia Washington

When the dark, well-dressed woman stepped off the stage, Rodantha immediately knew it was Cissy. They stood in a long embrace, tears of joy in their eyes. "But where is your Irish teacher friend, Cissy?" Rodantha said dabbing her eyes.

"Miss Roisin stopped at Council Grove to talk to some town speculators from Topeka who want to organize a freedmen's town further west. I felt safe to make the short trip here alone. I was so anxious to see you, I couldn't wait. Roisin will be over tomorrow on the next stage after her meeting. This new town, well, it is what I need your help with."

Rodantha, Cissy, and William talked for hours in the privacy of the caretaker's quarters, while Ellie and Jennie slept in the alcove. Mary Jane took care of the diners and hotel customers, and Riley did all the chores. Cissy explained, "This idea for a freedman's town would be like Canaan Land in the Bible, the promised land of the Israelites. Former slaves would be free there and able to start farms and build their own schools and churches out on the wide open and free prairies. To make this scheme work, we need some folks such as you to form a western underground railroad to give these people safe passage to Canaan. We know that the Missouri ruffians have been raiding out here from time to time. We hear reports of beatings, lynchings, and torture. Thankfully the sympathies of most local residents are for Kansas to be free soil, and many are willing to help us.

"Roisin wants to have white 'masters' in the guise of slave owners as they actually conduct the freedmen, women, and children to Canaan. Though the exact location has not been decided, we do know it will be west of Diamond Spring. We need safe stops along the way. Some might come very long distances from the plantations in the southern states."

William said, "One more thing there is that you need to figure into this plan of yours. There are native tribes all over the plains, and some are hostile to any invasion of their territory, by anyone, white or black skin. Single wagons on the trail are easy targets for the hostile bands of Indians to pick off. So, I recommend organizing some trains here at Diamond Spring like most Santa Fe teamsters and overlanders do for safety.

"I see," said Cissy. "That is something we didn't really understand very well."

William looked at Rodantha with a question in his eyes. "Do you think we could help with forming up the trains, Rodantha? Making sure the white 'conductors' band their wagons together into trains for protection."

"It is dangerous work, Will, but I do want to help Cissy build this Canaan Land. It's something we can do from right here. It is the right thing to do, shor. Like we talked about your dream of a world that is as friendly as a horseshoe game where all races are welcome to play together."

After Miss Roisin and Cissy left to return to Quindaro, William and Rodantha started stocking a small pantry with supplies that the Canaan travelers might need to build a new town. The Hywells paid Waldo-Hall out of their earnings for everything intended to help the former slaves to freedom. Miss Roisin would send a letter when the first "shipment" was to arrive.

-47-

Buffalo and Indians

April 1859

As if to entertain the little Hywell girls, a flock of Carolina Parakeets chattered outside the station caretaker's apartment with their flamboyant yellow and green feathers, long pointed tails, and orange heads. They flitted back and forth, to the trees along Diamond Creek. While Rodantha watched the colorful birds out the upstairs apartment window, an ominous moving black mass appeared on the horizon, and the floor began to shake. The roar moved toward the hotel over the new spring green of the hills. A customer's mules boarding in the corral began to bray loudly.

William had gone out early, so Rodantha guided the two toddlers downstairs as fast as their little legs could go. In the kitchen, the dishes in the cupboards rattled, and Piper barked in the yard. She quickly opened the door to look out as William ran up the front steps onto the front porch.

"Buffalo herd coming fast, get inside!" he yelled. He followed her in and bolted the door behind him. "They are moving northwest. We'll be safe inside but stay away from the windows."

But just as quickly as it had started, the rumbling ceased. They watched as the huge herd of shaggy headed bulls slowed to a walk and crossed the trail at an angle. This went on for more than hour as the herd of thousands walked by, grunting and snorting and leaving clumps of their heavy winter coats here and there. "I'll make some coffee, Will. I think they've gone now."

But a while later, after she had made and baked biscuits, Rodantha looked out to see why Piper was barking frantically again. Another herd of bison, this time obviously smaller cows and calves, crossed the trail at the same angle, but at a much slower pace, often stopping and browsing on the roadside grasses that had not been trampled. William came back inside from the front porch where he sat to eat his breakfast and watch the buffalo parade past.

"Never realized that the bulls traveled ahead like that," Will mused. But it makes sense that the calves can't move as fast, and the mothers stay behind with them. Moving to their northern pastures for the summer, they are. From the look of that huge herd of mothers and calves coming from the south, it will probably be several hours before they are gone on north of us."

At daybreak next morning, William went downstairs to find six Indians standing in the dining room. They had not rung the desk bell or in any way given a signal or clue that they were there. William's heart raced, but he gazed calmly at the interlopers and gave no sign of his distress. Ebenezer had warned that Indians often walked into homes and buildings, never knocking or calling out a greeting.

These tall bare-chested bronze warriors wore moccasins, breech cloths, and leggings trimmed with scalp-locks. They wore bracelets above their elbows and many rings in their ears. One was tattooed on both face and chest. They had no facial hair, their eyebrows shaved or plucked clean. The only hair on their heads was a row of long spiked hair down the center of their heads from forehead to back, which made them look even taller by several inches. They carried weapons—lances, bows, arrows, and old muskets. The tattooed man stepped forward, hand across his stomach, palm up, indicating hunger. He said, "Heap hungry, you feed."

William said nothing but held up two fingers pointing upward to indicate "friend." He nodded yes and pointed up the stairs. He ran upstairs to awaken Rodantha. As the little girls slept, Rodantha stirred the firebox and threw in kindling to get a fire going in the big stove, heated the left-over buffalo stew, and made coffee. William fried johnnycakes as fast as he could. The Indians stood on the porch silently waiting and stood outside while they ate. Rodantha sat down in her rocker and held her coffee cup tightly in her trembling hands. She slowly sipped and didn't look up.

The Indians left their dishes on the porch and came back through the open doorway. "You give toe-back." the tattooed one said.

"In the store." William pointed out the door. "Follow me." The Indians walked away slowly, regally, erect and stately on their long legs, and Rodantha watched them from the windows as they followed William to the storehouse. He soon returned alone.

"They left their horses behind the barn, that's why we didn't hear them, made their arrival silent. Say they are on a buffalo hunt following their quarry toward the Smoky Hill River bend. That matches the direction those buffalo were headed yesterday. They call themselves O-Wah-SAY-Ja. Say their home is south. I think they are what folks around here call Osage. They live on a treaty reservation down south, at least sometimes of the year. I think we have seen the last of them now, Danna. You can relax."

-48-

Hunters

April 1859

Two days later, another hunting party arrived at Diamond Spring, white men this time. They came in just after the stage pulled out carrying the previous night's guests. Mary Jane cared for the twins while Rodantha laundered bed linens in the alcove just off the kitchen. Danna had baked a double recipe of cornbread and left it to cool while she did the washing. William talked with the hunters and served up the warm cornbread with fresh coffee.

She caught bits and pieces of conversation as she scurried back and forth to the wash tubs, in between hanging the sheets and towels out on drying ropes in the side yard. "Name's James Mead … these friends … some sport among the buffalo … my ranch on the Saline River … have eight teams … your corral for …"

Rodantha heard William say, "Yes, we have rooms for you fellas … Mr. Kilborn … Campbell … Mr. Phillips … supper … Rodantha's Road House." She knew she would be cooking for a crowd this evening.

"The Bishop brothers decided to come too … huge herd going northwest … Osages trailing them …" The voices blended, indistinct as the men asked many questions. "Ammunition … strapping leathers … blacksmith … buffalo … prairie chickens … turkeys … antelope … next stage tomorrow … Santa Fe trade."

Rodantha hurried up the back stairs. She had no more time to listen in on their conversations as it was time to feed the twins and get them down for a nap. Mary Jane took over the chores, finished the laundry, and made up the beds for the hunters with her usual confidence. Rodantha came back down

221

and put the turkey stuffed with onions in the oven, and scrubbed potatoes to bake.

After supper one of the hunters, Mr. Campbell, asked Will, "Has there been trouble on this part of the trail with the Missouri ruffians? I heard that Bloody Bill Barber has been raiding around here lately. I figure the locals all know that you are a Free-Soil man and let you know if they have trouble. Plus, you have guests to think of."

Will said, "Bloody Bill and the other bands of Missouri bushwhackers have mostly been at Council Grove and east. They don't really want to mix it up with the tribes out here."

"We just wanted to know, so we can avoid any trouble while we are out hunting. We will be watchful."

"You fellas are experienced hunters and know to stay together. The most vulnerable to bushwhackers are lone travelers. The ruffians just shoot them and leave them where they fall, they do. Just yesterday one of the teamsters brought a body and buried it up behind the barn. They had no idea who it was." William paused and took a big gulp of coffee.

"I know that you are well armed, so can defend yourselves. Those bushwhackers don't like a lop-sided fight."

The Mead hunting party left early next morning as Rodantha sat the toddlers down for their oatmeal. She cooked eggs and bacon and served several other travelers in the dining room. When William came in from seeing the hunters off, he filled her in on what he had learned from Mead and another man in the party, a Mr. William A. Phillips.

"You remember, Danna, when we ran into those Missouri ruffians at Boone's store in Westport? The bounty hunter with the turkey feathered hat was with them. The other bushwhackers called him Deke. You got us out of there fast when he acted like he knew you."

"That really scared me, Will. I'll never forget that day."

"Well, that day they apparently were looking for this Mr. Phillips who stayed here last night. I thought about those wild bushwhackers when Phillips began to tell me his story. Do you remember I told you then? They wanted to hang him for his abolitionist stand. They were angry and stirred up and really scared me.

"Well, come to find out this Mr. Phillips is a lawyer and author of a book. He gave me a copy yesterday. It's called *The Conquest of Kansas* and details the wars and battles fought between the Jayhawkers and those bloody southern pro-slavery ruffians." He held up the sizable, black-bound book and rushed excitedly on with his story.

"I have only had time to read small portions of the many events he writes about, but there are chapters on the Wakarusa War, the sacking of Lawrence. You remember the burned-out hotel in Lawrence that we saw when we were there? He has written about hundreds of horrible unthinkable incidents, killings, and burnings in his book—Battle of Black Jack, rigged elections, and bogus legislatures.

"Worst of all they stripped off all his clothes, tarred and feathered him. He said he was near death after they dragged him around the streets and publicly humiliated him. He is just now recovering from the poisoning effects of the tar and the wounds to his chest and back. He only escaped because they wanted him to be an example. But he said that writing this book, it was sweet revenge."

Rodantha sat down and began to rock in the rocking chair. She shook her head and clasped her hands together tightly. "He looks like a common everyday fella in his hunting clothes. How horrible to be tarred and feathered. So cruel. When will this fighting over slavery end, Will?"

"I realize now how lucky we were to come along into Kansas in the fall," William continued. "Since during the summer, many settlers were being turned back at the Missouri border and not even allowed into Kansas. We would have been forced to lie about ourselves, or be turned back. Or worse, killed.

"Mr. Phillips' last comment to me was that this hunting trip was the best medicine he could have. Oh, and he said to give you his regards for a clean fresh bed and comfortable room last night."

"How about I put the book under our bed upstairs for safe keeping?" Rodantha said. "You don't know the minds of the folks who stop here, who might see it—southern sympathizers. Don't want to get in any trouble, Will. I'm afraid for the girls, my little ones. Cain't have nothing bad happen to them, no…" her voice trailed off and she blew her nose.

She stood and shook out her apron and stuffed her handkerchief in the pocket. "But for me, I still ain't scared of anything, except crossing rivers. Just afraid for my little ones." She took a ragged breath. "Well, I reckon it's about time to start supper."

Fire

Late April 1859

About midnight, Rodantha suddenly awoke. She smelled smoke and went immediately into the little alcove where the twins slept to make sure they were all right. William was up, pulling on his trousers and boots. She looked out of the upstairs windows to see a line of bright yellow fire glowing orange above. The smoke billowed up in orange clouds over the distant hills. The flames flared up high into the horizon to the southwest and lit up the dark sky.

She quickly dressed and wet several towels. She draped them over the cribs to keep the smoke out of her children's lungs. Rodantha followed William down the stairs and rang the triangle dinner bell to awaken the two guests, Mr. and Mrs. Morris, who were staying at the hotel. She stoked the stove fire to heat some water.

William called over his shoulder as he raced out toward the barn, "I will check on the animals and start filling all the buckets and troughs from the water barrels." Mary Jane had stayed the night and appeared dressed and ready to help, but she couldn't quit coughing. Rodantha tied a wet bandana around Mary Jane's nose and mouth and gave her a long drink.

William appeared again at the door and hollered, "Our only luck is that the spring and creek are between us and the fire. It should be some protection. I hope the firebreaks will be enough to stop it!"

As they all went out into the smoky night, William yelled again. "Just keep filling the trenches from the barrels."

As the fire raced toward the station, Rodantha, Mary Jane, and William worked frantically. The trenches drained the water out to the plowed strips on the perimeter of the station grounds where William had also burned a fire break into the tall grass for several yards beyond the plowed strip. He had been preparing the fire break for the last month after hearing reports from the teamsters traveling through about the blackened areas obvious along the trail to the west.

With wet kerchiefs tied around their mouths and noses, the three of them worked feverishly to prevent the station from burning. Rodantha sent Mary Jane back inside to check on the twins and make sure all the doors and windows were shut tight, and said, "Just stuff old rags from my rag bag anywhere the smoke could leak in. And make sure the guests are all right. They were just standing around on the porch in a daze coughing into their handkerchiefs when we came out. I don't think they understand what is going on."

Rodantha watched the fire rage up to the firebreak. It jumped the plowed ground, igniting the dry haystack in the middle of it. When it exploded in a huge ball of fire, she ran back to the hotel. She soon saw that it was contained there by the plowed ground, not spreading outward. Several times she caught glimpses of William running back and forth through the smoke. She swallowed hard and silently said a prayer. *Hear me, Lord! Keep him safe. I cain't survive without him!*

The horses in the barn screamed and stamped and tried to break down their stalls. All that Rodantha could do now was pray that their efforts would protect them from the flames. She watched helplessly as the fire burned all around the plowed and back-fired perimeter and continued its wild fury on east toward Council Grove. Soon only smoldering prairie remained, blackened into ash. The haystack continued to burn and smoke for hours, but the smoke mostly trailed off in the stiff breeze.

When it was safer to breathe the air, Rodantha and Mary Jane briefly roused the sleeping children to make sure they were unharmed. The two women fell asleep, exhausted, in their sooty, smoky clothes on the floor by their cribs. Next morning they found William on the porch asleep in the old rocking chair, his face and hands blackened with soot.

Miraculously, the hotel, storehouse, and barn were left standing, unharmed. The haystack still smoldered. William's precautions had worked well. The fire stayed mostly on the outside of the plowed and backfired lines.

The guests had gone back up to their room when the danger passed but now came down looking for their morning Diamond coffee. They were in remarkably good spirits and marveled at the spectacle they had witnessed during the night.

Mrs. Morris, who was traveling to Leavenworth, said out loud what Rodantha had been thinking. "That fire was almost magical as it raced toward us in the blackness. I was both afraid and in awe. I couldn't look away."

All around them were blackened rolling hills, the scattered surface rocks now clearly visible. A hint of green was visible in the morning sun where the new spring grass shoots of April had withstood the heat.

Rodantha stoked the fire in the stove under the water kettle and fetched some cold mason jars of the strong syrupy coffee from the spring house to make some quick hot cups to boost spirits. The Carolina Parakeets chattered away in the trees at the creek as though nothing had happened.

Cowboys and Coffee

1860

A dark leathery-skinned fellow sat down in the dining room early Monday morning as Rodantha was roasting coffee. She hadn't seen him in the dining room, but recognized him from the saloon the night before, drinking with a cowboy. He looked like an Indian, but when he spoke, he sounded like a Scotsman, faintly like William's Welsh accent. He said, "Good morning, ma'am. Name's Jesse Chisholm. Terrible dry weather we are having. The grass crunches underfoot. I knew there would be water here at the Diamond Spring, so decided to come this way. Hear tell there's not a drop of rain since last summer, '59."

"That's right, sir! Hot winds and sun been baking everything. Crops are dead and grass is drying up too, like you said. We supply water to everyone here abouts, and of course the travelers depend on us so much. We are starting to fear for the fires that have been starting up all around. I can barely keep my garden alive with spring water as it is. I put all my laundry rinse water on my garden too. Some folks have nothing, no reserves left. Newspapers say thousands have gone back east already."

"Well, I smelled your coffee out in the yard there," Mr. Chisholm said pointing toward the door, "and had to come in for a cup before I hit the trail. I already loaded up all the water I can carry."

"Shor, right away, sir. Would you like some oatmeal too? It's hot and ready."

"I'll just stick with the coffee, ma'am, thank you," he said. "I'm on my way through to Fort Leavenworth with a load of wolf pelts. I plan to trade for some store goods to trade with the Indians down in Texas when I go back."

Rodantha set the cup of coffee in front of him. He held it to his nose and then blew across it before he took a drink. He set the cup down and said, "Well, ma'am, that is undoubtedly the best coffee I ever drunk. I'll have another when I finish this one."

"Why, thank you kindly, sir! I only use the Ariosa, you know."

"Well, now that I know you make this, I may change my route to come back by here. I might be able to trade with the local Osage and Kaw too."

"How can you trade with all these tribes with their many languages? That seems near impossible to me, sir."

"I have been a trader amongst the Indians a good bit of my life, and I know upwards of ten of their languages. I use some Mexican Spanish or signs when all else fails. I am also an interpreter down in Texas for the government of the States from time to time. I haven't come this way since Waldo opened this station again. I have trading posts myself down in Indian territory near the Cherokees."

As he drank the second cup a little more slowly, he told her a story about an Indian named Toshe. "Everyone believed him to be over one-hundred years of age because he always boasted that he had grown sons when the 'stars fell' in 1833."

"What does that mean, 'the stars fell?'" Rodantha wanted to know.

"That is Indian talk for a shower of falling stars called meteors. The Indians mark time before and after the meteors as they consider it a sacred event. But the curious thing about Toshe is that he and his equally-ancient wife had never cut their hair. They each braided their gray hair in one long rope that dragged on the ground when they walked. I think it was a sign of their importance to their people."

Jesse Chisholm took the last gulp of his coffee, abruptly stood, and replaced his chair under the table. "I must be on my way, but please tell me your name."

"Rodantha Hywell. Most people call me Danna. I have enjoyed making your acquaintance, Mr. Chisholm."

"Thank you, Danna. I will be back for some more of this excellent coffee." He flipped out a gold Spanish coin onto the table. He gazed out the window for a moment and then headed toward the door. He turned back toward her, pointed to the window, and said, "Looks like that scruffy blond cowboy is headed out north with that little herd of longhorns, just like he said. I told him how to get to Montana. Hope he makes it."

"Mr. Chisholm, your change, sir." but he was already gone.

Rodantha had seen the blond cowboy the night before in the saloon when she took some biscuits over there for one of the customers. She remembered him well and wrote in her diary that night about him.

I hear many tales around the dining room table, and more around the fireplace after supper or in the saloon when tongues are loosened. Women don't really go into saloons, so I am privy to some tales that are not meant for my ears. Being a server, the men mostly ignore me and forget themselves.

The saloon draws a breed that never even comes into the hotel. They usually camp out beyond the spring, and if I wasn't serving drinks or taking food over, I would miss some of the most interesting folks to cross the trail.

One fellow, I don't know his name, was in there late last night when Will was tending the bar and asked me to bring over an order of biscuits. This cowboy was already drunk, talking loud, laughing and showing his black teeth. He smelled bad (like a lot of these fellows) and had a long dirty blond handlebar mustache that hung below his chin, fiery wild eyes, and long matted blond hair under the biggest hat I ever saw. He wore a dirty checkered scarf. His bowlegs made me wonder how he could stand at the bar at all, and his spurs clanked and pinged every time he moved. A huge side arm was strapped down in a holster, over-sized for his thin wiry body. I stayed in the back storeroom and listened.

He came up from Baxter Springs down near Indian Territory. He had been with an outfit driving several thousand cattle up from Texas to Kansas City. He said they were on the trail "from see to can't see" every day. They got stopped by a bunch of local cattlemen at Baxter, who claimed that the Texas cattle had cow fever and would spread the ticks to the local cattle. After a couple of gun battles, this cowboy escaped with about a hundred longhorns and headed away from the usual route of the Shawnee Trail toward the northwest. He just kept going and finally crossed the Santa Fe here at Diamond. He wanted to go on to Montana if the Pawnee didn't get him first. I peeked out at him just in time to see him spit out black tobacco juice on my clean floor. He staggered out the door. Will closed up and shooed all the customers out. I cleaned the floor right away.

The next morning, Jesse Chisholm pointed the cowboy out to me—driving those longhorns away over the ridge. When I looked out it seemed to me the blond cowboy had about half the number of cattle he said there was.

Mr. Chisholm gave him directions to Montana. If anyone knows the way to Montana it would be Mr. Chisholm. Seemed to me he's been everywhere, blazing trails to trade with Indians or to just find out what was at the end.

Kansas - A New State

1861

William was elated when the Eastern newspapers carried the news that Kansas had joined the Union as a free state. He had gone over to Council Grove to cast his vote for a free state in the territorial election. The bogus Lecompton legislature was gone and a legitimate government set up in Topeka under the Wyandotte Constitution, allowing all white males twenty-one years of age and older to vote. It reset the western Kansas boundary at the 25th Meridian. Beyond that was the territory of Colorado.

He read some of the newspaper article to Rodantha as she worked in the kitchen and then said, "I was so disappointed that Kansas statehood got bogged down in the legislature before the election. Would have cast my vote for Mr. Lincoln, if our territorial status had ended."

1861 Diary

In April, southern troops fired on Fort Sumpter, a Union stronghold, and two days later President Lincoln called for volunteers to stop the "insurrection." The bleeding of Kansas has now become a WAR since some southern states seceded from the Union. This is exactly what Mr. Majors warned us about.

This is the worst trouble I ever seen in my life, and I seen plenty. There is quite a lot of talk among the travelers that come through Diamond station about Missouri ruffians. Teamsters witness or hear about the attacks on various towns and people in Kansas.

William prays every night for President Lincoln. But I pray for my girls and for William. He is known all around here because

of the Waldo-Hall station and his duty as the agent. He has never
hid the fact that he is a Free-Soil man. I will admit in this diary that
I am truly scared of what might happen, but I will not let on.

Rodantha brought cold leftovers from the hotel over to the saloon and
set them behind the partition wall dividing the bar and the workroom until
Will could return to serve the customers. She heard a couple of men talking
over in the corner of the saloon but decided to stay in the back to mend the
tablecloth that Will had asked her about earlier. When she heard one of them
say William's name, she moved closer to the end of the partition so that she
could hear what they were saying.

"I seen that station man, Hywell, talking to some overlanders who
stopped by a couple of hours ago. They was certainly the types we been
looking for, Deke. They ain't got no slaves with them. Thinks they're gonna
settle in this free state to farm, they was saying. We got to stop that."

A deep growling voice said, "Some of the boys say Hywell's a damn
Jayhawker, from somewhere back East. Even a Quaker maybe. He might not
put up a fight, so pretty easy to bag. Hywell looks familiar to me, but I reckon
similar to a lot of the English. I vaguely remember a bounty notice about him
when I was in Maryland a few years ago, but I ain't had time to go back to
find out what was on his head. Not worth as much as these slaves we been
catching for sure. But he's been getting other folk to agree with his perverted
way of thinking."

The other voice said, "These bleeding hearts think they can come in
here and tell us what we can and cain't do. High and mighty, they are. The
best way is to kill all these here Free Soilers, no matter what their religion.
That'll turn the country and this new state around our way. We can move in
here with our darkies and build fine farms and plantations. It's the only way
I tell you, Deke. Only way to get Kansas turned back to a slave state and sede
from the Yankee states." The voices went silent for a while, and Rodantha
realized she had been holding her breath.

"You just want to string that old Hywell up tonight, Deke? We could do
it pretty quick."

Deep-throated Deke said, "Nah, we need more fire power. What with
all these guests around—and there's women and children, so we got to plan

it good, to get them all at once."

Rodantha heard their spurs clanking and chairs scuffing the floor. Deke said, "Looks like we ain't getting no vittles here tonight. Let's ride on over to Council Grove. The boys got a camp around there and least some coffee and beans. They got a little slave gal that can't be tamed. Damaged she is. We can all have some fun before I send her straight to hell."

The door banged shut, letting in the stench of rotting flesh. Rodantha could hear them mounting up outside. She moved quickly to the back window, waiting behind the curtain to get a look at them as they rode past. The deep voice yelled out, "Death to the Jayhawkers!"

As a horse and rider trotted past illuminated by the tall windows, she saw who it was—the bounty hunter riding the same roan horse with a turkey feather in his hat. He was leading a pack horse with a body crudely slung over it. The other man soon followed, hollering, "Wait up, Deke."

Rodantha trembled as she repeated everything she had heard to William. He quickly closed the saloon, and they hurried over to the hotel to check on the guests, children, Mary Jane, and Riley. There had been threats before, but this one seemed more ominous, especially since it was coming from the bounty hunter they had seen many times on the roan horse. Since this Deke said that William looked familiar, she was finding it hard to breathe. She didn't sleep at all, getting up several times to check on her children. She made some mint tea to calm her nerves. She couldn't help thinking of Cissy and Moss somewhere out there in a world bent on their destruction.

The next day, nothing happened out of the ordinary, and the two bad characters didn't come around. Weeks slipped by and she worried less about Deke. The ache in her heart and butterflies in her stomach subsided a little. William started wearing his pistol in his belt during the day and keeping it near his pillow at night.

She was extra busy. Volunteer dragoons were being sent west to build and man forts since Indian tribes were retaliating, trying to keep settlers out of their reserves. Most of the conscripted soldiers were fighting bloody battles in the war between the states. The dragoons usually camped near Diamond Spring and came up to the hotel looking for coffee. Many were just boys, wishing for their mothers. So Rodantha gave away gallons of coffee, to ease their homesickness a little. She understood this as she had the same feelings for her quieter life before all the wars, hatred, and suspicion in the country now.

Dark Turbulence

May 1863

After Mary Jane took the twins upstairs to bed, Rodantha followed William out onto the front porch of Rodantha's Road House to see what the commotion was. Danna thought it was one of those unscheduled Waldo-Hall Stagecoach runs, with folks looking for some hot Diamond Coffee and a trip to the privies. Riley was busy filling the copper boiler to heat more water for a bath. She called back through the open door, "Fill the kettle too, Riley, for some fresh coffee."

As her eyes adjusted to the darkness outside, Rodantha could see at least a dozen riders coming up the trail. It was not teamsters or a stagecoach. A couple of the riders carried torches that soon illuminated the stage yard. All had their pistols drawn. They yelled obscenities and began shooting directly at the hotel as they came closer. The bullets zinged off the rock walls of the hotel. Dust kicked up all around and blew into Rodantha's face. She blinked and tried to wipe her eyes.

A deep voice yelled out, "William Hywell, this is your last goddam day on earth."

She heard the sharp crack, saw the wild bright flash from a pistol, followed by intense pain in her head. Then a shotgun blast hit the porch post above her and rained hot shot down that burned her cheeks. Rodantha instinctively whirled around in front of William to protect him as several more shots rang out through the black night. William sank to the floor. Blood pulsed out of his leg.

He yelled out, "Danna, Danna! It's that Bloody Bill Barber and his bushwhackers! Get away! Quick as you can!" William screamed in pain and pressed on his mangled leg to stop the blood from gushing out. She quickly loosened his necktie, took it off, and tied it around his upper leg, ignoring the pain in her head and ear.

"Goddamn Jayhawkers, kill 'em all." She heard the ruffians laughing wildly. "Let's string 'em up, Barber."

The horses screamed in a thunder of hooves, whistles, cracks, and curses. In the moonlight she could just make out the dreaded Missouri ruffians as they circled in a frenzy around the stage yard. She grabbed William's belt and pulled him toward the open door of the hotel to get off the porch. He moaned piteously. But she couldn't get William through the door.

She grabbed the Navy pistol out of his waistband where he had been carrying it all day. She fired several times toward the circling mob, and one man went down, the one with a turkey feather in his hat. He was an easy target. In the moonlight she could see he rode a roan horse—light body and dark legs. Just for a moment, she was elated, amazed that she had brought down the bounty hunter that she had feared night and day.

In an instant, two masked bushwhackers caught William by the heels and dragged him out into the yard, where they tied a rope to his leg and started dragging him away.

"William!" she screamed into the night. "No, no, Will. No! William!" Her head throbbed. She felt faint.

The raging fire leapt up around her, engulfing the hotel, the store, and blacksmith shop. The heat sucked the air from her lungs. She couldn't move. She thought, *This might be the end of the road for me.* But then she thought of Jennie and Ellie. *Where are they? I have to find them!*

Rodantha was aware of someone leaning over her. "Ma'am. Mrs. Hywell. Ma'am, can you stand? Ma'am! Can you see me?" Smoke choked her and heat burned through her body. Her head ached, and she could feel the blood running down her neck.

Riley Storrs helped Rodantha to her feet and led her off the porch, away from the burning buildings toward the barn. "I saw the whole thing, ma'am. I hid until the ruffians cleared out. Looks like you shot one of them. They threw him up on his roan and led him away as fast as they came in. I tried to shoot a couple more with Will's Navy, but they were too far away by that time."

"Riley! Riley! Where are my girls?" she screamed.

"Safe with Mary Jane in the wagon," Riley said. "We all ran out the back door and hid in the barn. They didn't bother it none. Mary Jane wrapped the little ones in quilts and threw a bunch of your stuff out the back window. She said you wouldn't want the treasure box to burn up, but I'm not sure what that means.

"Sit here," he said pointing to the wagon tongue. "I'll get cold water. Wait quiet till I get back from the spring."

Riley held a cold, wet handkerchief to her ear and dabbed the blood on her neck. "This will stop the bleeding, ma'am. Looks like a bullet caught the top of your ear and sliced off a little of your hair. Better now."

Riley helped Rodantha climb into her old wagon. He put a little tuft of prairie hay under her head and let Jennie and Ellie snuggle in close under the salvaged quilts. Mary Jane watched over them as they slept until daybreak.

Mary Jane whispered, "Wake up, Danna! Ellie, Jennie! Wake up girls, here's some water. The ruffians are coming back! We have to hide and be quiet. Shhhhh now. Stay down inside the wagon."

Rodantha's head throbbed, and she could taste blood in her mouth. But as she lay breathlessly listening to the commotions outside, she recognized the sounds she had grown to know well. It was a wagon train. Whips cracked and popped, wagon wheels creaked and rumbled. There were shouts of many voices and sharp whistles—"Circle up … haw … gee … step up, step up … sharp eyes now … load your guns … hotel on fire boys … careful now."

She sat up straight, and yelled into the quiet barn, "Where is Will? Where is Will?" Her five-year-old daughters began to cry, and Mary Jane tried to sooth them over their mother's frantic cries.

Rodantha's head throbbed. She sank back into the hay, closed her eyes, and held onto Mary Ann's hand. When she opened her eyes, she was shocked to see Mr. Majors there smiling down at her in his kindly way. She thought it must be a dream. But then he offered a real cup, and she was surprised to feel its warmth.

"Some Ariosa, Mrs. Hywell. Will help you to rights again. Drink up."

Rodantha gratefully took the cup of hot coffee and drank the whole thing before she could get the words out. "William was shot by bushwhackers in the night. They drug him off. We got to find him. He is hurt bad. Please, Alexander, find him."

"We already sent men out to look for him. Riley told us the whole story. Don't you worry, Rodantha."

"Well, wh…" Rodantha stammered, "why are you here, Mr. Majors? How?"

"We're on a run out to supply the military at the new fort being built at Dodge and then will take the Pike's Peak Trail to Denver City. Gold strike out there has the whole place building out and needing supplies. A good opportunity for an old trader like me. But we had no idea about your trouble here till we started our drop down into the Diamond Valley. We could see smoke, so we came on the double, as fast as our teams would go."

Mr. Majors pointed to her empty cup. "More coffee?"

"No," Rodantha sobbed, "I'll just rest my sore head, if you promise to find him!"

"Promise," Mr. Majors said.

-53-

Gone

May 1863

Mary Jane woke Rodantha and gave her some cool spring water to drink.

"Danna … uh … they found him. He's gone." Mary Jane choked and cleared her throat. "I cleaned him up a little and wrapped him in one of the quilts."

"No, that cain't be right, Mary, I just spoke to him, and he said he got lost in the timber, but was coming back to me right away."

"I'm so sorry, Danna," Mary Jane sobbed. "But I … I think you were dreaming." Mary Jane recovered slightly and helped Rodantha to sit up. "Please, now, please … can you come out? I am afraid you have to see for yourself."

The story the teamsters told wrapped its icy fingers around her heart and threatened to squeeze the life out of her. Mr. Majors' men found William in a little dry creek bed covered by overhanging branches, where he had crawled up and died, necktie still tied tightly around his leg. They brought him to the barn where Rodantha and her children were asleep in the back of the Hywells' old overland wagon, which had carried them a thousand miles.

One young man gave her a big turkey feather found during the search and said, "We heard the story of how you avenged your husband, ma'am. More than most folks can say. An honorable thing it is."

Rodantha handed the feather to Mr. Majors and said, "Throw this in the cook's fire over there, so I can watch it burn."

Mr. Majors walked slowly to the fire, lit the end of the turkey feather, and held it high before shoving in down into the depths of the burning logs.

He walked slowly back to where William lay covered on the ground. Alexander uncovered William's head, careful not to reveal his bloody mangled leg. He waited a moment for realization to show on Rodantha's tear-stained face and then covered William again with Aunt Zelda's quilt.

Rodantha crumbled to the ground and sobbed. "I can't go on without you, Will. This can't be true. These ruffians has taken away my soul, my life. Cruel slavery is the end of me, sure as I was a slave myself. Everything is gone!"

Mr. Majors knelt there beside her, with a reassuring hand on her head, and alternately held her trembling hands. He wisely let her spend herself until she curled exhausted into a fetal position, barely able to breathe. Alexander Majors picked her up off the hard ground and put her on the tailgate of the wagon on the soft hay. Mary Jane comforted the children in the wagon the best she could and dozed as they all slept. Mr. Majors sat up all night and talked quietly off and on with some of his men. He watched her sleep until she awakened with a start.

After Rodantha drank some coffee, Mr. Majors gently said, "We have a special burial place for William. The boys are laying up a rock fence around his grave, just the way he built the big corral. We will wall it up tight, so no wolves can get in. We'll use the zigzag fence boards for a door. I'll say a few words from my favorite scripture and my boys will sing. We are a god-fearing outfit. You rest now, Rodantha. We'll take care of things."

Alexander majors read passages from his well-worn Bible. "From the Old Testament we read, Genesis 3:19, 'In the sweat of thy face shalt thou eat your bread till thou return unto the ground, for out of it wast thou taken; for dust thou art and unto dust shalt thou return.' From the New Testament, Christ comforts his disciples, in John, Chapter 14—'Let not your heart be troubled; ye believe in God, believe also in me. In my Father's house are many mansions. I go to prepare a place for you. I will come again and receive you unto myself and where I am there ye may be also.'

"Lord, we know that William is with you today, and we celebrate his homecoming. For you have told us in First Thessalonians '...concerning them which are asleep that ye sorrow not, even as others which have no hope. For if we believe that Jesus died and rose again, even so them also which sleep in Jesus will God bring with him.'"

Alexander Majors looked up from his Bible and continued, "So we gather here to remember William Hywell. He was our friend, and to this family gathered, husband and father."

Jennie and Ellie stood with Rodantha near the open grave holding prairie flowers they had picked. Ellie cried out, "Daddy, Daddy, don't go." Jennie wailed in unashamed grief as only a child would do. The twins continued sobbing until Rodantha crouched between them to hug them close. They lay their heads on her shoulders and shuddered ragged gulps of air.

Mr. Majors continued, "William was an immigrant from Wales, who brought his beloved bride, Rodantha, to Kansas in 1856. He worked hard and provided a good life for his family. He was fair and honest in all his business dealings. In his lifetime he stood for peace and goodwill to all he knew, learned from his Quaker mother's teachings. He considered all races his brothers and sisters and treated all with respect. His caring example toward the enslaved and the native will never be forgotten. He was an honorable man."

He closed the Bible and looked skyward. "Receive our brother unto yourself, Lord. And now a benediction for we who are left to mourn. God be with you and comfort you. And all the people said…"

All the people standing on that prairie said, "Amen."

Mr. Majors picked up a handful of prairie dust and gently sifted it through his fingers over William wrapped in Aunt Zelda's quilt surrounded by the rock fence. Rodantha dropped in a bouquet of prairie flowers, and after some coaxing, Jennie and Ellie relinquished their bouquets also. The gathered teamsters each brought a single blade of tall grass from the surrounding hills. While Ellie and Jennie sobbed and whimpered and wiped their noses on the hems of their dresses, a small group of the teamsters harmonized on two verses of "Amazing Grace."

Then it was all over. Mary Jane led the children to the wagon where Henry waited to drive them all south to their house on Stribby Creek, but they ran back and threw their arms around Rodantha, refusing to let go of their mother. Rodantha said, "There, there. It's all right now, you go on with Auntie Jane. I'll come down to see you soon my sweets." She hugged the little ones and waved goodbye until they were out of sight.

Riley stood outside the rock wall with shovel in hand. Only Rodantha was left at the rock-fenced grave. She sat down on the prairie and looked up at the wind-blown clouds, on the run across the intense blue sky, alternately casting shadows and light down on her. She simultaneously held in her heart all the joys and sorrows of her life with William, so like the dark and light of those clouds chasing across the sky. She wept. Her heart was broken. Dark turbulence engulfed her.

As she left the gravesite, the profound silence of the prairie was interrupted by the swish-swish of the shovel as Riley shoveled the fresh mound of prairie soil into William's grave. A meadowlark perched on the top of the new rock fence and sang sweetly. The tall grass whispered in the gentle May breeze. A hawk circled, and occasionally she could hear the spring as it bubbled and gurgled its Diamonds out of the earth. She thought, *William is now part of these hills and the spring itself.*

-54-

Life in a Treasure Box

May 1863

Not much was left of Rodantha's life at Diamond Spring. The rock walls of the Waldo-Hall hotel, eatery, and store house were all that was left standing. Almost everything inside was reduced to ash. Her old metal treasure box, several of Aunt Zelda's quilts, and a bundle of rag rug materials had been thrown out the window as Mary Jane and Riley ran away from the burning buildings, taking the little girls to safety in the barn. She found a hairbrush, comb, and Ellie's rag doll on the charred ground.

The treasure box was dented but held together by one of William's worn-out braces (the green ones his Quaker mother made him out of old canvas awnings). The latch had broken off long ago, and the lid no longer closed securely.

The covered wagon, four oxen, Molly, Dollar, and Dalia were her worldly possessions. The wagon's canvas top was tattered and needed repair. Piper could not be found, though the teamsters looked everywhere for him as they searched for William. Rodantha repeatedly called him, but he was gone. She missed his friendly black and white tail wagging.

She half-heartedly tried to set up for living in the wagon once again with a few metal pans, buckets, and utensils that had not been burned up in the fire. The bullwhackers brought a few useful things to her from the ruins and filled a bucket with sweet Diamond Spring water to drink. As she cleared away the hay they had used for bedding after the fire, she found a treasure. William must have left his hat as he worked from the back of the wagon the day he died. There it was—his hat crushed and sweat stained. She inhaled the familiar smell of him and sobbed.

Mr. Majors stationed a young teamster, Vander, outside her tailgate at night with a pistol, and she slept from exhaustion in the salvaged quilts, hay stuffed in a stained pillowcase under her head. She was glad she had saved it in her rag bag. Next morning Alexander brought johnnycakes and coffee. "Just keep the dishes, Rodantha, we have plenty," he said in his kind way.

Like my own Pa, he is, she thought.

Rodantha opened the treasure box and saw the hymnal on top. She longed to hear William playing his pipe. She would never hear it again. She quickly checked to see that the Spanish gold pieces were there in the bottom. The bright white limestone chip was still there. The one William had given her from the Ohio State House. This brought a flood of memories with it. She closed the lid and tied the brace securely around it again. She stowed it in the corner of the wagon as she always had out on the roads and trails.

Rodantha looked through the bundle of torn cloth and old clothes meant for rag rugs. The pin cushion was there with needles and thread, and the large crochet hook was stuck into a small, just-started rug. She put these sewing tools into the treasure box for safekeeping. She found William's worn-out trousers and shirt that had yet to be torn into strips. Finding them mostly serviceable, she patched the holes and resewed some of the seams. Rodantha changed her singed blue calico dress for William's cast-off clothes and felt grateful for her laziness in getting another rug started. She took William's old hat to the creek and washed it with some lye soap brought by one of the teamsters. Staked overnight, it shrank and hardened out of shape.

About noon, Mr. Majors came back with the news that he and his outfit would be moving on to keep their schedules and commitments. "I know how hard this is, but you have to think about what you will do now, Rodantha."

"My little girls is the most precious to me. I will go down to Stribby Creek to get them as soon as I can."

"I have a wife and children of my own in Nebraska, so I do understand. But I have to ask—do you have a place to live? Could you stay with Mary Jane Pracht?"

"Well … no… don't think so. Mary Jane and Henry have been living with some of his relations, and having my girls is enough of a crowd in that small place they got. The school is used every day for school and Sunday services. Only possible I can think of is maybe Ebenezer Storrs."

"How can he help?"

"Riley says Ebenezer is about finished building his new bank down in Elmdale and has a little caretaker room in it. I think Riley has been pestering his Dad to let him stay there. Riley is wanting to be on his own. You know how boys is. Maybe I could rent the caretaker's room. I got a little saved, and I could make rugs to sell."

"How far is that?"

"Oh, I don't rightly know, but Riley comes over here, in a half-days' travel, so I think I could take Molly and ride down there."

"Or if you would rather, I could have Vander take you to Elmdale in your wagon and help with yoking the team. That way you wouldn't have to leave anything behind. You and Van seem to be getting along pretty well."

"Yes, but then what if that don't work out and I am stuck here after you leave for Colorado Territory? Don't think I could manage the team by myself. And mind you, I'm just going on what Riley said. He could be stretching the truth about the bank building being finished. Besides I have these cows too, Dollar and Dalia, to care for. I don't rightly know if there is even any place to camp or corral the stock at Elmdale or any hay and feed for them. I don't rightly know what I should do."

"You know, Rodantha, that I will help you with whatever you decide to do. You are like my own daughter. I want you and your family to be safe and looked after. You cannot stay here alone, though. It is too dangerous. But just remember that tomorrow should be our last full day here. The next day we will start for Fort Dodge with much needed supplies. I am supposed to be there in less than two weeks.

"I will leave Van here with you until you find out about the situation with Mr. Storrs' bank building. I'll send Van over here in a little while to help you get your wagon and gear ready." Mr. Majors put his hands on her shoulders, looked squarely into her eyes and said, "You must start preparing to leave here, Rodantha."

Vander showed up a half hour later, out of breath and wiping his red face with a kerchief. "Sorry ma'am, I had to chase down a bull. Boss said I was to come over here straight away to help you."

"Just catch your breath, Vander. Sit here and have a drink out of this pail of cool water first." He sat dutifully on the wagon tongue and drained the dipper.

"Well, I can see right now that your wheels need a good soaking in the creek, ma'am." These won't last an hour out on the trail. All dried out and shrunk from sitting too long in the barn."

"First off, don't call me ma'am. My name is Rodantha, Danna for short. And second, I am curious about your name—Vander? Mr. Majors calls you

Van. What should I call you? Got a last name?"

Well, ma'am … er… Rodantha. My name is really George Vander-walker, but that is a mouthful for most of these bullwhackers, so they just call me Vander or Walker. You can just call me Van."

"All right then, Van, let's start with those wheels just like you said. There is some tar left in the bucket over there to grease the hubs."

Van Walker pulled each wheel in turn, soaked them in Diamond Creek, and put them back on the wagon. He was finished by the time the mess cooks were clanging their dinner triangles for supper. He scurried off and brought back plates of beans, cornbread, and roasted apples. They sat and devoured this simple meal like it was the food of kings.

-55-

Mind Made Up

Last Day of May 1863

Two days later when Mr. Majors brought johnnycakes and coffee out to her wagon in the barn, Rodantha was dressed in William's tattered, but mended trousers and shirt. Her wounded scalp and ear were healing so she could wear William's old hat perched lightly on her head. She sat on the high seat of her wagon explaining to her young guardian bullwhacker, Vander, about how the rig should be put together.

"Now, just take Curly, George, Dollar, and Dalia to the cavey yard," she bossed. "Dollar and Dalia belong to you now, Van, so take good care of them."

Vander had yoked Dutch and Shire and tied Molly to the back of the wagon. The water barrel stood on the outside dripping Diamond Spring water until the staves could swell shut.

"Well, I see that you are ready to go," Mr. Majors said with a smile as he handed her the coffee. "Van will go along with you down to the Pracht's place on Stribby Creek, to be with your children. I know you are anxious to see them. We will look after your animals until he catches back up to us. He is taking a good fast horse."

"I have a little different idea to propose, Alexander. Now hear me out. I have done considerable thinking about all this and hope you can agree with what I want to do." Rodantha nodded toward Vander and continued.

"Van has been a God-send sir. He knows his way around all the wagon parts, and animal choring. He wakes early and stays late, ever watchful and helpful. His ma and pa should be right proud of such a boy as they raised." Vander hung his head and shuffled his boots in the dust.

"I am ever so grateful to have him along with me down to Stribby Creek but would also like to keep him with me back to Council Grove. I have decided what I want to do about a place to live and get a new start."

"Well, that might take a couple days longer, Rodantha. We might be all the way to Fort Dodge by the time he gets back to us. Humm, let me think. Do go on with your plan, though."

"I have money saved from our Waldo-Hall wages that was safe in my treasure box on the night of the fire. I want to take a room at the Hays House for a week, look for kitchen or hotel work there, maybe for room and board. I'll talk to Aunt Sally first. Maybe help Ebenezer Storrs at the Council Grove stage stop. I know he hates that mail work. I could sweep up at his bank or other places, maybe clean houses, or feed horses at the stable. I'll start selling my rugs right away. I been working on new ones the last couple of nights with the rug scraps that weren't burned up."

Mr. Majors rubbed his jaw in thought and then smiled at Rodantha. "Tell you what. I can go along with your plan, because I have another company train coming along the trail, bringing more supplies out to Colorado territory. Van might have to wait on them a couple extra days, but he might be wanting some time off to hang around at the dance hall anyway. I'll send a pony dispatch, so the train foreman knows to pick Van up on the way through the Grove."

"I can hardly believe what you are saying, Alexander," she gushed. "I thought you was going to turn me down." She flung her arms around him impulsively.

"Now, I got one more thing in mind. Vander don't know anything about this yet, but I think he will go along with it. In fact, this works perfect now that he can join back up with another train." She paused and looked at young Vander who was again studying his boots.

"I want you to have my wagon and oxen, Alexander, if Van will take them back with him to meet up with you in Colorado. I done give Van my milk cow, Dollar, and her calf, Dalia. They are on the way out to your cavey yard. So, this is maybe a little payment for all you have done for me Alexander, helping me get on my feet after … well … now that Will is gone … your loaning me Van and all." She paused and looked at Alexander, who didn't object.

"Besides I cain't take care of no oxen and my wagon wheels will just break apart from disuse. So, you'll be helping me out. I judge I will miss that old Dutch though. I'll just keep his big rattle-y bell to remind me of him. I'll keep Molly in the town stable if I can, and my treasure box, of course."

"Well, Van, we've got our marching orders," Mr. Majors said with a grin. "Don't forget to take that bell off Dutch and give it to Miss Rodantha now."

In the next two hours, the twenty-six wagons of the Russell, Majors and Waddell freighting company headed west, each pulled by six yoke of oxen. As they moved into action, this became a long, three-track snake, crossing the open prairie at the slow ox pace of three miles an hour, followed by the trailing loose animals of the cavey yard.

Rodantha's wagon headed south toward Stribby Creek and her children. Vander Walker stayed out in front of the oxen and kept a steady pace. The rattle of Amish cow bells provided a comforting accompaniment.

"Oh William…" Tears welled in Rodantha's eyes. She shut them tight and tried to get her breath. When she opened her eyes again, her mind was made up, even though tears often trailed down her cheeks.

June 2 Diary Entry

I had to say goodbye to the Diamond station, my home for the last few years. The burned ruins of the hotel and storehouse are like shadows of the past, only the remainders of my life now far away. But the Spring—well, Diamond Spring is exactly as it was the day I arrived there several years ago. I dipped up a cup of the cold clear sweet water and picked a sprig of mint from the hillside before I left. Diamond is a part of the everlasting earth and God that made it all. It never fails, it never ceases, it never disappoints. The spring never made anyone sick and needs no boiling. It calls to all who pass to partake of its fountain and is truly a treasure of the new state of Kansas. I will go back to visit William's grave, and I know Diamond Spring will be there with William—forever. It is comforting.

-56-

Letter from Cissy

1863

Rodantha's most interesting job was for Waldo-Hall Company Depot at Council Grove, meeting stages when Ebenezer Storrs was away attending to his banking and cattle businesses. She watched the stage schedules closely and arrived at the station before the stage pulled in. In this way, she met many new people and got to know most of the town's people as well. She also sorted, stamped, and filed mail on the days she met the stages. This was the most dependable work she had found.

One day, when a few Kanza women and girls gathered in front of the depot waiting for their men to finish drinking at the saloon two doors down, Rodantha stood out front. The stage arrived, and two finely dressed ladies alighted and stepped down from the stage, kicking up their hoop skirts a little. An Indian girl of about ten ran up and lifted their skirts high to look at the petticoats and bloomers underneath. The Kaw women gathered around immediately and stooped to look under the skirts also. They ran their hands all around the hoops that swayed and bounced.

The Indian girls giggled, and the women laughed and laughed until this brought tears to their eyes. The fine ladies stood still with fear and shock on their faces. They made no protest about this indignity and waited until the laughter died down to move. The Indian women moved off down the street a little way, shaking their heads and speaking to each other in the Kanza language, still laughing. The fine ladies shook down their skirts, adjusted their bonnets, and tried to act as though nothing had happened.

Rodantha punched their tickets and tried to keep from laughing too. That was the talk of the town all day. It was plain to see that the Kanza had

249

a great sense of humor.

Rodantha also did laundry and cleaned rooms at Hays House and washed glasses and dishes at the saloon for room and board. The twins were sometimes on their own more than she liked and had to amuse themselves in the hotel room.

A little later she moved to the caretaker's apartment at the back of Ebenezer's Peoples Exchange Bank where he trained her as a part-time teller when he had to be away. The apartment had a little sleeping porch for the twins and a private outhouse. She could watch her children more easily there. She opened and closed the bank for Ebenezer, who built a new house in Elmdale so Riley could have his own room.

She spent evenings after the girls were in bed making rugs, saddle pads, and chair pads that she consigned to the local mercantile. Sometimes Ebenezer came to call and sat on the extra chair in her apartment while she made coffee. They talked of many things. She looked forward more and more to these social visits.

Artistically talented Jennie drew little pictures on her slate to show him. Ellie had taken up crocheting rugs and made a tiny one in a crude heart shape for him. Rodantha's heart swelled with pride when Ebenezer complimented them and brought little gifts. This kindly man was the nearest thing they had to a real father.

When Riley came with his father, he gave the girls piggyback rides through the big bank lobby after hours and read dime novels, portraying characters in funny voices. Often, the twins would say, almost in unison, "Is Riley coming too, Mother?"

While sorting the mail, Rodantha saw her own name on a letter. The return address said, *Cecilia Washington*. Rodantha and Cissy had kept up an intermittent correspondence as the mail service between Quindaro and Diamond Spring improved. Rodantha knew from the letters that the effort to start a Canaan Land town for former slaves had stalled for lack of funds, inability to find appropriate land on which to build, trouble with Indian hostilities, and a full-blown War of Secession.

Rodantha wrote to tell Cissy about all the happenings at Diamond Spring, William's murder at the hand of bushwhackers, her move to Council

Grove after the fire, her growing daughters, and her various jobs working at the Hays House with former slave, Aunt Sally. Since the beginning of the war between the states in 1860, there had been no way for Cissy to come out to Diamond Spring. Cissy wrote a long letter this time, in her beautiful penmanship.

Dearest Sister,

Thank you for your letter. I am in deepest sympathy with you over William's sudden and tragic death. He was a towering figure in my life. He saved my life and that of old father. I owe him a debt of gratitude that can never be repaid. I have great sorrow in my heart and pray for you every day.

I am, however, very relieved and happy that you have recovered from your wounds and that your girls are doing so well. Your opportunities for work in Council Grove are encouraging, especially the bank work for your good friend, Ebenezer. He sounds like an enterprising fellow with his farm mortgages, cattle business, and opening the new bank building.

As you know, I have now been teaching for four years, off and on, when children can come here from the war-torn areas of the South, escaping with their parents (or sometimes without). More and more are escaping and crossing into Kansas at Quindaro, where we have organized a workable underground railroad system. The Emancipation Proclamation was signed by President Lincoln in January, and the Union cause has been strengthened. Now more than ever we need a place where former slaves can build new lives.

Sadly, Roisin died a few months back, so I have been trying to carry on with the Canaan Land work that she was so committed to. I promised her I would come out to see you when the last term was over. Your willingness to help was so encouraging and she admired your courage in the face of danger. So do I.

I have secured a ticket to catch the Mahaffie Stage in August and should be in Council Grove by August 15. I do hope this will be convenient for you. Please inquire if there are accommodations at Hays House on that day. I have funds enough to cover a week or two there.

A new group of investors has prospects for a Canaan Land townsite further west from you. And the most encouraging of all is a large donation from the Plymouth Congregational Church in Lawrence. The Bandage Roller ladies' group there have been going door to door asking for help to build Canaan. This is a good sign. Many people who normally don't do anything to promote the abolitionist cause besides sit around in a circle and roll bandages for wounded soldiers are now getting involved. Now that the Diamond Spring station is gone, new safe houses will need to be found in your area. There are many challenges.

I am hoping that you are still doing well. I plan to see you soon.

I am ever your sister,
Cecilia Washington

Old Friends

August 15, 1863

Rodantha studied the stage schedules and logs as she always did on the days she was working for Ebenezer to meet the stages and sort the mail. About noon, the stage from Mahaffie via Council Grove arrived with three passengers. Cissy was one of them. She was dressed in white lightweight linen and looked cool and calm despite the brutally-hot weather. She carried a large folding fan and a small hand-held purse. She had only one large piece of luggage. The two gentlemen also getting off carried their own valises. Rodantha punched their tickets and pointed them toward the Hays House bar. "I hear the beer is cold today, gentlemen."

"May I have your ticket please, ma'am?" Rodantha said to Cissy with ridged formality and a wide grin.

"Why, thank you so much, miss," Cissy replied, handing over her ticket. "Where might a lady find some iced lemonade today?"

"Just two doors down." At this they both burst into laughter and hugged each other in a little dance of joy.

Rodantha had recently learned how to take charge of things when receiving stages, ticketing, and directing people where they wanted to go. In her most emphatic and assertive tone, Rodantha said to the stage driver, "Please deliver this lady's luggage to the Hays House. It is will-call for Cecilia Washington. She will be coming along directly." Rodantha handed the stage driver a bank note, saying, "This is good for dinner and beer, compliments of Waldo-Hall Company. The stable man is here to take care of the horses and get a fresh team up when you are ready. No passengers are going on through, so you can take your time." The driver took off at a trot, carrying Cissy's luggage toward the Hays House.

"How about that lemonade now, Cissy?"

"I thought you would never ask, Danna." The two old friends took their lemonade to the second-floor porch, where they might catch a cooling breeze. They sat under the shade of a big striped awning. Cissy fanned them both with her big fan, and they talked incessantly, but quietly, so as not to draw too much attention to a white woman sitting with a Black woman in a public place.

When the ice was melted and the lemonade gone, Rodantha ensured that there was no fuss from the hotel clerk about the reservation. "This guest is a very important teacher, writer, and scholar, who will be staying for a week, maybe two. She will require the very highest level of service befitting her station. Please have the will-call for Cecilia Washington taken to her room."

Danna walked her old friend arm-in-arm up the stairs and said, "Rest a while, Cissy, and I'll be back at supper time to collect you. I'll get the girls from school, and we'll all go to my apartment at the Elmdale bank so that we can talk freely. Ebenezer is out on bank business right now, but he lets me use his horse and buggy to go back and forth on business. Right now, though, I have to receive and sort the mail that just came in."

Cissy and Rodantha talked and talked, and the twin girls listened politely for a while as they ate their supper of baked potatoes and ham slices with cinnamon apples. Jennie finally said, "Ma, may we be excused? We have cyphers to do."

Rodantha nodded and the girls got up and put their plates in the dishpan. Ellie said, "Miss Cecilia, just one thing. Is your dark color all the way through or does it wash off when you take a bath?"

Unflappable Cissy replied, "It's all the way through dearie, and there's a big advantage too!"

"What's that? Ellie wanted to know.

"Well, other people can't tell when you *need* to take a bath. You can get away with not scrubbing behind your ears for ever so long."

"I think I would like that a lot," Ellie said as the little girls disappeared into the alcove to do their homework.

"I'm sorry, Cissy," Rodantha said. "The girls have never really been up close to a person of color, and I did not think to prepare them in any way."

"It's actually good for them to see that we are all the same humans but just come in different colors. Your girls will soon be the ones to take the lead in equalizing the races. This is a good start."

After the girls were sleeping soundly in the alcove, Danna made up the day bed along one side of the main room with fresh linens for Cissy. Danna slept on a cot pulled up next to the day bed. Cissy and Rodantha talked nearly all night. "We four in these tiny rooms are the future of this country, Danna. We must try to make it a good future."

-58-

Bad News

August 26, 1863

The news of William Quantrill's raid on Lawrence Kansas on August 21 reached the town of Council Grove five days later. Several Eastern newspapers carrying the news were delivered by the regular stage mail drop. When Rodantha saw the headlines, she ran over to the Hays House and banged on Cissy's door.

"Sorry to bother you, Cissy, I know you are busy writing your article, but I have to let you know the bad news."

"What has happened? Are your girls okay?"

"Yes, the twins are fine. The news is about a horrible attack on Lawrence by that evil ruffian, William Quantrill. He and his Confederate militia burned buildings and killed people of Lawrence. Here is the article in the newspaper that just came on the stage. The newspaper has printed an eyewitness account by Rev. Richard Cordley, the paster of the Congregational Church." Cissy sat down and read:

No one expected indiscriminate slaughter. When it was known that the town was in their possession, everybody expected that they would rob and burn the town, kill all military men they could find, and a few marked characters. But few expected a wholesale murder. ... A gentlemen who was concealed where he could see the whole, said the scene presented was the most perfect realization of the slang phrase, "Hell let loose," that could ever be imagined.

As the scene at their entrance was one of the wildest, the scene after their departure was one of the saddest that ever met mortal gaze. Massachusetts Street was one bed of embers. On this street seventy-five buildings, containing at least twice that number of places of business and offices, were destroyed. The dead lay all along the side-walk, many of them so burned that they could not be recognized and could scarcely be taken up. Here and there among the embers could be seen the bones of those who had perished in the buildings and had been consumed. On two sides of another block lay seventeen bodies. Almost the first sight that met our gaze was a father almost frantic, looking for the remains of his son among the embers of his office. The work of gathering and burying the dead soon began. From every quarter they were being brought in, until the floor of the Methodist Church, which was taken as a sort of a hospital, was covered with dead and wounded. In almost every house could be heard the wail of the widow and orphan. The work of burying was sad and wearying. Coffins could not be procured. Many carpenters were killed and most of the living had lost their tools. But they rallied nobly and worked day and night, making pine and walnut boxes, fastening them together with the burnt nails gathered from the ruins of the stores. It sounded rather harsh to the ear of the mourner, to have the lid <u>nailed</u> over the bodies of their loved ones; but it was the best that could be done. Thus the work went on for three days, til one hundred and twenty-two were deposited in the Cemetery, and many others in their own yard. Fifty-three were buried in one long grave. Early on the morning after the massacre, our attention was attracted by loud wailings. We went in the direction of the sound, and among the ashes of a building, sat a woman, holding in her hands the blackened skull of her husband, who was shot and burned at that place.

Another article gave a grim synopsis of what had happened.

At dawn on August 21, 1863, Quantrill and 400 Confederate guerrillas rode into the sleeping town of Lawrence, where they began to ransack homes, shoot civilians, loot stores, and set fire to buildings including the Eldridge Hotel. One of the first casualties was Reverend Snyder, shot as he was milking his cow outside his home.

Most of the town was burned and between 160 and 190 men and boys were killed. There are at least 80 widows and 250 orphaned children. This raid is part of an ongoing conflict between the Free-State forces who control Lawrence and the proslavery partisans who live in nearby Missouri. Even though Kansas entered the Union as a free state in 1861 the territorial animosities have continued all during the war between the states now raging.

George Ellis, a free black man, was outside working on his family's farm. George hid in a dense thicket near the Kansas River. After Quantrill's men set his house afire, his sister Jane successfully dragged her brother Ben out of the burning house and concealed him underneath a mattress. The raiders killed George's father.

Purportedly the raiders were hunting for Free-State leader, James H. Lane, commander of the Jayhawkers, a military regiment who have looted, raided and killed slavery sympathizers in Missouri. He hid in a West Lawrence cornfield to escape detection, along with several of his neighbors. Free-State leader and former state governor, Charles Robinson escaped with his life as well.

When Cissy finished reading the articles, she looked at Rodantha with daggers in her eyes. Rodantha pounded her fist down hard on the washstand, upsetting the water pitcher and spilling a little on the floor.

Rodantha spoke first saying, "This Reverend Cordley, in that article, is now the pastor of the Plymouth Congregation Church where Will played his pipe and where we found out about the job building fence for Waldo-Hall Company at Diamond Spring. That church might be all burned up now. The men of that church now murdered?

"Will gave the church the remaining funds from our wagon purchase to help other emigrants coming to Kansas. That money, a considerable sum, could be all burned up too." Rodantha shuddered and tried to catch her breath. "Aside from Will's murder at the hands of the ruffians, this is by far the worst human cruelty I ever heard of."

"And I am sure the article does not tell even half of the evil deeds. I know from writing articles how much is left out," Cissy replied.

"I need to do something about this, Cissy!"

"So do I," Cissy said empathically.

"What? Get some guns and go after them?"

"Well, that would feel good, wouldn't it?" Cissy agreed. "But I think we have a more powerful revenge. Why not strike at their very foundations?"

"What are you thinking of, Cissy?"

"Missouri ruffians and the people in the slave states are willing to wage war, kill abolitionists, kill emigrants to Kansas in favor of Free Soil, or freedmen, women, and children. They kill slave runaways or anyone that they even suspect is sympathetic to the cause of freeing slaves.

"So, what I say is, instead, we resist, not kill. What if we could somehow help abolitionists, emigrants, and freedmen, and give them a chance to survive?" Cissy stood up and walked over to where Rodantha stood, fist still on the washstand. Cissy put her hands on Danna's shoulders and looked into her eyes.

"The more free-soil emigrants and slaves *alive* increases our power and diminishes the killers' power over us. It would be our resistance against their army of destruction. And, for all we know, you and I may be next on their list, or your innocent children who just get in their way."

"You are right, Cissy," Rodantha said quietly. "Until today I have been afraid to speak, afraid to draw attention, afraid to really do anything about the abuse of emigrants and slaves. Will and I spent so much time running from the law, I kind of got used to it. But I truly want to resist these evils as you say. This Lawrence massacre has gone too far. It is more than I can take."

Cissy mused, "If escaping slaves had a safe place to go, that would solve so many problems. That seems nearly impossible right now. So far, a town, a Canann Land, has not been organized. That takes a lot of money we don't have. My dear friend, Roisin, died before she could realize this dream."

"What if it was not just one town, but many places spread out all over? Rodantha asked. "Spread out like emigrants do when they are starting farms and ranches. What if it was a real Canaan *Land*, like the … like the prairie, for instance?"

"The trouble with that idea is we still need people who will help get escaping slaves to the safe places, like the underground railroad worked back East. Remember that escaping slaves have nothing, and are often sick, lame, or injured."

"I … I think I know what we can do, Cissy!" Rodantha said, flinging her arms around her friend. "If we could find emigrants who need the help and connect them with a former slave to share the work of starting a farm or ranch, then that would turn them *all* into emigrants, equally sharing the hard life on the frontier. Emigrants get help, escaping slaves get protected. This is like what happened when we took you and Moss with us to Indiana."

"I don't think most settlers would be willing to do this," Cissy said, shaking her head. "Only people already committed to the abolitionist cause would take a chance on an unknown slave being attached to their party."

Cissy was quiet for a moment. "But wait, it might work if we were to *pay* emigrants to do this. Use that big donation from Plymouth Congregational Bandage Rollers to *pay the emigrants* instead of trying to buy *land* for a Canaan town. Remember I wrote you about this in my letter? It's your Canaan *land,* idea instead of Canaan *town*. There would have to be rules about length of service and terminating partnerships."

Rodantha said, "That's exactly what it would be—partners—not just emigrant *aid*."

-59-

Emigrant Partners

1863

As soon as Cissy returned to Quindaro and her classroom, Miss Cecilia Washington sent the first partner "package" to Rodantha in Council Grove. She chose a brave and intelligent teenage boy, Toby, from her class of students, who she thought could endure the journey. He was the last of his family and had survived by eating grasshoppers. He would be shuffled through the established Underground Railroad safe houses.

One man in the safe house network knew of a Mexican bull train coming through, since he was buying some wool from them. Toby would be hidden in the back of wool trader, Senior Perea's wagon, and stuffed in among the bolts of bayetta cloth and sacks of potatoes.

Miss Cecilia, in teacherly fashion, told the boy, "Now Toby, jump free of the wagon when you hear the signal—three long rings of a rattle-y Amish cow bell. Miss Rodantha will be there ringing that Dutch bell. You go with her."

By some miracle this plan worked, and Toby was the first former slave freed by their emigrant partner scheme. Overlanders, Mr. and Mrs. Bowman, were paid two dollars to take Toby with them to work their claim to the south along the Cottonwood River. Rodantha watched them go, Toby riding proudly on the back of their biggest mule.

In Council Grove where many emigrants crossed or used the Santa Fe commercial trail, settlers and former slaves could cross paths naturally. Settlers knew that water and supplies could be found in the trading lanes of the Santa Fe Trail before they struck out north and south to lands they were preempting or purchasing for farms and ranches.

Rodantha operated her end of the enterprise from the Council Grove Waldo-Hall stage stop. Her job was to pair up former slaves with westering settlers and teamsters. Both emigrants and former slaves could easily find her on the main street through Council Grove.

She looked for opportunities to talk to overlanders who stopped to get directions, mail a letter, or ask advice. She asked plainly, "Would you like to have an emigrant partner? I know of someone who is looking for work and might be available. We will pre-pay fair compensation that you would receive up front. In return, your helper could travel along with you and work on your claim. You can set the length of service and expected duties."

If the overlander showed some interest, Rodantha always said. "Just so you understand how this works. This partner is a *former* slave, now free. We are paying you for this woman's labor, you do not own her. She is free to go, any time." Often partnerships were made on the spot. Hard working pioneers had so much in common with hard working slaves.

Most times she knew when "packages" were to be delivered, and she could match up the partners quickly. Sometimes when escaping slaves had to wait for a partner, Rodantha supplied some food and shelter at a local safe house. The whole enterprise was funded by the donation from the Bandage Rollers of Plymouth Church. She even matched up a former slave with one of the teamster outfits. She kept a record of each name in a little logbook to record the partner name, emigrant name, date, direction/destination. There were seven names on the list. There should have been eight, but one poor woman died of cholera in one of the safe house cellars.

Ebenezer was resistant to the whole idea at first. He thought it would cut into her time working for him to meet stages and receive and sort mail, but she proved him wrong over time. Rodantha began to keep more regular hours and was able to get letters back and forth to Cissy about "packages" being shipped to her.

One day, when Ebenezer was returning from the Elmdale Peoples Exchange Bank, he stopped in to see her. He brought her some flowers and asked if he could call the next day, when he had more time. He had some business to speak to her about.

As soon as Ebenezer was settled at her table with some coffee he said, "This emigrant partner scheme is all right by me, Danna. I haven't had to meet a stage or sort mail since you started doing this. You keep your dealings quiet, so townspeople don't get alarmed. You have done well.

"But there have been changes in the company since Jacob Hall bought out Dr. Waldo. Hall has a new partner now, Mr. Hockaday. I am not sure what the company will do next, but Mr. Hall has asked me if you would be interested in being the full-time postmistress. I have told him that you were already doing the job through me, so I have recommended you. The job is yours if you want it. Of course, you will be paid more for all the responsibility. Let me know if you want to do this. I am just not sure they will want you involved in this emigrant partner scheme. It's a risk they might not want. Chances are you could continue unless there is some trouble. Think it over and let me know." When he left, he held her hand a long time and acted like he wanted to say something further. He waved and smiled from the buggy as he took off.

Rodantha learned that her pay would be nearly double, so she took the job. Mr. Hall formally hired her when he came along the trail in November, but he said nothing about her work with the emigrants. She didn't bring up the subject and decided she would continue unless there was some objection.

Rodantha had arranged for seven former slaves to partner with overlanders or teamsters. In a letter to Cissy she wrote:

> I feel like we have been successful, Cissy. The slaves you smuggled out here are now free and living somewhere on the prairie away from cruel masters. The emigrants now have some help to make life easier. Our scheme of revenge by resisting evil makes me proud and happy. I hope you feel the same way.

Rodantha's world began to change rapidly. She could now afford a "store-bought" dress, that she ordered from a catalog. It came on the mail stage. The dress was black and white pinstripe in two pieces. The blouse had a high collar and pleats at the shoulder, long sleeves, and button cuffs. The skirt buttoned at various waist sizes for a perfect fit. She thought it looked like proper attire for a postmistress. She wore it when she worked in the mail office and washed it on days off. Ellie and Jennie got new dresses too, made by a local seamstress, a little too large, so they could grow into them.

The weather turned bitterly cold, and almost all traffic on the Santa Fe

Trail stopped. There was snow every day for a week. The school and most businesses were closed. Rodantha crocheted rugs and enjoyed playing games with her girls by the fire.

A few months later the Hall-Hockaday Company moved their operations to a larger building in Council Grove. Mr. Hall wrote to her that they expected the volume of mail to increase and there might be an extra stage put on the line. The new building had a large waiting area in the front for stage customers and an apartment in the rear for the postmistress/stage clerk.

Rodantha moved out of the Elmdale Bank caretaker quarters and into the Hall-Hockaday Company apartment at the back of the new station. Ellie and Jennie had a real, though tiny, bedroom. New furniture was also provided with nice feather beds. The girls loved living in the bustling town where many of their school friends were.

Since moving to the new stage stop, no partner "packages" had come, and there were no letters from Cissy. Postmistress Hywell was at the new stage stop full time now and was glad she didn't have to take the buggy back and forth to the Elmdale Bank. She handled all the mail, talked to the townspeople when they came in to pick up letters and packages, met all the stages, and handled ticketing, plus she did her own cooking, cleaning, laundry, and caring for Jennie and Ellie. Her rug making was often neglected, and she treasured her day off on Sunday.

Eb called on Rodantha regularly and always brought flowers or candies. He brought hair ribbons for the girls or bright shiny pennies from the bank. He often patted their heads and always shook hands when he said hello and bowed when he left. He started kissing Rodantha on the cheek as he left and she grew more and more fond of him, even though he was far more reserved and formal than William. He was a good friend. He was fond of the twins and very successful in business.

Now that Riley was old enough, Ebenezer trained him to be the teller at the Elmdale Bank. Riley soon took over this job and relieved Ebenezer of having to be there at the posted banker's hours. Riley looked so grown up in his suit and tie.

But the emigrant partners never got started again. So many things had changed. Cissy wrote a long letter explaining that she would be going back to her old school, Eleutherian, to teach. She would be teaching young adults now, men and women, black and white. She was a published writer and journalist and so was hired to teach those subjects. Her experience as a former slave and graduate of the school made her a most valued asset to their curriculum.

Since there was no one to carry on smuggling slaves out of Quindaro, the emigrant partners could not continue. Cissy's letter said, "A new teacher has been hired for the Freedman's School, but she may not be brave enough to be a smuggler."

By the newspaper reports, the war between the states was starting to turn against the Confederacy and in favor of the Union. General Grant was wearing down General Lee's confederates in Virginia and Lincoln was favored to win re-election. William would have been happy to hear this.

A package with a letter inside came from Mr. Majors. Rodantha cried when she read the part about Dutch.

Since Van returned to us with your oxen, he has had Dutch and Shire as part of his team. Two more hard-working animals cannot be found on the earth. But sadly, Dutch died during the night about a few weeks ago. He was old and worn out by a life of service.

Out of respect, Van and some of the boys dug a hole and buried him. Van thinks Dutch wanted you to have his horns. So here they are, now made into this beautiful, polished horn-shaped box by a local Shoshone woman. One of the French traders supplied the little brass hinges and clasp.

Rodantha put the horn box on the top of the chest of drawers and filled it with some of the small keepsakes from the tin seed box turned treasure box: the Peterson's silver bell, the penny from the pork farmer, the limestone chip from the Ohio state house, and the portrait buttons of her family from the lace cape she wore at her wedding. Ellie and Jennie often took out the little treasures and discussed the stories their mother told them about each one.

Rodantha learned that the Eldridge Hotel in the town of Lawrence Kansas was being rebuilt, and that much of the town was slowly recovering from the devastating attack by Quantrill and his marauders. She wrote a letter of thanks to the Bandage Roller ladies in care of the Plymouth

Congregational Church and could only hope that it would find its way to the women whose generous donation had helped to save the lives of seven slaves.

-60-

Back to Diamond Spring

1864

Amid all the turmoil, Rodantha returned to Diamond Spring when the weather warmed and the hills turned green again. Riley drove her over there on Sunday while the twins went with Ebenezer to visit his sister, Mary Jane Pracht and husband Henry. They had a new baby girl, Miranda. Ellie and Jennie were so excited to see Auntie Jane again, especially now that there was also a baby to play with.

Rodantha headed straight for the small rock-fenced square at the side of William's four-acre stone corral. She could feel his presence, watching over the place like a guardian. She longed to see him walk out to meet her, hair brushing his collar, and boot laces flapping. As she walked out to his grave, she saw wildflowers bunched against the fence, the tall grass prairie's version of a garden: gay feather, sunflower, butterfly milkweed, and purple coneflower. She cleared the tall grass away from the bottom of the heavy wood gate to open it and then chased out a packrat foraging for nesting materials.

Inside the enclosure, she sat on the prairie next to William's grave and leaned against the rock fence in its shade. She was at peace. She was at home. She lost track of earth time, living all her adventures with William once again. She was sure that the very same meadowlark came to sing on the top of the rock fence. The one that sang the day he died. That bird knew the right song to sing. Her mind drifted with the windblown clouds. She closed her eyes. God was in heaven, and all was right with the world.

Before Riley drove her back home, they dipped up a bucket of clear cold Diamond Spring water and picked a sprig of mint from the hillside. On the drive back to Council Grove, the sun chased clouds on the run over the prairie hills.

Later, after much thought and many erasures, Rodantha wrote one last entry in her diary.

June 1, 1864

I am not quite sure how a young backwoods girl could travel a road, a thousand miles long, come out here to the untamed lands of the buffalo, meet up with Kanza and Osage Indians, Spanish traders, teamsters, slaves, and all manner of folks from everywhere, traveling along the Santa Fe Trail, some good and some bad. Then to lose everything in the struggle against slavery and live to see a day where I am a postmistress, earning enough to support my children. It does not seem possible. I am most proud that Cissy and I freed slaves from their bondage. I thank God for this miracle.

As I have read all that I wrote since I started this diary eight years ago, I have thought of how to say what is in my heart. I see at least I have learned to write and spell better.

I am not that same girl of eighteen—so full of myself. But I am still in awe of the freedom and adventure that William and I had when we started. I can barely believe that I did all those things, the hard work it took, the great sorrows and losses, but also happy times.

At the start, I did not know I was an emigrant, nor even know the meaning of the word. All the people from the eastern states and many countries, who have come (and are still coming in great numbers) looking for better lives—are emigrants all. We are a country of emigrants. Some came by force and some came by choice.

I am in sympathy with the slaves who have endured the worst cruelty known to mankind. I remain abolitionist as I promised William, though this has proven very hard. Though I know I should, I find it impossible to forgive those evil ruffian bushwhackers for taking Will from me. I understand hatred now, and how it has engulfed the whole country.

My feeling toward the native tribes is a jumble. We have treated them badly, cruelly, and taken their land by force. We have crowded them together unnaturally. They have been killed by greed and disease as we have come into their homelands. But Indians have been equally cruel and savage toward emigrants—murdering, burning, scalping, stealing children. I know only one solution to these many troubles—try to love one another as the Quakers believe. This is hard, maybe impossible, for generations to come. I pray for peace with the native people.

I also pray for peace in the war between the states and the end of slavery. I hope to see Cissy again one day and maybe go to her Eleutherian school back in Indiana.

I am thankful for my healthy children and grateful to Ebenezer for helping me. Maybe love can blossom again. He is a kind and caring man. I look forward to what is on the road ahead. I guess I should say, Rodantha's Road, as Will named it years ago.

I am reminded of the clouds pushed by the prairie winds on bright sunny days. They hold a deep meaning for me since the day Will died. I see dark and light as the cloud shadows run across the sunny land, exchanging places. Like the dark and light of my life.

Reader's Resource
for
Rodantha's Road

Check out the author's website for a FREE PDF of this educational resource that includes a discussion guide, terms and definitions, reference material, and supplemental reading.

www.joycehilliardstotts.com

Rodantha's Road
Music

Listen to this music on YouTube at:
www.youtube.com/@JoyceHilliardStotts

Clouds On The Run

Scottish Tune, O Waly, Waly
Also known as The Water is Wide

Joyce Hilliard Stotts

Music adapted and arranged by Joyce Hilliard Stotts. Lyrics by Joyce Hilliard Stotts, 2024

Suo Gan
Welsh Lull Song

Traditional

The Welsh name Suo Gan is pronounced See-O-Gahn and means lullaby or literally, Lull Song. This traditional tune by an anonymous composer is in the public domain, presented here with English words.

MEADOWLARKS AT HOME

Medium Tempo

Lyrics - Joyce Hilliard Stotts

This tune called Cranham (a village in Glochestershire, England) was written by Gustav Holst in 1906, published in The English Hymnal, and set to Christina Rossetti's 1872 poem, In the Bleak Mid-Winter. The original was sung slowly, solemnly and was appropriate for congregational singing. This tune is in the public domain.

WHERE THE WEST BEGINS

Up Tempo, Western Two-Step

Tune, **We** *are Climbing Jacob's Ladder* is a Public Domain spiritual
Lyrics by Joyce Hilliard Stotts, based on the Public Domain poem by
Arthur Chapman, *Out Where the West Begins*, 1917.

* Sing **bold font** as Coda/Outro after last verse.

Alternate key A – Chords: A, E7, D

**Out Where the West Begins
by Arthur Chapman, 1917**

Out where the handclasp's a little stronger,
Out where the smile dwells a little longer,
That's where the West begins;
Out where the sun is a little brighter,
Where the snows that fall are a trifle whiter,
Where the bonds of home are a wee bit tighter,
That's where the West begins.

Out where the skies are a trifle bluer,
Out where the friendship's a little truer,
That's were the West Begins;
Out where a fresher breeze is blowing,
Where there's laughter in every streamlet flowing
Where there's more of reaping and less of sowing,
That's where the West begins.

Out where the world is in the making,
Where fewer hearts in despair are aching.
That's where the West begins.
Where there's more of singing and less of sighing
Where there's more of giving and less of buying
And a man makes a friend without half trying
That's where the West begins.

Music Arranged and adapted by Joyce Hilliard
Stotts, 2019. YouTube Music Video produced
by Richard (Dick) Montgomery, 2024.

Acknowledgments

Thanks to the Dunedin writers group for encouragement and inspiration during the writing of this book. Thanks to my husband, Gary, and the extended families of Stotts, Hilliards, Bowmans, and Andersons for believing in me. Thanks to first readers David Bowman, Dave Lynch, Kylie Watts, Carol Ball and Jon-Michael (Mike) Miller for great suggestions and generous commentary; to Dave Hutchinson for digital photo of the Diamond Spring painting; to Richard (Dick) Montgomery for his musical expertise, advice, and great patience in producing the music included in the book and understanding that creative work is never really finished

About the Author

Joyce Hilliard Stotts grew up in Wyandotte and Leavenworth counties of Kansas, earned a B.S. from Emporia State University in 1970, and taught junior/senior high school English and Social Studies in Topeka, Kansas. She earned an M.S. degree from Kansas University and was an Instructional Designer/Technical Writer for FlightSafety International in Wichita, Kansas.

In 2023 Joyce renovated two historic buildings in downtown Cottonwood Falls, Kansas that are now a vacation home and commercial space. She is currently a partner in a family business, *Spice of the Harbor* in Safety Harbor, Florida where she lives part of the year.

www.joycehilliardstotts.com